PENGUIN BOOKS

# After You

# After You

### JOJO MOYES

PENGUIN BOOKS

PENGUIN BOOKS

UK | USA | Canada | Ireland | Australia
India | New Zealand | South Africa

Penguin Books is part of the Penguin Random House group of companies
whose addresses can be found at global.penguinrandomhouse.com.

First published in Great Britain by Michael Joseph 2015
First published in Penguin Books 2016
006

Set in 11.21/13.30 pt Garamond MT Std
Typeset by Penguin Books
Printed in Great Britain by Clays Ltd, St Ives plc

A CIP catalogue record for this book is available from the British Library

B FORMAT ISBN: 978–1–405–90907–5
A FORMAT ISBN: 978–1–405–92675–1

www.greenpenguin.co.uk

For my grandmother, Betty McKee

# Chapter One

The big man at the end of the bar is sweating. He holds his head low over his double Scotch, but every few minutes he glances up and out, behind him, towards the door. A fine sheen of perspiration glistens under the strip-lights. He lets out a long, shaky breath, disguised as a sigh, and turns back to his drink.

'Hey. Excuse me?'

I look up from polishing glasses.

'Can I get another one here?'

I want to tell him it's really not a good idea, that it won't help. That it might even put him over the limit. But he's a big guy and it's fifteen minutes till closing time and, according to company guidelines, I have no reason to tell him no, so I walk over, take his glass and hold it up to the optic. He nods at the bottle. 'Double,' he says, and slides a fat hand down his damp face.

'That'll be seven pounds twenty, please.'

It's a quarter to eleven on a Tuesday night and the Shamrock and Clover, East City Airport's Irish-themed pub, which is as Irish as Mahatma Gandhi, is winding down for the night. The bar closes ten minutes after the last plane takes off, and right now it's just me, an intense young man with a laptop, the cackling women at table two and the man nursing a double Jameson's waiting for either the SC107 to Stockholm or the DB224 to Munich – the latter has been delayed for forty minutes.

I've been on since midday, as Carly has a stomach-ache and went home. I don't mind. I never mind staying late. Humming softly to *Celtic Pipes of the Emerald Isle, Vol. III*, I walk over and

1

he glasses from the two women, who are peering
at some video footage on a phone. They laugh the
easy laugh of the well lubricated.

'My granddaughter. Five days old,' says the blonde woman,
as I reach over the table for her glass.

'Lovely.' I smile. All babies look like currant buns to me.

'She lives in Sweden. I've never been. But I have to go and
see my first grandchild, don't I?'

'We're wetting the baby's head.' They burst out laughing
again. 'Join us in a toast? Go on, take a load off for five minutes. We'll never finish this bottle in time.'

'Oops! Here we go. Come on, Dor.' Alerted by a screen,
they gather up their belongings, and perhaps it's only me who
notices a slight stagger as they brace themselves for the walk
towards security. I place their glasses on the bar, scan the
room for anything else that needs washing.

'You never tempted, then?' The smaller woman has turned
back for her scarf.

'I'm sorry?'

'To just walk down there, at the end of a shift. Hop on a
plane. I would.' She laughs again. 'Every bloody day.'

I smile, the kind of professional smile that might convey
anything at all, and turn back towards the bar.


Around me the concession stores are closing up for the
night, steel shutters clattering down over the overpriced
handbags and emergency-gift Toblerones. The lights flicker
off at gates three, five, eleven, the last of the day's travellers
winking their way into the night sky. Violet, the Congolese
cleaner, pushes her trolley towards me, her walk a slow sway,
her rubber-soled shoes squeaking on the shiny Marmoleum.

'Evening, darling.'

'Evening, Violet.'

'You shouldn't be here this late, sweetheart. You should be home with your loved ones.'

She says exactly the same thing to me every night. 'Not long now.' I respond with these exact words every night. Satisfied, she nods and continues on her way.

Intense Young Laptop Man and Sweaty Scotch Drinker have gone. I finish stacking the glasses, and cash up, checking twice until the till roll matches what is in the drawer. I note everything in the ledger, check the pumps, jot down what we need to reorder. It is then that I notice the big man's coat is still over his bar stool. I walk over, and glance up at the monitor. The flight to Munich would be just boarding, if I felt inclined to run his coat down to him. I look again, then walk slowly to the Gents.

'Hello? Anyone in here?'

The voice that emerges is strangled, bears a faint edge of hysteria. I push the door.

The Scotch Drinker is bent low over the sinks, splashing his face. His skin is chalk-white. 'Are they calling my flight?'

'It's only just gone up. You've probably got a few minutes.' I make to leave, but something stops me. The man is staring at me, his eyes two tight little buttons of anxiety. 'I can't do it.' He grabs a paper towel and pats at his face. 'I can't get on the plane.'

I wait.

'I'm meant to be travelling over to meet my new boss, and I can't. I haven't had the guts to tell him I'm scared of flying.' He shakes his head. 'Not scared. Terrified.'

I let the door close behind me. 'What's your new job?'

He blinks. 'Uh ... car parts. I'm the new Senior Regional Manager, bracket Spares close bracket, for Hunt Motors.'

'Sounds like a big job,' I say. 'You have ... brackets.'

'I've been working for it a long time.' He swallows hard.

3

'Which is why I don't want to die in a ball of flame. I really don't want to die in an airborne ball of flame.'

I am tempted to point out that it wouldn't actually be an airborne ball of flame, more a rapidly descending one, but suspect it wouldn't really help. He splashes his face again and I hand him another paper towel.

'Thank you.' He lets out a shaky breath, and straightens, attempting to pull himself together. 'I bet you never saw a grown man behave like an idiot before, huh?'

'About four times a day.'

His tiny eyes widen.

'About four times a day I have to fish someone out of the men's loos. And it's usually down to fear of flying.'

He blinks at me.

'But, you know, like I say to everyone else, no planes have ever gone down from this airport.'

His neck shoots back in his collar. 'Really?'

'Not one.'

'Not even . . . a little crash on the runway?'

I shrug. 'It's actually pretty boring here. People fly off, go to where they're going, come back again a few days later.' I lean against the door to prop it open. These lavatories never smell any better by the evening. 'And anyway, personally, I think there are worse things that can happen to you.'

'Well. I suppose that's true.' He considers this, looks sideways at me. 'Four a day, uh?'

'Sometimes more. Now, if you wouldn't mind, I really have to get back. It's not good for me to be seen coming out of the men's loos too often.'

He smiles, and for a minute I can see how he might be in other circumstances. A naturally ebullient man. A cheerful man. A man at the top of his game of continentally manufactured car parts. 'You know, I think I hear them calling your flight.'

4

'You reckon I'll be okay?'

'You'll be okay. It's a very safe airline. And it's just a couple of hours out of your life. Look, the SK491 landed five minutes ago. As you walk to your departure gate, you'll see the air stewards and stewardesses coming through on their way home and you'll see them all chatting and laughing. For them, getting on these flights is pretty much like getting on a bus. Some of them do it two, three, four times a day. And they're not stupid. If it wasn't safe, they wouldn't get on, would they?'

'Like getting on a bus,' he repeats.

'Probably an awful lot safer.'

'Well, that's for sure.' He raises his eyebrows. 'Lot of idiots on the road.'

I nod.

He straightens his tie. 'And it's a big job.'

'Shame to miss out on it, for such a small thing. You'll be fine once you get used to being up there again.'

'Maybe I will. Thank you . . .'

'Louisa,' I say.

'Thank you, Louisa. You're a very kind girl.' He looks at me speculatively. 'I don't suppose . . . you'd . . . like to go for a drink some time?'

'I think I hear them calling your flight, sir,' I say, and I open the door to allow him to pass through.

He nods, to cover his embarrassment, makes a fuss of patting his pockets. 'Right. Sure. Well . . . off I go, then.'

'Enjoy those brackets.'

It's two minutes after he has left that I discover he has been sick all over cubicle three.

I arrive home at a quarter past one and let myself into the silent flat. I change into my pyjama bottoms and a hooded sweatshirt, then open the fridge, pull out a bottle of white and pour a glass. It is lip-pursingly sour. I study the label and realize I must have opened it the previous night, and forgotten to put the top in the bottle. Then I decide it's never a good idea to think about these things too hard. I slump into a chair with it.

On the mantelpiece there are two cards. One is from my parents, wishing me a happy birthday. That 'best wishes' from Mum is as piercing as any stab wound. The other is from my sister, suggesting she and Thom come down for the weekend. It is six months old. Two voicemails on my phone, one from the dentist. One not.

*Hi, Louisa. It's Jared here. We met in the Dirty Duck? Well, we hooked up* [muffled, awkward laugh]. *It was just . . . you know . . . I enjoyed it. Thought maybe we could do it again? You've got my digits . . .*

When there is nothing left in the bottle, I consider buying another, but I don't want to go out again. I don't want Samir at the twenty-four-hour grocery to make one of his jokes about my endless bottles of Pinot Grigio. I don't want to have to talk to anyone. I am suddenly bone-weary, but it is the kind of head-buzzing exhaustion that tells me if I go to bed I won't sleep. I think briefly about Jared and that he had oddly shaped fingernails. Am I bothered about oddly shaped fingernails? I stare at the bare walls of the living room and realize suddenly that what I actually need is air. I really need air. I open the hall window and climb unsteadily up the fire escape until I am on the roof.

The first time I came up, nine months previously, the estate agent showed me how the previous tenants had made a small terrace garden up there, dotting around a few lead planters and a small bench. 'It's not officially yours, obviously,' he'd said, 'but yours is the only flat with direct access to it. I think it's pretty nice. You could even have a party up here!' I had

6

gazed at him, wondering if I really looked like the kind of person who held parties.

The plants have long since withered and died. I am apparently not very good at looking after things. Now I stand on the roof, staring out at London's winking darkness below. Around me a million people are living, breathing, eating, arguing. A million lives completely divorced from mine. It is a strange sort of peace.

The sodium lights glitter as the sounds of the city filter up into the night air, engines revving, doors slamming. Several miles south, the distant brutalist thump of a police helicopter, its beam scanning the dark for some vanished miscreant in a local park. Somewhere in the distance a siren. Always a siren. 'Won't take much to make this feel like home,' the estate agent had said. I had almost laughed. The city feels as alien to me as it always has. But, then, everywhere does, these days.

I hesitate, then take a step out onto the parapet, my arms lifted out to the side, a slightly drunken tightrope walker. One foot in front of the other, edging along the concrete, the breeze making the hairs on my outstretched arms prickle. When I first moved down here, when it all hit me hardest, I would sometimes dare myself to walk from one end to the other of my block. When I reached the other end I would laugh into the night air. *You see? I'm here – staying alive – right out on the edge. I'm doing what you told me!*

It has become a secret habit, me, the city skyline, the comfort of the dark, the anonymity, and the knowledge that up here nobody knows who I am. I lift my head, feeling the night breezes, hearing laughter below, the muffled smash of a bottle breaking, the traffic snaking up towards the city, seeing the endless red stream of tail-lights, an automotive blood supply. Only the hours between three and five a.m. are relatively peaceful, the drunks having collapsed into bed, the restaurant chefs having peeled off their whites, the pubs having barred their doors. The silence of those hours is interrupted only sporadically, by the night tankers, the opening up of the Jewish bakery along the street, the soft thump of the newspaper delivery vans dropping their paper bales. I know the subtlest movements of the city because I no longer sleep.

Somewhere down there a lock-in is going on in the White Horse, full of hipsters and East-Enders, and a couple are arguing outside, and across the city the general hospital is picking up the pieces of the sick and the injured and those who have just about scraped through another day. Up here is just the air, the dark and somewhere the FedEx freight flight from LHR to Beijing, and countless travellers, like Mr Scotch Drinker, on their way to somewhere new.

'Eighteen months. Eighteen whole months. So when is it going to be enough?' I say, into the darkness. And there it is – I can feel it boiling up again, the unexpected anger. I take two steps along, glancing down at my feet. 'Because this doesn't feel like living. It doesn't feel like anything.'

Two steps. Two more. I will go as far as the corner tonight.

'You didn't give me a bloody life, did you? Not really. You just smashed up my old one. Smashed it into little pieces. What am I meant to do with what's left? When is it going to feel –' I stretch out my arms, feeling the cool night air against my skin, and realize I am crying again. 'Fuck you, Will,' I whisper. 'Fuck you for leaving me.'

Grief wells up again, like a sudden tide, intense, overwhelming. And just as I feel myself sinking into it, a voice says, from the shadows, 'I don't think you should stand there.'

I half turn, and catch a flash of a small pale face on the fire escape, dark eyes wide open. In shock, my foot slips on the parapet, my weight suddenly the wrong side of the drop. My

8

heart lurches, a split second before my body follows. And then, like a nightmare, I am weightless, in the abyss of the night air, my legs flailing above my head as I hear the shriek that may be my own –

*Crunch*

And then all is black.

# Chapter Two

'What's your name, sweetheart?'

A brace around my neck.

A hand feeling around my head, gently, swiftly.

I am alive. This is actually quite surprising.

'That's it. Open your eyes. Look at me, now. Look at me. Can you tell me your name?'

I want to speak, to open my mouth, but my voice emerges muffled and nonsensical. I think I have bitten my tongue. There is blood in my mouth, warm and tasting of iron. I cannot move.

'We're going to put you onto a spinal board, okay? You may be a bit uncomfortable for a minute, but I'm going to give you some morphine to make the pain a bit easier.' The man's voice is calm, level, as if it is the most normal thing in the world to be lying broken on concrete, staring up at the dark sky. I want to laugh. I want to tell him how ridiculous it is that I am here. But nothing seems to work as it should.

The man's face disappears from view. A woman in a neon jacket, her dark curly hair tied back in a ponytail, looms over me and shines a thin torch abruptly in my eyes, gazing at me with the same detached interest as if I was a specimen, not a person.

'Do we need to bag her?'

I want to speak but I'm distracted by the pain in my legs. *Jesus*, I say, but I'm not sure if I say it aloud.

'Multiple fractures. Pupils normal and reactive. BP ninety

over sixty. She's lucky she hit that awning. What are the odds of landing on a daybed, eh? . . . I don't like that bruising, though.' Cold air on my midriff, the light touch of warm fingers. 'Internal bleeding?'

'Do we need a second team?'

'Can you step back, please, sir? Right back?'

Another man's voice: 'I came outside for a smoke, and she dropped on to my bloody balcony. She nearly bloody landed on me.'

'Well, there you go – it's your lucky day. She didn't.'

'I got the shock of my life. You don't expect people to just drop out of the bloody sky. Look at my chair. That was eight hundred pounds from the Conran Shop . . . Do you think I can claim for it?'

A brief silence.

'You can do what you want, sir. Tell you what, you could charge her for cleaning the blood off your balcony while you're at it. How about that?'

The first man's eyes slide towards his colleague. Time slips, I tilt with it. I've fallen off a roof? My face is cold and I realize distantly that I'm starting to shake.

'She's going into shock, Sam.'

A van door slides open somewhere below. And then the board beneath me moves and briefly *the pain the pain the pain* – Everything turns black.

A siren and a swirl of blue. Always a siren in London. We are moving. Neon slides across the interior of the ambulance, hiccups and repeats, illuminating the unexpectedly packed interior, the man in the green uniform, who is tapping something into his phone, before turning to adjust the drip above my head. The pain has lessened – morphine? – but with consciousness comes growing terror. A giant airbag is inflating slowly inside me, steadily blocking out everything else. *Oh, no. Oh, no.*

'Egcuse nge?'

It takes two goes for the man, his arm braced against the back of the cab, to hear me. He turns and stoops towards my face. He smells of lemons and he has missed a bit when shaving. 'You okay there?'

'Ang I –'

The man leans down. 'Sorry. Hard to hear over the siren. We'll be at the hospital soon.' He places a hand on mine. It is dry and warm and reassuring. I'm suddenly panicked in case he decides to let go. 'Just hang on in there. What's our ETA, Donna?'

I can't say the words. My tongue fills my mouth. My thoughts are muddled, overlapping. Did I move my arms when they picked me up? I lifted my right hand, didn't I?

'Ang I garalysed?' It emerges as a whisper.

'What?' He drops his ear to somewhere near my mouth.

'Garalysed? Ang I garalysed?'

'Paralysed?' The man hesitates, his eyes on mine, then turns and looks down at my legs. 'Can you wiggle your toes?'

I try to remember how to move my feet. It seems to require several more leaps of concentration than it used to. The man reaches down and lightly touches my toe, as if to remind me where they are. 'Try again. There you go.'

Pain shoots up both my legs. A gasp, possibly a sob. Mine.

'You're all right. Pain is good. I can't say for sure, but I don't think there's any spinal injury. You've done your hip, and a few other bits besides.'

His eyes are on mine. Kind eyes. He seems to understand how much I need convincing. I feel his hand close on mine. I have never needed a human touch more.

'Really. I'm pretty sure you're not paralysed.'

'Oh, thang Gog.' I hear my voice, as if from afar. My eyes brim with tears. 'Please don' leggo ogme,' I whisper.

He moves his face closer. 'I am not letting go of you.'

I want to speak, but his face blurs, and I am gone again.

Afterwards they tell me I fell two floors of the five, busting through an awning, breaking my fall on a top-of-the-range outsized canvas and wicker-effect waterproof-cushioned sun-lounger on the balcony of Mr Antony Gardiner, a copyright lawyer, and neighbour I have never met. My hip smashed into two pieces and two of my ribs and my collarbone snapped straight through. I broke two fingers on my left hand, and a metatarsal, which poked through the skin of my foot and caused one of the medical students to faint. My X-rays are a source of some fascination.

I keep hearing the voice of the paramedic who treated me: *You never know what will happen when you fall from a great height.* I am apparently very lucky. They tell me this and wait, smiling, as if I should respond with a huge grin, or perhaps a little tap dance. I don't feel lucky. I don't feel anything. I doze and wake, and sometimes the view above me is the bright lights of an operating theatre, and then it is a quiet, still room. A nurse's face. Snatches of conversation.

*Did you see the mess the old woman on D4 made? That's some end of a shift, eh?*

*You work up at the Princess Elizabeth, right? You can tell them we know how to run an ER. Ha-ha-ha-ha-ha.*

*You just rest now, Louisa. We're taking care of everything. Just rest now.*

The morphine makes me sleepy. They up my dose and it's a welcome cold trickle of oblivion.

\*

I open my eyes to find my mother at the end of my bed.

'She's awake. Bernard, she's awake. Do we need to get the nurse?'

She's changed the colour of her hair, I think distantly. And then: Oh. It's my mother. My mother doesn't talk to me any more.

'Oh, thank God. Thank God.' My mother reaches up and touches the crucifix around her neck. It reminds me of someone but I cannot think who. She leans forward and lightly strokes my cheek. For some reason this makes my eyes fill immediately with tears. 'Oh, my little girl.' She is leaning over me, as if to shelter me from further damage. I smell her perfume, as familiar as my own. 'Oh, Lou.' She mops my tears with a tissue. 'I got the fright of my life when they called. Are you in pain? Do you need anything? Are you comfortable? What can I get you?'

She talks so fast that I cannot answer.

'We came as soon as they said. Treena's looking after Granddad. He sends his love. Well, he sort of made that noise, you know, but we all know what he means. Oh, love, how on earth did you get yourself into this mess? What on earth were you *thinking*?'

She doesn't seem to require an answer. All I have to do is lie here.

My mother dabs at her eyes, and again at mine. 'You're still my daughter. And . . . and I couldn't bear it if something happened to you and we weren't . . . you know.'

'Ngung –' I swallow the words. My tongue feels ridiculous. I sound drunk. 'I ngever wanged –'

'I know. But you made it so hard for me, Lou. I couldn't –'

'Not now, love, eh?' Dad touches her shoulder.

She looks away into the middle distance, and takes my hand. 'When we got the call. Oh. I thought – I didn't know –' She is sniffing again, her handkerchief pressed to her lips. 'Thank God she's okay, Bernard.'

'Of course she is. Made of rubber, this one, eh?'

Dad looms over me. We had last spoken on the telephone two months previously, but I haven't seen him in person for the eighteen months since I left my home town. He looks enormous and familiar, and desperately, desperately tired.

'Shorry,' I whisper. I can't think what else to say.

'Don't be daft. We're just glad you're okay. Even if you do look like you've done six rounds with Mike Tyson. Have you seen yourself in a mirror since you got here?'

I shake my head.

'Maybe . . . I might just hold off a bit longer. You know Terry Nicholls, that time he went right over his handlebars by the mini-mart? Well, take off the moustache, and that's pretty much what you look like. Actually,' he peers closer at my face, 'now you mention it . . .'

'Bernard.'

'We'll bring you some tweezers tomorrow. Anyway, the next time you decide you want flying lessons, let's head down the ole airstrip, yes? Jumping and flapping your arms is plainly not working for you.'

I try to smile.

They both bend over me. Their faces are strained, anxious. My parents.

'She's got thin, Bernard. Don't you think she's got thin?'

Dad leans closer, and then I see his eyes are a little watery, his smile a bit wobblier than usual. 'Ah . . . she looks beautiful, love. Believe me. You look bloody beautiful.' He squeezes my hand, then lifts it to his mouth and kisses it. My dad has never done anything like that to me in my whole life.

It is then that I realize they thought I was going to die and a sob bursts unannounced from my chest. I shut my eyes against the hot tears and feel his large, wood-roughened palm around mine.

'We're here, sweetheart. It's all right now. It's all going to be okay.'

They make the fifty-mile journey every day for two weeks, catching the early train down, and then after that, every few days. Dad gets special dispensation from work, because Mum won't travel by herself. There are, after all, all sorts in London. This is said more than once and always accompanied by a furtive glance behind her, as if a knife-wielding hood is even now sneaking into the ward. Treena is staying over to keep an eye on Granddad. There is an edge to the way Mum says it that makes me think this might not be my sister's first choice of arrangements.

Mum brings homemade food, and has done so since the day we all stared at my lunch and, despite five minutes of intense speculation, couldn't work out what it was. 'And in plastic trays, Bernard. Like a prison.' She prodded it sadly with a fork, then sniffed it. Since then she has arrived with enormous sandwiches, thick slices of ham or cheese in white bloomer bread, homemade soups in flasks. 'Food you can recognize,' and feeds me like a baby. My tongue slowly returns to its normal size. Apparently I'd almost bitten through it when I landed. It's not unusual, they tell me.

I have two operations to pin my hip, and my left foot and left arm are in plaster up to the joints. Keith, one of the porters, asks if he can sign my casts – apparently it's bad luck to have them virgin white – and promptly writes a comment so filthy that Eveline, the Filipina nurse, has to put a plaster on it before the consultant comes around. When he pushes me to X-ray, or to the pharmacy, he tells me the gossip from around the hospital. I could do without hearing about the patients who die slowly and horribly, of which there seem to be an endless number, but it keeps him happy. I sometimes wonder what he tells people about me. I am the girl who fell off a five-storey building and lived. In hospital status, this apparently puts me some way above the compacted bowel in C ward, or That Daft Bint Who Accidentally Took Her Thumb Off with Pruning Shears.

It's amazing how quickly you become institutionalized. I wake, accept the ministrations of a handful of people I now recognize, try to say the right thing to the consultants, and wait for my parents to arrive. My parents keep busy with small tasks in my room, and become uncharacteristically deferential in the face of the doctors. Dad apologizes repeatedly for my inability to bounce, until Mum kicks him, quite hard, in the ankle.

After the rounds are finished, Mum usually has a walk around the concourse shops downstairs and returns exclaiming in hushed tones at the number of fast-food outlets. 'That one-legged man from the cardio ward, Bernard. Sitting down there stuffing his face with cheeseburger and chips, like you wouldn't believe.'

Dad sits and reads the local paper in the chair at the end of my bed. The first week he keeps checking it for reports of my accident. I try to tell him that in this part of the city even double murders barely merit a News In Brief, but in Stortfold the previous week the local paper's front page ran with 'Supermarket Trolleys Left in Wrong Area of Car Park'. The week before that it was 'Schoolboys Sad at State of Duck Pond' so he has yet to be convinced.

On the Friday after the final operation on my hip, my mother brings a dressing-gown that is one size too big for me, and a large brown-paper bag of egg sandwiches. I don't have to ask what they are: the sulphurous smell floods the room as soon as she opens her bag. My father wafts his hand in front of his nose. 'The nurses'll be blaming me, Josie,' he says, opening and closing my door.

'Eggs will build her up. She's too thin. And, besides, you can't talk. You were blaming the dog for your awful smells two years after he'd actually died.'

'Just keeping the romance alive, love.'

Mum lowers her voice: 'Treena says her last fellow put the blankets over her head when he broke wind. Can you imagine!'

Dad turns to me. 'When I do it, your mother won't even stay in the same postcode.'

There is tension in the air, even as they laugh. I can feel it. When your whole world shrinks to four walls, you become acutely attuned to slight variations in atmosphere. It's in the way consultants turn away slightly when they're examining X-rays or the nurses cover their mouths when they're talking about someone nearby who has just died.

'What?' I say. 'What is it?'

They look awkwardly at each other.

'So . . .' Mum sits on the end of my bed. 'The doctor said . . . the consultant said . . . it's not clear how you fell.'

I bite into an egg sandwich. I can pick things up with my left hand now. 'Oh, that. I got distracted.'

'While walking around a roof.'

I chew for a minute.

'Is there any chance you were sleepwalking, sweetheart?'

'Dad – I've never sleepwalked in my life.'

'Yes, you have. There was that time when you were thirteen and you sleepwalked downstairs and ate half of Treena's birthday cake.'

'Um. I may not have actually been asleep.'

'And there's your blood-alcohol level. They said . . . you had drunk . . . an awful lot.'

'I'd had a tough night at work. I had a drink or two and I just went up on the roof to get some air. And then I got distracted by a voice.'

'You heard a *voice*.'

'I was standing on the top – looking out. I do it sometimes. And there was this girl's voice behind me and it gave me a shock and I lost my footing.'

'A girl?'

'I only really heard her voice.'

Dad leans forward. 'You're sure it was an actual girl? Not an imaginary –'

'It's my hip that's mashed up, Dad, not my brain.'

'They did say it was a girl who called the ambulance.' Mum touches Dad's arm.

'So you're saying it really *was* an accident,' he says.

I stop eating. They look away from each other guiltily.

'What? You . . . you think I jumped off?'

'We're not saying anything.' Dad scratches his head. 'It's just – well – things had all gone so wrong since . . . and we hadn't seen you for so long . . . and we were a bit surprised that you'd be up walking on the roof of a building in the wee small hours. You used to be afraid of heights.'

'I used to be engaged to a man who thought it was normal to calculate how many calories he'd burned while he slept. Jesus. This is why you've been so nice to me? You think I tried to kill myself?'

'It's just he was asking us all sorts . . .'

'Who was asking what?'

'The psychiatrist bloke. They just want to make sure you're okay, love. We know things have been all – well, you know – since –'

'Psychiatrist?'

'They're putting you on the waiting list to see someone. To

talk, you know. And we've had a long chat with the doctors and you're coming home with us. Just while you recover. You can't stay by yourself in that flat of yours. It's –'

'You've been in my flat?'

'Well, we had to fetch your things.'

There is a long silence. I think of them standing in my doorway, my mother's hands tight on her bag as she surveyed the unwashed bed-linen, the empty wine bottles lined up in a row on the mantelpiece, the solitary half-bar of Fruit and Nut in the fridge. I picture them shaking their heads, looking at each other. *Are you sure we've got the right place, Bernard?*

'Right now you need to be with your family. Just till you're back on your feet.'

I want to say I'll be fine in my flat, no matter what they think of it. I want to do my job and come home and not think until my next shift. I want to say I can't come back to Stortfold and be *that girl* again, *the one who*. I don't want to have to feel the weight of my mother's carefully disguised disapproval, of my father's cheerful determination that *it's all okay, everything is just fine*, as if saying it enough times will actually make it okay. I don't want to pass Will's house every day, to think about what I was part of, the thing that will always be there.

But I don't say any of it. Because suddenly I'm tired and everything hurts and I just can't fight any more.

Dad brings me home two weeks later in his work van. There is only room for two in the front, so Mum has stayed behind to prepare the house, and as the motorway speeds beneath us, I find my stomach tightening nervously.

The cheerful streets of my hometown feel foreign to me now. I look at them with a distant, analytical eye, noting how small everything looks, how tired, how *twee*. I realize this is how Will must have seen it when he first came home after his accident, and push the thought away. As we drive down our street, I find myself sinking slightly in my seat. I don't want to make polite conversation with neighbours, to explain myself. I don't want to be judged for what I did.

'You okay?' Dad turns, as if he guesses something of what's going through my head.

'Fine.'

'Good girl.' He puts a hand briefly on my shoulder.

Mum is already at the door as we pull up. I suspect she has been standing by the window for the past half-hour. Dad puts one of my bags on the step, then comes back to help me out, hoisting the other over his shoulder.

I place my cane carefully on the paving stones, and feel the twitching of curtains behind me as I make my way slowly up the path. *Look who it is*, I can hear them whispering. *What do you think she's done now?*

Dad steers me forward, watching my feet carefully, as if they might suddenly shoot out and go somewhere they shouldn't. 'Okay there?' he keeps saying. 'Not too fast now.'

I can see Granddad hovering behind Mum in the hall, wearing his checked shirt and his good blue jumper. Nothing has changed. The wallpaper is the same. The hall carpet is the same, the lines in the worn pile visible from where Mum must have vacuumed that morning. I can see my old blue anorak hanging on the hook. Eighteen months. I feel as if I have been away for a decade.

'Don't rush her,' Mum says, her hands pressed together. 'You're going too fast, Bernard.'

'She's hardly flipping Mo Farah. If she goes any slower we'll be moonwalking.'

'Watch those steps. Should you stand behind her, Bernard, coming up the steps? You know, in case she falls backwards?'

'I know where the steps are,' I say, through gritted teeth. 'I only lived here for twenty-six years.'

'Watch she doesn't catch herself on that lip there, Bernard. You don't want her to smash the other hip.'

*Oh, God*, I think. *Is this what it was like for you, Will? Every single day?*

And then my sister is in the doorway, pushing past Mum. 'Oh, for God's sake, Mum. Come on, Hopalong. You're turning us into a freaking sideshow.'

Treena wedges her shoulder under my armpit and turns briefly to glare out at the neighbours, her eyebrows raised as if to say, *Really?* I can almost hear the swishing of curtains as they close.

'Bunch of bloody rubberneckers. Anyway, hurry up. I promised Thomas he could see your scars before I take him to youth club. God, how much weight have you lost? Your boobs must look like two tangerines in a pair of socks.'

It's hard to laugh and walk at the same time. Thomas runs to hug me so that I have to stop and put a hand against the wall to keep my balance as we collide. 'Did they really cut you open and put you back together?' he says. His head comes up to my chest. He's missing four front teeth. 'Grandpa says they probably put you back together all the wrong way. And God only knows how we'll tell the difference.'

'Bernard!'

'I was *joking*.'

'Louisa.' Granddad's voice is thick and hesitant. He reaches forward unsteadily and hugs me and I hug him back. He pulls away, his old hands gripping my arms surprisingly tightly, and frowns at me, a mock anger.

'I know, Daddy. I know. But she's home now,' says Mum.

'You're back in your old room,' says Dad. 'I'm afraid we

redecorated with Transformers wallpaper for Thom. You don't mind the odd Autobot and Predacon, right?'

'I had worms in my bottom,' says Thomas. 'Mum says I'm not to talk about it outside the house. Or put my fingers up my –'

'Oh, good Lord,' says Mum.

'Welcome home, Lou,' says Dad, and promptly drops my bag on my foot.

# Chapter Three

Looking back, for the first nine months after Will's death I was in a kind of daze. I went straight to Paris and simply didn't go home, giddy with freedom, with the appetites that Will had stirred in me. I got a job at a bar favoured by expats where they didn't mind my terrible French, and I grew better at it. I rented a tiny attic room in the 16th, above a Middle Eastern restaurant, and I would lie awake, listening to the sound of the late drinkers and the early-morning deliveries, and every day I felt like I was living someone else's life.

Those early months, it was as if I had lost a layer of skin – I felt everything more intensely. I woke up laughing, or crying, saw everything as if a filter had been removed. I ate new foods, walked strange streets, spoke to people in a language that wasn't mine. Sometimes I felt haunted by him, as if I was seeing it all through his eyes, heard his voice in my ear.

*What do you think of that, then, Clark?*
*I told you you'd love this.*
*Eat it! Try it! Go on!*

I felt lost without our daily routines. It took weeks for my hands not to feel useless without daily contact with his body: the soft shirt I would button, the warm, motionless hands I would wash gently, the silky hair I could still feel between my fingers. I missed his voice, his abrupt, hard-earned laugh, the feel of his lips against my fingers, the way his eyelids would lower when he was about to drop off to sleep. My mother, still aghast at what I had been part of, had told me that while she loved me, she could not reconcile this Louisa with the

24

daughter she had raised, so with the loss of my family, as well as the man I had loved, every thread that had linked me to who I was had been cut. I felt as if I had simply floated off, untethered, to some unknown universe.

So I acted out a new life. I made casual, arm's-length friendships with other travellers: young English students on gap years, Americans retracing the steps of literary heroes, certain that they would never return to the Midwest, wealthy young bankers, day-trippers, a constantly changing cast that drifted in and through and past; escapees from other lives. I smiled and I chatted and I worked, and I told myself I was doing what he wanted. That there had to be comfort, at least, in that.

Winter loosened its grip and the spring was beautiful. Then almost overnight I woke up one morning and realized I had fallen out of love with the city. Or, at least, I didn't feel Parisian enough to stay. The stories of the expats began to sound wearyingly similar, the Parisians to seem unfriendly – or, at least, I noticed, several times a day, the myriad ways in which I would never quite fit in. The city, compelling as it was, felt like a glamorous couture dress that I had bought in haste but didn't quite fit me after all. I handed in my notice and went travelling around Europe.

No two months had ever left me feeling more inadequate. I was lonely almost all the time. I hated not knowing where I was going to sleep each night, was permanently anxious about train timetables and currency, found it difficult to make friends when I didn't trust anyone I met. And what could I say about myself, anyway? When people asked me, I could give them only the most cursory details. All the stuff that was important or interesting about me was what I couldn't share. Without someone to talk to, every sight I saw – whether it was the Trevi Fountain or a canal in Amsterdam – felt simply like a box I'd needed to tick on a list. I spent the last week on a beach in Greece that reminded me too much of a beach I had been on with Will not too long before, and finally, after a week of sitting on the sand fending off bronzed men, who all seemed to be called Dmitri, and trying to tell myself I was actually having a good time, I gave up and returned to Paris. Mostly because that was the first time it had occurred to me that I had nowhere else to go.

For two weeks I slept on the sofa of a girl I'd worked with at the bar, while I tried to decide what to do next. Recalling a conversation I'd had with Will about careers, I wrote to several colleges about fashion courses, but I had no history of work to show them and they rebuffed me politely. The place on the course I had originally won after Will died had been awarded to someone else because I had failed to defer. I could apply again next year, the administrator said, in the tones of someone who knew I wouldn't.

I looked online at jobs websites and saw that, despite everything I had been through, I was still unqualified for the kind of jobs I might be interested in doing. And then by chance, just as I was wondering what to do next, Michael Lawler, Will's lawyer, rang me and suggested it was time to do something with the money Will had left. It was the excuse to move that I needed. He helped me negotiate a price on a scarily expensive two-bedroomed flat on the edge of the Square Mile, which I bought largely because I remembered Will once talking about the wine bar on the corner, which made me feel a bit closer to him; there was a little left over with which to furnish it. Six weeks later I came back to England, got a job at the Shamrock and Clover, slept with a man called Phil I would never see again, and waited to feel as if I had really started living.

Nine months on I was still waiting.

*

I didn't go out much that first week home. I was sore, and grew tired quickly, so it was easy to lie in bed and doze, wiped out by extra-strength painkillers, and tell myself that letting my body recover was all that mattered. In a weird way, being back in our little family house suited me: it was the first place I had managed to sleep more than four hours at a stretch since I had left; it was small enough that I could always reach out for a wall to support myself. Mum fed me, Granddad kept me company (Treena had gone back to college, taking Thom with her), and I watched a lot of daytime television, marvelling at its never-ending advertisements for loan companies and stair lifts, and its preoccupations with minor celebrities that the best part of a year abroad had left me unable to recognize. It was like being in a little cocoon, one that, admittedly, had a whacking great elephant squatting in its corner.

We didn't talk about anything that might upset this delicate equilibrium. I would watch whatever celebrity news daytime television threw up and then say, at supper, 'Well, what about that Shayna West, then, eh?' And Mum and Dad would leap on the topic gratefully, remarking that she was a trollop or had nice hair or that she was no better than she should be. We covered *Bargains In Your Attic* ('I always wonder what that Victorian planter of your mother's would have been worth . . . ugly old thing.') and *Ideal Homes in the Country* ('I wouldn't wash a dog in that bathroom'). I didn't think beyond each mealtime, beyond the basic challenges of getting dressed, brushing my teeth and completing whatever tiny tasks my mother set me ('You know, love, when I'm out, if you could sort your washing, I'll do it with my coloureds').

But, like a creeping tide, the outside world insisted steadily on intruding. I heard the neighbours asking questions of my mother as she hung out the washing. *Your Lou home, then, is she?*

And Mum's uncharacteristically curt response: *She is.* I found myself avoiding the rooms in the house from which I could see the castle. But I knew it was there, the people in it living, breathing links to Will. Sometimes I wondered what had happened to them; while in Paris I had been forwarded a letter from Mrs Traynor, thanking me formally for everything I had done for her son. 'I am conscious that you did everything you could.' But that was it. That family had gone from being my whole life to a ghostly remnant of a time I wouldn't allow myself to remember. Now, as our street sat moored in the shadow of the castle for several hours every evening, I felt the Traynors' presence like a rebuke.

I'd been there two weeks before I realized that Mum and Dad no longer went to their social club. 'Isn't it Tuesday?' I said, on the third week, as we sat around the dinner table. 'Shouldn't you be gone by now?'

They glanced at each other. 'Ah, no. We're fine here,' Dad said, chewing a piece of his pork chop.

'I'm fine by myself, honestly,' I told them. 'I'm much better now. And I'm quite happy watching television.' I secretly longed to sit, unobserved, with nobody else in the room. I had barely been left alone for more than half an hour at a time since I'd come home. 'Really. Go out and enjoy yourselves. Don't mind me.'

'We . . . we don't really go to the club any more,' said Mum, as she sliced through a potato.

'People . . . they had a lot to say. About what went on.' Dad shrugged. 'In the end it was easier just to stay out of it.' The silence that followed this lasted a full six minutes.

And there were other, more concrete, reminders of the life I had left behind. Ones that wore skin-tight running pants with special wicking properties.

It was on the fourth morning Patrick jogged past our house

28

that I thought it might be more than coincidence. I had heard his voice the first day and limped blearily to the window, peering through the blind. And there he was below me, stretching out his hamstrings while talking to a blonde girl with a ponytail; she was clad in matching blue Lycra so tight I could pretty much work out what she'd had for breakfast. They looked like two Olympians missing a bobsleigh.

I stood back from the window in case he looked up and saw me, and within a minute, they were gone again, jogging down the road, backs erect, legs pumping, like a pair of glossy turquoise carriage ponies.

Two days later I was getting dressed when I heard them. Patrick was saying something loudly about carb-loading, and this time the girl flicked a suspicious glance towards my house, as if she were wondering why they had stopped in exactly the same place twice.

On the third day I was in the front room with Granddad when they arrived. 'We should practise sprints,' Patrick was saying loudly. 'Tell you what, you go to the third lamppost and back and I'll time you. Two-minute intervals. Go!'

Granddad rolled his eyes meaningfully.

'Has he been doing this the whole time I've been back?'

Granddad's eyes rolled pretty much into the back of his head.

I watched through the net curtains as Patrick stood, eyes fixed on his stopwatch, his best side presented to my window. He was wearing a black fleece zip-up top and matching Lycra shorts, and as he stood, a few feet the other side of the curtain, I was able to gaze at him, quietly amazed that this was someone I had been sure, for so long, I loved.

'Keep going!' he yelled, looking up from the stopwatch. And, like an obedient gun dog, the girl touched the lamppost beside him and bolted away again. 'Forty-two point three eight seconds,' he said approvingly, when she returned, panting. 'I reckon you could shave another point five of a second off that.'

'That's for your benefit,' said my mother, who had walked in bearing two mugs.

'I did wonder.'

'His mother asked me in the supermarket were you back and I said you were. Don't look at me like that – I could hardly lie to the woman.' She nodded towards the window. 'That one's had her boobs done. They're the talk of Stortfold. Apparently you could rest two cups of tea on them.' She stood beside me for a moment. 'You know they're engaged?'

I waited for the pang, but it was so mild it could have been wind. 'They look . . . well suited.'

My mother stood there for a moment, watching him. 'He's not a bad sort, Lou. You just . . . changed.' She handed me a mug and turned away.

Finally, on the morning he stopped to do press-ups on the pavement outside the house, I opened the front door and stepped out. I leaned against the porch, my arms folded across my chest, watching until he looked up. 'I wouldn't stop there for too long. Next door's dog is a bit partial to that bit of pavement.'

'Lou!' he exclaimed, as if I was the very last person he expected to see standing outside my own house, which he had visited several times a week for the seven years we had been together. 'Well . . . I'm surprised to see you back. I thought you were off to conquer the big wide world!'

His fiancée, who was doing press-ups beside him, looked up, then back down at the pavement. It might have been my imagination, but her buttocks might have clenched even more tightly. Up, down, she bobbed furiously. Up and down.

I found myself worrying slightly for the welfare of her new bosom.

He bounced to his feet. 'This is Caroline, my fiancée.' He kept his eyes on me, perhaps waiting for some kind of reaction. 'We're training for the next Ironman. We've done two together already.'

'How . . . romantic,' I said.

'Well, Caroline and I feel it's good to do things together,' he said.

'So I see,' I replied. 'And his and hers turquoise Lycra!'

'Oh. Yeah. Team colour.'

There was a short silence.

I gave a little air punch. 'Go, team!'

Caroline sprang to her feet and began to stretch out her thigh muscles, folding her leg behind her like a stork. She nodded towards me, the least civility she could reasonably get away with.

'You've lost weight,' he said.

'Yeah, well. A saline-drip diet will do that to you.'

'I heard you had an . . . accident.' He cocked his head sideways, sympathetically.

'News travels fast.'

'Still. I'm glad you're okay.' He sniffed, looked down the road. 'It must have been hard for you this past year. You know. Doing what you did and all.'

And there it was. I tried to keep control of my breathing. Caroline resolutely refused to look at me, extending her leg in a hamstring stretch. Then, 'Anyway . . . congratulations on the marriage.'

He surveyed his future wife proudly, lost in admiration of her sinewy leg. 'Well, it's like they say – you just know when you know.' He gave me a *faux*-apologetic smile. And that was what finished me off.

'I'm sure you did. And I guess you've got plenty put aside to pay for the wedding – they're not cheap, are they?'

They both looked at me.

'What with selling my story to the newspapers. What did they pay you, Pat? A couple of thousand? Treena never could find out the exact figure. Still, Will's death should be good for a few matching Lycra onesies, right?'

The way Caroline's face shot towards his told me this was one particular part of Patrick's history that he had not yet got round to sharing.

He stared at me, two pinpricks of colour bleeding onto his face. 'That was nothing to do with me.'

'Of course not. Nice to see you, anyway, Pat. Good luck with the wedding, Caroline! I'm sure you'll be the . . . firmest bride around.' I turned and walked slowly back inside. I closed the door, resting against it, heart thumping, until I could be sure that they had finally jogged on.

'Arse,' said Granddad, as I limped back into the living room. And again, glancing dismissively at the window: 'Arse.' Then he chuckled.

I stared at him. And, completely unexpectedly, I found I had started to laugh, for the first time in as long as I could remember.


'So did you decide what you're going to do? When you're better?'

I was lying on my bed. Treena was calling from college, while she waited for Thomas to come out of his football club. I stared up at the ceiling, on which Thomas had stuck a whole galaxy of Day-glo stickers, which, apparently, nobody could remove without bringing half the ceiling with them. 'Not really.'

'You've got to do something. You can't sit around here on your backside for all eternity.'

'I won't sit on my backside. Besides, my hip still hurts. The physio said I'm better off lying down.'

'Mum and Dad are wondering what you're going to do. There are no jobs in Stortfold.'

'I do know that.'

'But you're drifting. You don't seem to be interested in anything.'

'Treen, I just fell off a building. I'm recuperating.'

'And before that you were wafting around travelling. And then you were working in a bar until you knew what you wanted to do. You'll have to sort your head out at some point. If you're not going back to school, you have to figure out what it is you're actually going to do with your life.

'I'm just saying. Anyway, if you're going to stay in Stortfold, you need to rent out that flat. Mum and Dad can't support you for ever.'

'This from the woman who has been supported by the Bank of Mum and Dad for the past eight years.'

'I'm in full-time education. That's different. So, anyway, I went through your bank statements while you were in hospital, and after I'd paid all your bills, I worked out you've got about fifteen hundred pounds left over, including statutory sick pay. By the way, what the hell were all those transatlantic phone calls? They cost you a fortune.'

'None of your business.'

'So, I made you a list of estate agents in the area who do rentals. And then I thought maybe we could take another look at college applications. Someone might have dropped out of that course you wanted.'

'Treen. You're making me tired.'

'No point hanging around. You'll feel better once you've got some focus.'

For all it was annoying, there was something reassuring

about my sister nagging at me. Nobody else dared to. It was as if my parents still believed there was something very wrong at the heart of me, and that I must be treated with kid gloves. Mum laid my washing, neatly folded, on the end of my bed and cooked me three meals a day, and when I caught her watching me she would smile, an awkward half-smile, which covered everything we didn't want to say to each other. Dad took me to my physio appointments, sat beside me on the sofa to watch television and didn't even take the mickey out of me. Treena was the only one who treated me like she always had.

'You know what I'm going to say, don't you?'

I turned onto my side, wincing.

'I do. And don't.'

'Well, you know what Will would have said. You had a deal. You can't back out of it.'

'Okay. That's it, Treen. We're done with this conversation.'

'Fine. Thom's just coming out of the changing rooms. See you Friday!' she said, as if we had just been talking about music, or where she was going on holiday, or soap.

And I was left staring at the ceiling.

*You had a deal.*

Yeah. And look how that turned out.

For all Treena moaned at me, in the weeks that had passed since I'd come home I had made some progress. I'd stopped using the cane, which had made me feel around eighty-nine years old, and which I had managed to leave behind in almost every place I'd visited since coming home. Most mornings I took Granddad for a walk around the park, at Mum's request. The doctor had instructed him to take daily exercise but when she had followed him one day she had found he was simply walking to the corner shop to buy a bumper pack of pork scratchings and eating them on a slow walk home.

We walked slowly, both of us with a limp and neither of us with any real place to be.

Mum kept suggesting we do the grounds of the castle 'for a change of scene', but I ignored her, and as the gate shut behind us each morning Granddad nodded firmly in the direction of the park. It wasn't just because this way was shorter, or closer to the betting shop. I think he knew I didn't want to go back there. I wasn't ready. I wasn't sure I would ever be ready.

We did two slow circuits of the duck pond, and sat on a bench in the watery spring sunshine to watch the toddlers and their parents feeding the fat ducks, and the teenagers smoking, yelling and whacking each other; the helpless combat of early courtship. We took a stroll over to the bookie's so Granddad could lose three pounds on an each-way bet on a horse called Wag The Dog. Then, as he crumpled up his betting slip and threw it into the bin, I said I'd buy him a jam doughnut from the supermarket.

'Oh fat,' he said, as we stood in the bakery section.

I frowned at him.

'Oh fat,' he said, pointing at our doughnuts, and laughed.

'Oh. Yup. That's what we'll tell Mum. Low-fat doughnuts.'

Mum said his new medication made him giggly. I had decided there were worse things that could happen to you.

Granddad was still giggling at his own joke as we queued at the checkout. I kept my head down, digging in my pockets for change. I was thinking about whether I would help Dad with the garden that weekend. So it took me a minute to grasp what was being said in whispers behind me.

'It's the guilt. They say she tried to jump off a block of flats.'

'Well, you would, wouldn't you? I know I couldn't live with myself.'

'I'm surprised she can show her face around here.'

I stood very still.

'You know, poor Josie Clark is still mortified. She goes to confession every single week, and you know that woman is as blameless as a line of clean laundry.'

Granddad was pointing at the doughnuts and mouthing at the checkout girl: 'Oh fat.'

She smiled politely. 'Eighty-six pence, please.'

'The Traynors have never been the same.'

'Well, it destroyed them, didn't it?'

'Eighty-six pence, please.'

It took me several seconds to register that the checkout girl was looking at me, waiting. I pulled a handful of coins from my pocket. My fingers fumbled as I tried to sort through them.

'You'd think Josie wouldn't dare leave her in sole charge of her granddaddy, wouldn't you?'

'You don't think she'd . . .'

'Well, you don't know. She's done it the once, after all . . .'

My cheeks were flaming. My money clattered onto the counter. Granddad was still repeating, 'OH FAT. OH FAT,' at the bemused checkout girl, waiting for her to get the joke. I pulled at his sleeve. 'Come on, Granddad, we have to go.'

'Oh fat,' he insisted, again.

'Right,' she said, and smiled kindly.

'*Please, Granddad.*' I felt hot and dizzy, as if I might faint. They might still have been talking but my ears were ringing so loudly I couldn't tell.

'Bye-bye,' he said.

'Bye then,' said the girl.

'Nice,' said Granddad, as we emerged into the sunlight. Then, looking at me: 'Why you crying?'

So here is the thing about being involved in a catastrophic, life-changing event. You think it's just the catastrophic life-changing event that you're going to have to deal with: the flashbacks, the sleepless nights, the endless running over events in your head, asking yourself if you had done the right thing, said the things you should have said, whether you could have changed things, had you done it even a degree differently.

My mother had told me that being with Will at the end would affect the rest of my life, and I had thought she meant me, psychologically. I'd thought she meant the guilt I would have to learn to get over, the grief, the insomnia, the weird, inappropriate bursts of anger, the endless internal dialogue with someone who wasn't even there. But now I saw it wasn't just me: in a digital age, I would be that person for ever. Even if I managed to wipe the whole thing from my memory, I would never be allowed to disassociate myself from Will's death. My name would be tied to his for as long as there were pixels and a screen. People would form judgements about me, based on the most cursory knowledge – or sometimes no knowledge at all – and there was nothing I could do about it.

I cut my hair into a bob. I changed the way I dressed, bagging up everything that had ever made me distinctive and stuffing it into the back of my wardrobe. I adopted Treena's uniform of jeans and a generic T-shirt. Now, when I read newspaper stories about the bank teller who had stolen a fortune, the woman who had killed her child, the sibling who had disappeared, I found myself not shuddering in horror, as I once might have, but wondering instead at the story that hadn't made it into black and white.

What I felt with them was a weird kinship. I was tainted. The world around me knew it. Worse, I had started to know it too.

I tucked what remained of my dark hair into a beanie, put my sunglasses on, and walked to the library, doing everything I could not to let my limp show, even though it made my jaw ache with concentration.

I made my way past the singing-toddler group in the children's corner, and the silent genealogy enthusiasts trying to confirm that, yes, they were distantly connected to King Richard III, and sat down in the corner with the files of local papers. It wasn't hard to locate August 2009. I took a breath, then opened them halfway and flicked through the headlines.

## Local Man Ends His Life at Swiss Clinic

### Traynor Family Ask for Privacy at 'Difficult Time'

*The 35-year-old son of Steven Traynor, custodian of Stortfold Castle, has ended his life at Dignitas, the controversial centre for assisted suicide. Mr Traynor was left quadriplegic after a traffic accident in 2007. He apparently travelled to the clinic with his family and his carer, Louisa Clark, 27, also from Stortfold.*

*Police are investigating the circumstances surrounding the death. Sources say they have not ruled out the possibility that a prosecution may arise.*

*Louisa Clark's parents, Bernard and Josephine Clark, of Renfrew Road, refused to comment.*

*Camilla Traynor, a Justice of the Peace, is understood to have stood down from the bench following her son's suicide. A local source said her position, given the actions of the family, had become 'untenable'.*

And then there it was, Will's face, looking out from the grainy newspaper photograph. That slightly sardonic smile, the direct gaze. I felt, briefly, winded.

*Mr Traynor's death ends a successful career in the City, where he was known as a ruthless asset stripper, but also as someone with a sure eye for a corporate bargain. His colleagues yesterday lined up to pay tribute to a man they described as*

I closed the newspaper. When I could be sure that I had got my face under control, I looked up. Around me the library hummed with quiet industry. The toddlers kept singing, their reedy voices chaotic and meandering, their mothers clapping fondly around them. The librarian behind me was discussing *sotto voce*, with a colleague, the best way to make Thai curry. The man beside me ran his finger down an ancient electoral roll, murmuring, 'Fisher, Fitzgibbon, Fitzwilliam . . .'

I had done nothing. It was more than eighteen months and I had done nothing, bar sell drinks in two different countries and feel sorry for myself. And now, after four weeks back in the house I'd grown up in, I could feel Stortfold reaching out to suck me in, to reassure me that I could be fine here. It would be all right. There might be no great adventures, sure, and a bit of discomfort as people adjusted to my presence again, but there were worse things, right, than to be with your family, loved and secure? Safe?

I looked down at the pile of newspapers in front of me. The most recent front-page headline read:

## ROW OVER DISABLED PARKING SPACE IN FRONT OF POST OFFICE

I thought back to Dad, sitting on my hospital bed, looking in vain for a report of an extraordinary accident.

*I failed you, Will. I failed you in every way possible.*

You could hear the shouting all the way up the street when I finally arrived home. As I opened the door my ears were filled with the sound of Thomas wailing. My sister was scolding him, her finger wagging, in the corner of the living room. Mum was leaning over Granddad with a washing-up bowl of water and a scouring pad, while Granddad politely batted her away.

'What's going on?'

Mum moved to the side and I saw Granddad's face clearly for the first time. He was sporting a new set of jet black eyebrows and a thick black slightly uneven moustache.

'Permanent pen,' said Mum. 'From now on nobody is to leave Granddad napping in the same room as Thomas.'

'You have to stop drawing on things,' Treena was yelling. 'Paper only, okay? Not walls. Not faces. Not Mrs Reynolds's dog. Not my pants.'

'I was doing you days of the week!'

'I don't need days-of-the-week pants!' she shouted. 'And if I did I would spell Wednesday correctly!'

'Don't scold him, Treen,' said Mum, leaning back to see if she'd had any effect. 'It could be a lot worse.'

In our little house, Dad's footsteps coming down the stairs sounded like a particularly emphatic roll of thunder. He barrelled into the front room, his shoulders hunched in frustration, his hair standing up on one side. 'Can't a man get a nap in his own house on his day off? This place is like a ruddy madhouse.'

We all stopped and stared at him.

'What? What did I say?'

'Bernard –'

'Ah, come on. Our Lou doesn't think I mean *her* –'

'Oh, my sweet Lord.' Mum's hand flew to her face.

My sister had started to push Thomas out of the room. 'Oh, boy,' she hissed. 'Thomas, you'd better get out of here right now. Because I swear when your grandpa gets hold of you –'

'What?' Dad frowned. 'What's the matter?'

Granddad barked a laugh. He held up a shaking finger.

It was almost magnificent. Thomas had coloured in the whole of Dad's face with blue marker pen. His eyes emerged like two gooseberries from a sea of cobalt blue. 'What?'

Thomas's voice, as he disappeared down the corridor, was a wail of protest. 'We were watching *Avatar*! He said he wouldn't mind being an avatar!'

Dad's eyes widened. He strode to the mirror over the mantelpiece.

There was a brief silence. 'Oh, my God.'

'Bernard, don't take the Lord's name in vain.'

'He's turned me bloody blue, Josie. I think I'm entitled to take the Lord's name to Butlins in a flipping wheelbarrow. Is this permanent pen? THOMMO? IS THIS PERMANENT PEN?'

'We'll get it off, Dad.' My sister closed the door to the garden behind her. Beyond it you could just make out Thomas's wailing.

'I'm meant to be overseeing the new fencing at the castle tomorrow. I have contractors coming. How the hell am I meant to deal with contractors if I'm *blue*?' Dad spat on his hand and started to rub at his face. The faintest smudging appeared, but mostly seemed to spread onto his palm. 'It's not coming off. Josie, *it's not coming off*!'

Mum shifted her attention from Granddad and set about Dad with the scouring pad. 'Just stay still, Bernard. I'm doing what I can.'

Treena went for her laptop bag. 'I'll go on the internet. I'm sure there's something. Toothpaste or nail-polish remover or bleach or –'

'You are not putting bleach on my ruddy face!' Dad roared. Granddad, with his new pirate moustache, sat giggling in the corner of the room.

I began to edge past them.

Mum was holding Dad's face with her left hand as she scrubbed. She turned, as if she'd only just seen me. 'Lou! I didn't ask – are you okay, love? Did you have a nice walk?' Everyone stopped abruptly to smile at me; a smile that said, *Everything's okay here, Lou. You don't have to worry.* I hated that smile.

'Fine.'

It was the answer they all wanted. Mum turned to Dad. 'That's grand. Isn't it grand, Bernard?'

'It is. Great news.'

'If you sort out your whites, love, I'll pop them in the wash with Daddy's later.'

'Actually,' I said, 'don't bother. I've been thinking. It's time for me to go home.'

Nobody spoke. Mum glanced at Dad. Granddad let out another little giggle and clamped his hand over his mouth.

'Fair enough,' said Dad, with as much dignity as a middle-aged, blueberry-coloured man could muster. 'But if you go back to that flat, Louisa, you go on one condition . . .'

# Chapter Four

'My name is Natasha and I lost my husband to cancer three years ago.'

On a humid Monday night, the members of the Moving On Circle sat in a ring of orange office chairs in the Pentecostal Church Hall, alongside Marc, the leader, a tall, moustachioed man, whose whole being exuded a kind of exhausted melancholy, and one empty chair.

'I'm Fred. My wife, Jilly, died in September. She was seventy-four.'

'Sunil. My twin brother died of leukaemia two years ago.'

'William. Dead father, six months ago. All a bit ridiculous, frankly, as we never really got on when he was alive. I keep asking myself why I'm here.'

There was a peculiar scent to grief. It smelt of damp, imperfectly ventilated church halls and poor-quality teabags. It smelt of meals for one and stale cigarettes, smoked hunched against the cold. It smelt of spritzed hair and armpits, little practical victories against a morass of despair. That smell alone told me I did not belong there, whatever I had promised Dad.

I felt like a fraud. Plus they all looked so . . . . *sad*.

I shifted uneasily in my seat, and Marc caught me. He gave me a reassuring smile. *We know*, it said. *We've been here before.*

*I bet you haven't*, I responded silently.

'Sorry. Sorry I'm late.' The door opened, letting in a blast of warm air, and the empty chair was taken by a mop-headed teenager, who folded his limbs into place as if they were always somehow too long for the space they were in.

43

'Jake. You missed last week. Everything okay?'

'Sorry. Dad messed up at work and he couldn't get me here.'

'Don't worry. It's good you made it. You know where the drinks are.'

The boy glanced around the room from under his long fringe, hesitating slightly when his gaze landed on my glittery green skirt. I pulled my bag onto my lap in an attempt to hide it and he looked away.

'Hello, dear. I'm Daphne. My husband took his own life. I don't think it was the nagging!' The woman's half-laugh seemed to leak pain. She patted her carefully set hair and peered down awkwardly at her knees. 'We were happy. We were.'

The boy's hands were tucked under his thighs. 'Jake. Mum. Two years ago. I've been coming here for the past year because my dad can't deal with it, and I needed someone to talk to.'

'How is your dad this week, Jake?' said Marc.

'Not bad. I mean, he brought a woman home last Friday night but, like, he didn't sit on the sofa and cry afterwards. So that's something.'

'Jake's father is handling his own grief in his own way,' Marc said in my direction.

'Shagging,' said Jake. 'Mostly shagging.'

'I wish I was younger,' said Fred, wistfully. He was wearing a collar and tie, the kind of man who considers himself undressed without one. 'I think that would have been a marvellous way to handle Jilly dying.'

'My cousin picked up a man at my aunt's funeral,' said a woman in the corner who might have been called Leanne; I couldn't remember. She was small and round and had a thick fringe of chocolate-coloured hair.

'Actually during the funeral?'

'She said they went to a Travelodge after the sandwiches.' She shrugged. 'It's the heightened emotions, apparently.'

I was in the wrong place. I could see that now. Surreptitiously, I gathered my belongings, wondering whether I should announce my leaving or whether it would be simpler just to run.

Then Marc turned to me expectantly.

I stared blankly at him.

He raised his eyebrows.

'Oh. Me? Actually, I was just leaving. I think I've . . . I mean, I don't think I'm –'

'Oh, everyone wants to leave on their first day, dear.'

'I wanted to leave on my second and third too.'

'That's the biscuits. I keep telling Marc we should have better ones.'

'Just tell us the bare bones of it, if you like. Don't worry. You're among friends.'

They were all waiting. I couldn't run. I hunched back into my seat. 'Um. Okay. Well, my name's Louisa and the man I . . . I loved . . . died at thirty-five.'

There were a few nods of sympathy.

'Too young. When did this happen, Louisa?'

'Twenty months ago. And a week. And two days.'

'Three years, two weeks and two days.' Natasha smiled at me from across the room.

There was a low murmur of commiseration. Daphne, beside me, reached out a plump, beringed hand and patted my leg.

'We've had many discussions in this room about the particular difficulties when someone dies young,' said Marc. 'How long were you together?'

'Uh. We . . . well . . . a little less than six months.'

A few barely hidden looks of surprise.

'That's – quite brief,' a voice said.

'I'm sure Louisa's pain is just as valid,' said Marc, smoothly. 'And how did he pass, Louisa?'

'Pass what?'

'Die,' said Fred, helpfully.

'Oh. He – uh – he took his own life.'

'That must have been a great shock.'

'Not really. I knew he was planning it.'

There is a peculiar sort of silence, it turns out, when you tell a room full of people who think they know everything there is to know about the death of a loved one that they don't.

I took a breath. 'He knew he wanted to do it before I met him. I tried to change his mind and I couldn't. So I went along with it, because I loved him, and it seemed to make sense at the time. And now it makes a lot less sense. Which is why I'm here.'

'Death never makes sense,' said Daphne.

'Unless you're Buddhist,' said Natasha. 'I keep trying to think Buddhist thoughts but I'm worried that Olaf is going to come back as a mouse or something and I'm going to poison him.' She sighed. 'I have to put poison down. We have a terrible mouse problem in our block.'

'You'll never get rid of them. They're like fleas,' said Sunil. 'For every one you see, there are hundreds of them behind the scenes.'

'You might want to think about what you're doing, Natasha, love,' said Daphne. 'There could be hundreds of little Olafs running around. My Alan could be one of them. You could actually be poisoning the both of them.'

'Well,' said Fred, 'if it's Buddhist, he'd just come back as something else, wouldn't he?'

'But what if it's a fly or something and Natasha kills that too?'

'I'd hate to come back as a fly,' said William. 'Horrible black hairy things.' He shuddered.

'I'm not, like, some mass murderer,' said Natasha. 'You're

46

making it sound like I'm out there slaughtering everyone's reincarnated husbands.'

'Well, that mouse might be someone's husband. Even if it isn't Olaf.'

'I think we should try to steer this session back on track,' said Marc, rubbing his temple. 'Louisa, it's brave of you to come and tell your story. Why don't you tell us a bit more about how you and – what was his name? – how you met. You're in a circle of trust. We've all pledged that our stories go no further than these walls.'

It was at this point that I happened to catch Jake's eye. He glanced at Daphne, then at me, and shook his head subtly.

'I met him at work,' I said. 'And his name was . . . Bill.'

Despite what I had promised Dad, I wasn't planning to attend the Moving On Circle. But my return to work had been so awful that by the time the day ended I hadn't been able to face going home to an empty flat.

'You're back!' Carly had placed the cup of coffee on the bar, taken the businessman's change, and hugged me, all while dropping the coins into the correct sections of the till drawer, in one fluid motion. 'What the hell happened? Tim just told us you had an accident. And then he left so I wasn't even sure you were coming back.'

'Long story.' I stared at her. 'Uh . . . what are you wearing?'

Nine o'clock on Monday morning and the airport had been a blue-grey blur of men charging laptops, staring into iPhones, reading the City pages or talking discreetly into handsets about market share. Carly caught the eye of some-one on the other side of the till. 'Yeah. Well, things have changed since you've been gone.'

I turned to see a businessman standing on the wrong side of the bar. I blinked at him and put my bag down. 'Um – if you'd like to wait there, I'll serve you –'

'You must be Louise.' His handshake was emphatic and without warmth. 'I'm the new bar manager. Richard Percival.' I took in his slick hair, his suit, his pale blue shirt, and wondered what kind of bars he had actually managed.

'Nice to meet you.'

'You're the one who's been off for two months.'

'Well. Yes. I –'

He walked along the optics, scanning each bottle. 'I just want you to know that I'm not a fan of people taking endless sick leave.'

My neck shifted a few centimetres back in my collar.

'I'm just laying down a marker, Louise. I'm not one of those managers who turn a blind eye. I know that in many companies time off is pretty much considered a staff perk. But not in companies where I work.'

'Believe me, I've not thought of the last nine weeks as a perk.'

He examined the underside of a tap, and rubbed at it meditatively with his thumb.

I took a breath before I spoke. 'I fell off a building. Perhaps I could show you my surgery scars. So, you know, you can be reassured that I'm unlikely to want to do it again.'

He stared at me. 'There's no need to be sarcastic. I'm not saying you're about to have other accidents, but your sick leave is, *pro rata*, at an unusually high level for someone who has worked for this company a relatively short time. That's all I wanted to point out. That it has been noted.'

He wore cufflinks with racing cars on them.

'Message received, Mr Percival.' I said. 'I'll do my best to avoid further near-fatal accidents.'

'You'll need a uniform. If you give me five minutes I'll get one out of the stockroom. What size are you? Twelve? Fourteen?'

I stared at him. 'Ten.'

He raised an eyebrow. I raised one back. As he walked to his office, Carly leaned over from the coffee machine and smiled sweetly in his direction. 'Utter, utter bellend,' she said, from the side of her mouth.

She wasn't wrong. From the moment I returned, Richard Percival was, in the words of my father, all over me like a bad suit. He measured my measures, checked every corner of the bar for molecular peanut crumbs, was in and out of the loos checking on hygiene and wouldn't let us leave until he had stood over us cashing up and ensuring each till roll matched takings to the last penny.

I no longer had time to chat to the customers, to look up departure times, hand over lost passports, contemplate the planes we could see taking off through the great glass window. I didn't even have time to be irritated by *Celtic Pan Pipes, Vol. III*. If a customer was left waiting to be served for more than ten seconds Richard would magically appear from his office, sighing ostentatiously, then apologize loudly and repeatedly because they had been kept waiting *so long*. Carly and I, usually busy with other customers, would exchange secret glances of resignation and contempt.

He spent half the day meeting reps, the rest on the phone to Head Office, bleating about Footfall and Spend Per Head. We were encouraged to upsell with every transaction, and taken to one side for a talking-to if we forgot. All that was bad enough.

But then there was the uniform.

Carly came into the Ladies as I was finishing getting changed and stood beside me in front of the mirror. 'We look like a pair of eejits,' she said.

Not content with dark skirts and white shirts, some marketing genius high up the corporate ladder had decided that the atmosphere of the Shamrock and Clover chain would benefit from genuine Irish clothing. This genuine Irish clothing had evidently been thought up by someone who believed that across Dublin, right this minute, businesswomen and check-out girls were pirouetting across their workplaces dressed in embroidered tabards, knee-high socks and laced-up dancing shoes, all in glittering emerald green. With accompanying ringlet wigs.

'Jesus. If my boyfriend saw me dressed like this he'd dump me.' Carly lit a cigarette, and climbed up on the sink to disable the smoke alarm on the ceiling. 'Mind you, he'd probably want to do me first. The perv.'

'What do the men have to wear?' I pulled my short skirt out at the sides and eyed Carly's lighter nervously, wondering how flammable I was.

'Look outside. There's only Richard. And he has to wear that shirt with a green logo. The poor thing.'

'That's it? No pixie shoes? Or little leprechaun hat?'

'Surprise, surprise. It's only us girls who have to work look-ing like porno Munchkins.'

'I look like Dolly Parton: The Early Years in this wig.'

'Grab a red one. Lucky us, we have a choice of three colours.'

From somewhere outside we could hear Richard calling. My stomach had begun to clench reflexively when I heard his voice.

'Anyway, I'm not staying. I'm going to *Riverdance* my way out of this place and into another job,' Carly said. 'He can stick his bloody shamrocks up his tight little corporate arse.' She had given what I could only describe as a sarcastic skip, and left the Ladies. I spent the rest of the day getting little electric shocks from the static.

*

The Moving On Circle ended at half past nine. I walked out into the humid summer evening, exhausted by the twin trials of work and the evening's events. I took off my jacket, too hot, feeling suddenly that, having laid myself bare in front of a room full of strangers, being seen in a *faux*-Irish dancer uniform, which was, in truth, ever so slightly too small, didn't really make much difference.

I hadn't been able to talk about Will – not the way they talked, as if their loved ones were still part of their lives, perhaps in the next room.

– *Oh yes, my Jilly used to do that all the time.*

– *I can't delete my brother's voicemail message. I have a little listen to his voice when I feel like I'm going to forget what he sounded like.*

– *Sometimes I can hear him in the next room.*

I could barely even say Will's name. And listening to their tales of family relationships, of thirty-year marriages, shared houses, lives, children, I felt like a fraud. I had been a carer for someone for six months. I'd loved him, and watched him end his life. How could these strangers possibly understand what Will and I had been to each other during that time? How could I explain the way we had so swiftly understood each other, the shorthand jokes, the blunt truths and raw secrets? How could I convey the way those short months had changed the way I felt about everything? The way he had skewed my world so totally that it made no sense without him in it?

And when it came down to it, what was the point in re-examining your sadness all the time anyway? It was like picking at a wound and refusing to let it heal. I knew what I had been part of. I knew what my role was. What was the point in going over and over it?

I wouldn't come next week, I knew now. I would find an excuse for Dad.

I walked slowly across the car park, rummaging in my bag for my keys, telling myself it had at least meant that I hadn't had to spend another evening alone in front of my television, dreading the passing of the twelve hours until I had to return to work.

'His name wasn't really Bill, right?'

Jake fell into step alongside me.

'Nope.'

'Daphne's like a one-woman broadcasting corporation. She means well, but your personal story will be all over her social club before you can say Rodent Reincarnation.'

'Thanks for that.'

He grinned at me, and nodded towards my Lurex skirt. 'Nice threads, by the way. It's a good look for a grief-counselling session.' He stopped briefly to retie a shoelace.

I stopped with him. I hesitated, then said: 'I'm sorry about your mum.'

His face was sombre. 'You can't say that. It's like prison – you can't ask someone what they're in for.'

'Really? Oh, I'm sorry. I didn't –'

'I'm joking. See you next week.'

A man leaning against a motorbike lifted a hand in greeting. He stepped forward as Jake crossed the car park and enveloped him in a bear hug, kissing his cheek. I stopped to watch, mostly because it was rare to see a man hug his son like that in public, once they were over satchel-carrying age.

'How was it?'

'Okay. The usual.' Jake gestured to me. 'Oh, this is . . . Louisa. She's new.'

The man squinted at me. He was tall and broad-shouldered. A nose that might once have been broken gave him the faintly bruising appearance of a former boxer.

I nodded a polite greeting. 'It was nice to meet you, Jake.

Bye then.' I lifted a hand, and began to make my way to my car. But as I passed the man he kept staring at me, and I felt myself colour under the intensity of his gaze. 'You're that girl,' he said.

*Oh, no*, I thought, slowing suddenly. *Not here too.*

I stared at the ground for a moment and took a breath. Then I turned back to face them both. 'Okay. As I've just made clear in the group, my friend made his own decisions. All I ever did was support them. Not that, if I'm honest, I really want to get into this right here and with a complete stranger.'

Jake's father continued to squint at me. He lifted his hand to his head.

'I understand that not everybody will get it. But that's the way it was. I don't feel I have to debate my choices. And I'm really tired and it's been a bit of a day, and I think I'm going to go home now.'

He cocked his head to one side. And then he said, 'I have no idea what you're talking about.'

I frowned.

'The limp. I noticed you have a limp. You live near that massive new development, right? You're the girl who fell off the roof. March. April.'

And suddenly I recognized him. 'Oh – you were –'

'The paramedic. We were the team who picked you up. I'd been wondering what happened to you.'

I almost buckled with relief. I let my gaze run over his face, his hair, his arms, suddenly recalling with Pavlovian accuracy his reassuring manner, the sound of the siren, the faint scent of lemons. And I let out a breath. 'I'm good. Well. Not good exactly. I have a shot hip and a new boss who's an utter arse and – you know – I'm at a grief-counselling club in a damp church hall with people who are just really, really . . .'

'Sad,' said Jake, helpfully.

'The hip will get better. It's plainly not hindering your dance career.'

My laugh emerged as a honk.

'Oh. No. This is . . . The outfit is related to the boss who is an arse. Not my normal mode of dress. Anyway. Thank you. Wow . . .' I put my hand to my head. 'This is weird. You saved me.'

'It's good to see you. We don't often get to see what happens afterwards.'

'You did a great job. It was . . . Well, you were really kind. I remember that much.'

'*De nada.*'

I stared at him.

'*De nada.* Spanish. "It was nothing."'

'Oh, okay, then. I take it all back. Thanks for nothing.'

He smiled and raised a paddle-sized hand.

Afterwards, I didn't know what made me do it. 'Hey.'

He looked back towards me. 'It's Sam, actually.'

'Sam. I didn't jump.'

'Okay.'

'No. Really. I mean, I know you've just seen me coming out of a grief-counselling group and everything but it's – well, I just – I wouldn't jump.'

He gave me a look that seemed to suggest he had seen and heard everything.

'Good to know.'

We gazed at each other for a minute. Then he lifted his hand again. 'Nice to see you, Louisa.'

He pulled on a helmet and Jake slid onto the bike behind him. I found myself watching as they pulled out of the car park. And because I was still watching I caught Jake's exaggerated eye roll as he pulled on his own helmet. And then I remembered what he had said in the session.

*The compulsive shagger.*

'Idiot,' I told myself, and limped across the rest of the tarmac to where my car was boiling gently in the evening heat.

# Chapter Five

I lived on the edge of the City. In case I was in any doubt, across the road stood a huge office-block-sized crater, surrounded by a developer's hoarding, upon which was written: FARTHINGATE – WHERE THE CITY BEGINS. We existed at the exact point where the glossy glass temples to finance butted up against the grubby old brick and sash-windows of curry shops and twenty-four-hour grocers, of stripper pubs and minicab offices that resolutely refused to die. My block sat among those architectural refuseniks, a lead-stained, warehouse-style building staring at the steady onslaught of glass and steel and wondering how long it could survive, perhaps rescued by a hipster juice bar or pop-up retail experience. I knew nobody except Samir who ran the convenience store and the woman in the bagel bakery, who smiled at me in greeting but didn't seem to speak any English.

Mostly this anonymity suited me. I had come here, after all, to escape my history, from feeling as if everyone knew every thing there was to know about me. And the City had begun to alter me. I had come to know my little corner of it, its rhythms and its danger points. I learned that if you gave money to the drunk at the bus station he would come and sit outside your flat for the next eight weeks; that if I had to walk through the estate at night it was wise to do it with my keys lodged between my fingers; that if I was walking out to get a late-night bottle of wine it was probably better not to glance at the group of young men huddled outside Kebab Korner.

I was no longer disturbed by the persistent *whump whump whump* of the police helicopter overhead.

I could survive. Besides, I knew, more than anyone, that worse things could happen.

'Hey.'

'Hey, Lou. Can't sleep again?'

'It's just gone ten o'clock here.'

'So, what's up?'

Nathan, Will's former physio, had spent the last nine months working in New York for a middle-aged CEO with a Wall Street reputation, a four-storey townhouse and a muscular condition. Calling him in my sleepless small hours had become something of a habit. It was good to know there was someone who understood, out there in the dark, even if sometimes his news felt tinged with a series of small blows – *everyone else has moved on. Everyone else has achieved something.*

'So how's the Big Apple?'

'Not bad?' His Antipodean drawl made every answer a question.

I lay down on the sofa, pushing my feet up on the armrest. 'Yeah. That doesn't tell me a whole lot.'

'Okay. Well, got a pay rise, so that was cool. Booked myself a flight home in a couple of weeks to see the olds. So that'll be good. They're over the moon because my sister's having a baby. Oh, and I met a really fit bird in a bar down on Sixth Avenue and we were getting on real well so I asked her out, and when I told her what I did, she said sorry but she only went out with guys who wore suits to work.' He laughed.

I found I was smiling. 'So scrubs don't count?'

'Apparently not. Though she did say she might have changed her mind if I was an actual doctor.' He laughed again. Nathan was made of equanimity. 'It's cool. Girls like that get all picky if you don't take them to the right restaurants and stuff. Better to know sooner, right? How about you?'

I shrugged. 'Getting there. Sort of.'

'You still sleeping in his T-shirt?'

'No. It stopped smelling of him. And it had started to get a bit unsavoury, if I'm honest. I washed it and I've packed it in tissue. But I've got his jumper for bad days.'

'Good to have back-up.'

'Oh, and I went to the grief-counselling group.'

'How was it?'

'Crap. I felt like a fraud.'

Nathan waited.

I shifted the pillow under my head. 'Did I imagine it all, Nathan? Sometimes I think I've made what happened between Will and me so much bigger in my head. Like how can I have loved someone that much in such a short time? And all these things I think about the two of us – did we actually feel what I remember? The further we get from it, the more those six months just seems like this weird . . . dream.'

There was a tiny pause before Nathan responded. 'You didn't imagine it, mate.'

I rubbed my eyes. 'Am I the only one? Still missing him?'

Another short silence.

'Nah. He was a good bloke. The best.'

That was one of the things I liked about Nathan. He didn't mind a lengthy phone silence. I finally sat up and blew my nose. 'Anyway. I don't think I'll go back. I'm not sure it's my thing.'

'Give it a go, Lou. You can't judge anything from one session.'

'You sound like my dad.'

'Well, he always was a sensible fella.'

I started at the sound of the doorbell. Nobody ever rang my doorbell, aside from Mrs Nellis in flat twelve, when the postman had accidentally swapped our mail. I doubted she was up at this hour. And I certainly was not in receipt of her *Elizabethan Doll* partwork magazine.

It rang again. A third time, shrill and insistent.

'I've got to go. Someone's at the door.'

'Keep your pecker up, mate. You'll be okay.'

I put the phone down and stood up warily. I had no friends nearby. I hadn't worked out how you actually made them when you moved to a new area and spent most of your upright hours working. And if my parents had decided to stage an intervention and bring me back to Stortfold, they would have organized it between rush-hours as neither of them liked driving in the dark.

I waited, wondering if whoever it was would simply realize their mistake and go away. But it rang again, jarring and end-less, as if they were now leaning against the bell.

I got up and walked to the door. 'Who is it?'

'I need to talk to you.'

A girl's voice. I peered through the spy-hole. She was look-ing down at her feet, so I could only make out long chestnut hair, an oversized bomber jacket. She swayed slightly, rubbed at her nose. Drunk?

'I think you have the wrong flat.'

'Are you Louisa Clark?'

I paused. 'How do you know my name?'

'I need to talk to you. Can you just open the door?'

'It's almost half past ten at night.'

'Yeah. That's why I'd rather not be standing here in your corridor.'

I had lived there long enough to know not to open my door to strangers. In that area of town it was not unusual to get the odd junkie ringing bells speculatively in the hope of cash. But this was a well-spoken girl. And young. Too young to be one of the journalists who had briefly fixated on the story of the handsome former whizz-kid who had decided to end his life. Too young to be out this late? I angled my head, trying to see if there was anyone else in the corridor. It appeared to be empty. 'Can you tell me what it's about?'

'Not out here, no.'

I opened the door to the length of the safety chain, so that we were eye to eye. 'You're going to have to give me more than that.'

She couldn't have been more than sixteen, the dewy plumpness of youth still visible in her cheeks. Her hair long and lustrous. Long skinny legs in tight black jeans. Flicky eyeliner, in a pretty face. 'So . . . who did you say you were?' I asked.

'Lily. Lily Houghton-Miller. Look,' she said, and lifted her chin an inch, 'I need to talk to you about my father.'

'I think you have the wrong person. I don't know anyone called Houghton-Miller. There must be another Louisa Clark you've confused me with.'

I made to shut the door, but she had wedged the toe of her shoe in it. I looked down at it, and slowly back up at her.

'Not *his* name,' she said, as though I was stupid. And when she spoke, her eyes were both fierce and searching. 'His name is Will Traynor.'

Lily Houghton-Miller stood in the middle of my living room and surveyed me with the detached interest of a scientist gazing at a new variety of manure-based invertebrate. 'Wow. What are you wearing?'

'I – I work in an Irish pub.'

'Pole dancing?' Having apparently lost interest in me, she pivoted slowly, gazing at the room. 'This is where you actually live? Where's your furniture?'

'I just moved in.'

'One sofa, one television, two boxes of books?' She nodded towards the chair on which I sat, my breathing still unbalanced, trying to make any kind of sense out of what she had just told me.

I stood up. 'I'm going to get a drink. Would you like something?'

'I'll have a Coke. Unless you've got wine.'

'How old are you?'

'Why do you want to know?'

'I don't understand . . .' I went behind the kitchen counter. 'Will didn't have children. I would have known.' I frowned at her, suddenly suspicious. 'Is this some kind of joke?'

'A joke?'

'Will and I talked . . . a lot. He would have told me.'

'Yeah. Well, turns out he didn't. And I need to talk about him to someone who is not going to totally freak out every time I even mention his name, like the rest of my family.'

She picked up the card from my mother and put it down again. 'I'm hardly going to say it as a *joke*. I mean, yeah. My real dad, some sad bloke in a wheelchair. Like *that*'s funny.'

I handed her a glass of water. 'But who . . . who is your family? I mean, who is your mother?'

'Have you got any cigarettes?' She had started pacing around the room, touching things, picking up the few belongings I had and putting them down. When I shook my head, she said, 'My mother is called Tanya. Tanya Miller. She's married to my stepdad, who is called Francis Stupid Fuckface Houghton.'

'Nice name.'

She put down the water and pulled a packet of cigarettes from her bomber jacket and lit one. I was going to say she couldn't smoke in my home, but I was too taken aback, so I simply walked over to the window and opened it.

I couldn't take my eyes off her. I could maybe see little hints of Will. It was in her blue eyes, that vaguely caramel colouring. It was in the way she tilted her chin slightly before she spoke, her unblinking stare. Or was I seeing what I wanted to see? She gazed out of the window at the street below.

'Lily, before we go on there's something I need to –'

'I know he's dead,' she said. She inhaled sharply and blew the smoke into the centre of the room. 'I mean, that was how I found out. There was some documentary on television about assisted suicide and they mentioned his name and Mum totally freaked out for no reason and ran to the bathroom and Fuckface went after her so obviously I listened outside. And she was in total shock because she hadn't even known that he'd ended up in a wheelchair. I heard the whole thing. I mean, it's not like I didn't know Fuckface wasn't my real dad. It's just that my mum only ever said my real dad was an asshole who didn't want to know me.'

'Will wasn't an asshole.'

She shrugged. 'He sounded like one. But, anyway, when I tried to ask her questions she just started totally flipping out and said that I knew everything about him that I needed to know and Fuckface Francis had been a better dad to me than Will Traynor ever would have been and I really should leave it alone.'

I sipped my water. I had never wanted a glass of wine more. 'So what did you do?'

She took another drag of her cigarette. 'I Googled him, of course. And I found you.'

I needed to be alone to digest what she had told me. It was too overwhelming. I didn't know what to make of the spiky girl, who walked around my living room, making the air around her crackle.

'So did he not say anything about me *at all*?'

I was staring at her shoes: ballerina pumps, heavily scuffed as if they had spent too much time shuffling around London streets. I felt as if I was being reeled in. 'How old are you, Lily?'

'Sixteen. Do I at least look like him? I saw a picture on Google images, but I was thinking maybe you had a photograph.' She gazed around the living room. 'Are all your photographs in boxes?'

She eyed the cardboard crates in the corner, and I wondered whether she would actually open them and start going through them. I was pretty sure the one she was about to go into contained Will's jumper. And I felt a sudden panic. 'Um. Lily. This is all . . . quite a lot to take in. And if you are who you say you are, then we – we do have a lot to discuss. But it's nearly eleven o'clock, and I'm not sure this is the time to start. Where do you live?'

'St John's Wood.'

'Well. Uh. Your parents are going to be wondering where you are. Why don't I give you my number and we –'

'I can't go *home*.' She faced the window, flicked the ash out with a practised finger. 'Strictly speaking, I'm not even meant to be here. I'm meant to be at school. Weekly boarding. They'll all be freaking out now because I'm not there.' She pulled out her phone, as an afterthought, and grimaced at whatever she saw on its screen, then shoved it back in her pocket.

'Well, I'm . . . not sure what I can do other than –'

'I thought maybe I could stay here? Just tonight? And then you could tell me some more stuff about him?'

'Stay *here*? No. No. I'm sorry, you can't. I don't know you.'

'But you did know my dad. Did you say you think he didn't actually know about me?'

'You need to go home. Look, let's call your parents. They can come and collect you. Let's do that and I –'

She stared at me. 'I thought you'd help me.'

'I will help you, Lily. But this isn't the way to –'

'You don't believe me, do you?'

'I – I have no idea what to –'

'You don't want to help. You don't want to do anything. What have you actually told me about my dad? Nothing. How have you actually helped? You haven't. Thanks.'

'Hold on! That's not fair – we've only just –'

But the girl flicked her cigarette butt out of the window and turned to walk past me out of the room.

'What? Where are you going?'

'Oh, what do *you* care?' she said, and before I could say anything more, the front door had slammed and she was gone.

I sat very still on my sofa, trying to digest what had just happened for the best part of an hour, Lily's voice ringing in my ears. Had I heard her correctly? I went over and over what she had told me, trying to recall it through the buzz in my ears.

*My father was Will Traynor.*

Lily's mother had apparently told her Will had not wanted anything to do with her. But surely he would have mentioned something to me. We had no secrets from each other. Weren't we the two people who had managed to talk about everything? For a moment I wobbled: had Will not been as honest with me as I'd believed? Had he actually possessed the ability simply to airbrush an entire daughter out of his conscience?

My thoughts were chasing each other in circles. I grabbed my laptop, sat cross-legged on the sofa and typed 'Lily Hawton Miller' into a search engine, and when that came up with no results, I tried again with various spellings, settling on 'Lily Houghton-Miller', which brought up a number of hockey-fixture results posted by a school called Upton Tilton in

Shropshire. I called up some of the images, and as I zoomed in, there she was, an unsmiling girl in a row of smiling hockey players. *Lily Houghton-Miller played a brave, if unsuccessful defence.* It was dated two years ago. Boarding-school. She'd said she was meant to be at boarding-school. But it still didn't mean she was any relation of Will or, indeed, that her mother had been telling the truth about her parentage.

I altered the search to just the words 'Houghton-Miller', which brought up a short diary item about Francis and Tanya Houghton-Miller attending a banking dinner at the Savoy, and a planning application from the previous year for a wine cellar under a house in St John's Wood.

I sat back, thinking, then did a search on 'Tanya Miller' and 'William Traynor'. It turned up nothing. I tried again, using 'Will Traynor', and suddenly I was on a Facebook thread for alumni of Durham University, on which several women, all of whose names seemed to end in '-ella' – Estella, Fenella, Arabella – were discussing Will's death.

I couldn't believe it when I heard it on the news. Him of all people! RIP Will.

Nobody gets through life unscathed. You know Rory Appleton died in the Turks and Caicos, in a speed-boating accident?

Didn't he do geography? Red hair?

No, PPE.

I'm sure I snogged Rory at the Freshers' Ball. Enormous tongue.

I'm not being funny, Fenella, but that's rather bad taste. The poor man is dead.

Wasn't Will Traynor the one who went out with Tanya Miller for the whole of the third year?

I don't see how it's in poor taste to mention that I may have kissed
    someone just because they then went on to pass away.

I'm not saying you have to rewrite history. It's just his wife might be
    reading this and she might not want to know that her beloved stuck
    his tongue in the face of some girl on Facebook.

I'm sure she knows his tongue was enormous. I mean, she married him.

Rory Appleton got married?

Tanya married some banker. Here's a link. I always thought she and Will
    would get married when we were at uni. They were so gorgeous.

I clicked on the link, which showed a picture of a reed-thin
blonde woman with an artfully tousled chignon smiling as she
stood on the steps of a register office with an older, dark-
haired man. A short distance away, at the edge of the picture,
a young girl in a white tulle dress was scowling. She bore a
definite resemblance to the Lily Houghton-Miller I had met.
But the image was seven years old, and in truth it could have
portrayed any grumpy young bridesmaid with long mid-
brown hair.

I reread the thread, and closed my laptop. What should I
do? If she really was Will's daughter, should I call the school?
I was pretty sure there were rules about strangers who tried
to contact teenage girls.

And what if this really was some elaborate scam? Will had
died a wealthy man. It wasn't beyond the realm of possibility
that somebody could think up an intricate scheme by which
to leach money from his family. When Dad's mate Chalky died
of a heart attack, seventeen people had turned up at the wake
telling his wife he owed them betting money.

I would steer clear, I decided. There was too much potential for pain and disruption if I got this wrong.

But when I went to bed it was Lily's voice I heard, echoing into the silent flat.

*Will Traynor was my father.*

# Chapter Six

'Sorry. My alarm didn't go off.' I rushed past Richard and hung my coat on the peg, pulling my synthetic skirt down over my thighs.

'Three-quarters of an hour late. This is not acceptable.'

It was eight thirty a.m. We were, I noted, the only two people in the bar.

Carly had left: she hadn't even bothered telling Richard to his face. She simply sent a text message telling him she would drop the sodding uniform in at the end of the week, and that as she was owed two weeks' sodding holiday pay she was taking her sodding notice in lieu. *If she had bothered to read the employment handbook*, he had fumed, *she would have known that taking notice in lieu of holiday was completely unacceptable. It was there in Section Three, as clear as day*, if *she had cared to look. And the sodding language was simply unnecessary.*

He was now going through the due processes to find a replacement. Which meant that until due processes were completed it was just me. And Richard.

'I'm sorry. Something . . . came up at home.'

I had woken with a start at seven thirty, unable for several minutes to recall what country I was in or what my name was, and had lain on my bed, unable to move, while I mulled over the previous evening's events.

'A good worker doesn't bring their home life to the workplace with them,' Richard intoned, as he pushed past me with his clipboard. I watched him go, wondering if he even had a home life. He never seemed to spend any time there.

'Yeah. Well. A good employer doesn't make his employee wear a uniform Stringfellow's would have rejected as tacky,' I muttered, as I tapped my code into the till, pulling the hem of my Lurex skirt down with my free hand.

He turned swiftly, and walked back across the bar. 'What did you say?'

'Nothing.'

'Yes, you did.'

'I said I'll remember that for next time. Thank you very much for reminding me.'

I smiled sweetly at him.

He looked at me for several seconds longer than was comfortable for either of us. And then he said, 'The cleaner is off sick again. You'll need to do the Gents before you start on the bar.'

His gaze was steady, daring me to say something. I reminded myself that I could not afford to lose this job. I swallowed. 'Right.'

'Oh, and cubicle three's a bit of a mess.'

'Jolly good,' I said.

He turned on his highly polished heel and walked back into the office. I sent mental voodoo arrows into the back of his head the whole way.


'This week's Moving On Circle is about guilt, survivor's guilt, guilt that we didn't do enough . . . It's often this that keeps us from moving forward.'

Marc waited as we handed around the biscuit tin, then leaned forward on his plastic chair, his hands clasped in front of him. He ignored the low rumbling of discontent that there were no bourbon creams.

'I used to get ever so impatient with Jilly,' Fred said, into the silence. 'When she had the dementia, I mean. She would put dirty plates back in the kitchen cupboards and I would find them days later and . . . I'm ashamed to say, I did shout at her a couple of times.' He wiped at an eye. 'She was such a houseproud woman, before. That was the worst thing.'

'You lived with Jilly's dementia for a long time, Fred. You'd have to have been superhuman not to find it a strain.'

'Dirty plates would drive me mad,' said Daphne. 'I think I would have shouted something terrible.'

'But it wasn't her fault, was it?' Fred straightened on his chair. 'I think about those plates a lot. I wish I could go back. I'd wash them up without saying a word. Just give her a nice cuddle instead.'

'I find myself fantasizing about men on the tube,' said Natasha. 'Sometimes when I'm riding up an escalator, I exchange a look with some random man going down. And before I've even got to the platform I'm building a whole relationship with him in my head. You know, where he runs back down the escalator because he just knows there's something magical between us, and we stand there, gazing at each other, amid the crowds of commuters on the Piccadilly Line, and then we go for a drink, and before you know it, we're –'

'Sounds like a Richard Curtis movie,' said William.

'I like Richard Curtis movies,' said Sunil. 'Especially that one about the actress and the man in his pants.'

'Shepherd's Bush,' said Daphne.

There was a short pause. 'I think it's *Notting Hill*, Daphne,' Marc said.

'I preferred Daphne's version. What?' said William, snorting. 'We're not allowed to laugh now?'

'So in my head we're getting married,' said Natasha. 'And then when we're standing at the altar, I think, What am I doing? Olaf only died three years ago and I'm fantasizing about other men.'

Marc leaned back in his chair. 'You don't think that's natural, after three years by yourself? To fantasize about other relationships?'

'But if I had really loved Olaf, surely I wouldn't think about anyone else.'

'It's not the Victorian age,' said William. 'You don't have to wear widow's weeds till you're elderly.'

'If it was me that died, I'd hate the thought of Olaf falling in love with someone else.'

'You wouldn't know,' said William. 'You'd be dead.'

'What about you, Louisa?' Marc had noticed my silence. 'Do you suffer feelings of guilt?'

'Can we – can we do someone else?'

'I'm Catholic,' said Daphne. 'I feel guilty about everything. It's the nuns, you know.'

'What do you find difficult about this subject, Louisa?'

I took a swig of coffee. I felt everyone's eyes on me. *Come on*, I told myself. I swallowed. 'That I couldn't stop him,' I said. 'Sometimes I think if I had been smarter, or . . . handled things differently . . . or just been more – I don't know. More anything.'

'You feel guilty about Bill's death because you feel you could have stopped him?'

I pulled at a thread. When it came away in my hand it seemed to loosen something in my brain. 'Also that I'm living a life that is so much less than the one I promised him I'd live. And guilt over the fact that he basically paid for my flat when my sister will probably never be able to afford one of her own. And guilt that I don't even really like living in it, because it doesn't feel like mine, and it feels wrong to make it nice because all I associate it with is the fact that W— Bill is dead and somehow I benefited from that.'

There was a short silence.

'You shouldn't feel guilty about property,' said Daphne.

'I wish someone would leave me a flat,' said Sunil.

'But that's just a fairy tale ending, isn't it? Man dies, everyone learns something, moves on, creates something wonderful out of his death.' I was speaking without thinking now. 'I've done none of those things. I've basically just failed at all of it.'

'My dad cries nearly every time he shags someone who isn't my mum,' Jake blurted, twisting his hands together. He stared out from under his fringe. 'He charms women into sleeping with him and then he gets off on being sad about it. It's like as long as he feels guilty about it afterwards it's okay.'

'You think he uses his guilt as a crutch.'

'I just think either you have sex and feel glad that you're having all the sex –'

'I wouldn't feel guilty about having all the sex,' said Fred.

'Or you treat women like human beings and make sure you don't have anything to feel guilty about. Or don't even sleep with anyone, and treasure Mum's memory until you're actually ready to move on.'

His voice broke on *treasure* and his jaw tautened. We were used, by then, to the sudden stiffening of expressions, and an unspoken group courtesy meant that we each looked away until any potential tears subsided.

Marc's voice was gentle. 'Have you told your father how you feel, Jake?'

'We don't talk about Mum. He's fine as long as, you know, we don't actually mention her.'

'That's quite a burden for you to carry alone.'

'Yeah. Well . . . That's why I'm here, isn't it?'

There was a short silence.

'Have a biscuit, Jake darling,' said Daphne, and we passed the tin back around the circle, vaguely reassured, in some way nobody could quite define, when Jake finally took one.

I kept thinking about Lily. I barely registered Sunil's tale of weeping in the baked-goods section of the supermarket, and just about raised a sympathetic expression for Fred's solitary marking of Jilly's birthday with a bunch of foil balloons. For days now the whole episode with Lily had taken on the tenor of a dream, vivid and surreal.

*How could Will have had a daughter?*

'You look happy.'

Jake's father was leaning against his motorbike as I walked across the church hall's car park.

I stopped in front of him. 'It's a grief-counselling session. I'm hardly going to come out tap-dancing.'

'Fair point.'

'It's not what you think. I mean, it's not me,' I said. 'It's . . . to do with a teenager.'

He tipped his head backwards, spying Jake behind me. 'Oh. Right. Well, you have my sympathies there. You look young to have a teenager, if you don't mind me saying.'

'Oh. No. Not mine! It's . . . complicated.'

'I'd love to give you advice. But I don't have a clue.' He stepped forward and enveloped Jake in a hug, which the boy tolerated glumly. 'You all right, young man?'

'Fine.'

'Fine,' Sam said, glancing sideways at me. 'There you go. Universal response of all teenagers to everything. War, famine, lottery wins, global fame. It's all *fine*.'

'You didn't need to pick me up. I'm going to Jools's.'

'You want a lift?'

'She lives, like, there. In that block.' Jake pointed. 'I think I can manage that by myself.'

Sam's expression remained even. 'So, maybe text me next time? Save me coming here and waiting?'

Jake shrugged, and walked off, his rucksack slung over his shoulder. We watched him go in silence.

'I'll see you later, yes, Jake?'

Jake lifted a hand without looking back.

'Okay,' I said. 'So now I feel a tiny bit better.'

Sam gave the slightest shake of his head. He watched his son go, as if, even now, he couldn't bear to just leave him. 'Some days he feels it harder than others.' And then he turned to me. 'You want to grab a coffee or something, Louisa? Just so I don't have to feel like the world's biggest loser? It *is* Louisa, right?'

I thought of what Jake had said in that evening's session. *On Friday Dad brought home this psycho blonde called Mags who is obsessed with him. When he was in the shower she kept asking me if he talked about her when she wasn't there.*

The compulsive shagger. But he was nice enough, and he had helped put me back together in the ambulance, and the alternative was another night at home wondering what had been going on in Lily Houghton-Miller's head. 'If we can talk about anything but teenagers.'

'Can we talk about your outfit?'

I looked down at my green Lurex skirt and my Irish dancing shoes. 'Absolutely not.'

'It was worth a try,' he said, and climbed onto his motorbike.

We sat outside a near-empty bar a short distance from my flat. He drank black coffee, and I had fruit juice.

I had time to study him surreptitiously now that I wasn't dodging cars in a car park or lying strapped to a hospital gurney. His nose held a tell-tale ridge, and his eyes crinkled in a way that suggested there was almost no human behaviour he hadn't seen and, perhaps, been slightly amused by. He was tall and broad, his features coarser than Will's somehow, yet he moved with a kind of gentle economy, as if he had absorbed the effort of not damaging things just from his size. He was evidently more comfortable with listening than talking, or perhaps it was just that it was unsettling to be on my own with a man after so much time because I found I was gabbling. I talked about my job at the bar, making him laugh about Richard Percival and the horrors of my outfit, and how strange it had been to live briefly at home again, and my father's bad jokes, and Granddad and his doughnuts, and my nephew's unorthodox use of a blue marker pen. But I was conscious as I spoke, as so often these days, of how much I didn't say: about Will, about the surreal thing that had happened to me the previous evening, about me. With Will I had never had to consider what I said: talking to him was as effortless as breathing. Now I was good at not really saying anything about myself at all.

He just sat, and nodded, watched the traffic go by and sipped his coffee, as if it were perfectly normal for him to be passing the time with a feverishly chatting stranger in a green Lurex mini-skirt.

'So, how's the hip?' he asked, when finally I ground to a halt.

'Not bad. I'd quite like to stop limping, though.'

'You'll get there, if you keep up the physio.' For a moment, I could hear that voice from the back of the ambulance. Calm, unfazed, reassuring. 'The other injuries?'

I peered down at myself, as if I could see through what I was wearing. 'Well, other than the fact that I look like someone's drawn all over bits of me with a particularly vivid red pen, not bad.'

Sam nodded. 'You were lucky. That was quite a fall.'

And there it was again. The sick lurch in my stomach. The air beneath my feet. *You never know what will happen when you fall from a great height.* 'I wasn't trying to –'

'You said.'

'But I'm not sure anyone believes me.'

75

We exchanged an awkward smile and for a minute I wondered if he didn't either.

'So . . . do you pick up many people who fall off the tops of buildings?'

He shook his head, gazed out across the road. 'I just pick up the pieces. I'm glad that, in your case, the pieces fitted back together.'

We sat in silence for a while longer. I kept thinking about things I should say, but I was so out of practice at being alone with a man – while sober at least – that I kept losing my nerve, my mouth opening and closing like that of a goldfish.

'So you want to tell me about the teenager?' Sam said.

It was a relief to explain it to someone. I told him about the late-night knock at the door, and our bizarre meeting and what I had found on Facebook, and the way she had run away before I'd had a chance to work out what on earth to do.

'Whoa,' he said when I'd finished. 'That's . . .' He gave a little shake of his head. 'You think she is who she says she is?'

'She does look a bit like him. But I don't honestly know. Am I looking for signs? Am I seeing what I want to see? It's possible. I spend half my time thinking how amazing that there's something of him left behind, and the other half wondering if I'm being a complete sucker. And then there's this whole extra layer of stuff in the middle – like if this is his daughter then how is it fair that he never even got to meet her? And how are his parents supposed to cope with it? And what if meeting her would actually have changed his mind? What if that would have been the thing that convinced him . . .' My voice tailed away.

Sam leaned back in his chair, his brow furrowed. 'And this man would be the reason you're attending the group.'

'Yes.'

I could feel him studying me, perhaps reassessing what Will had meant to me.

'I don't know what to do,' I said. 'I don't know whether to seek her out, or whether I should just leave well enough alone.'

He looked out at the city street, thinking. And then he said: 'Well, what would he have done?'

And just like that, I faltered. I gazed up at that big man with his direct gaze, his two-day stubble, and his kind, capable hands. And all my thoughts evaporated.

'You okay?'

I took a deep gulp of my drink, trying to hide what I felt was written clearly on my face. Suddenly, for no reason I could work out, I wanted to cry. It was too much. That odd, unbalancing night. The fact that Will had loomed up again, ever-present in every conversation. I could see his face suddenly, that sardonic eyebrow raised, as if to say, *What on earth are you up to now, Clark?*

'Just . . . a long day. Actually, would you mind if I –'

Sam pushed his chair back, stood up. 'No. No, you go. Sorry. I didn't think –'

'This has been really nice. It's just –'

'No problem. A long day. And the whole grief thing. I get it. No, no – don't worry,' he said, as I reached for my purse. 'Really. I can stand you an orange juice.'

I think I might have run to my car, in spite of my limp. I felt his eyes on me the whole way.

I pulled up in the car park, and let out a breath I felt as if I'd been holding all the way from the bar. I glanced over at the corner shop, then back at my flat, and decided I didn't want to be sensible. I wanted wine, several large glasses of it, until I could persuade myself to stop looking backwards. Or maybe not look at anything at all.

My hip ached as I climbed out of the car. Since Richard had arrived, it hurt constantly; the physio at the hospital had told me not to spend too much time on my feet. But the thought of saying as much to Richard filled me with dread.

*I see. So you work in a bar but you want to be allowed to sit down all day, is that it?*

That milk-fed, preparing-for-middle-management face; that carefully nondescript haircut. That air of weary superiority, even though he was barely two years older than me. I closed my eyes, and tried to make the knot of anxiety in my stomach disappear.

'Just this, please,' I said, placing a bottle of cold Sauvignon Blanc on the counter.

'Party, is it?'

'What?'

'Fancy dress. You going as – Don't tell me.' Samir stroked his chin. 'Snow White?'

'Sure,' I said.

'You want to be careful with that. Empty calories, innit? You want to drink vodka. That's a clean drink. Maybe a bit of lemon. That's what I tell Ginny, across the road. You know she's a lap-dancer, right? They got to watch their figures.'

'Dietary advice. Nice.'

'It's like all this stuff about sugar. You got to watch the sugar. No point buying the low-fat stuff if it's full of sugar, right? There's your empty calories. Right there. And them chemical sugars are the worst. They stick to your gut.'

He rang up the wine, handed me my change.

'What's that you're eating, Samir?'

'Smoky Bacon Pot Noodle. It's good, man.'

I was lost in thought – somewhere in the dark crevasse between my sore pelvis, existential job-related despair, and a weird craving for a Smoky Bacon Pot Noodle – when I saw her.

She was in the doorway of my block, sitting on the ground, her arms wrapped around her knees. I took my change from Samir, and half walked, half ran across the road. 'Lily?'

She looked up slowly.

Her voice was slurred, her eyes bloodshot, as if she had been crying. 'Nobody would let me in. I rang all the bells but nobody would let me in.'

I wrestled the key into the door and propped it with my bag, crouching down beside her. 'What happened?'

'I just want to go to sleep,' she said, rubbing her eyes. 'I'm so, so tired. I wanted to get a taxi home but I hadn't got any money.'

I caught the sour whiff of alcohol. 'Are you drunk?'

'I don't know.' She blinked at me, tilting her head. I wondered then if it was just alcohol. 'If I'm not, you've totally turned into a leprechaun.' She patted her pockets. 'Oh, look – look what I've got!' She held up a half-smoked roll-up that even I could smell was not just tobacco. 'Let's have a smoke, Lily,' she said. 'Oh, no. You're Louisa. I'm Lily.' She giggled and, pulling a lighter clumsily from her pocket, promptly tried to light the wrong end.

'Okay, you. Time to go home.' I took it from her hand, and, ignoring her vague protests, squashed it firmly under my foot. 'I'll call you a taxi.'

'But I don't –'

'Lily!'

I glanced up. A young man stood across the street, his hands in his jeans pockets, watching us steadily. Lily looked up at him and then away.

'Who is that?' I said.

She stared at her feet.

'Lily. Come here.' His voice held the surety of possession. He stood, legs slightly apart, as if even at that distance he expected her to obey him. Something made me instantly uneasy.

Nobody moved.

'Is he your boyfriend? Do you want to talk to him?' I said quietly.

The first time she spoke I couldn't make out what she said. I had to lean closer and ask her to repeat herself.

'Make him go away.' She closed her eyes, and turned her face towards the door. 'Please.'

He began to walk across the street towards us. I stood, and tried to make my voice sound as authoritative as possible. 'You can go now, thanks. Lily's coming inside with me.'

He stopped halfway across the road.

I held his gaze. 'You can speak to her some other time. Okay?'

I had my hand on the buzzer, and now muttered at some imaginary, muscular, short-tempered boyfriend. 'Yeah. Do you want to come down and give me a hand, Dave? Thanks.'

The young man's expression suggested this was not the last of it. Then he turned, pulled his phone from his pocket and began a low, urgent conversation with someone as he walked away, ignoring the beeping taxi that had to swerve around him, and casting us only the briefest of backwards looks.

I sighed, a little more shakily than I'd expected, put my hands under her armpits and, with not very much elegance and a fair amount of muffled swearing, managed to haul Lily Houghton-Miller into the lobby.

That night she slept at my flat. I couldn't think what else to do with her. She was sick twice in the bathroom, batting me away when I tried to hold her hair up for her. She refused to give me a home phone number, or maybe couldn't remember it, and her mobile phone was pin-locked.

I cleaned her up, helped her into a pair of my jogging bottoms and a T-shirt, and led her into the living room. 'You tidied up!' she said, with a little exclamation, as if I had done it just for her. I made her drink a glass of water and put her on the sofa in the recovery position, even though I was pretty sure by then that there was nothing left inside her to come out.

As I lifted her head and placed it on the pillow, she opened her eyes, as if recognizing me properly for the first time. 'Sorry.' She spoke so quietly that, for a moment, I couldn't be entirely sure that that was what she had said, and her eyes brimmed briefly with tears.

I covered her with a blanket and watched her as she fell asleep – her pale face, the blue shadows under her eyes, the eyebrows that followed the same curve that Will's had, the same faint sprinkling of freckles.

Almost as an afterthought I locked the flat door and brought the keys into my bedroom with me, tucking them under my pillow to stop her stealing anything, or simply to stop her leaving, I wasn't sure. I lay awake, my mind still busy with the sound of the sirens and the airport and the faces of the grieving in the church hall and the hard, knowing stare of the young man across the road, and the knowledge that I had someone who was essentially a stranger sleeping under my roof. And all the while a voice kept saying: *What on earth are you doing?*

But what else could I have done? Finally, some time after the birds started singing, and the bakery van unloaded its morning delivery downstairs, my thoughts slowed, and stilled, and I fell asleep.

# Chapter Seven

I could smell coffee. It took me several seconds to consider why the smell of coffee might be filtering through my flat, and when the answer registered I sat bolt upright and leaped out of bed, hauling my hoodie over my head.

She was cross-legged on the sofa, smoking, using my one good mug as an ashtray. The television was on – some manic children's confection of brightly clad, gurning presenters – and two Styrofoam cups sat on the mantelpiece.

'Oh, hi. That one on the right's yours,' she said, turning briefly towards me. 'I didn't know what you liked so I got you an Americano.'

I blinked, wrinkling my nose against the cigarette smoke. I crossed the room and opened a window. I looked at the clock. 'Is that the time?'

'Yeah. The coffee might be a bit cold. Didn't know whether to wake you.'

'It's my day off,' I said, reaching for the coffee. It was warm enough. I took a slug gratefully. Then I stared at the cup. 'Hang on. How did you get these? I locked the front door.'

'I went down the fire escape,' she said. 'I didn't have any money so I told the guy at the bakery whose flat it was and he said you could bring it in later. Oh, and you also owe him for two bagels with smoked salmon and cream cheese.'

'I do?' I wanted to be cross, but I was suddenly really hungry.

She followed my gaze. 'Oh. I ate those.' She blew a smoke ring into the centre of the room. 'You didn't have anything much in your fridge. You really do need to sort this place out.'

The Lily of this morning was such a different character from the girl I had picked off the street last night that it was hard to believe they were the same person. I walked back into the bedroom to get dressed, listening to her watching television, padding into the kitchen to fetch herself a drink.

'Hey, thingy . . . Louise. Could you lend me some money?' she called out.

'If it's to get off your face again, no.'

She walked into my bedroom without knocking. I pulled my sweatshirt up to my chest. 'And can I stay tonight?'

'I need to talk to your mum, Lily.'

'What for?'

'I need to know a little bit more about what's actually going on here.'

She stood in the doorway. 'So you don't believe me.'

I gestured to her to turn around, so I could finish putting my bra on. 'I do believe you. But that's the deal. You want something from me, I need to know a bit more about you first.'

Just as I pulled my T-shirt over my head, she turned back again. 'Suit yourself. I need to pick up some more clothes anyway.'

'Why? Where have you been staying?'

She walked away from me, as if she hadn't heard, sniffing her armpit. 'Can I use your shower? I absolutely reek.'

An hour later, we drove to St John's Wood. I was exhausted, both by the night's events and the strange energy Lily gave off beside me. She fidgeted constantly, smoked endless cigarettes, then sat in a silence so loaded I could almost feel the weight of her thoughts.

'So who was he? That guy last night?' I kept my face to the front, my voice neutral.

'Just someone.'

'You told me he was your boyfriend.'

'Then that's who he was.' Her voice had hardened, her face closed. As we drew nearer to her parents' house, she crossed her arms in front of her, bringing her knees up to her chin, her gaze set and defiant, as if already in silent battle. I had wondered if she had been telling me the truth about St John's Wood, but she gestured to a wide, tree-lined street, and told me to take the third left, and we were in the kind of road where diplomats or expat American bankers live, the kind of road that nobody ever seems to go in or come out of. I pulled the car up, gazing out of the window at the tall white stucco buildings, the carefully trimmed yew hedging, and immaculate window boxes.

'You live *here*?'

She slammed the passenger door behind her so hard that my little car rattled. 'I don't live here. *They* live here.'

She let herself in and I followed awkwardly, feeling like an intruder. We were in a spacious, high-ceilinged hallway, with parquet flooring and a huge gilt mirror on the wall, a slew of white-card invitations jostling for space in its frame. A vase of beautifully arranged flowers sat on a small antique table. The air was scented with their perfume.

From upstairs came the sound of commotion, possibly children's voices – it was hard to tell.

'My half-brothers,' Lily said dismissively, and walked through to the kitchen, apparently expecting me to follow. It was enormous, in modernist grey, with an endless mushroom-coloured polished-concrete worktop. Everything in it screamed money, from the Dualit toaster to the coffee-maker, which was large and complicated enough not to be out of place in a Milanese café. Lily opened the fridge and scanned it, finally pulling out a box of fresh pineapple pieces that she started to eat with her fingers.

'Lily?'

A voice from upstairs, urgent, female.

'Lily, is that you?' The sound of footsteps racing down.

Lily rolled her eyes.

A blonde woman appeared in the doorway. She stared at me, then at Lily, who was dropping a piece of pineapple languidly into her mouth. She walked over and snatched the container from her hands. 'Where the *hell* have you been? The school is beside themselves. Daddy was out driving round the neighbourhood. We thought you'd been murdered! Where *were* you?'

'He's not my dad.'

'Don't get smart with me, young lady. You can't just walk back in here like nothing's happened! Do you have any idea of the trouble you've caused? I was up with your brother half the night, and then I couldn't sleep for worrying about what had happened to you. I've had to cancel our trip to Granny Houghton's because we didn't know where you were.'

Lily stared at her coolly. 'I don't know why you bothered. You don't usually care where I am.'

The woman stiffened with rage. She was thin, the kind of thin that comes with faddy diets or compulsive exercise; her hair was expensively cut and coloured so that it looked neither, and she was wearing what I assumed were designer jeans. But her face, tanned as it was, betrayed her: she looked exhausted.

She spun round to me. 'Is it you she's been staying with?'

'Well, yes, but –'

She looked me up and down, and apparently decided she was not enamoured of what she saw. 'Do you know the trouble you're causing? Do you have any idea how old she is? What the hell do you want with a girl that young anyway? You must be, what, thirty?'

'Actually, I –'

85

'Is this what it's about?' she asked her daughter. 'Are you having a relationship with this woman?'

'Oh, Mum, shut *up*.' Lily had picked up the pineapple again, and was fishing around in it with her forefinger. 'It's not what you think. She hasn't caused any of it.' She lowered the last piece of pineapple into her mouth, pausing to chew, perhaps for dramatic effect, before she spoke again. 'She's the woman who used to look after my dad. My real dad.'

Tanya Houghton-Miller sat back in the endless cushions of her cream sofa and stirred her coffee. I perched on the edge of the sofa opposite, gazing at the oversized Diptyque candles and the artfully placed *Interiors* magazines. I was slightly afraid that if I sat back as she had, my coffee would tip into my lap.

'How did you meet my daughter?' she said wearily. Her wedding finger sported two of the biggest diamonds I'd ever seen.

'I didn't, really. She turned up at my flat. I had no idea who she was.'

She digested that for a minute. 'And you used to look after Will Traynor.'

'Yes. Until he died.'

There was a brief pause as we both studied the ceiling – something had just crashed above our heads. 'My sons.' She sighed. 'They have some behavioural issues.'

'Are they from your . . . ?'

'They're not Will's, if that's what you're asking.'

We sat there in silence. Or as near to silence as it could get when you could hear furious screaming upstairs. There was another thud, followed by an ominous silence.

'Mrs Houghton-Miller,' I said. 'Is it true? Is Lily Will's daughter?'

She raised her chin slightly. 'Yes.'

I felt suddenly shaky, and put my coffee cup on the table. 'I don't understand. I don't understand how –'

'It's quite simple. Will and I were together during the last year of uni. I was totally in love with him, of course. Everyone was. Although I should say it wasn't all one-way traffic – you know?' She raised a small smile and waited, as if expecting me to say something.

I couldn't. How could Will not have told me he had a daughter? After everything we had been through?

Tanya drawled on: 'Anyway. We were the golden couple of our group. Balls, punting, weekends away, you know the drill. Will and I – well, we were everywhere.' She told the story as if it were still fresh to her, as if it were something she had gone over and over in her head. 'And then at our Founders' Ball, I had to leave to help my friend Liza, who had got herself into a bit of a mess, and when I came back, Will was gone. No idea where he was. So I waited there for ages, and all the cars came and took everyone home, and finally a girl I didn't even know very well came up to me and told me that Will had gone off with a girl called Stephanie Loudon. You won't know her but she'd had her eye on him for ever. At first I didn't believe it, but I drove to her house anyway, and sat outside, and sure enough, at five a.m. he came out and they stood there kissing on the doorstep, like they couldn't care who saw. And when I got out of the car and confronted him, he didn't even have the grace to be ashamed. He just said there was no point in us getting emotional as we were never going to last beyond college anyway.

'And then, of course, college finished, which was something of a relief, to be honest, because who wants to be the girl Will Traynor dumped? But it was so hard to get over, because it had ended so abruptly. After we left and he started work in the City I wrote to him asking if we could at least meet for a drink so I could work out what on earth had gone wrong. Because, as far as I was concerned, we had been really happy, you know? And he just got his secretary to send this – this *card*, saying she was very sorry but Will's diary was absolutely full and he didn't have time right now but he wished me all the best. "All the best".' She grimaced.

I winced internally. Much as I wanted to discount her story, this version of Will held a horrible ring of truth. Will himself had looked back at his earlier life with utter clarity, had confessed how badly he had treated women when he was younger. (His exact words were: 'I was a complete arse.')

Tanya was still talking. 'And then, about two months later, I discovered I was pregnant. And it was already awfully late because my periods had always been erratic and I hadn't realized I'd already missed two. So I decided to go ahead and have Lily. But –' here she lifted her chin again, as if braced to defend herself – 'there was no point in telling him. Not after everything he'd said and done.'

My coffee had gone cold. 'No point in telling him?'

'He'd as good as said he didn't want anything to do with me. He would have acted as if I'd done it deliberately, to trap him or something.'

My mouth was hanging open. I closed it. 'But you – you don't think he had the right to know, Mrs Houghton-Miller? You don't think he might have wanted to meet his child? Regardless of what had happened between the two of you?'

She put down her cup.

'She's *sixteen*,' I said. 'She would have been fourteen, fifteen when he died. That's an awful long –'

'And by that time she had Francis. He was her father. And he has been very good to her. We were a family. Are a family.'

'I don't understand –'

'Will didn't *deserve* to know her.'

The words settled in the air between us.

'He was an arsehole. Okay? Will Traynor was a selfish arsehole.' She pushed a strand of hair back from her face. 'Obviously I didn't know what had happened to him. That came as a complete shock. But I can't honestly say it would have made a difference.'

It took me a moment to find my voice. 'It would have made every difference. To him.'

She looked at me sharply.

'Will killed himself,' I said, and my voice cracked a little. 'Will ended his life because he couldn't see any reason to go on. If he'd known he had a daughter –'

She stood up. '*Oh*, no. You don't pin that on me, Miss Whoever-you-are. I am not going to be made to feel responsible for that man's suicide. You think my life isn't complicated enough? Don't you dare come here judging me. If you'd had to cope with half of what I cope with . . . No. Will Traynor was a horrible man.'

'Will Traynor was the finest man I ever knew.'

She let her gaze run up and down me. 'Yes. Well, I can imagine that's probably true.'

I thought I had never been filled with such an instant dislike for someone.

I had stood to leave when a voice broke into the silence. 'So my dad really didn't know about me.'

Lily was standing very still in the doorway. Tanya Houghton-Miller blanched. Then she recovered herself. 'I was saving you from hurt, Lily. I knew Will very well, and I was not prepared to put either of us through the humiliation of trying to persuade him to be part of a relationship he wouldn't have wanted.' She smoothed her hair. 'And you really must stop this awful eavesdropping habit. You're likely to get quite the wrong end of the stick.'

I couldn't listen to any more. I walked to the door as a boy began shouting upstairs. A plastic truck flew down the stairs and crashed into pieces somewhere below. An anxious face – Filipina? – gazed at me over the banister. I began to walk down the stairs.

'Where are you going?'

'I'm sorry, Lily. We'll – perhaps we'll talk some other time.'

'But you've hardly told me anything about my dad.'

'He wasn't your father,' Tanya Houghton-Miller said. 'Francis has done more for you since you were little than Will ever would have done.'

'Francis is not my *dad*,' Lily roared.

Another crash from upstairs, and a woman's voice, shouting in a language I didn't understand. A toy machine-gun sent tinny blasts into the air. Tanya put her hands to her head. 'I can't cope with this. I simply can't cope.'

Lily caught up with me at the door. 'Can I stay with you?'

'What?'

'At your flat? I can't stay here.'

'Lily, I don't think –'

'Just for tonight. Please.'

'Oh, be my guest. Have her stay with you for a day or two. She's just delightful company.' Tanya waved a hand. 'Polite, helpful, loving. A dream to have around!' Her face hardened. 'Let's see how that works out. You know she drinks? And smokes in the house? And that she was suspended from school? She's told you all this, has she?'

Lily seemed almost bored, as if she had heard this a million times before.

'She didn't even bother turning up for her exams. We've done everything possible for her. Counsellors, the best schools, private tutors. Francis has treated her as if she were his own. And she just throws it all back in our faces. My husband is having a very difficult time at the bank right now, and the boys have their issues, and she doesn't give us an inch. She never has.'

'How would you even *know*? I've been with nannies half my life. When the boys were born, you sent me to boarding-school.'

'I couldn't cope with all of you! I did what I could!'

'You did what you *wanted*, which was to start your perfect family all over again, without me.' Lily turned back to me. 'Please? Just for a bit? I promise I won't get under your feet at all. I'll be really helpful.'

I should have said no. I knew I should. But I was so angry with that woman. And just for a moment I felt as if I had to stand in for Will, to do the thing he couldn't do. 'Fine,' I said, as a large Lego creation whistled past my ear and smashed into tiny coloured pieces by my feet. 'Grab your things. I'll be waiting outside.'

The rest of the day was a blur. We moved my boxes out of the spare room, stacking them in my bedroom, and made the room hers, or at least less of a storage area, putting up the blind I had never quite got round to fixing, and moving in a lamp and my spare bedside table. I bought a camp bed, and we carried it up the stairs together, with a hanging rail for her few things, a new duvet cover and pillow cases. She seemed to like having a purpose, and was completely unfazed at the idea of moving in with somebody she hardly knew. I watched her arranging her few belongings in the spare room that evening and felt oddly sad. How unhappy did a girl have to be to want to leave all that luxury for a box room with a camp bed and a wobbly clothes rail?

I cooked pasta, conscious of the strangeness of having someone to cook for, and we watched television together. At half past eight her phone went off and she asked for a piece of paper and a pen. 'Here,' she said, scribbling on it. 'This is my mum's mobile number. She wants your phone number and address. In case of emergencies.'

I wondered fleetingly how often she thought Lily was going to stay.

At ten, exhausted, I told her I was turning in. She was still watching television, sitting cross-legged on the sofa, and messaging someone on her little laptop. 'Don't stay up too late, okay?' It sounded fake on my lips, like someone pretending to be an adult.

Her eyes were still glued to the television.

'Lily?'

She looked up, as if she'd only just noticed I was in the room. 'Oh, yeah, I meant to tell you. I was there.'

'Where?'

'On the roof. When you fell. It was me who called the ambulance.'

I saw her face suddenly, those big eyes, that skin, pale in the darkness. 'But what were you doing up there?'

'I found your address. After everyone at home had gone nutso, I just wanted to work out who you were before I tried to talk to you. I saw I could get up there by the fire escape and your light was on. I was just waiting, really. But when you came up and started messing about on the edge I suddenly thought if I said anything I'd freak you out.'

'Which you did.'

'Yeah. I didn't mean to do that. I actually thought I'd killed you.' She laughed, nervously.

We sat there for a minute.

'Everyone thinks I tried to jump.'

Her face swivelled towards me. 'Really?'

'Yeah.'

92

She thought about this. 'Because of what happened to my dad?'

'Yes.'

'Do you miss him?'

'Every single day.'

She was silent. Eventually she said, 'So when is your next day off?'

'Sunday. Why?' I said, dragging my thoughts back.

'Can we go to your home town?'

'You want to go to Stortfold?'

'I want to see where he lived.'

# Chapter Eight

I didn't tell Dad we were coming. I wasn't entirely sure how to have that conversation. We pulled up outside our house and I sat for a minute, conscious, as she peered out of the window, of the small, rather weary appearance of my parents' house in comparison with her own. She had suggested we bring flowers when I told her my mother would insist we stay for lunch, and got cross when I suggested petrol-station carnations, even though they were for someone she'd never met.

I had driven to the supermarket on the other side of Stortfold, where she had chosen a huge hand-tied bouquet of freesias, peonies and ranunculus. Which I had paid for.

'Stay here a minute,' I said, as she started to climb out. 'I'm going to explain before you come in.'

'But –'

'Trust me,' I said. 'They're going to need a minute.'

I walked up the little garden path and knocked on the door. I could hear the television in the living room, and pictured Granddad there, watching the racing, his mouth working silently along with the horses' legs. The sights and sounds of home. I thought of the months I had kept away, no longer sure I was even welcome, of how I had refused to allow myself to think of how it felt to walk up this path, the fabric-conditioned scent of my mother's embrace, my father's distant bellow of laughter.

Dad opened the door, and his eyebrows shot up. 'Lou! We weren't expecting you! . . . Were we expecting you?' He stepped forward and enveloped me in a hug.

I realized I liked having my family back. 'Hi, Dad.'

He waited on the step, arm outstretched. The smell of roast chicken wafted down the corridor. 'You coming in, then, or are we going to have a picnic out on the front step?'

'I need to tell you something first.'

'You lost your job.'

'No, I did not lose my –'

'You got another tattoo.'

'You knew about the tattoo?'

'I'm your father. I've known about every bloody thing you and your sister have done since you were three years old.' He leaned forward. 'Your mother would never let me have one.'

'No, Dad, I don't have another tattoo.' I took a breath. 'I . . . I have Will's daughter.'

Dad stood very still. Mum appeared behind him, with her apron on. 'Lou!' She caught the look on Dad's face. 'What? What's wrong?'

'She says she has Will's daughter.'

'She has Will's *what*?' Mum squawked.

Dad had gone quite white. He reached behind him for the radiator and clutched it.

'What?' I said, anxious. 'What's the matter?'

'You – you're not telling me you harvested his . . . you know . . . his little fellas?'

I pulled a face. 'She's in the *car*. She's sixteen years old.'

'Oh, thank God. Oh, Josie, thank God. These days, you're so . . . I never know what –' He composed himself. 'Will's *daughter*, you say? You never said he –'

'I didn't know. Nobody knew.'

Mum peered around him to my car, where Lily was trying to act as if she didn't know she was being talked about.

'Well, you'd better bring her in,' said Mum, her hand to her neck. 'It's a decent-sized chicken. It will do all of us if I add a few more potatoes.' She shook her head in amazement. 'Will's *daughter*. Well, goodness, Lou. You're certainly full of surprises.' She waved at Lily, who waved back tentatively. 'Come on in, love!'

Dad lifted a hand in greeting, then murmured quietly, 'Does Mr Traynor know?'

'Not yet.'

Dad rubbed his chest. 'Is there anything else?'

'Like what?'

'Anything else you need to tell me. You know, apart from jumping off buildings and bringing home long-lost children. You're not joining the circus, or adopting a kid from Kazakhstan or something?'

'I promise I am doing none of the above. Yet.'

'Well, thank the Lord for that. What's the time? I think I'm ready for a drink.'


'So where'd you go to school, Lily?'

'It's a small boarding-school in Shropshire. No one's ever heard of it. It's mostly posh retards and distant members of the Moldavian royal family.'

We had crammed ourselves around the dining-table in the front room, the seven of us knee to knee, and six of us praying that nobody needed the loo, which would necessitate everyone getting up and moving the table six inches towards the sofa.

'Boarding-school, eh? Tuck shops and midnight feasts and all that? I bet that's a gas.'

'Not really. They shut the tuck shop last year because half the girls had eating disorders and were making themselves sick on Snickers bars.'

'Lily's mother lives in St John's Wood,' I said. 'She's staying with me for a couple of days while she . . . while she gets to know a bit about the other side of her family.'

Mum said, 'The Traynors have lived here for generations.'

'Really? Do you know them?'

Mum froze. 'Well, not as such . . .'

'What's their house like?'

Mum's face closed. 'You'd be better asking Lou about that sort of thing. She's the one who spent . . . all the time there.'

Lily waited.

Dad said, 'I work with Mr Traynor, who is responsible for the running of the estate.'

'Granddad!' exclaimed Granddad, and laughed. Lily glanced at him, then back at me. I smiled, although even the mention of Mr Traynor's name made me feel oddly unbalanced.

'That's right, Daddy,' said Mum. 'He'd be Lily's granddad. Just like you. Now who wants some more potatoes?'

'Granddad,' Lily repeated quietly, clearly pleased.

'We'll ring them and . . . tell them,' I said. 'And if you like we can drive past their house when we leave. Just so you can see a bit of it.'

My sister sat silently throughout this exchange. Lily had been placed next to Thom, possibly in an attempt to get him to behave better, although the risk of him starting a conversation related to intestinal parasites was still quite high. Treena watched Lily. She was more suspicious than my parents, who had just accepted everything I'd told them. She had hauled me upstairs while Dad was showing Lily the garden, and asked all the questions that had flown wildly around my head, like a trapped pigeon in a closed room. *How did I know she was who she said? What did she want?* And then, finally, *Why on earth would her own mother want her to come and live with* you?

'So how long is she staying?' she said, at the table, while Dad was telling Lily about working with green oak.

'We haven't really discussed it.'

She pulled the kind of face at me that told me simultaneously that I was an eejit, and also that this was no surprise to her whatsoever.

'She's been with me for two nights, Treen. And she's only young.'

'My point exactly. What do you know about looking after children?'

'She's hardly a child.'

'She's *worse* than a child. Teenagers are basically toddlers with hormones – old enough to want to do stuff without having any of the common sense. She could get into all sorts of trouble. I can't believe you're actually doing this.'

I handed her the gravy boat. '"Hello, Lou. Well done on keeping your job in a tough market. Congratulations on getting over your terrible accident. It's really lovely to see you."'

She passed me the salt, and muttered, under her breath, 'You know, you won't be able to cope with this, as well as . . .'

'As well as what?'

'Your depression.'

'I don't *have* depression,' I hissed. 'I'm not depressed, Treena. For crying out loud, I did not throw myself off a building.'

'You haven't been yourself for ages. Not since the whole Will thing.'

'What do I have to do to convince you? I'm holding down a job. I'm doing my physio to get my hip straight and going to a flipping grief-counselling group to get my mind straight. I think I'm doing pretty well, okay?' The whole table was now listening to me. 'In fact – here's the thing. Oh, yes. Lily was there. She saw me fall. It turns out she was the one who called the ambulance.'

Every member of my family looked at me. 'You see, it's true. She saw me fall. I didn't jump. Lily, I was just telling my

98

sister. You were there when I fell, weren't you? See? I told you all I heard a girl's voice. I wasn't going mad. She actually saw the whole thing. I slipped, right?'

Lily looked up from her plate, still chewing. She had barely stopped eating since we sat down. 'Yup. She totally wasn't trying to kill herself.'

Mum and Dad exchanged a glance. My mother sighed, crossed herself discreetly and smiled. My sister lifted her eyebrows, the closest I was going to get to an apology. I felt, briefly, elated.

'Yeah. She was just shouting at the sky.' Lily lifted her fork. 'And really, really pissed.'

There was a brief silence.

'Oh,' said Dad. 'Well, that's –'

'That's . . . good,' said Mum.

'This chicken's great,' said Lily. 'Can I have some more?'

We stayed until late afternoon, partly because every time I got up to leave, Mum kept pressing more food on us, and partly because having other people to chat to Lily made the situation seem a little less weird and intense. Dad and I moved out to the back garden and the two deckchairs that had somehow failed to rot during another winter (although it was wisest to stay almost completely still once you were in them, just in case).

'You know your sister has been reading *The Female Eunuch*? And some old shite called *The Women's Bedroom* or something. She says your mother is a classic example of oppressed womanhood, and that the fact your mother disagrees shows how oppressed she is. She's trying to tell her I should be doing the cooking and cleaning and making out I'm some fecking caveman. But if I dare to say anything back she keeps telling me to "check my privilege". Check my privilege! I told her I'd be happy to check it if I knew where the hell your mother had put it.'

'Mum seems fine to me,' I said. I took a swig of my tea, feeling a faintly guilty pang that the sounds I could hear were Mum washing up.

He looked sideways at me. 'She hasn't shaved her legs in three weeks. Three weeks, Lou! If I'm really honest it gives me the heebie-jeebies when they touch me. I've been on the sofa for the last two nights. I don't know, Lou. Why are people never happy just to let things *be* any more? Your mum was happy, I'm happy. We know what our roles are. I'm the one with hairy legs. She's the one who fits the rubber gloves. Simple.'

Down the garden, Lily was teaching Thom to make bird-calls using a thick blade of grass. He held it up between his thumbs, but it's possible that his four missing teeth hampered any sound production, as all that emerged was a raspberry and a light shower of saliva.

We sat in companionable silence for a while, listening to the squawks of the birdcalls, Granddad whistling, and next door's dog yelping to be let in. I felt happy to be home.

'So how is Mr Traynor?' I asked.

'Ah, he's grand. You know he's going to be a daddy again?'

I turned, carefully, in my chair. 'Really?'

'Not with Mrs Traynor. She moved out straight after . . . you know. This is with the red-headed girl, I forget her name.'

'Della,' I said, remembering suddenly.

'That's the one. They seem to have known each other quite a while, but I think the whole, you know, having-a-baby thing was a bit of a surprise to the both of them.' Dad cracked open another beer. 'He's cheerful enough. I suppose it's nice for him to have a new son or daughter on the way. Something to focus on.'

Some part of me wanted to judge him. But I could too

easily imagine the need to create something good out of what had happened, the desire to climb back out, by whatever means.

*They're only still together because of me*, Will had told me, more than once.

'What do you think he'll make of Lily?' I asked.

'I have no idea, love.' Dad thought for a bit. 'I think he'll be happy. It's like he's getting a bit of his son back, isn't it?'

'What do you think Mrs Traynor will think?'

'I don't know, love. I have no idea where she even lives these days.'

'Lily's . . . quite a handful.'

Dad burst out laughing. 'You don't say! You and Treena drove your mother and me half demented for years with your late nights and your boyfriends and your heartbreaks. It's about time you had some of it coming back your way.' He took a swig of his beer and chuckled again. 'It's good news, love. I'm glad you won't be on your own in that empty old flat of yours.'

Thom's grass let out a squawk. His face lit up, and he thrust his blade skyward. We raised our thumbs in salute.

'Dad.'

He turned to me.

'You know I'm fine, right?'

'Yes, love.' He gave me a gentle shoulder bump. 'But it's my job to worry. I'll be worrying till I'm too old to get out of my chair.' He looked down at it. 'Mind you, that might be sooner than I'd like.'

We left shortly before five. In the rear-view mirror Treena was the only one of the family not waving. She stood there, her arms crossed over her chest, her head moving slowly from side to side as she watched us go.

*

When we got home, Lily disappeared onto the roof. I hadn't been up there since the accident. I'd told myself the spring weather had made it pointless to try, that the fire escape would be slippery because of the rain, that the sight of all those pots of dead plants would make me feel guilty, but, really, I was afraid. Even thinking about heading up there again made my heart thump harder; it took nothing for me to recall that sense of the world disappearing from beneath me, like a rug pulled from under my feet.

I watched her climb out of the landing window and shouted up that she should come down in twenty minutes. When twenty-five had gone by, I began to get anxious. I called out of the window but only the sound of the traffic came back to me. At thirty-five minutes I found myself, swearing under my breath, climbing out of the hall window onto the fire escape.

It was a warm summer evening and the rooftop asphalt radiated heat. Below us the sounds of the city spelled a lazy Sunday in slow-moving traffic, windows down, music blaring, youths hanging out on street corners, and the distant char-grilled smells of barbecues on other rooftops.

Lily sat on an upturned plant pot, looking out over the City. I stood with my back to the water tank, trying not to feel a reflexive panic whenever she leaned towards the edge.

It had been a mistake to go up there. I felt the asphalt listing gently underneath my feet, like the deck of a ship. I made my way unsteadily to the rusting iron seat, lowering myself into it. My body knew exactly how it felt to stand on that ledge; how the infinitesimal difference between the solid business of living, and the lurch that would end everything could be measured in the smallest of units, in grams, in millimetres, in degrees, and that knowledge made the hairs on my arms prickle and a fine sweat seep through the skin on the back of my neck.

'Can you come down, Lily?'

'All your plants have died.' She was picking at the dead leaves of a desiccated shrub.

'Yes. Well, I haven't been up here for months.'

'You shouldn't let plants die. It's cruel.'

I looked at her sharply, to see if she was joking, but she didn't seem to be. She stooped, breaking off a twig and examining the dried-up centre. 'How did you meet my dad?'

I reached for the corner of the water tank, trying to stop my legs shaking. 'I just applied for a job to look after him. And I got it.'

'Even though you weren't medically trained.'

'Yes.'

She considered this, flicked the dead stem away into the air, then got up, walked to the far end of the terrace, and stood, her hands on her hips, legs braced, a skinny Amazon warrior. 'He was handsome, wasn't he?'

The roof was swaying under me. I needed to go downstairs. 'I can't do this up here, Lily.'

'Are you really frightened?'

'I'd just really rather we went down. Please.'

She tilted her head and watched me, as if trying to work out whether to do as I asked. She took a step towards the wall, and put her foot up speculatively, as if to jump onto the edge, just long enough to make me break out into a spontaneous sweat. Then she turned to me, grinned, put her cigarette between her teeth and walked back across the roof towards the fire escape. 'You won't fall off again, silly. Nobody's that unlucky.'

'Yeah. Well, right now, I don't really want to test the odds.'

Some minutes later, when I could make my legs obey my brain, we went down the two flights of iron steps. We stopped outside my window when I realized I was shaking too much to climb through and I sat down on the step.

Lily rolled her eyes, waiting. Then, when she grasped I couldn't move, she sat down on the steps beside me. We were only, perhaps, ten feet lower than we had been, but with my hallway visible through the window, and a rail on each side, I began to breathe normally again.

'You know what you need,' she said, and held up her roll-up.

'Are you seriously telling me to get stoned? Four floors up? You know I just fell off a roof?'

'It'll help you relax.'

And then, when I didn't take it, 'Oh, come *on*. What – are you seriously the straightest person in the whole of London?'

'I'm not from London.'

Afterwards, I couldn't believe I had been manipulated by a sixteen-year-old. But Lily was like the cool girl in class, the one you found yourself trying to impress. Before she could say anything else, I took it from her and had a tentative drag, trying not to cough when it hit the back of my throat. 'Anyway, you're sixteen,' I muttered. 'You shouldn't be doing this. And where is someone like you getting this stuff?'

Lily peered over the railing. 'Did you fancy him?'

'Fancy who? Your dad? Not at first.'

'Because he was in a wheelchair.'

*Because he was doing an impression of Daniel Day-Lewis in* My Left Foot *and it scared the bejaysus out of me*, I wanted to say, but it would have taken too much explaining. 'No. The wheelchair was the least important thing about him. I didn't fancy him because . . . he was very angry. And a bit intimidating. And those two things made him quite hard to fancy.'

'Do I look like him? I Googled him but I can't tell.'

'A bit. Your colouring is the same. Maybe your eyes.'

'My mum said he was really handsome and that was what made him such an arsehole. One of the things. Whenever I'm getting on her nerves now she tells me I'm just like him. *Oh,*

*God, you're just like Will Traynor.'* She always calls him Will Traynor, though. Not "your father". She's determined to make out like Fuckface is my dad, even though he is patently not. It's like she thinks she can just make a family by insisting that we are one.'

I took another drag. I could feel myself getting woozy. Apart from one night at a house party in Paris, it had been years since I'd had a joint. 'You know, I think I'd enjoy this more if there wasn't a small possibility of me falling off this fire escape.'

She took it from me. 'Jeez, Louise. You need to have some fun.' She inhaled deeply, and leaned her head back. 'Did he tell you about how he was feeling? Like the real stuff?' She inhaled again and handed it back to me. She seemed totally unaffected.

'Yes.'

'Did you argue?'

'Quite a lot. But we laughed a lot, too.'

'Did he fancy you?'

'Fancy me? . . . I don't know if "fancy" is the right word.'

My mouth worked silently around words I couldn't find. How could I explain to this girl what Will and I had been to each other, the way I felt that no person in the world had ever understood me like he did or ever would again? How could she understand that losing him was like having a hole shot straight through me, a painful, constant reminder, an absence I could never fill?

She stared at me. 'He did! My dad fancied you!' She started to giggle. And it was such a ridiculous thing to say, such a useless word, faced with what Will and I had been to each other, that, despite myself, I giggled too.

'My dad had the hots for you. How mad is that?' She gasped. 'Oh, my God! In a different universe, you could have been MY STEPMUM.'

We gazed at each other in mock-horror and somehow this fact swelled between us until a bubble of merriment lodged in my chest. I began to laugh, the kind of laugh that verges on hysteria, that makes your stomach hurt, where the mere act of looking at someone sets you off again.

'Did you have sex?'

And that killed it.

'Okay. This conversation has now got weird.'

Lily pulled a face. 'Your whole relationship sounds weird.'

'It wasn't at all. It . . . it . . .'

It was suddenly too much: the rooftop, the questions, the joint, the memories of Will. We seemed to be conjuring him out of the air between us: his smile, his skin, the feel of his face against mine, and I wasn't sure I wanted to do it. I let my head fall slightly between my knees. *Breathe*, I told myself.

'Louisa?'

'What?'

'Did he always plan to go to that place? Dignitas?'

I nodded. I repeated the word to myself, trying to quell my rising sense of panic. In. Out. *Just breathe.*

'Did you try to change his mind?'

'Will was . . . stubborn.'

'Did you argue about it?'

I swallowed. 'Right up until the last day.'

*The last day.* Why had I said that? I closed my eyes.

When I finally opened them again, she was watching me.

'Were you with him when he died?'

Our eyes locked. The young are terrifying, I thought. They are without boundaries. They fear nothing. I could see the next question forming on her lips, the faint searching in her gaze. But perhaps she was not as brave as I'd thought.

Finally she dropped her gaze. 'So when are you going to tell his parents about me?'

My heart lurched. 'This week. I'll call this week.'

She nodded, turned her face away so that I couldn't see her expression. I watched as she inhaled again. And then, abruptly, she dropped the joint through the bars of the fire-escape steps, stood up and climbed inside without a backward look. I waited until my legs felt as if they could support me again, then followed her through the window.

# Chapter Nine

I called on Tuesday lunchtime, when a joint one-day strike by French and German air-traffic control had left the bar almost empty. I waited until Richard had disappeared to the wholesaler's, then stood out on the concourse, outside the last Ladies before security, and searched my phone for the number I had never been able to delete.

The phone rang three, four times, and just for a moment I was filled with the overwhelming urge to press END CALL. But then a man's voice answered, his vowels clipped, familiar. 'Hello?'

'Mr Traynor? It – it's Lou.'

'Lou?'

'Louisa Clark.'

A short silence. I could hear his memories thudding down on him along with the simple fact of my name and felt oddly guilty. The last time I had seen him had been at Will's graveside, a prematurely aged man, repeatedly straightening his shoulders as he struggled under the weight of his grief.

'Louisa. Well . . . Goodness. This is – How are you?'

I shifted to allow Violet to sway past with her trolley. She gave me a knowing smile, adjusting her purple turban with her free hand. I noticed she had little Union Jacks painted on her fingernails.

'I'm very well, thank you. And how are you?'

'Oh – you know. Actually, I'm very well, too. Circumstances have changed a little since we last saw each other, but it's all . . . you know . . .'

That temporary and uncharacteristic loss of bonhomie almost caused me to falter. I took a deep breath. 'Mr Traynor, I'm ringing because I really need to talk to you about something.'

'I thought Michael Lawler had sorted out all the financial matters.' His tone altered just slightly.

'It's not to do with money.' I closed my eyes. 'Mr Traynor, I had a visitor a short time ago and it's someone I think you need to meet.'

A woman bumped into my legs with her wheeled case, and mouthed an apology.

'Okay. There's no simple way of doing this, so I'm just going to say it. Will had a daughter and she turned up on my doorstep. She's desperate to meet you.'

A long silence this time.

'Mr Traynor?'

'I'm sorry. Can you repeat what you just said?'

'Will had a daughter. He didn't know about her. The mother is an old girlfriend of his, from university, who took it upon herself not to tell him. He had a daughter and she tracked me down and she really wants to meet you. She's sixteen. Her name is Lily.'

'Lily?'

'Yes. I've spoken to her mother and she seems genuine. A woman called Miller. Tanya Miller.'

'I – I don't remember her. But Will did have an awful lot of girlfriends.'

Another long silence. When he spoke again his voice cracked. 'Will had . . . a daughter?'

'Yes. Your granddaughter.'

'You – you really think she is his daughter?'

'I've met her mother, and heard what she had to say and, yes, I really think she is.'

'Oh. Oh, my.'

I could hear a voice in the background: 'Steven? *Steven? Are you all right?*'

Another silence.

'Mr Traynor?'

'I'm so sorry. It's just – I'm a little . . .'

I put my hand to my head. 'It's a huge shock. I know. I'm sorry. I couldn't think of the best way to tell you. I didn't want to just turn up at your house in case . . .'

'No. No, don't be sorry. It's good news. Extraordinary news. A *granddaughter*.'

'What's going on? Why are you sitting down like that?' The voice in the background sounded concerned.

I heard a hand go over the receiver, then: 'I'm fine, darling. Really. I – I'll explain everything in a minute.'

More muffled conversation. And then back to me, his voice suddenly uncertain: 'Louisa?'

'Yes?'

'You're absolutely sure? I mean, this is just so –'

'As sure as I can be, Mr Traynor. I'm happy to explain more to you, but she's sixteen and she's full of life and she's . . . well, she's just very keen to find out about the family she never knew she had.'

'Oh, my goodness. Oh, my . . . Louisa?'

'I'm still here.'

When he spoke again I found my eyes had filled unexpectedly with tears.

'How do I meet her? How do we go about meeting . . . Lily?'

We drove up the following Saturday. Lily was afraid to go alone, but wouldn't say as much. She just told me it was better if I explained everything to Mr Traynor because 'Old people are better at talking to each other.'

We drove in silence. I felt almost sick with nerves at having to enter the Traynor house again, not that I could explain it to the passenger beside me. Lily said nothing.

*Did he believe you?*

Yes, I told her. I think he did. Although she might be wise to have a blood test, just to reassure everyone.

*Did he actually ask to meet me, or did you suggest it?*

I couldn't remember. My brain had set up a kind of static buzz just speaking to him again.

*What if I'm not what he's expecting?*

I wasn't sure he was expecting anything. He'd only just discovered he had a grandchild.'

Lily had turned up on Friday night, even though I hadn't expected her until Saturday morning, saying that she'd had a massive row with her mother and that Fuckface Francis had told her she had some growing up to do. She sniffed. 'This from a man who thinks it's normal to have a whole room devoted to a *train set*.'

I had told her she was welcome to stay as long as (a) I could get confirmation from her mother that she always knew where she was, (b) she didn't drink and (c) she didn't smoke in my flat. Which meant that while I was in the bath she walked across the road to Samir's shop and chatted to him for the length of time it took to smoke two cigarettes, but it seemed churlish to argue. Tanya Houghton-Miller wailed on for almost twenty minutes about the impossibility of everything, told me four times I would end up sending Lily home within forty-eight hours and only got off the phone when a child started screaming in the background. I listened to Lily clattering around in my little kitchen, and music I didn't understand vibrating the few bits of furniture in my living room.

*Okay, Will*, I told him silently. *If this was your idea of pushing me into a whole new life you certainly pulled a blinder.*

\*

The next morning I walked into the spare room to wake Lily and found her already awake, her arms curled round her legs, smoking by my open window. An array of clothes was tossed around on the bed, as if she had tried on a dozen outfits and found them all wanting.

She glared at me, as if daring me to say anything. I had a sudden image of Will, turning from the window in his wheelchair, his gaze furious and pained, and just for a moment it took my breath away.

'We leave in half an hour,' I said.

We reached the outskirts of town shortly before eleven. Summer had brought the tourists flocking back to the narrow streets of Stortfold, like clumps of earthbound, gaudily coloured swallows, clutching guidebooks and ice creams, weaving their way aimlessly past the cafés and seasonal shops full of castle-imprinted coasters and calendars that would be swiftly placed in drawers at home and rarely looked at again. I drove slowly past the castle in the long queue of National Trust traffic, wondering at the Pac-a-macs, the anoraks and sunhats that seemed to stay the same every year. This year was the five-hundredth anniversary of the castle, and everywhere we looked there were posters advertising events linked to it: morris dancers, hog roasts, fêtes . . .

I drove up to the front of the house, grateful that we weren't facing the annex where I had spent so much time with Will. We sat in the car and listened to the engine ticking down. Lily, I noticed, had bitten away nearly all of her nails. 'You okay?'

She shrugged.

'Shall we go in, then?'

She stared at her feet. 'What if he doesn't like me?'

'Why wouldn't he?'

'Nobody else does.'

'I'm sure that's not true.'

'Nobody at school likes me. My parents can't wait to get rid of me.' She bit savagely at the corner of a remaining thumbnail. 'What kind of mother lets her daughter go and live at the mouldy old flat of someone they don't even know?'

I took a deep breath. 'Mr Traynor's a nice man. And I wouldn't have brought you here if I thought it wouldn't go well.'

'If he doesn't like me, can we just leave? Like, really quickly?'

'Of course.'

'I'll know. Just from how he looks at me.'

'We'll skid out on two wheels if necessary.'

She smiled reluctantly.

'Okay,' I said, trying not to show her that I was almost as nervous as she was. 'Let's go.'

I stood on the step, watching Lily so that I wouldn't think too hard about where I was. The door opened slowly, and there he stood, still in the same cornflower blue shirt I remembered from two summers previously, but a newer, shorter haircut, perhaps a vain attempt to combat the ageing effects of extreme grief. He opened his mouth as if he wanted to say something to me but had forgotten what it was, and then he looked at Lily and his eyes widened just a little. 'Lily?'

She nodded.

He gazed at her intently. Nobody moved. And then his mouth compressed, and tears filled his eyes, and he stepped forward and swept her into his arms. 'Oh, my dear. Oh, my goodness. Oh, it's so very good to meet you. Oh, my goodness.'

His grey head came down to rest against hers. I wondered, briefly, if she would pull back: Lily was not someone who encouraged physical contact. But as I watched, her hands crept out and she reached around his waist and clutched his shirt, her knuckles whitening and her eyes closing as she let herself be held by him. They stood like that for what seemed an eternity, the old man and his granddaughter, not moving from the front step.

He leaned back, and there were tears running down his face. 'Let me look at you. Let me look.'

She glanced at me, embarrassed and pleased at the same time.

'Yes. Yes, I can see it. Look at you! Look at you!' His face swung towards mine. 'She looks like him, doesn't she?'

I nodded.

She was staring at him, too, searching, perhaps, for traces of her father. When she looked down, they were still holding each other's hands.

Until that moment, I hadn't realized I was crying. It was the naked relief on Mr Traynor's battered old face, the joy of something he had thought lost and partially recaptured, the sheer unexpected happiness of both of them in finding each other. And as she smiled back at him – a slow, sweet smile of recognition – my nervousness, and any doubts I'd had about Lily Houghton-Miller, were banished.

It had been less than two years, but Granta House had changed significantly since I had last been there. Gone were the enormous antique cabinets, the trinket boxes on highly polished mahogany tables, the heavy drapes. It took the waddling figure of Della Layton to indicate why that might be. There were still a few glowing pieces of antique furniture, yes, but everything else was white or brightly coloured – new sunshine yellow Sanderson curtains and pale rugs on the old wood floors, modern prints in unmoulded frames. She moved towards us slowly and her smile was faintly guarded, like something she had forced herself to wear. I found myself moving back involuntarily as she approached: there was something oddly shocking about such a very pregnant woman – the sheer bulk of her, the almost obscene curve of her stomach.

'Hello, you must be Louisa. How lovely to meet you.'

Her lustrous red hair was pinned up in a clip, a pale blue linen shirt rolled up around slightly swollen wrists. I couldn't help noticing the enormous diamond ring cutting into her wedding finger, and wondered with a vague pang what the last months had been like for Mrs Traynor.

'Congratulations,' I said, indicating her belly. I wanted to say something else, but I could never work out whether it was appropriate to say a heavily pregnant woman was 'large', 'not large', 'neat', 'blooming', or any of the other euphemisms people seemed to use to disguise what they wanted to say, which was essentially along the lines of *Bloody hell*.

'Thank you. It was a bit of a surprise, but a very welcome one.' Her gaze slid away from me. She was watching Mr Traynor and Lily. He still had one of her hands encased in his, patting it for emphasis, and was telling her about the house, how it had been passed through the family for so many generations. 'Would everyone like tea?' she asked. And then, again, 'Steven? Tea?'

'Lovely, darling. Thank you. Lily, do you drink tea?'

'Could I have juice, please? Or some water?' Lily smiled.

'I'll help you,' I said to Della. Mr Traynor had begun to point out ancestors in the portraits on the wall, his hand at Lily's elbow, remarking on the similarity of her nose to this one, or the colour of her hair to that one over there.

Della watched them for a moment, and I thought I noticed something close to dismay flicker across her features. She caught me looking, and smiled briskly, as if embarrassed to have her feelings so nakedly on display. 'That would be lovely. Thank you.'

We moved around each other in the kitchen, fetching milk, sugar, a teapot, exchanging polite queries about biscuits. I stooped to get the cups out of the cupboard when Della couldn't comfortably reach that low, and placed them on the kitchen worktop. New cups, I noticed. A modern, geo-metrical design, instead of the worn flowery porcelain her predecessor had favoured, all delicately painted wild herbs and flowers with Latin names. All traces of Mrs Traynor's thirty-eight-year tenure here seemed to have been swiftly and ruthlessly erased.

'The house looks . . . nice. Different,' I said.

'Yes. Well, Steven lost a lot of his furniture in the divorce. So we had to change the look a bit.' She reached for the tea caddy. 'He lost things that had been in his family for genera-tions. Of course, she took everything she could.'

She flashed me a look, as if assessing whether I could be considered an ally.

'I haven't spoken to Mrs . . . Camilla since Will . . .' I said, feeling oddly disloyal.

'So. Steven said this girl just turned up on your doorstep.' Her smile was small and fixed.

'Yes. It was a surprise. But I've met Lily's mother, and she . . . well, she was obviously close to Will for some time.'

Della put her hand to the small of her back, then turned back to the kettle. Mum had said she headed a small solicitors' practice in the next town. *You've got to wonder about a woman who hasn't been married by thirty,* she had said sniffily, and then, after a quick look in my direction, *Forty. I meant forty.*

'What do you think she wants?'

'I'm sorry?'

'What do you think she wants? The girl?'

I could hear Lily in the hall, asking questions, childish and interested, and felt oddly protective. 'I don't think she *wants* anything. She just discovered she had a father she hadn't known about and wants to get to know his family. *Her* family.'

Della warmed and emptied the teapot, measured out the tea-leaves (loose, I noted, just as Mrs Traynor would have had). She poured the boiling water slowly, careful not to splash herself. 'I have loved Steven for a very long time. He – he – has had a very hard time this last year or so. It would be . . .' she didn't look at me as she spoke '. . . very difficult for him if Lily were to complicate his life at this point.'

'I don't think Lily wants to complicate either of your lives,' I said carefully. 'But I do think she has a right to know her own grandfather.'

'Of course,' she said smoothly, that automatic smile in place. I realized, in that instant, that I had failed some internal test, and also that I didn't care. And then, with a final murmured check of the tray, Della picked it up and, accepting my offer to bring the cake and the teapot, carried it through to the drawing room.

'And how are you, Louisa?'

Mr Traynor leaned back in his easy chair, a broad smile breaking his saggy features. He had talked to Lily almost constantly throughout tea, asking questions about her mother, where she lived, what she was studying (she didn't tell him about the problems at school), whether she preferred fruit cake or chocolate ('Chocolate? Me too!') or ginger (no), and cricket (not really – 'Well, we'll have to do something about that!'). He seemed reassured by her, by her likeness to his son. At that point, he probably wouldn't have cared if she had announced that her mother was a Brazilian lap-dancer.

I watched him sneaking looks at Lily, when she was talking, studying her in profile, as if perhaps he could see Will there too. Other times I caught a flicker of melancholy in his expression.

I suspected that he was thinking what I had thought: this new grief that his son would never know her. Then he would almost visibly pull himself together, forcing himself a little more upright, a ready smile back upon his face.

He had walked her around the grounds for half an hour, exclaiming when they returned that Lily had found her way out of the maze 'on your first go! It must be a genetic thing.' Lily had smiled as broadly if she had won a prize.

'And, Louisa? What is happening in your life?'

'I'm fine, thank you.'

'Are you still working as a . . . carer?'

'No. I – I went travelling for a bit, and now I'm working at an airport.'

'Oh! Good! British Airways, I hope?'

I felt my cheeks colour.

'Management, is it?'

'I work in a bar. At the airport.'

He hesitated, just a fraction of a second, and nodded firmly. 'People always need bars. Especially at airports. I always have a double whisky before I get on a plane, don't I, darling?'

'Yes, you do,' replied Della.

'And I suppose it must be rather interesting watching everyone fly off every day. Exciting.'

'I have other things in the pipeline.'

'Of course you do. Good. Good . . .'

There was a short silence.

'When is the baby due?' I said, to shift everybody's attention away from me.

'Next month,' said Della, her hands resting on the swell of her belly. 'It's a girl.'

'How lovely. What are you going to call her?'

They exchanged the glances that parents-to-be do when they have chosen a name but don't want to tell anyone.

'Oh . . . we don't know.'

'Feels most odd. To be a father again, at my age. Can't quite imagine it. You know, changing nappies, that sort of thing.' He glanced at Della, then added reassuringly, 'It's marvellous, though. I'm a very lucky man. We're both very lucky, aren't we, Della?'

She smiled at him.

'I'm sure,' I said. 'How's Georgina?'

Perhaps only I would have noticed how Mr Traynor's expression changed, just a degree. 'Oh, she's fine. Still in Australia, you know.'

'Right.'

'She did come over a few months ago . . . but she spent most of her time with her mother. She was very busy.'

'Of course.'

'I think she's got a boyfriend. I'm sure someone told me she had a boyfriend. So that's . . . that's nice.'

Della's hand reached across and touched his.

'Who's Georgina?' Lily was eating a biscuit.

'Will's younger sister,' said Mr Traynor, turning to her. 'Your aunt! Yes! In fact, she looked a little like you when she was your age.'

'Can I see a picture?'

'I'll find you one.' Mr Traynor rubbed the side of his face. 'I'm trying to remember where we put that graduation photo.'

'Your study,' said Della. 'Stay there, darling. I'll get it. Good for me to keep moving.' She levered herself out of the sofa and walked heavily out of the room. Lily insisted on going with her. 'I want to see the rest of the photographs. I want to see who I look like.'

Mr Traynor watched them go, still smiling. We sat and sipped our tea in silence. He turned to me. 'Have you spoken to her yet? . . . Camilla?'

'I don't know where she lives. I was going to ask you for her details. I know Lily wants to meet her, too.'

'She's had a difficult time of it. George says so, anyway. We haven't really spoken. It's all a bit complicated because of . . .' He nodded towards the door and let out an almost imperceptible sigh.

'Would you like to tell her? About Lily?'

'Oh, no. Oh . . . No. I – I'm not sure she'd really want . . .' He ran a hand over his brow. 'Probably better if you do it.'

He copied out the address and phone number on a piece of paper and handed it to me. 'It's some distance away,' he noted, and smiled apologetically. 'Think she wanted a fresh start. Give her my best, won't you? It's odd . . . to finally have a grandchild, in these circumstances.' He lowered his voice. 'Funnily enough, Camilla is the only person who could really understand how I'm feeling right now.'

If he had been anybody else I might have hugged him just then, but we were English and he had once been my boss of sorts, so we simply smiled awkwardly at each other. And possibly wished we were somewhere else.

Mr Traynor straightened in his chair. 'Still. I'm a lucky man. A new start, at my age. Not sure I really deserve it.'

'I'm not sure happiness is a matter of what you deserve.'

'And you? I know you were very fond of Will . . .'

'He's a hard act to follow.' I was conscious of a lump in my throat. When it cleared, Mr Traynor was still looking at me.

'My son was all about living, Louisa. I don't need to tell you that.'

'That's the thing, though, isn't it?'

He waited.

'He was just better at it than the rest of us.'

'You'll get there, Louisa. We all get there. In our ways.' He touched my elbow, his expression soft.

Della, arriving back in the room, began to load the tray, stacking the cups so ostentatiously that it could only have been a signal.

'We'd better get going,' I said to Lily, standing as she came in, holding out the framed photograph.

'She does look like me, doesn't she? Do you think our eyes are a bit the same? Do you think she'd want to speak to me? Is she on email?'

'I'm sure she will,' said Mr Traynor. 'But if you don't mind, Lily, I'll speak to her myself first. It's quite big news for us all to digest. Best give her a few days to get used to it.'

'Okay. So when can I come and stay?'

To my right, I heard the clatter of Della almost dropping a cup. She stooped slightly, righting it on the tray.

'Stay?' Mr Traynor bent forward, as if he weren't sure he'd heard her correctly.

'Well. You're my grandfather. I thought maybe I could come and stay for the rest of the summer? Get to know you. We've got so much to catch up on, haven't we?' Her face was alight with anticipation.

Mr Traynor looked towards Della, whose expression halted whatever he might have been about to say.

'It would be lovely to have you at some point,' Della said, holding the tray in front of her, 'but we have other things going on just now.'

'It's Della's first child, you see. I think she'd like –'

'I just need a little time by myself with Steven. And the baby.'

'I could help. I'm really good with babies,' Lily said. 'I used to look after my brothers all the time when they were babies. And they were awful. Really horrible babies. They screamed, like, all the time.'

Mr Traynor looked at Della. 'I'm sure you'll be simply

brilliant, Lily darling,' he said. 'It's just that right now is not a very good time.'

'But you've got loads of room. I can just stay in one of the guest rooms. You won't even know I'm here. I'll be really helpful with nappies and stuff and I could babysit so you could still go out. I could just . . .' Lily trailed off. She glanced from one to the other, waiting.

'Lily . . .' I said, hovering uncomfortably near the door.

'You don't want me here.'

Mr Traynor stepped forward, made as if to put a hand on her shoulder. 'Lily darling. That's not –'

She ducked away. 'You like the idea of having a granddaughter, but you don't actually want me in your life. You just – you just want a *visitor*.'

'It's the timing, Lily,' said Della, calmly. 'It's just – well, I waited a long time for Steven – your grandfather – and this time with our baby is very precious to us.'

'And I'm not.'

'That's not it at all.' Mr Traynor moved towards her again.

She batted him off. 'Oh, God, you're all the same. You and your perfect little families, all closed off. Nobody has any room for me.'

'Oh, come on. Let's not be dramatic about –' Della began.

'*Get lost*,' Lily spat. And as Della shrank back, and Mr Traynor's eyes widened in shock, she ran, and I left them in the silent drawing room to race after her.

# Chapter Ten

I emailed Nathan. The answer came back:

Lou, have you started on strong meds? WTAF?

I sent him a second email, filling in a little more detail, and his normal equanimity seemed to return.

Well, the old dog. Still had some surprises for us, eh?

I didn't hear from Lily for two days. Half of me was concerned, the other a tiny bit relieved just to have a brief interlude of calm. I wondered if, once she was free of any fairytale ideas about Will's family, she might be more inclined to build bridges with her own. Then I wondered whether Mr Traynor would call her directly to smooth things over. And I wondered where Lily was, and whether her absence involved the young man who had stood and watched her in my doorway. There had been something about him – about Lily's evasiveness when I asked about him – that had stayed with me.

I had thought a lot about Sam, regretting my rapid exit. With hindsight, it had all seemed a bit overemotional and weird, running away from him like that. I must have seemed the exact person I kept protesting I wasn't. I resolved that the next time I saw him outside the Moving On Circle I would react very calmly, perhaps say hello with an enigmatic, non-depressed-person smile.

Work sagged and dragged. A new girl had started: Vera, a stern Lithuanian, who completed all the bar's tasks wearing the kind of peculiar half-smile of someone contemplating the fact that they had planted a dirty bomb nearby. She called all men 'filthy, filthy beasts' when out of earshot of Richard.

He had begun giving morning 'motivational' chats, after which we all had to pump the air and jump and shout, 'YEAH!' which always dislodged my curly wig, at which he would frown, as if it was somehow a failure indicative of my personality, not an inbuilt hazard of wearing a nylon hairpiece that didn't actually stick to my head. Vera's wig stayed immobile on hers. Perhaps it was too afraid to fall off.

One night when I got home I did an internet search on teenagers' problems, trying to work out whether I could help to repair the damage of the weekend. But it had quite a lot on hormonal breakouts and nothing on what to do when you had introduced a sixteen-year-old you had just met to her dead quadriplegic father's surviving family. At half past ten I gave up, gazed around at the bedroom in which half my clothes were still stored in boxes, promised myself that this would be the week I did something about it, and then, having reassured myself that I totally would, fell asleep.

I was woken at half past two in the morning by the sound of someone trying to force my front door. I stumbled out of bed, grabbed a mop, then put my eye to the spy-hole, my heart thumping. 'I'm calling the police!' I yelled. 'What do you want?'

'It's Lily. *Duh.*' She fell through the door as I opened it, half laughing, reeking of cigarettes, her mascara smeared around her eyes.

I wrapped my dressing-gown around myself, and locked the door behind her. 'Jesus, Lily. It's the middle of the night.'

'Do you want to go dancing? I thought we could go dancing. I love dancing. Actually, that's not entirely true. I do like dancing but that's not why I'm here. Mum wouldn't let me in. They've changed the locks. Can you believe it?'

I was tempted to answer that, with my alarm clock set for six a.m., funnily enough, I could.

Lily bumped heavily against the wall. 'She wouldn't even open the stupid door. Just shouted through the letterbox at me. Like I was some kind of . . . vagrant. So . . . I thought I'd stay here. Or we could go dancing . . .' She swayed past me and headed for the music system, where she turned up the sound to a deafening level. I raced towards it to turn it down, but she grabbed my hand. 'Let's dance, Louisa! You need to bust some moves! You're so sad all the time! Cut loose! C'mon!'

I wrenched my hand away, and rushed to the volume button, just in time for the first thumps of outrage to land from downstairs. When I turned, Lily had disappeared into the spare room, where she teetered and finally collapsed, face down, on the camp bed.

'Oh. My. God. This bed is *soooooo* rubbish.'

'Lily? You can't just come in here and – Oh, for God's sake.'

'Just for a minute,' came the muffled answer. 'Literally a stopover. And then I'm going dancing. We're going dancing.'

'Lily. I have work tomorrow morning.'

'I love you, Louisa. Did I tell you that? I really do love you. You're the only one who . . .'

'You can't just collapse here like –'

'Mmph . . . disco nap . . .'

She didn't move.

I touched her shoulder. 'Lily . . . Lily?'

She let out a small snore.

I sighed, waited a few minutes, then carefully removed her tatty pumps, and the contents of her pocket (cigarettes, mobile phone, a crumpled fiver), which I took into my room. I propped her on her side in the recovery position, and finally, wide awake at three a.m., knowing I would probably not sleep for fear she would choke, sat on the chair, to watch her.

Lily's face was peaceful. The wary scowl and the manic, overeager smile had stilled into something unearthly and beautiful, her hair fanned around her shoulders. Maddening as her behaviour was, I couldn't be angry. I kept recalling the hurt on her face that Sunday. Lily was my polar opposite. She didn't nurse a hurt, or contain it. She lashed out, got drunk, did God-knew-what to try to forget. She was more like her father than I'd thought.

*What would you have made of this, Will?* I asked him silently.

But, just as I had struggled to help him, I didn't know what to do for her. I didn't know how to make it better.

I thought of my sister's words: *You won't be able to cope, you know.* And just for a few still, pre-dawn moments, I hated her for being right.

We developed a routine of sorts, in which Lily would turn up to see me every few days. I was never certain which Lily I would find at my door: manically cheerful Lily, demanding that we go out and eat at this restaurant or look at the totally gorgeous cat outside on the wall downstairs, or dance in the living room to some band she'd just discovered; or subdued, wary Lily, who would nod a silent greeting on her way in, then lie on my sofa and watch television. Sometimes she would ask random questions about Will – what programmes did he like? (He barely watched television; he preferred films.) Did he have a favourite fruit? (Seedless grapes. Red ones.) When was the last time I'd seen him laugh? (He didn't laugh much. But his smile . . . I could picture it now, a rare flash of even white teeth, his eyes crinkling.) I was never sure whether she found my answers satisfactory.

And then, every ten days or so, there was drunk Lily, or

worse (I was never sure), who would hammer on my door in the small hours, ignoring my protests about time and lost sleep, stumble past me with mascara-smudged cheeks and missing shoes and pass out on the little camp bed, refusing to wake when I left in the morning.

She seemed to have no hobbies, and few friends. She would talk to anyone in the street, asking favours with the unembarrassed insouciance of a feral kid. But she wouldn't answer the phone at home and seemed to expect everyone she met to dislike her.

Given that most private schools had finished for the summer, I asked her where she was when she wasn't at my flat or visiting her mother, and after a brief pause, she said, 'Martin's.' When I asked if he was her boyfriend, she pulled the universal teenage face in response to an adult who had said something not just spectacularly stupid but revolting, too.

Sometimes she would be angry, at others rude. But I could never refuse her. Chaotic as her behaviour was, I got the feeling my flat was a safe haven. I found myself searching for clues: examining her phone for messages (pin-locked), her pockets for drugs (none, apart from that one joint) and once, ten minutes after she had come in, tear-stained and drunk, staring down at the car outside my block, its horn blaring intermittently for the best part of three-quarters of an hour. Eventually one of my neighbours went downstairs and thumped on the window so hard that the occupant had driven off.

'You know, I'm not judging, but it's not a good idea to get so drunk that you don't know what you're doing, Lily,' I said one morning, as I made us both coffee. Lily spent so much time with me now that I'd had to adjust the way I lived: shopping for two, picking up mess that wasn't my own, making twice the hot drinks, remembering to lock the bathroom door to avoid shrieks of *Oh, my God. Gross!*

'You are totally judging. That's exactly what "it's not a good idea" means.'

'I'm serious.'

'Do I tell you how to live your life? Do I tell you that this flat is depressing, and you dress like someone who has lost the will to live, apart from when you're being a gammy-legged porno pixie? Do I? Do I? No. I don't say anything, so just leave me alone.'

I wanted to tell her then. I wanted to tell her what had happened to me nine years previously, on a night when I had drunk too much, and how my sister had led me home, shoeless and crying silently, in the early hours. But she would no doubt greet it with the same childish scorn with which she greeted most of my revelations, and it was a conversation I had only ever managed to have with one person. And he wasn't here any more. 'It's also not fair to wake me up in the middle of the night. I have to get up early for work.'

'So give me a key. Then I won't wake you up, will I?'

She blasted me with that winning smile. It was rare and dazzling, and enough like Will's that I found myself giving the key to her. Even as I handed it over, I knew what my sister would say.

I spoke to Mr Traynor twice during that time. He was anxious to know Lily was well, had started to worry about what she was going to do with her life. 'I mean, she's plainly a bright girl. It's not a good idea for her to drop out of school at sixteen. Do her parents not have anything to say about it?'

'They don't seem to speak very much.'

'Should I have a word with them? Do you think she needs a university fund? I have to say, things are a tad tighter than they were since the divorce, but Will left a fair bit. So I thought that might be . . . an appropriate use for it.' He lowered his voice. 'It might be wise, though, for us not to mention anything to Della just now. I don't want her getting the wrong idea.'

I resisted the urge to ask what the right idea might be.

'Louisa, do you think you could persuade Lily to come back? I keep thinking about her. I'd like us to all try again. I know Della would love to get to know her better too.'

I remembered Della's expression as we had tiptoed around each other in the kitchen, and wondered whether Mr Traynor was wilfully blind or just an eternal optimist.

'I'll try,' I promised.

There is a peculiar sort of silence in a flat when you are on your own in a city on a hot summer weekend. I was on earlies, finished my shift at four, arrived home by five, exhausted, and was secretly grateful that, for a few brief hours, I had my home to myself. I showered, ate some toast, took a look online to see if there were any jobs that either paid more than the minimum wage or were not zero-hours contracts, then sat in the living room with all the windows open to encourage a breeze, listening to the sounds of the city filtering in on the warm air.

Most of the time, I was reasonably content with my life. I had been to enough group sessions now to know that it was important to be grateful for simple pleasures. I was healthy. I had my family again. I was working. If I hadn't made peace with Will's death, I did at least feel like I might be crawling out from under its shadow.

And yet.

On evenings like this, when the streets below were filled with couples strolling, and laughing people spilled out of pubs, already planning meals, nights out, trips to clubs, something ached inside me; something primal telling me that I was in the wrong place, that I was missing something.

These were the moments when I felt most left behind.

I tidied up a little, washed my uniform, and then, just as I was sinking into a kind of quiet melancholy, my buzzer went. I stood and picked up the entry-phone wearily, expecting a request for directions from a UPS driver, or some misdirected Hawaiian pizza, but instead I heard a man's voice.

'Louisa?'

'Who is this?' I said, though I knew immediately who it was.

'Sam. Ambulance Sam. I was just passing on the way home from work, and I just . . . Well, you left in such a hurry the other night, I thought I'd make sure you were okay.'

'A fortnight later? I could have been eaten by cats by now.'

'I'm guessing you weren't.'

'I don't have a cat.' A short silence. 'But I'm fine, Ambulance Sam. Thanks.'

'Great . . . That's good to hear.'

I shifted, so I could see him through the grainy black and white of the little entry video screen. He was wearing a biker jacket instead of his paramedic uniform, and had one hand resting against the wall, which he now removed, and turned to face the road. I saw him let out a breath, and that small motion prompted me to speak. 'So . . . what are you up to?'

'Not much. Trying and failing to chat someone up through an entry-phone, mostly.'

My laugh was too quick. Too loud. 'I gave up on that ages ago,' I said. 'It makes buying them a drink really, really hard.'

I saw him laugh. I looked around at my silent flat. And I spoke before I could think: 'Stay there. I'll come down.'

I was going to bring my car, but when he held out a spare motorbike helmet, it seemed prissy to insist on my own transport. I stuffed my keys into my pocket and stood waiting for him to motion me aboard.

'You're a paramedic. And you ride a motorbike.'

'I know. But, as vices go, she's pretty much the only one I have left.' He grinned wolfishly. Something inside me lurched unexpectedly. 'You don't feel safe with me?'

There was no appropriate answer to that question. I held his gaze and climbed onto the back. If he did anything dangerous he had the skills to patch me up again afterwards.

'So what do I do?' I said, as I pulled the helmet over my head. 'I've never been on one of these before.'

'Hold on to those handlebars on the seat, and just move with the bike. Don't brace against me. If you're not happy, tap me on the shoulder and I'll stop.'

'Where are we going?'

'You any good at interior decorating?'

'Hopeless. Why?'

He fired up the ignition. 'I thought I'd show you my new house.'

And then we were in the traffic, weaving in and out of the cars and lorries, following signs to the motorway. I had to shut my eyes, press myself against his back and hope that he couldn't hear me squeal.


We went out to the very edge of the city, a place where the gardens grew larger, then morphed into fields, and houses had names instead of numbers. We came through a village that wasn't quite separate from the one before it, and Sam slowed the bike at a field gate and finally cut the engine, motioning for me to climb off. I removed the helmet, my heart still thumping in my ears, and tried to lift my sweaty hair from my head with fingers that were still stiff from gripping the pillion handlebars.

Sam opened the gate, and ushered me through. Half the field was grassland, the other an irregular mess of concrete and breeze blocks. In the corner beyond the building work, sheltered by a high hedge, stood a railway carriage and, beside it, a chicken run in which several birds stopped to look expectantly towards us.

'My house.'

'Nice!' I glanced around. 'Um . . . where is it?'

Sam began to walk down the field. 'There. That's the foundations. Took me the best part of three months to get those down.'

'You live here?'

'Yup.'

I stared at the concrete slabs. When I looked at him, something in his expression made me bite back what I was going to say. I rubbed at my head. 'So… are you going to stand there all evening? Or are you going to give me a guided tour?'

Bathed in the evening sun, and surrounded by the scents of grass and lavender, and the lazy hum of the bees, we walked slowly from one slab to another, Sam pointing to where the windows and doors would be. 'This is the bathroom.'

'Bit draughty.'

'Yeah. I need to do something about that. Watch out. That's not actually a doorway. You just walked into the shower.'

He stepped over a pile of breeze blocks onto another large grey slab, holding out his hand so that I could step safely over them too. 'And here's the living room. So if you look through that window there,' he held his fingers in a square, 'you get the views of the open countryside.'

I looked out at the shimmering landscape below. I felt as if we were a million miles out of the city, not ten. I took a deep breath, enjoying the unexpectedness of it all. 'It's nice, but I think your sofa's in the wrong place,' I said. 'You need two. One here, and maybe one there. And I'm guessing you have a window here?'

'Oh, yes. Got to be dual aspect.'

'Hmm. Plus you totally need to rethink your storage.'

The crazy thing was, within a few minutes of our walking and talking, I could actually see the house. I followed the line of Sam's hands, as he gestured towards invisible fireplaces, summoned staircases out of his imagination, drew lines across invisible ceilings. I could see its over-height windows, the banisters that a friend of his would carve from aged oak.

'It's going to be lovely,' I said, when we had conjured the last en-suite.

'In about ten years. But, yup, I hope so.'

I gazed around the field, taking in the vegetable patch, the chicken run, the birdsong. 'I have to tell you, this is not what I expected. You aren't tempted to, you know, get builders in?'

'I probably will eventually. But I like doing it. It's good for the soul, building a house.' He shrugged. 'When you spend all day patching up stab wounds and over-confident cyclists and the wives whose husbands have used them as a punch-bag and the kids with chronic asthma from the damp . . .'

'. . . and the daft women who fall off rooftops.'

'Those too.' He gestured towards the concrete mixer, the piles of bricks. 'I do this so I can live with that. Beer?' He climbed into the railway carriage, motioning for me to join him.

It was no longer a carriage inside. It had a small, immaculately laid-out kitchen area, and an L-shaped upholstered seat at the end, though it still carried the faint smell of beeswax and tweedy passengers. 'I don't like mobile homes,' he said, as if in explanation. He waved to the seat, 'Sit,' then pulled a cold beer from the fridge, cracking it open and handing me the bottle. He set a kettle on the stove for himself.

'You're not drinking?'

He shook his head. 'I found after a couple of years on the job that I'd come home and have a drink to relax. And then it was two. And then I found I couldn't relax until I'd had those two, or maybe three.' He opened a caddy, dropped a teabag into a mug. 'And then I . . . lost someone close to me, and I decided that either I stopped or I would never stop drinking again.' He didn't look at me while he said this, just moved around the railway carriage, a bulky, yet oddly graceful presence within its narrow walls. 'I do have the odd beer, but not tonight. I'm driving you home later.'

Comments like that took the weirdness out of sitting in a railway carriage with a man I didn't really know. How could you maintain a reserve with someone who had tended your broken, partially unclothed body? How could you feel anxious around a man who had already told you of his plan to take you home again? It was as if the manner of our first meeting had removed the normal, awkward obstacles to getting to know someone. He had seen me in my underwear. Hell, he had seen under my actual skin. It meant I felt at ease around Sam in a way I didn't with anyone else.

The carriage reminded me of the gypsy caravans I had read about in childhood, where everything had a place, and there was order in a confined space. It was homey, but austere, and unmistakably male. It smelt agreeably of sun-warmed wood, soap and bacon. A fresh start, I guessed. I wondered what had happened to his and Jake's old home. 'So . . . um . . . what does Jake think of it?'

He sat down at the other end of the bench with his tea. 'He thought I was mad at first. Now he quite likes it. He does the animals when I'm on shift. In return I've promised to teach him to drive around the field once he turns seventeen.' He lifted a mug. 'God help me.'

I raised my beer in return.

Perhaps it was the unexpected pleasure of being out on a warm Friday evening with a man who held your eye as he spoke and had the kind of hair you slightly wanted to ruffle with your fingers, or maybe it was just the second beer, but I finally started to enjoy myself. It got stuffy in the carriage, so we moved outside onto two fold-up chairs, and I watched the chickens peck around in the grass, which was oddly restful, and listened to Sam's tales of obese patients, who required four teams to lift them out of their homes, and young gang members, who tried to attack each other even as they were being stitched up in the back of his rig. As we talked I found myself sneaking surreptitious glances at him, at the way his hands held his mug, at his unexpected smiles, which caused three perfect lines to span out from the corner of each eye as if they had been drawn with fine-point precision.

He told me about his parents: his father a retired fireman, his mother a nightclub singer, who had given up her career for her children. ('I think it's why your outfit spoke to me. I'm comfortable with glitter.') He didn't mention his late wife by name, but observed that his mother worried about the on-going lack of a feminine influence in Jake's life. 'She comes and scoops him up once a month and takes him back to Cardiff so she and her sisters can coo over him and feed him up and make sure he has enough socks.' He rested his elbows on his knees. 'He moans about going, but he secretly loves it.'

I told him about Lily's return, and he winced at my tale of her meeting with the Traynors. I told him about her perplexing moods, and her erratic behaviour, and he nodded, as if this were all to be expected. When I told him about Lily's mother he shook his head. 'Just because they're wealthy doesn't make them better parents,' he said. 'If she was on benefits, that mother would probably get a little visit from Social Services.' He lifted a mug to me. 'It's a nice thing you're doing, Louisa Clark.'

'I'm not sure I'm doing it very well.'

'Nobody ever feels they're doing well with teenagers,' he said. 'I think that's kind of the point of them.'

It was hard to reconcile this Sam, at ease in his home, caring for his chickens, with the sobbing, skirt-chasing version we heard about in the Moving On Circle. But I knew very well how the persona you chose to present to the world could be very different from what was inside. I knew how grief could make you behave in ways you couldn't even begin to understand. 'I love your railway carriage,' I said. 'And your invisible house.'

'Then I hope you'll come again,' he said.

*The compulsive shagger.* If this was how he picked up women, I thought a little wistfully, then, boy, he was good. It was a potent mix: the gentlemanly grieving father, the rare smiles, the way he could scoop up a hen one-handed and the hen actually looked happy about it. I would not allow myself to become one of the psycho-girlfriends, I told myself repeatedly. But there was a sneaking pleasure to be had in just flirting gently with a handsome man. It was nice to feel something other than anxiety, or mute fury, the twin emotions that seemed to make up so much of my daily life. The only other encounters I'd had with the opposite sex over the last several months had been fuelled by alcohol and ended with a taxi and tears of self-loathing in the shower.

*What do you think, Will? Is this okay?*

It had grown darker, and we watched as the chickens clucked their way indignantly into their coop.

Sam watched them. He leant back in his chair. 'I get the feeling, Louisa Clark, that when you're talking to me there's a whole other conversation going on somewhere else.'

I wanted to come back with a smart answer. But he was right, and there was nothing I could say.

'You and I. We're both skirting around something.'

'You're very direct.'

'And now I've made you uncomfortable.'

'No.' I glanced at him. 'Well, maybe, a little.'

Behind us, a crow lifted noisily into the sky, its flapping wings sending vibrations through the still air. I fought the urge to smooth my hair and instead took a last swig of my beer. 'Okay. Well. Here's a real question. How long do you think it takes to get over someone dying? Someone you really loved, I mean.'

I'm not sure why I asked him. It was almost cruelly blunt, given his circumstances. Perhaps I was afraid that the compulsive shagger was about to come out to play.

Sam's eyes widened a little. 'Woah. Well . . .' he peered down at his mug, and then out at the shadowy fields '. . . I'm not sure you ever do.'

'That's cheery.'

'No. Really. I've thought about it a lot. You learn to live with it, with them. Because they do stay with you, even if they're not living, breathing people any more. It's not the same crushing grief you felt at first, the kind that swamps you, and makes you want to cry in the wrong places, and get irrationally angry with all the idiots who are still alive when the person you love is dead. It's just something you learn to accommodate. Like adapting around a hole. I don't know. It's like you become . . . a doughnut instead of a bun.'

There was such sadness in his face that I felt suddenly guilty. 'A doughnut.'

'Stupid analogy,' he said, with a half-smile.

'I didn't mean to –'

He shook his head. He looked at the grass between his feet, then sideways at me. 'C'mon. Let's get you home.'

We walked across the field to his bike. The air had cooled, and I crossed my arms over my chest. He saw, and handed me his jacket, insisting when I said I was okay. It was pleasingly heavy, and potently male. I tried not to inhale.

'Do you pick up all your patients like this?'

'Only the live ones.'

I laughed. It came out of me unexpectedly, louder than I had intended.

'We're not really meant to ask patients out on dates.' He held out the spare helmet. 'But I figure you're not my patient any more.'

I took it. 'And this isn't really a date.'

'It isn't?' He gave a small, philosophical nod as I climbed aboard. 'Okay.'

# Chapter Eleven

That week, when I arrived at the Moving On Circle Jake wasn't there. As Daphne discussed her inability to open jars without a man in her kitchen, and Sunil talked of the problems of dividing up his brother's few belongings among his remaining siblings, I found myself waiting for the heavy red doors to open at the end of the church hall. I told myself it was his welfare I was concerned about, that he needed to be able to express his discomfort at his father's behaviour in a safe place. I told myself firmly that it was not Sam I was hoping to see, leaning against his bike.

'What are the small things that trip you up, Louisa?'

Perhaps Jake had finished with the group, I thought. Perhaps he had decided he didn't need it any more. People did drop out, everyone said. And that would be it. I would never see either of them again.

'Louisa? The daily things? There must be something.'

I kept thinking about that field, the neat confines of the railway carriage, the way Sam had strolled down the field with a hen under one arm, as if he was carrying a precious parcel. The feathers on her chest had been as soft as a whisper.

Daphne nudged me.

'We were discussing the small things in day-to-day life that force you to contemplate loss,' said Marc.

'I miss sex,' said Natasha.

'That's not a small thing,' replied William.

'You didn't know my husband,' said Natasha, and snorted a laugh. 'Not really. That's a terrible joke to make. I'm sorry.

I don't know what came over me.'

'It's good to joke,' said Marc, encouragingly.

'Olaf was perfectly well endowed. Very well endowed, in fact.' Natasha's eyes flickered around us. When nobody spoke she held up her hands, a foot apart, and nodded emphatically. 'We were very happy.'

There was a short silence.

'Good,' said Marc. 'That's nice to hear.'

'I don't want anyone thinking . . . I mean, that's not what I want people thinking when they think of my husband. That he had a tiny –'

'I'm sure nobody thinks that about your husband.'

'I will, if you keep going on about it,' said William.

'I don't want you thinking about my husband's penis,' said Natasha. 'In fact, I forbid you to think about my husband's penis.'

'Stop going on about it then!' said William.

'Can we not talk about penises?' said Daphne. 'It makes me go a bit peculiar. The nuns used to smack us with rulers if we even used the word "undercarriage".'

Marc's voice was now tinged with desperation. 'Can we steer the conversation away from – back to symbols of loss. Louisa, you were about to tell us which small things brought your loss home to you.'

I sat there, trying to ignore Natasha holding up her hands again, silently measuring some unlikely invisible length.

'I think I miss having someone to discuss things with,' I said carefully.

There was a murmur of agreement.

'I mean, I'm not one of those people who has a massive circle of friends. I was with my last boyfriend for ages and we . . . we didn't really go out much. And then there was . . . Bill. We just used to talk all the time. About music, and people, and things we'd done and wanted to do, and I never worried about whether I was going to say the wrong thing or offend someone because he just "got" me, you know? And now I've moved to London and I'm sort of on my own, apart from my family, and talking to them is always . . . tricky.'

'Word,' said Sunil.

'And now there's something going on that I'd really like to chat to him about. I talk to him in my head, but it isn't the same. I miss having that . . . ability to just go, "Hey, what do you think of this?" And knowing that whatever he said was probably going to be the right thing.'

The group was silent for a minute.

'You can talk to us, Louisa,' said Marc.

'It's . . . complicated.'

'It's always complicated,' said Leanne.

I looked at their faces, kind and expectant, and completely unlikely to understand anything I told them. Not *really* understand it.

Daphne adjusted her silk scarf. 'What Louisa needs is another young man to talk to. Of course she does. You're young and pretty. You'll find someone else,' she said. 'And you, Natasha. Get back out there. It's too late for me, but you two shouldn't be sitting in this dingy old hall – Sorry, Marc, but they shouldn't. You should be out dancing, having a laugh.'

Natasha and I exchanged a look. Clearly, she wanted to go out dancing about as much as I did.

I had a sudden memory of Ambulance Sam and pushed the thought away.

'And if you ever do want another penis,' William said, 'I'm sure I could pencil in a –'

'Okay, everyone. Let's move on to wills,' said Marc. 'Anyone surprised by what turned up?'

*

I got home, exhausted, at a quarter past nine, to find Lily lying on the sofa in front of the television in her pyjamas. I dropped my bag. 'How long have you been here?'

'Since breakfast.'

'Are you okay?'

'Mm.'

Her face held a pallor that spoke of either illness or exhaustion.

'Not feeling well?'

She was eating popcorn out of a bowl and lazily scooped her fingers around the bottom of the bowl for crumbs. 'I just didn't feel like doing anything today.'

Lily's phone beeped. She stared listlessly at the message that came through, then pushed it away from her under a sofa cushion.

'Everything really okay?' I asked, after a minute.

'Fine.'

She didn't look fine.

'Anything I can help with?'

'I said I was fine.'

She didn't look at me as she spoke.

Lily spent that night at the flat. The following day, as I was leaving for work, Mr Traynor rang and asked to speak to her. She was stretched across the sofa and looked blankly up at me when I told her who was on the phone, then finally, reluctantly, held out a hand for the receiver. I stood there as she listened to him. I couldn't hear his words, but I could hear his tone: kind, reassuring, emollient. When he finished, she left a short pause, then said, 'Okay. Fine.'

'Are you going to see him again?' I said, as she handed back the phone.

'He wants to come to London to see me.'

'Well, that's nice.'

'But he can't be too far away from *her* just now in case she goes into labour.'

'Do you want me to take you back there to see him?'

'No.'

She tucked her knees underneath her chin, reached out the remote control and flicked through the channels.

'Do you want to talk about it?' I said, after a minute.

She didn't respond, and after a minute or two, I realized the conversation was over.

On Thursday, I went into my bedroom, closed the door and called my sister. We were speaking several times a week. It was easier now that my estrangement from our parents no longer hung between us, like a conversational minefield.

'Do you think it's normal?'

'Dad told me I once didn't speak to him for two whole weeks when I was sixteen. Only grunts. And I was actually quite happy.'

'She's not even grunting. She just looks miserable.'

'All teenagers do. It's their default setting. It's the cheerful ones you want to worry about – they're probably hiding some massive eating disorder or stealing lipsticks from Boots.'

'She's spent the last three days just lying on the sofa.'

'And your point is?'

'I think something's wrong.'

'She's sixteen years old. Her dad never knew she existed, and popped his clogs before she could meet him. Her mother married someone she calls Fuckface, she has two little brothers who sound like trainee Reggie and Ronnie Kray, and they changed the locks to the family home. I would probably lie on a sofa for a year if I was her.' Treena took a noisy slurp of her tea. 'Plus she's living with someone who wears glittery green Spandex to a bar job and calls it a career.'

'Lurex. It's Lurex.'

'Whatever. So when are you going to find yourself a decent job?'

'Soon. I just need to get this situation sorted first.'

'This situation.'

'She's really down. I feel bad for her.'

'You know what makes me feel down? The way you keep promising to live some kind of a life, then sacrifice yourself to every waif and stray who comes across your path.'

'Will was not a waif and stray.'

'But Lily is. You don't even *know* this girl, Lou. You should be focusing on moving forward. You should be sending off your CV, talking to contacts, working out where your strengths are, not finding yet another excuse to put your own life on hold.'

I stared outside at the city sky. In the next room, I could hear the television burbling away, then Lily getting up, walking to the fridge and flopping down again. I lowered my voice: 'So what would you do, Treen? The child of the man you loved turns up on your doorstep, and everyone else seems to have pretty much handed over responsibility for her. You'd walk away too, would you?'

My sister fell briefly silent. This was a rare enough occurrence that I felt obliged to keep talking. 'So if Thom, in eight years' time, had fallen out with you, for whatever reason – say he was pretty much on his own, and was going off the rails – you'd think it was great if the one person he asked for help decided it was altogether too much of a pain in the arse, would you? That they should just bugger off and suit themselves?' I rested my head against the wall. 'I'm trying to do the right thing here, Treen. Just cut me a break, okay?'

Nothing.

'It makes me feel better. Okay? It makes me feel better knowing I'm helping.'

My sister was silent for so long I wondered whether she had hung up. 'Treen?'

'Okay. Well, I do remember reading a thing in social psychology about how teenagers find too much face-to-face contact exhausting.'

'You want me to talk to her through a door?' One day I would have a telephone conversation with my sister that didn't involve the weary sigh of someone explaining something to a halfwit.

'No, doofus. What it means is that if you're going to get her to talk you need to be doing something together, side by side.'

On my way home on Friday evening I stopped off at the DIY superstore. Back at my block, I lugged the bags up the four flights of stairs, and let myself in. Lily was exactly where I was expecting to find her: stretched out in front of the television. 'What's that?' she asked.

'Paint. This flat's a bit tired. You keep telling me I need to brighten it up. I thought we could get rid of this boring old magnolia.'

She couldn't help herself. I pretended to be busy making myself a drink, watching out of the corner of my eye as she stretched, then walked over and examined the paint cans. 'That's hardly any less boring. It's basically pale grey.'

'I was told grey was the in thing. I'll take it back if you think it won't work.'

She peered at it. 'No. It's okay.'

'I thought the spare room could have cream on two, then one grey wall. Do you think they go?' I busied myself with unwrapping the paintbrushes and rollers as I spoke. I changed into an old shirt and some shorts and asked if she could put on some music.

'What sort?'

'You choose.' I hauled a chair off to one side and laid some dust sheets along the wall. 'Your dad said I was a musical Philistine.'

She didn't say anything, but I had her attention. I cracked open a paint tin and began to mix it. 'He made me go to my first ever concert. Classical, not pop. I only agreed because it meant he would leave the house. He didn't like going out much in the early days. He put on a shirt and a good jacket and it was the first time I had seen him look like . . .' I remembered the jolt as I had seen, emerging from the stiff blue collar, the man he had been before his accident. I swallowed. 'Anyway. I went preparing to be bored, and cried my way through the second half like a complete loon. It was the most amazing thing I'd ever heard in my life.'

A short silence.

'What was it? What did you listen to?'

'I can't remember. Sibelius? Does that sound right?'

She shrugged. I started painting, as she came up beside me. She picked up a brush. She said nothing at first, but she seemed to lose herself in the repetitive nature of the task. She was careful, too, adjusting the sheet so that she didn't spill paint on the floor, wiping her brush on the edge of the pot. We didn't speak, except for muttered requests: *Can you pass me the smaller brush? Do you think that will still show through on the second coat?* It took us just half an hour to do the first wall between us.

'So what do you think?' I said, admiring it. 'Think we can do another?'

She moved a dust sheet and started on the next wall. She had put on some indie band I had never heard of, light-hearted and agreeable. I started to paint again, ignoring the ache in my shoulder, the urge to yawn.

'You should get some pictures.'

'You're right.'

'I've got this big print at home of a Kandinsky. It doesn't really go in my room. You could have it if you want it.'

'That would be great.'

She was working faster now, speeding across the wall, carefully cutting in around the large window.

'So I was thinking,' I said, 'we should speak to Will's mum. Your grandmother. Are you okay if I write to her?'

She said nothing. She crouched down, apparently absorbed in carefully coating the wall to the skirting-board. Finally, she stood up. 'Is she like him?'

'Like who?'

'Mrs Traynor? Is she like Mr Traynor?'

I stepped down from the box I was using to stand on, and wiped my brush on the edge of the tin. 'She's . . . different.'

'That's your way of saying she's a cow.'

'She's not a cow. She's just – It takes longer to get to know her is all.'

'That's your way of telling me she's a cow and she's not going to like me.'

'I'm not saying that at all, Lily. But she is someone who doesn't show her emotions easily.'

Lily sighed and put down her paintbrush. 'I'm basically the only person in the world who could discover two grandparents I didn't know I had, then find out that neither of them even likes me.'

We stared at each other. And suddenly, unexpectedly, we started to laugh.

I put the lid on the paint. 'Come on,' I said. 'Let's go out.'

'Where?'

'You're the one who says I need to have some fun. You tell me.'

I pulled out a series of tops from one of my storage boxes until Lily finally determined which one was acceptable, and I let her take me to a tiny cavernous club in a back-street near the West End where the bouncers knew her by name and nobody seemed to consider for a minute that she might be under eighteen. 'It's nineties music. Olden-days stuff!' she said cheerfully, and I tried not to think too hard about the fact that I was, in her eyes, basically geriatric.

We danced until I stopped feeling self-conscious, sweat came through our clothes, our hair stuck out in fronds and my hip hurt so much that I wondered whether I would be able to stand up behind the bar the following week. We danced as if we had nothing to do but dance. Lord, it felt good. I had forgotten the joy of just existing; of losing yourself in music, in a crowd of people, the sensations that came with becoming one communal, organic mass, alive only to a pulsing beat. For a few dark, thumping hours, I let go of everything, my problems floating away like helium balloons: my awful job, my picky boss, my failure to move on. I became a thing, alive, joyful. I looked over the crowd at Lily, her eyes closed as her hair flew about her face, that peculiar mixture of concentration and freedom in her features that comes when someone loses themselves in rhythm. Then she opened her eyes and I wanted to be angry that her raised arm held a bottle that clearly wasn't cola, but I found myself smiling back at her – a broad, euphoric grin – and thinking how strange it was that a messed-up child who barely knew herself had so much to teach me about the business of living.

Around us London was shrill and heaving, even though it was two a.m. We paused for Lily to take joint selfies of us in front of a theatre, a Chinese sign and a man dressed as a large bear (apparently every event had to be marked by photographic evidence), then wove our way through crowded streets in search of a night bus, past the late-night kebab shops and the bellowing drunks, the pimps and the gaggles of screeching girls. My hip was throbbing badly, and sweat was cooling unpleasantly under my damp clothes, but I still felt energized, as if I had been snapped back on.

'God knows how we're going to get home,' Lily said cheerfully.

And then I heard the shout.

'Lou!' There was Sam, leaning out of the driver's window of an ambulance. As I lifted my hand in response, he pulled the truck across the road in a giant U-turn. 'Where you headed?'

'Home. If we can ever find a bus.'

'Hop in. Go on. I won't tell if you won't. We're just finishing our shift.' He looked at the woman beside him. 'Ah come on, Don. She's a patient. Broken hip. Can't leave her to walk home.'

Lily was delighted by this unexpected turn of events. And then the rear door opened and the woman, in a paramedic uniform, eyes rolling, was shepherding us in. 'You're going to get us sacked, Sam,' she said, and motioned for us to sit down on the gurney. 'Hiya. I'm Donna. Oh, no – I do remember you. The one who . . .'

'. . . fell off a building. Yup.'

Lily pulled me to her for an 'ambulance selfie' and I tried not to look as Donna rolled her eyes again.

'So where have you been?' Sam called through to the rear.

'Dancing,' said Lily. 'I've been trying to persuade Louisa to be less of a boring old fart. Can we put the siren on?'

'Nope. Where'd you go? That's from another boring old fart, by the way. I won't have a clue whatever you say.'

'The Twenty-two,' said Lily. 'Down the back of Tottenham Court Road?'

'That's where we had the emergency tracheotomy, Sam.'

'I remember. You look like you've had a good night.' He met my eye in the mirror and I coloured a little. I was suddenly glad to have been out dancing. It made me seem like I might be someone else altogether. Not just a tragic airport barmaid whose idea of a night out was falling off a roof.

'It was great,' I said, beaming.

Then he looked down at the computer screen on the dashboard. 'Oh, great. Got a Green One over at Spencer's.'

'But we're headed back in,' said Donna. 'Why does Lennie always do this to us? That man's a sadist.'

'No one else available.'

'What's going on?'

'A job's come up. I might have to drop you. It's not far from yours, though. Okay?'

'Spencer's,' said Donna, and let out a deep sigh. 'Oh, marvellous. Hold on tight, girls.'

The siren went on. And we were off, lurching through the London traffic with the blue light screaming above our head, Lily squealing with delight.

On any given week-night, Donna told us, as we clutched the handrails, the station would get calls from Spencer's, summoned to fix those who hadn't made it upright to closing time, or to stitch up the faces of young men for whom six pints in an evening left them combative and without any accompanying sense. 'These youngsters should be feeling great about life, but instead they're just knocking themselves out with every spare pound they earn. Every bloody week.'

We were there in minutes, the ambulance slowing outside to avoid the drunks spilling out onto the pavement. The signs in Spencer's nightclub's smoked windows advertised 'Free drinks for girls before 10 p.m.' Despite the stag and hen nights, the catcalling and gaudy clothes, the packed streets of the drinking zone had less of a carnival atmosphere than something tense and explosive. I found myself gazing out of the window warily.

Sam opened the rear doors and picked up his bag. 'Stay in the rig,' he said, and climbed out.

A police officer headed over to him, muttered something, and we watched as they walked over to a young man who was sitting in the gutter, blood streaming from a wound to his temple. Sam squatted beside him, while the officer attempted to keep back the drunken gawkers, the 'helpful' friends, the wailing girlfriends. He seemed to be surrounded by a bunch of well-dressed extras from *The Walking Dead*, swaying mindlessly and grunting, occasionally bloodied and toppling.

'I hate these jobs,' said Donna, checking briskly through her pack of plastic-wrapped medical supplies as we watched. 'Give me a woman in labour or a nice old granny with cardio-myopathy any day. Oh, flipping heck, he's off.'

Sam was tilting the young lad's face to examine it when another boy, his hair thick with gel and the collar of his shirt soaked in blood, grabbed at his shoulder. 'Oi! I need to go in the ambulance!'

Sam turned slowly towards the young drunk, who was spraying blood and saliva as he spoke. 'Back away now, mate. All right? Let me do my job.'

Drink had made the boy stupid. He glanced at his mates, and then he was in Sam's face, snarling, 'Don't you tell me to back away.'

Sam ignored him, and continued attending to the other boy's face.

'Hey! Hey you! I need to get to the hospital.' He pushed Sam's shoulder. 'Hey!'

Sam stayed crouched for a moment, very still. Then he

straightened slowly, and turned, so that he was nose to nose with the drunk. 'I'll explain something in terms you might be able to understand, son. You're not getting in the truck, okay? That's it. So save your energy, go finish your night with your mates, put a bit of ice on it, and see your GP in the morning.'

'You don't get to tell me *nothing*. I pay your wages. My *effing nose is broke.*'

As Sam gazed steadily back at him, the boy swung out a hand and pushed at Sam's chest. Sam looked down at it.

'Uh-oh,' said Donna, beside me.

Sam's voice, when it emerged, was a growl: 'Okay. I'm warning you now –'

'You don't warn me!' The boy's face was scornful. 'You don't warn me! Who do you think you are?'

Donna was out of the truck and jogging towards a cop. She murmured something in his ear and I saw them both look over. Donna's face was pleading. The boy was still yelling and swearing, now pushing at Sam's chest. 'So you sort *me* out before you deal with that *wanker.*'

Sam adjusted his collar. His face had become dangerously still.

And just as I realized I was holding my breath, the policeman was there, between them. Donna's hand was on Sam's sleeve and she was steering him back to the young lad on the kerb. The policeman muttered something into his radio, his hand on the drunk's shoulder. The boy swung round and spat on Sam's jacket. *'Fuck you.'*

There was a brief, shocked silence. Sam stiffened.

'Sam! Come on, give me a hand, yes? I need you.' Donna propelled him forwards. When I caught sight of Sam's face, his eyes glittered as cold and hard as diamonds.

'Come on,' said Donna, as they loaded the semi-comatose lad into the back of the truck. 'Let's get out of here.'

\*

He drove silently, Lily and I wedged into the front seat beside him. Donna cleaned the back of his jacket as he stared ahead, stubbly jaw jutting.

'Could be worse,' Donna said cheerfully. 'I had one throw up in my hair last month. And the little monster did it on purpose. Shoved his fingers down the back of his throat and ran up behind me, just because I wouldn't take him home, like I was some kind of bloody minicab.'

She stood up and motioned for the energy drink she kept in the front. 'It's a waste of resources. When you think what we could be doing, instead of scooping up a load of little . . .' She took a swig, then looked down at the barely conscious young boy. 'I don't know. You have to wonder what goes on in their heads.'

'Not much,' said Sam.

'Yeah. Well, we have to keep this one on a tight leash.' Donna patted Sam's shoulder. 'He got a caution last year.'

Sam glanced sideways at me, suddenly sheepish. 'We went to pick up a girl from the top of Commercial Street. Face smashed to a pulp. Domestic. As I went to lift her onto the gurney, her boyfriend came flying out of the pub and went for her again. Couldn't help myself.'

'You took a swing at him?'

'More than one,' Donna scoffed.

'Yeah. Well. It wasn't a good time.'

Donna shifted to grimace at me. 'Well, this one can't afford to get in trouble again. Or he's out of the service.'

'Thanks,' I said, as he let us out. 'For the lift, I mean.'

'Couldn't leave you in that open-air asylum,' he said.

His eyes briefly met mine. Then Donna shut the door and they were gone, heading for the hospital with their battered human cargo.

'You totally fancy him,' said Lily, as we watched the ambulance disappear.

I had forgotten she was even there. I sighed as I reached into my pockets for the keys. 'He's a shagger.'

'So? I would totally shag that,' Lily said, as I opened the door to let her in. 'I mean, if I was old. And a bit desperate. Like you.'

'I don't think I'm ready for a relationship, Lily.'

She was walking behind me, so there was no way I could actually prove it, but I swear I could feel her pulling faces at me the whole way up the stairs.

# Chapter Twelve

I wrote to Mrs Traynor. I didn't tell her about Lily, just that I hoped she was well, that I was back from my travels and would be in her area in a few weeks with a friend, and would like to say hello if possible. I sent it first class, and felt oddly excited as it plopped into the post-box.

Dad had told me over the phone that she had left Granta House within weeks of Will's death. He said the estate workers had been shocked, but I thought back to the time I had spotted Mr Traynor out with Della, the woman he was now about to have a baby with, and I wondered how many genuinely had been. There were few secrets in a small town.

'She took it all terrible hard,' Dad said. 'And once she was gone your redheaded woman there was in like Flynn. She saw her chance, all right. Nice auld fella, own hair, big house, he's not going to be single for long, eh? Speaking of which, Lou. You – you wouldn't have a word with your mother about her armpits, would you? She's going to be after plaiting it if she lets it all grow any longer.'

I kept thinking about Mrs Traynor, trying to imagine how she would react to the news about Lily. I remembered the joy and disbelief on Mr Traynor's face at their first meeting. Would Lily help to heal her pain a little? Sometimes I watched Lily laughing at something on television, or simply gazing steadily out of the window lost in thought, and I saw Will so clearly in her features – the precise angles of her nose, those almost Slavic cheekbones – that I forgot to breathe. (At this point she would usually grumble, 'Stop staring at me like a weirdo, Louisa. You're freaking me out.')

Lily had come to stay for two weeks. Tanya Houghton-Miller had called to say they were off on a family holiday to Tuscany and Lily didn't want to go with them. 'Frankly, the way she's behaving right now, as far as I'm concerned, that's fine. She's exhausting me.'

I pointed out that, given Lily was barely at home, and Tanya had changed the locks to her front door, it would be pretty hard for Lily to exhaust anyone unless she was tapping at their window and singing a lament. There was a short silence.

'When you have your own children, Louisa, you might eventually have some idea what I'm talking about.' Oh, the trump card of all parents. *How could I possibly understand?*

She offered me money to cover Lily's board and lodging while they were away. I took some pleasure in telling her I wouldn't dream of taking it, even though, frankly, it was costing me more than I had anticipated to have her there. Lily, it turned out, wasn't satisfied with my beans-on-toast or cheese-sandwich suppers. She would ask for cash, then return with artisan bread, exotic fruit, Greek yoghurt, organic chicken – the staples of a wealthy middle-class kitchen. I remembered Tanya's house, the way Lily had stood by the oversized fridge and thoughtlessly dropped chunks of fresh pineapple into her mouth.

'By the way,' I said, 'who is Martin?'

There was a short pause. 'Martin is my former partner. Lily apparently insists on seeing him, even though she knows I don't like it.'

'Could I have his number? I'd just like to make sure I know where she is. You know, while you're gone.'

'Martin's number? Why would I have Martin's number?' she squawked, and the phone went dead.

*

Something had changed since I'd met Lily. It wasn't just that I'd learned to accommodate the explosion of teenage-related mess in my near-empty flat, I had actually started to quite enjoy having Lily in my life, having someone to eat with, sit side by side with on the sofa, commenting on whatever we happened to be watching on the television, or keeping a poker face when she offered me some concoction she'd made. *Well, how should I know you have to cook the potatoes in a potato salad? It's a salad, for God's sake.*

At work I now listened to the fathers at the bar wishing their children goodnight as they flew off on business trips – *You be good for Mummy now, Luke . . . Did you? . . . You did? Aren't you a clever boy!* – and the custody arguments conducted in hissed telephone conversations: *No, I did not say I could pick him up from school that day. I was always due in Barcelona . . . Yes, I was . . . No, no, you just don't listen.*

I couldn't believe that you could give birth to someone, love them, nurture them, and by their sixteenth year claim that you were so exasperated that you'd change the locks of your house against them. Sixteen was still a child, surely. For all her posturing, I could see the child in Lily. It was there in the excitements and sudden enthusiasms. It was there in the sulks, the trying on of different looks in front of my bathroom mirror and the abrupt, innocent sleep.

I thought of my sister and her uncomplicated love for Thom. I thought of my parents, encouraging, worrying about and supporting Treena and me, even though we were both well into adulthood. And in those moments I felt Will's absence in Lily's life like I felt it in my own. *You should have been here, Will*, I told him silently. *It was you she really needed.*

I booked a day's holiday – an outrage, according to Richard. ('You've only been back five weeks. I really don't see why you need to disappear again.') I smiled, bobbed a curtsy in a grateful Irish-dancing-girl manner, and drove home later to find Lily painting one of the spare-room walls a particularly vivid shade of jade green. 'You said you wanted it brightening up,' she said, as I stood with my mouth open. 'Don't worry. I paid for the paint myself.'

'Well,' I pulled off my wig, and unlaced my shoes, 'just make sure you've finished by this evening because I've got the day off tomorrow,' I said, when I had changed into my jeans, 'and I'm going to show you some of the things your dad liked.'

She stopped, dripping jade paint onto the carpet. 'What things?'

'You'll see.'


We spent the day driving, our soundtrack a playlist on Lily's iPod that provided one minute a heart-breaking dirge of love and loss, the next an ear-perforating raging anthem of hatred against all mankind. I mastered the art, while on the motorway, of mentally rising above the noise and focusing on the road, while Lily sat beside me, nodding in time to the beat and occasionally performing an impromptu drum roll on the dashboard. It was good, I thought, that she was enjoying herself. And who needed both working eardrums anyway?

We started off in Stortfold, and took in the places Will and I used to sit and eat, the picnic spots in the fields above the town, his favourite benches around the grounds of the castle, and Lily had the grace to try not to look bored. To be fair, it was quite hard to work up enthusiasm about a series of fields. So I sat down and told her how, when I had first met him, Will had barely left the house, and how, through a mixture of subterfuge and bloody-mindedness, I had set about getting him out again. 'You have to understand,' I said, 'that your father hated to be dependent on anyone. And us going out didn't just mean that he had to rely on someone else but he had to be seen to be relying on someone else.'

'Even if it was you.'

'Even if it was me.'

She was thoughtful for a moment. 'I'd hate people seeing me like that. I don't even like people seeing me with wet hair.'

We visited the gallery where he had tried to explain to me the difference between 'good' and 'bad' modern art (I still couldn't tell), and she pulled a face at almost everything on its walls. We poked our heads into the wine merchant's where he had made me taste different sorts of wine ('No, Lily, we are *not* doing a wine-tasting today'), then walked to the tattoo shop where he had persuaded me to get my tattoo. She asked if I could lend her the money for one (I nearly wept with relief when the man told her no under-eighteens), then asked to see my little bumble bee. That was one of the few occasions when I felt I'd actually impressed her. She laughed out loud when I told her what he had chosen for himself: a Best Before date stencilled on his chest.

'You have the same awful sense of humour,' I said, and she tried not to look pleased.

It was then that the owner, overhearing our conversation, mentioned that he had a photograph. 'I keep pictures of all of my tattoos,' he said, from under a heavily waxed handlebar moustache. 'I like to have a record. Just remind me of the date?'

We stood there silently as he flicked through his laminated binder. And there it was, from almost two years previously, a close-up of that black and white design, neatly inked onto Will's caramel skin. I stood and stared at the photograph, its familiarity taking my breath away. The little black and white patterned block, the one I had washed with a soft cloth, which I had dried, rubbed sun cream into, rested my face against. I would have reached out to touch it, but Lily got there first, her fingers with their bitten nails tracing gently over the image of her father's skin. 'I think I'll get one,' she said. 'Like his, I mean. When I'm old enough.'

'So how is he?'

Lily and I turned. The tattooist was sitting on his chair, rubbing at a heavily coloured forearm. 'I remember him. We don't get many quadriplegics in here.' He grinned. 'He's a bit of a character, isn't he?'

A lump rose suddenly to my throat.

'He's dead,' said Lily, baldly. 'My dad. He's dead.'

The tattooist winced. 'Sorry, sweetheart. I had no idea.'

'Can I keep this?' Lily had started to work the photograph of Will's tattoo out of its plastic binder.

'Sure,' he said hurriedly. 'If you want it, take it. Here, have the plastic cover as well. Case it rains.'

'Thank you,' she said, tucking it neatly under her arm, and as the man stuttered another apology, we walked out of the shop.


We had lunch – an all-day breakfast – silently in a café. Feeling the day's mood leach away from us, I began to talk. I told Lily what I knew of Will's romantic history, about his career, that he was the kind of man who made you long for his approval, whether just by doing something that impressed him or making him laugh with some stupid joke. I told her how he was when I met him, and how he had changed, softened, starting to find joy in small things, even if many of those small things seemed to involve making fun of me. 'Like I wasn't very adventurous when it came to food. My mum basically has ten set meals which she's rotated for the past twenty-five years. And none of them involves quinoa. Or lemongrass. Or guacamole. Your dad would eat anything.'

'And now you do too?'

'Actually, I still try guacamole every couple of months or so. For him, really.'

'You don't like it?'

'It tastes okay, I suppose. I just can't get past the fact that it looks like something you blow out of your nose.'

I told her about his previous girlfriend, and how we had gatecrashed her wedding dance, me sitting on Will's lap as we turned his motorized wheelchair in circles on the dance floor, and she had snorted her drink through her nose. 'Seriously? Her wedding?' In the overheated confines of the little café, I conjured her father for her as best I could, and perhaps it was because we were away from all the complications of home, or because her parents were in a different country, or because, just for once, someone was telling her stories about him that were uncomplicated and funny, she laughed, and asked questions, nodding often as if my answers had confirmed something she already believed. *Yes, yes, he was like this. Yes, maybe I'm like that too.*

And as we talked well into the afternoon, letting our cups of tea cool in front of us, and the weary waitress offered yet again to remove the last of the toast we had taken two hours to eat, I grasped something else: for the first time, I was recalling Will without sadness.

'What about you?'

'What about me?' I put the last crust into my mouth, eyeing the waitress, who looked as if this was her trigger to come back again.

'What happened to you after Dad died? I mean, you seem to have done a lot more stuff when you were with him – even with him being stuck in a wheelchair – than you do now.'

The bread had turned claggy in my mouth. I struggled to swallow. Eventually, when the mouthful had gone down, I said, 'I do things. I've just been busy. Working. I mean, when you're on shifts, it's hard to make plans.'

She raised her eyebrows a fraction, but she didn't say anything.

'And my hip is still quite painful. I'm not really up to mountain-climbing yet.'

Lily stirred her tea idly.

'My life is eventful. I mean, falling off a roof isn't exactly humdrum. That's quite a lot of excitement for one year!'

'But it's hardly *doing* something, is it?'

We were silent for a moment. I took a breath, trying to quell the sudden buzzing in my ears. The waitress, arriving between us, swept up our empty plates, with a faint air of triumph, and took them to the kitchen.

'Hey,' I said. 'Did I tell you about the time I took your dad to the races?'

With immaculate timing, my car overheated on the motorway, forty miles from London. Lily was surprisingly sanguine about it. In fact, she was curious. 'I've never been in a car that broke down. I didn't know they even did that any more.'

At this statement my jaw dropped (my dad would regularly pray loudly to his old van, promising premium petrol, regular tyre-pressure checks, endless love, if she would make it back home again). Then she told me her parents traded up their Mercedes every year. Mostly, she added, because of the level of damage done to the leather interior by her half-brothers.

We sat by the side of the motorway, waiting for the breakdown truck to arrive, and feeling the little car judder sporadically as the lorries rumbled past. Eventually, deciding it would be safer for us to be out of the car, we scrambled up the embankment at the side of the motorway and sat on the grass, watching as the afternoon sun lost its heat and slid down the other side of the motorway bridge.

'So who is Martin?' I said, when we had exhausted all breakdown-related conversation.

Lily plucked at the grass beside her. 'Martin Steele? He's the man I grew up with.'

'I thought that was Francis.'

'No. Fuckface only came into the picture when I was seven.'

'You know, Lily, you might want to stop calling him that.'

She gave me a sideways look. 'Okay. You're probably right.' She lay back on the grass, and smiled sweetly. 'I'll call him Penisfeatures instead.'

'Let's stick with Fuckface then. So how come you still visit him?'

'Martin? He's the only dad I really remember. Mum got together with him while I was small. He's a musician. Very creative. He used to read stories and stuff and make up songs about me, that kind of thing. I just . . .' She trailed off.

'What happened? Between him and your mum?'

Lily reached into her bag, pulled out a packet of cigarettes and lit one. She inhaled and let out a long flute of smoke, almost dislocating her jawbone in the process. 'I came home from school one day with the au pair and Mum just announced that he'd gone. She said they'd agreed he had to go because they weren't getting on any more.' She inhaled again. 'Apparently he wasn't interested in her personal growth or he didn't share her vision of the future. Some bullshit. I think she just met Francis and knew Martin was never going to give her what she wanted.'

'Which was?'

'Money. And a big house. And the chance to spend her day shopping and bitching to her friends and aligning her *chakra*s or whatever. Francis earns a fortune doing private bank things in his private bank with all the other private bankers.' She turned to me. 'So, basically, one day Martin was my dad – I mean, I called him Daddy right up until the day he left – and the next he wasn't. He used to take me to nursery and primary school and everything – and then she decides she's had enough of him, and I get home and he's just . . . gone. It's her house, so he's gone. Just like that. And I'm not allowed to see him and I'm not even allowed to talk about him because I'm just *dredging things up* and *being difficult*. And obviously she is in *so much pain and emotional distress.*' Here Lily did a scarily good impression of Tanya's voice. 'And when I really did get mad at her, she told me there was no point in getting so upset because he wasn't even my real dad. So *that* was a nice way to find out.'

I stared at her.

'And the next thing, there's Francis turning up at our door, all over-the-top bunches of flowers and so-called family days out, where I'm basically playing gooseberry and sent off with the nannies while they're all over each other at some child-friendly luxury hotel. And then six months later she takes me to Pizza Express. I think it's some treat for me and that maybe Martin is coming back, but she says she and Francis are getting married and it's wonderful and he's going to be the most wonderful daddy to me and I "must love him very much".'

Lily blew a smoke ring up into the sky, watching as it swelled, wavered and evaporated.

'And you didn't.'

'I hated him.' She looked sideways at me. 'You can tell, you know, when someone's just putting up with you. Even if you're little. He never wanted me, only my mother. I can sort of understand it – who wants another man's kid hanging around? So when she had the twins they sent me away to boarding-school. Bang. Job done.'

Her eyes had filled with tears and I wanted to reach out to her, but she had wrapped her arms around her knees and stared straight ahead. We sat there in silence for a few minutes, watching the traffic start to build below us as the sun slid further down the sky.

'I found him, you know.'

I faced her.

'Martin. When I was eleven. I heard my nanny telling another one that she wasn't allowed to tell me he had called round. So I told her she had to tell me where he lived or I'd tell my mum she was stealing. I looked up the address and he lived about fifteen minutes' walk from where we were. Pye-croft Road – do you know it?'

I shook my head. 'Was he pleased to see you?'

She hesitated. 'So happy. He nearly cried, actually. He said he'd missed me so much, and that it was awful being away from me and that I could come around whenever I wanted. But he had hooked up with someone else and they had a baby. And when you turn up at someone's house and they have a baby and, like, a proper family of their own, you realize you're not part of his family any more. You're a leftover.'

'I'm sure nobody thought –'

'Yes, well. Anyway, he's really lovely and all, but I've told him I can't really see him. It's too weird. And, you know, like I said to him, *I'm not your real daughter*. He still calls me all the time, though. Stupid, really.' Lily shook her head furiously. We sat there for a while and then she looked up at the sky. 'You know the thing that really bugs me?'

I waited.

'She changed my name when she got married. My own name, and nobody ever even bothered to ask me.' Her voice cracked a little. 'I didn't even want to be a Houghton-Miller.'

'Oh, Lily.'

She wiped briskly at her face with the palm of her hand, as if embarrassed to be seen crying. She inhaled her cigarette, then ground it out on the grass and sniffed noisily. 'Mind you, these days Penisfeatures and Mum argue *all* the time. I wouldn't be surprised if they split up too. If that happens, no doubt we'll all have to move house again and change names and nobody will be able to say anything because of *her pain* and her need to *move forward emotionally* or whatever. And in two years' time there will be some other Fuckface and my brothers will be Houghton-Miller-Branson or Ozymandias or Toodlepip or whatever.' She half laughed. 'Luckily I'll be long gone by then. Not that she'll even notice.'

'You really believe she thinks that little of you?'

Lily's head swivelled round, and the look she gave me was both far too wise for her age and utterly heartbreaking. 'I think she loves me. But she loves herself more. Or how could she do what she does?'

# Chapter Thirteen

Mr Traynor's baby was born the following day. My phone rang at six thirty in the morning and, for a brief, awful moment, I thought something terrible had happened. But it was Mr Traynor, breathless and tearful, announcing, in slightly disbelieving, exclamatory tones, 'It's a girl! Eight pounds one ounce! And she's absolutely perfect!' He told me how beautiful she was, how like Will when he had been a baby, how I simply must come and see her, and then asked me to wake Lily, which I did, and watched her, sleepy and silent as he gave her the news that she had a . . . a . . . (they took a minute to work it out) an aunt!

'Okay,' she said finally. And then, having listened for a while: 'Yeah . . . sure.'

She ended the call and handed the phone back to me. Her eyes met mine, then she turned in her crumpled T-shirt and went back to bed, closing the door firmly behind her.

The well-lubricated health-plan salesmen were, I estimated at ten forty-five, one round off being barred from their flight, and I was wondering whether to point this out when a familiar reflective jacket appeared at the bar.

'No one in need of medical assistance here.' I walked over to him slowly. 'Yet, anyway.'

'I never get tired of that outfit. I have no idea why.'

Sam climbed up on a stool and rested his elbows on the counter. 'The wig is . . . interesting.'

I tugged at my Lurex skirt. 'The creation of static electricity is my superpower. Would you like a coffee?'

'Thanks. I can't hang around, though.' He checked his radio and put it back in his jacket pocket.

I made him an Americano, trying not to look as pleased as I felt to see him. 'How did you know where I worked?'

'We had a call-out at gate fourteen. Suspected heart attack. Jake reminded me you worked at the airport and, you know, you weren't exactly hard to track down . . .'

The businessmen were briefly muted. Sam was the kind of man, I had noticed, who made other men go a bit quiet. 'Donna's sneaking a look in Duty Free. Handbags.'

'I'm guessing you've seen your patient?'

He grinned. 'No. I was going to ask for directions to gate fourteen after I'd sat down with a coffee.'

'Funny. So did you save his life?'

'I gave her some aspirin, and advised her that drinking four double espressos before ten a.m. was not the best idea. I'm flattered that you have such an exciting view of my working day.'

I couldn't help but laugh. I handed him his coffee. He took a grateful swig. 'So. I was wondering . . . You up for another non-date some time soon?'

'With or without an ambulance?'

'Definitely without.'

'Can we discuss problem teenagers?' I found I was twirling a curly lock of nylon-fibre hair with my fingers. For crying out loud. I was playing with my hair and it wasn't even my actual hair. I dropped it.

'We can discuss whatever you like.'

'What did you have in mind?'

His pause was long enough to make me blush. 'Dinner? At mine? Tonight? I promise if it rains I won't make you sit in the dining room.'

'You're on.'

'I'll pick you up at seven thirty.'

He was just gulping down the last of his coffee when Richard appeared. He looked at Sam, then at me. I was still leaning against the bar, a few inches from him. 'Is there a problem?' he said.

'No problem whatsoever,' said Sam. When he stood up, he was a whole head taller than Richard.

A few fleeting thoughts flickered across Richard's face, so transparent that I could see the progression of each one. *Why is this paramedic here? Why is Louisa not doing something? I would like to tell Louisa off for not being obviously busy but this man is too big and there is a dynamic I do not entirely understand and I am a little bit wary of him.* It almost made me laugh out loud.

'So. Tonight.' Sam nodded at me. 'Keep the wig on, yes? I like you flammable.'

One of the businessmen, florid and pleased with himself, leaned back in his chair so that his stomach strained the seams of his shirt. 'Are you going to give us the lecture about alcohol limits now?'

The others laughed.

'No, you go ahead, gentlemen,' Sam said, saluting them. 'I'll just see you in a year or two.'

I watched him head off to Departures, joined by Donna outside the newsagent. When I turned back to the bar Richard was watching me. 'I have to say, Louisa, I don't approve of your conducting your social life in a work setting,' he said.

'Fine. Next time I'll tell him to ignore the heart attack at gate fourteen.'

Richard's jaw tightened. 'And what he said just then. About your wearing your wig later on. That wig is the property of Shamrock and Clover Irish Themed Bars Inc. You are not allowed to wear it in your own time.'

This time I couldn't help it. I started to laugh. 'Really?'

Even he had the grace to flush a little. 'It's company policy. It's classified as uniform.'

'Damn,' I said. 'I guess I'll just have to buy my own Irish-dancing-girl wigs in future. Hey, Richard!' I called, as he walked back into the office, bristling. 'For fairness, does that mean you can't get jiggy with Mrs Percival while wearing your polo-shirt?'

I arrived home to find no sign of Lily, other than a cereal packet on the kitchen counter and, inexplicably, a pile of dirt on the floor in the hallway. I tried her phone, got no response, and wondered how you were ever meant to find a balance between Over-anxious Parent, Normally Concerned Parent, and Tanya Houghton-Miller. And then I jumped into the shower and got ready for my date that absolutely, definitely, wasn't a date.

It rained, the heavens opening shortly after we arrived at Sam's field, and we were both soaked even running the short distance from his bike to the railway carriage. I stood dripping as he closed the door behind me, remembering how unpleasant the sensation of wet socks was.

'Stay there,' he said, brushing the drops from his head with a hand. 'You can't sit around in those wet clothes.'

'This is like the opening to a really bad porn movie,' I said. He stood very still and I realized I had actually said the words out loud. I gave him a smile that went a bit wonky.

'Okay,' he said, raising his eyebrows.

He disappeared into the back of the carriage and emerged a minute later with a jumper and what looked like some jogging bottoms.

'Jake's joggers. Freshly washed. Possibly not very porn star, though.' He handed them to me. 'My room's back there if you

170

want to get changed, or the bathroom's through that door, if you'd prefer.'

I walked into his bedroom and closed the door behind me. Above my head the rain beat noisily on the carriage roof, obscuring the windows with a never-ending stream of water. I wondered about drawing the curtains, then remembered there was nobody to see me, other than the hens, which were huddling out of the wet, grumpily shaking drops from their feathers. I pulled off my soaked top and jeans and dried myself with the towel he'd placed with the clothes. For fun, I flashed the hens through the window, something, I observed afterwards, Lily might do. They didn't look impressed. I held the towel to my face and sniffed it guiltily, like someone inhaling a forbidden drug. It was freshly laundered but somehow still managed to smell irrevocably male. I hadn't breathed in a scent like it since Will. It made me feel briefly unbalanced and I put it down.

The double bed filled most of the floor space. A narrow cupboard opposite acted as a wardrobe, and two pairs of work boots were neatly stacked in the corner. There was a book on the nightstand and beside it a photograph of Sam with a smiling woman, whose blonde hair was tied up in a messy knot. She had her arm around his shoulders and was grinning at the camera. She was not supermodel beautiful, but there was something compelling about her smile. She looked like the kind of woman who would have laughed a lot. She looked like a feminine version of Jake. I felt suddenly crushingly sad for him, and had to look away before I made myself sad, too. Sometimes I felt as if we were all wading around in grief, reluctant to admit to others how far we were waving or drowning. I wondered fleetingly whether Sam's reluctance to talk about his wife mirrored my own, the knowledge that the moment you opened the box, let out even a whisper of your sadness, it would mushroom into a cloud that overwhelmed all other conversation.

I checked myself, took a breath. 'Just have a nice evening,' I murmured, recalling the words of the Moving On Circle. *Allow yourself moments of happiness.*

I wiped the mascara smudges from under my eyes, observing in the small mirror that little could be done for my hair. Then I pulled Sam's oversized sweater over my head, trying to ignore the weird intimacy that came from wearing a man's clothes, pulled on Jake's joggers and gazed at my reflection.

*What do you think, Will? Just a nice evening. It doesn't have to mean anything, right?*

Sam grinned as I emerged, rolling up the sleeves of his jumper. 'You look about twelve.'

I went into the bathroom, wrung out my jeans, shirt and socks in the sink, then hung them over the shower curtain.

'What's cooking?'

'Well, I was going to do a salad, but it's not really salad weather any more. So I'm improvising.'

He had set a pot of water boiling on the stove, where it had fogged the windows. 'You eat pasta, right?'

'I eat anything.'

'Excellent.'

He opened a bottle of wine and poured me a glass, motioning me to the bench seat. In front of me the little table had been laid for two, and I felt a faint frisson at the sight. It was okay just to enjoy a moment, a small pleasure. I had been out dancing. I had flashed some hens. And now I was going to enjoy spending an evening with a man who wanted to cook me dinner. It was all progress, of sorts.

Perhaps Sam detected something of this internal struggle because he waited until I took my first sip, then said, while stirring something on the hob, 'Was that the boss you were talking about? That man today?'

The wine was delicious. I took another sip. I hadn't dared

drink while Lily had been with me: I might have let my guard down. 'Yup.'

'I know the type. If it's any consolation, within five years he'll either have a stomach ulcer or enough hypertension to cause erectile dysfunction.'

I laughed. 'Both those thoughts are oddly comforting.'

Finally he sat down, presenting me with a steaming bowl of pasta. 'Cheers,' he said, raising a glass of water. 'And now tell me what's going on with this long-lost girl of yours.'

Oh, but it was such a relief to have someone to talk to. I was so unused to people who actually listened – as opposed to those, at the bar, who only wanted to hear the sound of their own voices – that talking to Sam was a revelation. He didn't interrupt, or tell me what he thought, or what I should do. He listened, and nodded, and topped up my wine and said, finally, when it was long dark outside, 'It's quite a responsibility you've taken on.'

I leaned back on the bench and put my feet up. 'I don't feel like I have a choice. I keep asking myself what you said: what would Will want me to do?' I took another sip. 'It's harder than I'd imagined, though. I thought I'd just drop her in to meet her grandmother and grandfather and everyone would be delighted and it would be a happy ending, like those re-union programmes on television.'

He studied his hands. I studied him.

'You think I'm mad getting involved.'

'No. Too many people follow their own happiness without a thought for the damage they leave in their wake. You wouldn't believe the kids I pick up at the weekends, drunk, drugged, off their heads, whatever. The parents are wrapped up in their own stuff, or have disappeared completely, so they exist in a vacuum, and they make bad choices.'

'Is it worse than it used to be?'

'Who knows? I only know I see all these messed up kids. And that the hospital's young persons' psych has a waiting list as long as your arm.' He smiled wryly. 'Hold that soapbox. I need to shut the birds up for the night.'

I wanted to ask him then how someone so apparently wise could be so careless of his own son's feelings. I wanted to ask if he knew how unhappy Jake was. But it seemed a bit too confrontational, given the way he was talking, and the fact that he had just cooked me a very nice supper . . . I was distracted by the sight of the hens popping one at a time into their coop, and then he came back, bringing with him the faint scents of outside, and the cooler air, and the moment passed.

He poured more wine, and I drank it. I let myself take pleasure in the snugness of the little railway carriage, and the sensation of a properly full belly, and I listened to Sam talk. He told of nights holding the hands of elderly people who didn't want to make a fuss, and of management targets that left them all demoralized, feeling they weren't doing the job they'd been trained for. I listened, losing myself in a world far from my own, watching his hands draw animated circles in the air, his rueful smile when he felt he was taking himself too seriously. I watched his hands.

I coloured slightly as I realized where my thoughts were headed, and took another swig of my wine to hide it. 'Where's Jake tonight?'

'Barely seen him. At his girlfriend's, I think.' He looked rueful. 'She has this *Waltons*-style family, about a billion brothers and sisters and a mum who's home all day. He likes hanging out there.' He took another sip of his water. 'So where's Lily?'

'Don't know. I texted her twice but she hasn't bothered to reply.'

The sheer presence of him. It was like he was twice as large and twice as vivid as other men. My thoughts kept drifting, pulled on tides towards his eyes, which narrowed slightly as he listened, as if he were trying to ensure he had understood me perfectly . . . The faint hint of stubble on his jaw, the shape of his shoulder under the soft wool of his jumper. My gaze kept sliding downwards to his hands, resting on the table, fingers absently tapping on the surface. Such capable hands. I remembered the tenderness with which he had cradled my head, the way I had held on to him in the ambulance as if he were the only thing anchoring me. He looked at me and smiled, a gentle enquiry in it, and something in me turned molten. Would it be so bad, as long as my eyes were open?

'You want a coffee, Louisa?'

He had this way of looking at me. I shook my head.

'Do you want –'

Before I could think about it, I leaned across the little table, reached for the back of his head and kissed him. He hesitated for just a moment then shifted forward, and kissed me back. At some point I think someone knocked over a wineglass but I couldn't stop. I wanted to kiss him for ever. I blocked out all thoughts about what this was, what it might mean, what further mess I might create for myself. *C'mon, live*, I told myself. And I kissed him until reason seeped out through my pores and I became a living pulse, alive only to what I wanted to do to him.

He pulled back first, slightly dazed. 'Louisa –'

A piece of cutlery clattered to the floor. I stood and he stood, and pulled me to him. And suddenly we were crashing around the little railway carriage, all hands and lips and, oh God, the scent and taste and feel of him. It was like tiny fireworks going off all over me, bits of me I'd thought dead reigniting into life. He picked me up and I wrapped myself around him, all bulk and strength and muscle. I kissed his face, his ear, my fingers in his soft dark hair. And then he stood me back down and we were inches apart, his eyes on me, his expression a silent question.

I was breathing hard. 'I haven't taken my clothes off in front of anyone since . . . the accident,' I said.

'It's okay. I'm medically trained.'

'I'm serious. I'm a bit of a mess.' I felt suddenly, oddly tearful.

'You want me to make you feel better?'

'That's the cheesiest line I've –'

He lifted his shirt, revealing a two-inch purple scar across his stomach. 'There. Stabbed by an Australian with mental-health issues four years ago. Here.' He turned to reveal a huge green and yellow bruise across his lower back. 'Got a kicking from a drunk last Saturday. Woman.' He held out his hand. 'Broken finger. Caught in a gurney while lifting an overweight patient. And, oh, yes – here.' He showed me his hip, along which ran a short, silvery, jagged line with the stitch marks just about visible. 'Puncture wound, unknown provenance, nightclub fight in Hackney Road last year. The cops never worked out who did it.'

I looked at the solidity of him, at the smattering of scars. 'What's that one?' I said, gently touching a smaller scar on the side of his stomach. His skin was hot under his shirt.

'That? Oh. Appendix. I was nine.'

I gazed at his torso, then his face. Then holding his gaze, I lifted the jumper slowly over my head. I shivered involuntarily, whether from the cooler air or nerves I couldn't tell. He moved closer, so close that he was inches from me, and ran his finger gently along the line of my hip. 'I remember this. I remember I could feel the break here.' He ran it gently across my bare stomach, so that my muscles contracted. 'And there. You had this bloom of purple on your skin. I was afraid it was organ damage.' He placed his palm against it. It was warm, and my breath caught.

'I never thought the words "organ damage" could sound sexy before.'

'Oh, I haven't started yet.'

He walked me slowly backwards towards his bed. I sat down, my eyes on his, and he knelt, running his hands down my legs. 'And then there was that.' He picked up my right foot, with the vivid red scar across the top. He traced the line of it tenderly with his thumb. 'There. Broken. Soft tissue damage. That one would have hurt.'

'You remember a lot.'

'Most people I couldn't recognize in the street a day later. But you, Louisa, well, you kind of stuck.' He dipped his head and kissed the top of my foot, then slowly ran his hands up my leg and placed them either side of me, so that he was above me, supporting his own weight. 'Nothing hurts now, right?'

I shook my head, mute. I didn't care any more. I didn't care if he was a compulsive shagger or playing games. I was so overwhelmed with wanting him I didn't actually care if he broke my other hip.

He moved across me, inch by inch, like a tide, and I lay back so that I was flat on the bed. With each movement my breath became shallower until it was all I could hear in the silence. He gazed down at me, then closed his eyes and kissed me, slowly and tenderly. He kissed me and let his weight fall onto me just far enough that I felt the delicious powerlessness of lust, the hardness of a body against mine. We kissed, his lips on my neck, his skin against my skin, until I was giddy with it, until I was arching involuntarily against him, my legs wrapped around him.

'Oh, God,' I said, breathlessly, when we came up for air. 'I wish you weren't so totally wrong for me.'

His eyebrows shot up. 'That's – uh – seductive.'

'You're not going to cry afterwards, are you?'

He blinked. 'Er . . . no.'

'And just so you know, I'm not some weird obsessive. I'm not going to follow you around afterwards. Or ask Jake to tell me things about you while you're in the shower.'

'That's . . . that's good to know.'

And once we had established the ground rules, I flipped over so that I was on top of him and kissed him until I had forgotten everything we had just talked about.

An hour and a half later I was lying on my back and gazing dazedly up at the low ceiling. My skin buzzed, my bones hummed, I ached in places I hadn't known could ache, yet I was possessed with an extraordinary sense of peace, as if the core of me had simply melted and settled into a new shape. I wasn't sure I would ever get up again.

*You never know what will happen when you fall from a great height.*

That surely wasn't me. I coloured as I thought back to even twenty minutes previously. Did I really – and did I . . . Memories chased themselves in hot circles. I had never had sex like that. Not in seven years with Patrick. It was like comparing a cheese sandwich with . . . what? The most incredible *haute cuisine*? An enormous steak? I giggled involuntarily and clamped a hand over my mouth. I felt utterly unlike myself.

Sam had dozed off beside me and I turned my head to look at him. *Oh, my God*, I thought, marvelling at the planes of his face, his lips – it was impossible to look at him and not want to touch him. I wondered whether I should move my face a little bit closer and my hand so that I could –

'Hey,' he said softly, his eyes slanted with sleep.

. . . and then it hit me.

*Oh, God. I've become one of them.*

*

We dressed in near silence. Sam offered to make me tea, but I said I should probably get back as I needed to check whether Lily was home. 'Her family being on holiday and all.' I tugged my fingers through my now-matted hair.

'Sure. Oh. You want to go *now*?'

'Yes . . . please.'

I fetched my clothes from the bathroom, feeling self-conscious and suddenly sober. I couldn't let him see how unbalanced I was. Every bit of me was focused on trying to re-distance myself and it made me awkward. When I came out he was dressed and tidying up the last of the supper things. I tried not to look at him. It was easier that way.

'Could I borrow these clothes to go home? Mine are still damp.'

'Sure. Just . . . whatever.' He rifled in a drawer and held out a plastic bag.

I took it and we stood there in the dark space. 'It was a . . . nice evening.'

'"Nice".' He looked at me as if he were trying to work something out. 'Okay.'

As we rode through the damp night, I tried not to rest my cheek against his back. He insisted on lending me a leather jacket, although I had insisted I'd be fine. A few miles in, the air was cold and I was glad of it. We made it back to my flat by a quarter past eleven, although I had to check when I saw the clock. I felt like I'd lived several lifetimes since he'd picked me up.

I dismounted from the bike and started to take off his jacket. But he pushed down his kickstand with his heel. 'It's late. Let me at least see you upstairs.'

I hesitated. 'Okay. If you wait I can give you back your clothes.'

I tried to sound insouciant. He gave a shrug and followed me to the door.

We emerged from the stairwell to the sound of music thumping down the hallway. I knew immediately where it was coming from. I limped briskly down the corridor, paused outside the flat and opened the door slowly. Lily stood in the middle of the hall, cigarette in one hand, a glass of wine in the other. She was wearing a yellow flowered dress I had bought from a vintage boutique, back in the days when I cared about what I wore. I stared – and it's possible that when I registered what else she was wearing I stumbled: I felt Sam reach for my arm.

'Nice leathers, Louisa!'

Lily pointed her toe. She was wearing my green glittery shoes. 'Why don't you wear these? You have all these crazy outfits yet you just wear, like, jeans and T-shirts and stuff every day. *Sooo* boring!'

She walked back into my room and emerged a minute later, holding up a gold seventies lamé jumpsuit I used to pair with brown boots. 'I mean, look at this! I have total and utter jumpsuit envy right now.'

'Get them off,' I said, when I could speak.

'What?'

'Those tights. Get them off.' My voice emerged strangled and unrecognizable.

Lily looked down at the black and yellow tights. 'No, seriously though, you have some proper vintage gear in there. Biba, DVF. That purple Chanel type thing. Do you know what this stuff is worth?'

'Get them *off*.'

Perhaps registering my sudden rigidity, Sam began to propel me forwards. 'Look, why don't we go through to the living room and –'

'I'm not moving until she takes those tights off.'

Lily pulled a face.

'Jesus. No need to have a baby about it.'

I watched, vibrating with anger, as Lily began to peel down my bumble-bee tights, kicking at them when they wouldn't slide off her feet.

'Don't rip them!'

'It's just a pair of tights.'

'They are *not* just a pair of tights. They were . . . a gift.'

'Still a pair of tights,' she muttered.

She finally got them off, leaving them in a black and yellow heap on the floor. In the other room I could hear the clatter of hangers as the rest of my clothes were presumably being hastily replaced.

A moment later, Lily appeared in the living room. In her bra and knickers. She waited until she could be sure she had our attention, then pulled a short dress slowly and ostentatiously over her head, wiggling as it went over her slim, pale hips. Then she smiled at me sweetly. 'I'm going clubbing. Don't wait up. Nice to see you again, Mr –'

'Fielding,' said Sam.

'Mr Fielding.' She smiled at me. A smile that wasn't a smile at all. And with a slam of the door, she was gone.

I let out a shaky breath, then walked over and retrieved the tights. I sat down on the sofa and straightened them out, smoothing them until I could be sure there were no snags or cigarette burns.

Sam sat down beside me. 'You okay?' he said.

'I'm know you must think I'm crazy,' I said eventually, 'but they were a –'

'You don't have to explain.'

'I was a different person. They meant that – I was – he gave . . .' My voice was choked.

We sat there in the silent flat. I knew I should say something but I was lost for words, and there was an enormous lump in my throat.

I took Sam's jacket off, and held it out to him. 'It's fine,' I said. 'You don't have to stay.'

I felt his eyes on me but didn't raise mine from the floor.

'I'll leave you to it then.'

And then, before I could say anything else, he was gone.

# Chapter Fourteen

I was late to the Moving On Circle that week. Having left me a coffee, perhaps in lieu of an apology, Lily had subsequently spilt green paint on the hall floor, left a tub of ice cream to melt on the side in the kitchen, taken my door keys, with my car key attached, because she couldn't find her own, and borrowed my wig for a night out without asking. I had recovered it from the floor of her bedroom. When I put it on, I looked as if an Old English Sheepdog were doing something unmentionable to my head.

By the time I reached the church hall, everyone else was sitting down. Natasha moved obligingly so that I could take the plastic chair beside her.

'Tonight we're talking about signs that we might be moving on,' said Marc, who was holding a mug of tea. 'These don't have to be huge things – new relationships, or throwing out clothes or whatever. Just small things that make us see there may be a way through grief. It's surprising how many of these signs go unnoticed, or we refuse to acknowledge them because we feel guilty for moving forward.'

'I joined a dating website,' said Fred. 'It's called May to December.'

There was a low hum of surprise and approval.

'That's very encouraging, Fred.' Marc sipped his tea. 'What are you hoping to get from it? Some company? I remember you said you particularly missed having someone to go for a walk with on Sunday afternoons. Down by the duck pond, wasn't it, where you and your wife used to go?'

'Oh, no. It's for internet sex.'

Marc spluttered. There was a brief pause while someone handed him a tissue to mop the tea off his trousers.

'Internet sex. That's what they're all doing, isn't it? I've joined three sites.' Fred held up his hand, counting them off on his fingers. 'May to December, that's for young women who like older men, Sugar-Papas, for young women who like older men with money, and . . . um . . . Hot Studs.' He paused. 'They weren't specific.'

There was a short silence.

'It's nice to be optimistic, Fred,' said Natasha.

'How about you, Louisa?'

'Um . . .' I hesitated, given Jake was in front of me, and then thought, *What the hell?* 'I actually went on a date this weekend.'

There was a low *woo-hoo!* from other members of the group. I looked down a little sheepishly. I couldn't even think about that night without colour seeping into my face.

'And how did it go?'

'It was . . . surprising.'

'She shagged someone. She totally shagged someone,' said Natasha.

'She's got that glow,' said William.

'Did he have moves?' said Fred. 'Got any tips?'

'And you managed to not think about Bill too much?'

'Not enough to stop me . . . I just felt I wanted to do something that . . .' I shrugged '. . . I just wanted to feel alive.'

There was a murmur of agreement at that word. It was what we all wanted, ultimately, to be freed from our grief. To be released from this underworld of the dead, half our hearts lost underground, or trapped in little porcelain urns. It felt good to have something positive to say for once.

Marc nodded encouragingly. 'I think it sounds very healthy.'

I listened to Sunil say that he had started to listen to music again, and Natasha talk about how she had moved some of the pictures of her husband from the living room to her bedroom 'so that I don't end up talking about him every single time somebody comes round'. Daphne had stopped sniffing her husband's shirts, furtively, in his wardrobe. 'If I'm honest, they didn't really smell of him any more anyway. I think it was just a habit I'd got into.'

'And you, Jake?'

He still looked miserable. 'I go out more, I s'pose.'

'Have you talked to your father about your feelings?'

'No.'

I tried not to look at him as he spoke. I felt oddly raw, not knowing what he knew.

'I think he likes someone, though.'

'More shagging?' said Fred.

'No, I mean as in properly likes someone.'

I could feel myself blushing. I tried rubbing at an invisible mark on my shoe in an attempt to hide my face.

'What makes you think that, Jake?'

'He started talking about her over breakfast the other day. He was saying that he thought he was going to stop the whole picking-up-random-women thing. That he had met someone and he might want to make a go of it with her.'

I was glowing like a beacon. I couldn't believe that nobody else in the room was able to see it.

'So do you think he's finally worked out that rebound relationships are not the way forward? Perhaps he just needed a few partners before he fell in love with someone again.'

'He's done a lot of rebounding,' said William. 'Actual Space Hopper levels of rebounding.'

'Jake? How does that make you feel?' said Marc.

'A bit weird. I mean, I miss my mum, but I do think it's probably good that he's moving on.'

I tried to imagine what Sam had said. Had he mentioned me by name? I could picture the two of them in the kitchen of the little railway carriage, having this earnest discussion over tea and toast. My cheeks were aflame. I wasn't sure I wanted Sam to make assumptions about us so early on. I should have been clearer that it hadn't meant we were in a relationship. It was too soon. And too soon to have Jake discussing us in public.

'And have you met the woman?' said Natasha. 'Do you like her?'

Jake ducked his head. 'Yeah. That was the really crap bit.'

I glanced up.

'He asked her round for brunch on Sunday, and she was a total nightmare. She wore this super-tight top and she kept putting her arm around me like she knew me, and laughing too loudly, and then when my dad was in the garden she would look at me with these big round eyes and go, "And how *are* you?" with this really annoying head tilt.'

'Oh, the *head tilt*,' said William, and there was a low murmur of agreement. Everyone knew the head tilt.

'And when Dad was there she just giggled and flicked her hair all the time, like she was trying to be a teenager even though she was plainly at *least* thirty.' He wrinkled his nose in disgust.

'Thirty!' said Daphne, her gaze sliding sideways. 'Imagine!'

'I actually preferred the one who used to quiz me about what he was up to. At least she didn't pretend to be my best friend.'

I could barely hear the rest of what he said. A distant ringing had begun in my ears, drowning out all sound. How could I have been so stupid? I suddenly recalled Jake's eye roll the first time he had watched Sam chatting me up. There was my warning, right there, and I had been stupid enough to ignore it.

I felt hot and shaky. I couldn't stay there. I couldn't listen to any more. 'Um . . . I just remembered. I have an appointment,' I mumbled, gathering up my bag and bolting from my seat. 'Sorry.'

'Everything all right, Louisa?' said Marc.

'Totally fine. Got to dash.' I ran for the door, my fake smile plastered on my face so tightly that it was painful.

He was there. Of course he was. He had just pulled up on the bike in the car park and was removing his helmet. I emerged from the church hall and stopped at the top of the steps, wondering if there was any way I could get to my car without passing him, but it was hopeless. The physical part of my brain registered the shape of him before the remaining synapses caught up: a flush of pleasure, the flash of memory of how his hands had felt on me. And then that blazing anger, the blood pulse of humiliation.

'Hey,' he said, as he caught sight of me, his smile easy, his eyes crinkling with pleasure. The fecking charmer.

I slowed my step just long enough for him to register the hurt on my face. I didn't care. I felt like Lily suddenly. I was not going to internalize this. This had not been *me* climbing out of one person's bed and straight into another.

'Nice job, you utter, utter wanker,' I spat, then ran past him to my car before the choke in my voice could turn into an actual sob.

The week, as if in response to some unheard malign dog whistle, actually managed to go downhill from there. Richard grew ever pickier, complained that we didn't smile enough and that our lack of 'cheery bantz' with the customers was sending travellers along the way to the Wings in the Air Bar and Grill. The weather turned, sending the skies a gunmetal grey and delaying flights with tropical rainstorms, so the airport was filled with bad-tempered passengers, and then, with immaculate timing, the baggage handlers went on strike. 'What can you expect? Mercury is in retrograde,' said Vera, savagely, and growled at a customer who asked for less froth on his cappuccino.

At home, Lily arrived under her own dark cloud. She sat in my living room, glued to her mobile phone, but whatever was on it seemed to give her no pleasure. She would stare out of the window, stony-faced, as her father had, as if she were just as trapped as he had been. I had tried to explain that Will had given me the yellow and black tights, that their significance was not in the colour or the quality, but that they –

'Yeah, yeah, tights. Whatever,' she said.

For three nights I barely slept. I stared at my ceiling, fired by a stone-cold fury that lodged in my chest and refused to go away. I was so angry with Sam. But I was angrier with myself. He texted twice, a maddeningly *faux*-innocent '??', to which I didn't trust myself to respond. I had done the classic thing women do of ignoring everything a man says or does, preferring to listen to their own insistent drumbeat: *It will be different with me*. I had kissed him. I had made the whole thing happen. So I had only myself to blame.

I tried to tell myself I'd probably had a lucky escape. I told myself, with little internal exclamation marks, that it was better to find out now, rather than in six months' time! I tried to view it through Marc's eyes: it was good to have moved on! I could chalk this one up to experience! At least the sex was good! And then the stupid hot tears would leak out of my stupid eyes and I would screw them up and tell myself that this was what you got for letting anyone close.

Depression, we had learned in the group, loves a vacuum. Far better to be doing, or at least planning. Sometimes the illusion of happiness could inadvertently create it. Sick of coming home to find Lily prostrate on my sofa every evening, and just as sick of trying not to look irritated by it, on Friday night I told her that we would go to see Mrs Traynor the following day.

'But you said she didn't reply to your letter.'

'Maybe she didn't get it. Whatever. At some point Mr Traynor is going to tell his family about you, so we might as well go and see her before that happens.'

She didn't say anything. I took that as a tacit sign of agreement, and left her to it.

That night I found myself going through the clothes that Lily had pulled out of the packing case, the clothes I had ignored since leaving England for Paris two years previously. There had been no point in wearing them. I hadn't felt like that person since Will died.

Now, though, it felt important to put something on that was neither jeans nor a green Irish-dancing-girl outfit. I found a navy mini-dress I had once loved that seemed sober enough for a slightly formal visit, ironed it and put it to one side. I told Lily we would be leaving at nine the following morning and went to bed, wondering at how exhausting it was to live in a home with someone who believed that any speech more than a grunt was simply a superhuman step too far.

Ten minutes after I had closed my door, a handwritten note was pushed under it.

*Dear Louisa*

*I'm sorry I borrowed your clothes. And thanks for everything. I know I'm a pain sometimes.*

*Sorry.*

*Lily xxx*

*PS You should totally wear those clothes though. They are WAY better than that stuff you wear.*

I opened the door, and Lily was standing there, unsmiling. She stepped forwards and gave me a brief, emphatic hug, so tight that my ribs hurt. Then she turned and, without a word, disappeared back into the living room.

The day dawned brighter, and our mood lifted a little with it. We drove several hours to a tiny village in Oxfordshire, a place of walled gardens and mustard-tinted, sun-baked stone walls. I prattled on during the journey, mostly to hide my nerves about seeing Mrs Traynor again. The hardest thing about talking to teenagers, I had discovered, was that whatever you said inevitably came across like someone's elderly aunt at a wedding.

'So what things do you like doing? When you're not at school?'

She shrugged.

'What do you think you might want to do after you leave?'

She gave me the look.

'You must have had hobbies growing up?'

She reeled off a dizzying list: show-jumping, lacrosse, hockey, piano (grade five), cross-country running, county-level tennis.

'All that? And you didn't want to keep any of it up?'

She sniffed and shrugged simultaneously, then put her feet up on the dashboard, as if the conversation were closed.

'Your father loved to travel,' I remarked, a few miles on.

'You said.'

'He once told me he'd been everywhere except North Korea. And Disneyland. He could tell stories about places I'd never even heard of.'

'People my age don't go on adventures. There's nowhere left to discover. And people who backpack in their gap year are unbelievably tedious. Always yakking on about some bar they discovered on Ko Phang Yan, or how they scored amazing drugs in the Burmese rainforest.'

'You don't have to backpack.'

'Yeah, but once you've seen the inside of one Mandarin Oriental you've seen them all.' She yawned. 'I went to school near here once,' she observed later, peering out of the window. 'It was the only school I actually liked.' She paused. 'I had a friend called Holly.'

'What happened?'

'Mum got obsessed with the idea that it wasn't the *right sort of school*. She said they weren't far enough up the league tables or something. It was just some little boarding-school. Not academic. So they moved me. After that I couldn't be arsed making friends. What's the point if they're just going to move you on again?'

'Did you keep in touch with Holly?'

'Not really. There's no point when you can't actually see each other.'

I had a vague memory of the intensity of teenage female relationships, more of a passion than a normal friendship. 'What do you think you'll do? I mean if you really aren't going to go back to school.'

'I don't like thinking ahead.'

'But you're going to have to think about something, Lily.'

She closed her eyes for a minute, then put her feet down and peeled some purple varnish off her thumbnail. 'I don't know, Louisa. Perhaps I'll just follow your amazing example and do all the exciting things that you do.'

I took three deep breaths, just to prevent myself stopping the car on the motorway. Nerves, I told myself. It was just her nerves. And then, to annoy her, I turned on Radio 2 really loudly and kept it there the rest of the way.

*

We found Four Acres Lane with help from a local dog-walker, and pulled up outside Fox's Cottage, a modest white-rendered building with a thatched roof. Outside, scarlet roses tumbled around an iron arch at the start of the garden path, and delicately coloured blooms fought for space in neatly tended beds. A small hatchback sat in the drive.

'She's gone down in the world,' said Lily, peering out.

'It's pretty.'

'It's a shoebox.'

I sat, listening to the engine tick down. 'Listen, Lily. Before we go in. Just don't expect too much,' I said. 'Mrs Traynor's sort of formal. She takes refuge in manners. She'll probably speak to you like she's a teacher. I mean, I don't think she'll hug you, like Mr Traynor did.'

'My grandfather is a hypocrite.' Lily sniffed. 'He makes out like you're the greatest thing ever, but really he's just pussy-whipped.'

'And please don't use the term "pussy-whipped".'

'There's no point pretending to be someone I'm not,' Lily said sulkily.

We sat there for a while. I realized that neither of us wanted to be the one to walk up to the door. 'Shall I try to call her one more time?' I said, holding up my phone. I'd tried twice that morning but it had gone straight to voicemail.

'Don't tell her straight away,' she said suddenly. 'Who I am, I mean. I just . . . I just want to see who she is. Before we tell her.'

'Sure,' I said, softening. And before I could say anything else, Lily was out of the car and striding up towards the front gate, her hands bunched into fists, like a boxer about to enter a ring.

Mrs Traynor had gone grey. Her hair, which had been tinted dark brown, was now white and short, making her look much older than she actually was, or like someone recently recovered from a serious illness. She was probably a stone lighter than when I had last seen her, and there were liver-coloured hollows under her eyes. She looked at Lily with a confusion that told me she didn't expect any visitors, at any time. And then she saw me, and her eyes widened. 'Louisa?'

'Hello, Mrs Traynor.' I stepped forward and held out a hand. 'We were in the area. I don't know if you got my letter. I just thought I'd stop by and say hello . . .'

My voice – false and unnaturally cheery – tailed away. The last time she had seen me was when I helped clear her dead son's room; the time before that at his last breath. I watched her relive both those facts now. 'We were just admiring your garden.'

'David Austin roses,' said Lily.

Mrs Traynor looked at her as if noticing her for the first time. Her smile was slight and wavering. 'Yes. Yes, they are. How clever of you. It's – I'm very sorry. I don't have many visitors. What did you say your name was?'

'This is Lily,' I said, and watched as Lily took Mrs Traynor's hand and shook it, studying her intently as she did so.

We stood there on her front step for a moment, and finally, as if she thought she had no alternative, Mrs Traynor turned and pushed the door open. 'I suppose you'd better come in.'

The cottage was tiny, its ceilings so low that even I had to duck when moving from the hall to the kitchen. I waited as Mrs Traynor made tea, watching Lily walk restlessly around the tiny living room, navigating her way among the few bits of highly polished antique furniture that I remembered from my days in Granta House, picking things up and putting them down again.

'And . . . how have you been?'

Mrs Traynor's voice was flat, as if it were not a question she was really seeking an answer to.

'Oh, quite well, thank you.'

Long silence.

'It's a lovely village.'

'Yes. Well. I couldn't really stay in Stortfold . . .' She poured boiling water into the teapot and I couldn't help but be reminded of Della, moving heavily around Mrs Traynor's old kitchen.

'Do you know many people in the area?'

'No.' She said it as if that might have been the sole reason for her moving there. 'Would you mind taking the milk jug? I can't fit everything on this tray.'

There followed a painfully laboured half-hour of conversation. Mrs Traynor, a woman infused with the instinctive upper-middle-class skill of being all over any social situation, had apparently lost the ability to communicate. She seemed only half with us when I spoke. She asked a question, then asked it again ten minutes later, as if she had failed to register the answer. I wondered about the use of anti-depressants. Lily watched her surreptitiously, her thoughts ticking across her face, and I sat between them, my stomach in an increasingly tight knot, waiting for something to happen.

I chattered on into the silence, talking of my awful job, things I'd done in France, the fact that my parents were well, thank you – anything to end the awful, oppressive stillness that crept across the little room whenever I stopped. But Mrs Traynor's grief hung over the little house, like a fog. If Mr Traynor had seemed exhausted by sadness, Mrs Traynor appeared to be swallowed by it. There was almost nothing left of the brisk, proud woman I had known.

'What brings you to this area?' she said, finally.

'Um . . . just visiting friends,' I said.

'How do you two know each other?'

'I . . . knew Lily's father.'

'How nice,' said Mrs Traynor, and we smiled awkwardly. I watched Lily, waiting for her to say something, but she had frozen, as if she, too, were overwhelmed, faced with the reality of this woman's pain.

We drank a second cup of tea, and remarked upon her beautiful garden for the third, possibly fourth time, and I fought the sensation that our enduring presence was requiring a sort of superhuman effort on her behalf. She didn't want us there. She was far too polite to say so, but it was obvious that she really just wanted to be on her own. It was in every gesture – every forced smile, every attempt to stay on top of the conversation. I suspected that the moment we were gone she would simply retreat into a chair and stay there, or shuffle upstairs and curl up in her bed.

And then I noticed it: the complete absence of photographs. Where Granta House had been filled with silver-framed pictures of her children, of their family, ponies, skiing holidays, distant grandparents, this cottage was bare. A small bronze of a horse, a watercolour of some hyacinths, but no people. I found myself shifting in my seat, wondering if I had simply missed them, gathered on some occasional table or windowsill. But no: the cottage was brutally impersonal. I thought of my own flat, my utter failure to personalize it or allow myself to turn it into any kind of a home. And I felt suddenly leaden, and desperately sad.

*What have you done to us all, Will?*

'It's probably time to go, Louisa,' said Lily, looking pointedly at the clock. 'You did say we wouldn't want to hit traffic.'

I gazed at her. 'But –'

'You said we shouldn't stay too long.' Her voice was high and clear.

'Oh. Yes. Traffic can be very tedious.' Mrs Traynor began to rise from her chair.

I was glaring at Lily, about to protest again, when the phone rang. Mrs Traynor flinched, as if the sound were now unfamiliar. She looked at each of us, as if wondering whether to answer it, and then, perhaps realizing she couldn't ignore it while we were there, she excused herself and walked through to the other room, where we heard her answer.

'What are you doing?' I said.

'It just feels all wrong,' said Lily, miserably.

'But we can't go without telling her.'

'I just can't do this today. It's all . . .'

'I know it's scary. But look at her, Lily. I really think it might help her if you told her. Don't you?'

Lily's eyes widened.

'Tell me what?'

My head swivelled. Mrs Traynor was standing motionless by the door to the little hallway. 'What is it you need to tell me?'

Lily looked at me, then back towards Mrs Traynor. I felt time slow around us. She swallowed, then lifted her chin a little. 'That I'm your granddaughter.'

A brief silence.

'My . . . what?'

'I'm Will Traynor's daughter.'

Her words echoed into the little room. Mrs Traynor's gaze slid towards mine, as if to check that this was in fact some insane joke.

'But . . . you can't be.'

Lily recoiled.

'Mrs Traynor, I know this must have come as something of a shock –' I began.

She didn't hear me. She was staring fiercely at Lily. 'How could my son have had a daughter I didn't know about?'

'Because my mum didn't tell anyone.' Lily's voice emerged as a whisper.

'All this time? How can you have been a secret for all this time?' Mrs Traynor turned towards me. 'You knew about this?'

I swallowed. 'It was why I wrote to you. Lily came to find me. She wanted to know about her family. Mrs Traynor, we didn't want to cause you any more pain. It's just that Lily wanted to know her grandparents and it didn't go particularly well with Mr Traynor and . . .'

'But Will would have said something.' She shook her head. 'I know he would. He was *my son.*'

'I'll take a blood test if you really don't believe me,' said Lily, her arms folding across her chest. 'But I'm not after anything of yours. I don't need to come and stay with you or anything. I have my own *money*, if that's what you think.'

'I'm not sure what I –' Mrs Traynor began.

'You don't have to look horrified. I'm not, like, some contagious disease you've just inherited. Just, you know, a *granddaughter.* Jesus.'

Mrs Traynor sank slowly into a chair. After a moment, a trembling hand went to her head.

'Are you all right, Mrs Traynor?'

'I don't think I . . .' Mrs Traynor closed her eyes. She seemed to have retreated somewhere far inside herself.

'Lily, I think we should go. Mrs Traynor, I'm going to write down my number. We'll come back when this news has had a chance to sink in.'

'Says who? I'm not coming back here. She thinks I'm a liar. Jesus. This *family.*'

Lily stared at us both in disbelief, then pushed her way out of the little room, knocking over a small walnut occasional table as she went. I stooped, picking it up, and carefully replaced the little silver boxes that had been laid out neatly on its surface.

Mrs Traynor was gaunt with shock.

'I'm sorry, Mrs Traynor,' I said. 'I really did try to speak to you before we came.'

I heard the car door slam.

Mrs Traynor took a breath. 'I don't read things if I don't know where they've come from. I had letters. Vile letters. Telling me that I . . . I don't answer anything much now . . . It's never anything I want to hear.' She looked bewildered and old and fragile.

'I'm sorry. I'm really sorry.' I picked up my bag and fled.


'Don't say anything,' said Lily, as I got into the car. 'Just don't. Okay?'

'Why did you do that?' I sat in the driver's seat, keys in my hand. 'Why would you sabotage it all?'

'I could see how she felt about me from the moment she looked at me.'

'She's a mother, plainly still grieving her son. We had just given her an enormous shock. And you went off at her like a rocket. Could you not have been quiet and let her digest it all? Why do you have to push everyone away?'

'Oh, what the hell would you know about me?'

'You seem determined to wreck your relationship with every person who might get close to you.'

'Oh, *God*, is this about the stupid tights again? What do you know about anything? You spend your whole life alone in a crappy flat where nobody visits. Your parents plainly think you're a loser. You don't have the guts to walk out of even the world's most pathetic job.'

'You have no idea how hard it is to get any job, these days, so don't you tell me –'

'You're a *loser*. Worse than that you're a loser who thinks you can tell other people what to do. And who gives you the right? You sat there at my dad's bedside and you watched him die and you did nothing about it. Nothing! So I hardly think you're any great judge of how to behave.'

The silence in the car was as hard and brittle as glass. I stared at the wheel. I waited until I was sure I could breathe normally.

Then I started the car and we drove the 120 miles home in silence.

# Chapter Fifteen

I barely saw Lily for the next few days, and that suited me fine. When I came home from work a trail of crumbs or empty mugs confirmed that she had been there. A couple of times I walked in and the air felt oddly disturbed, as if something had taken place I couldn't quite identify. But nothing was missing and nothing obviously altered, and I put it down to the weirdness of sharing a flat with someone you weren't getting on with. For the first time I allowed myself to admit that I missed being on my own.

I called my sister, and she had the good grace not to say, 'I told you so.' Well, maybe just once.

'That is the worst thing about being a parent,' she said, as if I were one too. 'You're meant to be this serene, all-knowing, gracious person who can handle every situation. And sometimes when Thom is rude, or I'm tired, I just want to slam the door at him or stick my tongue out and tell him he's an arse.'

Which was pretty much how I felt.

Work had reached a misery point where I had to make myself sing show tunes in my car even to make myself drive to the airport.

And then there was Sam.

Who I didn't think about.

I didn't think about him in the morning, when I caught sight of my naked body in the bathroom mirror. I didn't remember the way his fingers had traced my skin and made my vivid red scars not so much invisible as part of a shared history – or how, for one brief evening, I had felt reckless and alive again.

I didn't think about him when I watched the couples, heads bowed together as they examined their boarding passes, off to share romantic adventures – or just hot monkey sex – in destinations far from there. I didn't think about him on the way to and from work, whenever an ambulance went screaming past. Which seemed to happen an inordinate number of times. And I definitely didn't think about him in the evening when I sat home alone on my sofa, gazing at a television show whose plot I couldn't have told you, and looking, I suspected, like the loneliest flammable porno pixie on the planet.

Nathan rang and left a message, asking me to call. I wasn't sure I could bear to hear the latest episode of his exciting new life in New York, and put it on my mental to-do list of things that would never actually get done. Tanya texted me to say the Houghton-Millers had come home three days early, something to do with Francis's work. Richard rang, telling me I was on the late shift from Monday to Friday. *And please don't be late, Louisa. I'd like to remind you again that you are on your final warning.*

I did the only thing I could think of: I went home, driving to Stortfold with the music turned up loud so that I didn't have to be alone with my thoughts. I felt grateful for my parents. I felt an almost umbilical pull towards home, the comfort offered by a traditional family and Sunday lunch on the table.

'Lunch?' said Dad, his arms crossed across his stomach, his jaw set in indignation. 'Oh, no. We don't do Sunday lunch any more. Lunch is a sign of patriarchal oppression.'

Granddad nodded mournfully from the corner.

'No, no, we can't have lunch. We do sandwiches on a Sunday now. Or soup. Soup is apparently agreeable to feminism.'

Treena, studying at the dining-table, rolled her eyes. 'Mum is doing a women's poetry class on Sunday mornings at the adult education centre. She's hardly turned into Andrea Dworkin.'

'See, Lou? Now I'm expected to know all about feminism and this Andrew Dorkin fella has stolen my bloody Sunday lunch.'

'You're being dramatic, Dad.'

'How is this dramatic? Sundays is *family* time. We should have family Sunday lunch.'

'Mum's entire life has been family time. Why can't you just let her have some time to herself?'

Dad pointed his folded-up newspaper at Treena. 'You did this. Your mammy and I were perfectly happy before you started telling her she wasn't.'

Granddad nodded in agreement.

'It's all gone pear-shaped around here. I can't watch the television without her muttering, "Sexist," at the yoghurt ads. This is sexist. That's sexist. When I brought home Ade Palmer's copy of the *Sun* just for a bit of a read of the sports pages she chucked it in the fire because of Page Three. I never know where she is from one day to the next.'

'One two-hour class,' said Treena, mildly, not looking up from her books. 'On a Sunday.'

'I'm not being funny, Dad,' I said, 'but those things on the end of your arms?'

'What?' Dad looked down. 'What?'

'Your hands,' I said. 'They're not painted on.'

He frowned at me.

'So I'm guessing you could make the lunch. Give Mum a surprise when she gets back from her poetry class?'

Dad's eyes widened. 'Me make the Sunday lunch? Me? We've been married nearly thirty years, Louisa. I don't do the bloody lunch. I do the earning, and your mother does the lunch. That's the deal! That's what I signed up for! What's the world coming to if I'm there with a pinny on, peeling spuds, on a Sunday? How is that fair?'

'It's called modern life, Dad.'

'Modern life. You're no help,' Dad said, and harrumphed. 'I'll bet you Mr bloody Traynor gets his Sunday lunch. That girl of his wouldn't be a feminist.'

'Ah. Then you need a castle, Dad. Castles trump feminism every time.'

Treena and I started to laugh.

'You know what? There's a reason why the two of you haven't got boyfriends.'

'Ooh. Red card!' We both held up our right hands. He shoved his paper up in the air and stomped off to the garden.

Treena grinned at me. 'I was going to suggest we cook lunch but . . . now?'

'I don't know. I wouldn't want to perpetuate patriarchal oppression. Pub?'

'Excellent. I'll text Mum.'

My mother, it emerged, had, at the age of fifty-six, begun to come out of her shell, first as tentatively as a hermit crab but now, apparently, with increasing enthusiasm. For years she hadn't left the house unaccompanied, had been satisfied with the little domain that was our three-and-a-half-bedroomed house. But spending weeks in London after I'd had my accident had forced her out of her normal routine and sparked some long-dormant curiosity about life beyond Stortfold. She had started flicking through some of the feminist texts Treena had been given at the GenderQuake awareness group at college, and these two alchemic happenings had caused my mother to undergo something of an awakening. She had ripped her way through *The Second Sex* and *Fear of Flying*, followed up with *The Female Eunuch*, and after reading *The Women's Room* had been so shocked at what she saw as the parallels to her own life that she had refused to cook for three days, until she had discovered Granddad was hoarding four-packs of stale doughnuts.

'I keep thinking about what your man Will said,' she remarked, as we sat around the table in the pub garden, watching Thom periodically butt heads with the other children on the sagging bouncy castle. 'You only get the one life – isn't that what he told you?' She was wearing her usual blue short-sleeved shirt, but she had tied her hair back in a way I hadn't seen before and looked oddly youthful. 'So I just want to make the most of things. Learn a little. Take the rubber gloves off once in a while.'

'Dad's quite pissed off,' I said.

'Language.'

'It's a sandwich,' said my sister. 'He's not trekking forty days through the Gobi desert for food.'

'And it's a ten-week course. He'll live,' said my mother, firmly, then sat back and surveyed the two of us. 'Well, now, isn't this nice? I'm not sure the three of us have been out together since . . . well, since you were teenagers and we would go shopping in town of a Saturday.'

'And Treena would complain that all the shops were boring.'

'Yeah, but that's because Lou liked charity shops that smelt of people's armpits.'

'It's nice to see you in some of your favourite things again.' Mum nodded at me admiringly. I had put on a bright yellow T-shirt in the hope that it would make me look happier than I felt.

They asked about Lily, and I told them she was spending more time with her mother, that she'd been a bit of a handful, and they exchanged looks, like that was pretty much what they had expected me to say. I didn't tell them about Mrs Traynor.

'That whole Lily thing was a very odd situation. I can't

think much of that mother just handing her daughter over to you.'

'Mum means that nicely, by the way,' said Treena.

'But that job of yours, Lou, love. I don't like the thought of you prancing around behind a bar in your next-to-nothings. It sounds like that place . . . What is it?'

'Hooters,' said Treena.

'It's not like Hooters. It's an airport. My hooters are fully suited and hooted.'

'Nobody toots those hooters,' said Treena.

'But you're wearing a sexist costume to serve drinks. If that's what you want to do, you could do that at . . . I don't know, Disneyland Paris. If you were Minnie, or Winnie the Pooh, you wouldn't even have to show your legs.'

'You'll be thirty soon,' said my sister. 'Minnie, Winnie or Nell Gwynnie. The choice is yours.'

'Well,' I said, as the waitress brought our chicken and chips, 'I've been thinking, and, yes, you're right. From now on I'm going to move on. Focus on my career.'

'Can you say that again?' My sister moved some of the chips from her plate on to Thom's. The pub garden had become noisier.

'Focus on my career,' I said, louder.

'No. That bit where you said I was right. I'm not sure you've said that since 1997. Thom, don't go back on the bouncy castle yet, sweetheart. You'll be sick.'

We sat there for a good part of the afternoon, avoiding Dad's increasingly cross texts demanding to know what we were doing. I had never sat with my mother and sister, like normal people, grown-ups, having conversations that didn't involve putting anything away or somebody being *so annoying*. We found ourselves surprisingly interested in each other's lives and opinions, as if we had suddenly realized each of us might have roles beyond *the brainy one*, *the chaotic one*, and *the one who does all the housework*.

It was an odd sensation, having to view my family as human beings.

'Mum,' I said, shortly after Thom had finished his chicken and run off to play, and about five minutes before he would lose his lunch on the bouncy castle and put it out of action for the rest of the afternoon, 'do you ever mind not having had a career?'

'No. I loved being a mum. I really did. But it's odd ... Everything that's happened over the past two years, it does make you think.'

I waited.

'I've been reading about all these women – these brave souls who made such a difference in the world to the way people think and do things. And I look at what I've done and wonder whether, well, whether anyone would notice a jot if I wasn't here.'

She said this quite evenly so I couldn't tell if she was actually much more upset about it than she was prepared to let on. 'We'd notice more than a jot, Mum,' I said.

'But it's not like I've made an impact on much, is it? I don't know. I've always been content. But it's like I've spent thirty years doing one thing and now everything I read, the television, the papers, it's like everyone's telling me it was worth nothing.'

My sister and I stared at each other.

'It wasn't nothing to us, Mum.'

'You're sweet girls.'

'I mean it. You ...' I thought suddenly of Tanya Houghton-Miller '... you made us feel safe. And loved. I liked you being there every day when we came home.'

Mum put her hand on mine. 'I'm fine. I'm so proud of the

pair of you, making your own way in the world. Really. But I just need to work out some things for myself. And it's an interesting journey, really it is. I'm loving the reading. Mrs Deans at the library is calling in all sorts of things she thinks I might be interested in. I'm going to move on to the American New Wave feminists next. Very interesting, all their theories.' She folded her paper napkin neatly. 'I do wish they'd all stop arguing with each other, though. I slightly want to smack their heads together.'

'And . . . are you really still not shaving your legs?'

I had gone too far. My mother's face closed off, and she gave me the fishy eye. 'Sometimes, it takes you a while to wake up to a true sign of oppression. I have told your father, and I'll tell you girls, the day he goes to the salon to have his legs covered with hot wax, then have it ripped off by a ruddy twenty-one-year-old is the day I'll start doing mine again.'

The sun eased down over Stortfold, like melting butter. I stayed much later into the evening than I had intended, said goodbye to my family, climbed into my car and drove home. I felt grounded, tethered. After the emotional turbulence of the past week, it was good to be surrounded by a bit of normality. And my sister, who never showed signs of weakness, had confessed that she thought she would remain single for ever, brushing away Mum's insistence that she was 'a gorgeous-looking girl'.

'But I'm a single mother,' she'd said. 'And, worse, I don't do flirting. I wouldn't know how to flirt with someone if Louisa stood behind them holding up placards. And the only men I've met in two years have either been frightened off by Thom or after one thing.'

'Oh, not –' my mother began.

'Free accounting advice.'

Suddenly, looking at her from the outside, I'd felt a sudden sympathy. She was right: I had been handed, against the odds, all the advantages – a home of my own, a future free of any responsibilities – and the only thing stopping me embracing them was myself. The fact that she wasn't eaten up with bitterness over our respective lots was pretty impressive. I hugged her before I left. She was a little shocked, then momentarily suspicious, patted her upper back to check for KICK ME signs, then finally hugged me back.

'Come and stay,' I said. 'Really. Come and stay. I'll take you dancing at this club I know. Mum can mind Thom.'

My sister laughed, and closed the door of the car as I started it. 'Yeah. You dancing? Like *that*'s going to happen.' She was still laughing as I drove away.

Six days later I returned home after a late shift to a nightclub of my own. As I came up the stairs of my block, instead of the usual silence, I could hear the distant sound of laughter, the irregular thump of music. I hesitated for a moment outside my front door, thinking that in my exhausted state I must be mistaken, then unlocked it.

The smell of weed hit me first, so strong I almost reflexively held my breath rather than inhale. I walked slowly to the living room, opened the door and stood there, not quite able to believe at first the scene that confronted me. In the dimly lit room, Lily was lying along my sofa, her short skirt rucked up somewhere just below her bottom, a badly rolled joint midway to her mouth. Two young men were sprawled against the sofa, islands amid a sea of alcoholic detritus, empty crisps packets and polystyrene takeaway cartons. Also seated on the floor were two girls of Lily's age; one, her hair pulled back tightly into a ponytail, looked at me with her eyebrows raised, as if to question what I was doing there. Music thumped from the sound system. The number of beer cans and overflowing ashtrays told of a long night.

'Oh,' Lily said, exaggeratedly. 'Hi-i-i.'

'What are you doing?'

'Yeah. We were out, and we sort of missed the late bus, so I thought it would be okay if we crashed here. You don't mind, do you?'

I was so stunned I could barely speak. 'Yes,' I said tightly. 'Actually, I do mind.'

'Uh-oh.' She began to cackle.

I dropped my bag with a thump at my feet. I gazed around me at the municipal rubbish dump that had once passed as my living room. 'Party's over. I'll give you five minutes to clear up your mess, and go.'

'Oh, God. I knew it. You're going to be boring about it, aren't you? Ugh. I *knew* it.' She threw herself back on the sofa melodramatically. Her voice was slurred, her actions thickened with – what? Drugs? I waited. For one brief, tense moment, the two men looked steadily at me and I could see they were assessing whether to get up or simply to sit there.

One of the girls sucked her teeth audibly.

'Four minutes,' I said slowly. 'I'm counting.'

Perhaps my righteous anger gave me some authority. Perhaps they were actually less brave than they appeared. One by one they clambered to their feet and sloped past me to the open front door. As the last of the boys left, he ostentatiously lifted his hand and dropped a can on the hall floor so that beer sprayed up the wall and over the carpet. I kicked the door shut behind them and picked it up. By the time I got to Lily, I was shaking with anger. 'What the *hell* do you think you're playing at?'

'Jesus. It was just a few friends, okay?'

'This is not your flat, Lily. It is not your place to bring

people back as you see fit . . .' A sudden flashback: that strange sense of dislocation when I had returned home a week ago. 'Oh, my God. You've done this before, haven't you? Last week. You had people home and then left before I got back.'

Lily climbed unsteadily to her feet. She pulled down her skirt and ran her hand through her hair, tugging at the tangles. Her eyeliner was smudged, and she had what could have been a bruise, or perhaps a hickey, on her neck. 'God. Why do you have to make such a big *deal* out of everything? They were just people, okay?'

'In *my home.*'

'Well, it's hardly a home, is it? It's got no furniture, and nothing personal. You haven't even got pictures on your walls. It's like . . . a garage. A garage without a car. I've actually seen homelier petrol stations.'

'What I do with my home is none of your business.'

She let out a small belch and fanned the air in front of her mouth. 'Ugh. Kebab breath.' She padded to the kitchen where she opened three cupboards until she found a glass. She filled it and gulped down the water. 'And you haven't even got a proper television. I didn't know people still had eighteen-inch televisions.'

I began to pick up the cans, shoving them into a plastic bag. 'So who were they?'

'I don't know. Just some people.'

'You don't *know*?'

'Friends.' She sounded irritated. 'People I know from clubbing.'

'You met them in a club?'

'Yes. Clubbing. Blah blah blah. It's like you're being deliberately thick. Yes. Just some friends I met in a club. It's what normal people do, you know? Have friends they go out with.'

She threw the glass into the washing-up bowl – I heard it crack – and stalked resentfully out of the kitchen.

I stared at her, my heart suddenly sinking. I ran next door to my room, and opened my top drawer. I riffled through my socks, looking for the little jewellery box that contained my grandmother's chain and wedding ring. I stopped and took a deep breath, telling myself I couldn't see them because I was panicking. It would be there. Of course it would. I began picking up the contents of the drawer, carefully checking through them and throwing them onto the bed.

'Did they come in here?' I shouted.

Lily appeared in the doorway. 'Did what?'

'Your friends. Did they come in my bedroom? Where's my jewellery?'

Lily seemed to wake up a little. 'Jewellery?'

'Oh, no. Oh, no.' I opened all my drawers, began dumping the contents on the floor. 'Where is it? And where's my emergency cash?' I turned to her. 'Who were they? What were their names?'

Lily had gone quiet.

'Lily!'

'I – I don't know.'

'What do you mean you don't know? You said they were your friends.'

'Just . . . clubbing friends. Mitch. And . . . Lise and – I can't remember.'

I ran for the door, belted along the corridor and hurled myself down the four flights of stairs. But by the time I reached the front door the corridor and the street beyond were empty, but for the late bus to Waterloo sailing gently, illuminated, down the middle of the dark road.

I stood in the doorway, panting. Then I closed my eyes, fighting back tears, dropping my hands to my knees as I realized what I had lost: my grandmother's ring, the fine gold chain, with the little pendant she had worn from when I was a child. I knew already I would never see them again. There were so few things to pass down in my family, and now even that was gone.

I walked slowly back up the stairs.

Lily was standing in the hallway when I opened the front door. 'I'm really sorry,' she said quietly. 'I didn't know they would steal your stuff.'

'Go away, Lily,' I said.

'They seemed really nice. I – I should have thought –'

'I've been at work for thirteen hours. I need to find out what I've lost and then I want to go to sleep. Your mother is back from her holiday. Please just go home.'

'But I –'

'No. No more.' I straightened up slowly, taking a moment to catch my breath. 'You know the real difference between you and your dad? Even when he was at his unhappiest he wouldn't have treated anyone like this.'

She looked as if I'd slapped her. I didn't care.

'I can't do this any more, Lily.' I pulled a twenty-pound note from my purse and handed it to her. 'There. For your taxi.'

She looked at it, then at me, and swallowed. She ran a hand through her hair and walked slowly back into the living room.

I took off my jacket, and stood staring at my reflection in the little mirror above my chest of drawers. I looked pale, exhausted, defeated. 'And leave your keys,' I said.

There was a short silence. I heard the clatter as they were dropped on the kitchen counter, and then, with a click, the front door closed and she was gone.

# Chapter Sixteen

*I messed it all up, Will.*

I hauled my knees up to my chest. I tried to imagine what he would have said if he could see me then, but I could no longer hear his voice in my head and that small fact made me even sadder.

*What do I do now?*

I understood I could not stay in the flat that Will's legacy had bought me. It felt as if it were steeped in my failures, a bonus prize I had failed to earn. How could you make a home in a place that had come to you for all the wrong reasons? I would sell it and invest the money somewhere. But where would I go instead?

I thought of my job, the reflexive way my stomach now clenched when I heard Celtic pan pipes, even on television; the way Richard made me feel useless, worthless.

I thought of Lily, noting the peculiar weight of the silence that resulted when you knew without doubt that nobody but you would be in your home. I wondered where she was, and pushed the thought away.

The rain eased off, slowing and ceasing almost apologetically, as if the weather were admitting it hadn't really known what had got into it. I pulled on some clothes, vacuumed the flat, and put out the bin-bags of party-related rubbish. I walked to the flower market, mostly to give myself something to do. *Always better to get out and about*, Marc said. I might feel better for being in the thick of Columbia Road, with its gaudy displays of blooms and its slow-moving crowds of shoppers. I fixed my face into a smile, frightened Samir when I bought myself an apple ('Are you on drugs, man?') and headed off into a sea of flowers.

I bought myself a coffee at a little coffee shop and watched the market through its steamed window, ignoring the fact that I was the only person in there on my own. I walked the length of the sodden market, breathed in the damp and heady scents of the lilies, admired the folded secrets of the peonies and roses, glass beads of rain still dotting their surfaces, and bought myself a bunch of dahlias and the whole time I felt as if I were acting, a figure in an advert: *Single city girl living the London dream.*

I walked home, cradling my dahlias in one arm, doing my best not to limp, all the while trying to stop the words *Oh, who do you think you're kidding?* popping repeatedly into my head.

The evening stretched and sagged, as lonely evenings do. I finished cleaning the flat, having fished cigarette butts out of the toilet, watched some television, washed my uniform. I ran a bath full of bubbles and climbed out of it after five minutes, afraid to be alone with my thoughts. I couldn't call my mother or my sister: I knew I wouldn't be able to keep up the pretence of happiness in front of them.

Finally, I reached into my bedside table, and pulled out the letter, the one Will had arranged for me to receive in Paris, back when I was still full of hope. I unfolded its well-worn creases gently. There were times, that first year, when I would read it nightly, trying to bring him to life beside me. These days I rationed myself: I told myself I didn't need to see it – I was afraid it would lose its talismanic power, the words become meaningless. Well, I needed them now.

The computer text, as dear to me as if he had been able to

handwrite it; some residual trace of his energy still in those laser-printed words.

*You're going to feel uncomfortable in your new world for a bit. It always does feel strange to be knocked out of your comfort zone . . . There is a hunger in you, Clark. A fearlessness. You just buried it, like most people do.*

*Just live well. Just live.*

I read the words of a man who had once believed in me, put my head on my knees and, finally, sobbed.

The phone rang, too loud, too close to my head, sending me lurching upright. I scrabbled for it, noting the time. Two a.m. The familiar reflexive fear. 'Lily?'

'What? Lou?'

Nathan's deep drawl rolled across the phone line.

'It's two a.m., Nathan.'

'Aw, man. I always mess up the time difference. Sorry. Want me to hang up?'

I pushed myself upright, rubbing at my face. 'No. No . . . It's good to hear from you.' I flicked on the bedside light. 'How are you?'

'Good! I'm back in New York.'

'Great.'

'Yeah. It was great to see the olds and all, but after a couple of weeks I was itching to get back here. This city is epic.'

I forced a smile, in case he could hear it. 'That's great, Nathan. I'm glad for you.'

'You still happy at that pub of yours?'

'It's fine.'

'You don't . . . want to do something else?'

'Well, you know when things are bad, and you tell yourself

stuff like, "Oh, it could be worse. I could be the person who cleans the poop out of the dog-poop bins"? Well, right now I'd rather be the person who picks up the poop out of the dog-poop bins.'

'Then I've got a proposition for you.'

'I get that a lot from customers, Nathan. And the answer is always no.'

'Ha. Well. There's a job opening out here, working for this family I live with. And you were the first person I thought of.'

Mr Gopnik's wife, he explained, was not a Wall Street Wife. She didn't do the whole 'shopping and lunches' thing; she was a Polish émigrée, prone to mild depression. She was lonely, and the help – a Guatemalan woman – wouldn't say two words to her.

What Mr Gopnik wanted was someone he could trust to keep his wife company and help with the children, to be an extra pair of hands when they travelled. 'He wants a sort of Girl Friday to the family. Someone cheerful and trustworthy. And someone who is not going to go blabbing about their private life.'

'Does he know –'

'I told him about Will at our first meeting, but he'd already done background. He wasn't put off. Far from it. He said he was impressed that we'd followed Will's wishes and never sold our stories.' Nathan paused. 'I've worked it out. At this level, Lou, people value trust and discretion over anything else. I mean, obviously you can't be an idiot, and have to do your job well, but, yeah, that's basically what matters.'

My mind was whirling, an out-of-control waltzer at a fairground. I held the phone in front of me and put it back to my ear. 'Is this . . . Am I actually still asleep?'

'It's not an easy ride. It's long hours and a lot of work. But I'll tell you, mate, I'm having the best time.'

I pushed my hand through my hair. I thought about the bar, with its huffing businessmen and Richard's gimlet stare. I thought about the flat, its walls closing in on me every evening. 'I don't know. This is . . . I mean it all seems –'

'It's a green card, Lou.' Nathan's voice dropped. 'It's your board and lodging. It's *New York*. Listen. This is a man who gets stuff done. Work hard, and he'll look after you. He's smart, and he's fair. Get out here, show him what you're worth, and you could end up with opportunities you wouldn't believe. Seriously. Don't think of this as a nanny job. Think of it as a *gateway*.'

'I don't know . . .'

'Some fella you don't want to leave?'

I hesitated. 'No. But so much has gone on . . . I've not been . . .' It seemed an awful lot to explain at two o'clock in the morning.

'I know you were knocked by what happened. We all were. But you've got to move on.'

'Don't say it's what he would have wanted.'

'Okay,' he said. We both listened, as he said it silently.

I tried to gather my thoughts. 'Would I have to go to New York for an interview?'

'They're in the Hamptons for the summer, so he's looking for someone to start in September. Basically, in six weeks. If you say you're interested, he'll interview you on Skype, sort out the paperwork to get you over, and then we go from there. There will be other candidates. It's too good a position. But Mr G trusts me, Lou. If I say someone's a good bet, they're in with a chance. So shall I throw your hat in the ring? Yes? It is a yes, right?'

I spoke almost before I could think. 'Uh . . . yes. Yes.'

'Great! Email me if you've got questions. I'll send you some pics.'

'Nathan?'

'Gotta go, Lou. The old man has just buzzed me.'

'Thank you. Thanks for thinking of me.'

There was a slight pause before he responded. 'No one I'd rather work with, mate.'

I couldn't sleep after he rang off, wondering whether I had imagined the whole conversation, my mind humming with the enormity of what might lie in front of me if I hadn't. At four, I sat up and emailed Nathan a handful of questions, and the answers came straight back.

> The family is okay. The rich are never normal (!) but these are good people. Minimal drama.

> You'd have your own room and bathroom. We'd share a kitchen with the housekeeper. She's all right. Bit older. Keeps herself to herself.

> Hours regular. Eight – at worst ten – a day. You get time off in lieu. You might want to learn a bit of Polish!

I finally fell asleep as it grew light, my mind full of Manhattan duplexes and bustling streets. And when I woke up, an email was waiting for me.

> Dear Ms Clark,
>
> Nathan tells me you might be interested in coming to work in our household. Would you be available for a Skype interview on Tuesday evening at 5 p.m. GMT (midday EST)?
>
> Yours sincerely,
>
> Leonard M. Gopnik

I stared at it for a full twenty minutes, proof that I hadn't dreamed the whole thing. And then I got up and showered, made myself a strong mug of coffee and typed my reply. It wouldn't hurt to have the interview, I told myself. I wouldn't get the job, if there were lots of highly professional New York candidates. But it was good practice, if nothing else. And it would make me feel as if I were finally doing something, moving forward.

Before I left for work, I took Will's letter carefully from the bedside table. I pressed my lips to it, then folded it carefully and put it back in the drawer.

*Thank you*, I told him silently.

It was a slightly thinned-out version of the Moving On Circle that week. Natasha was on holiday, as was Jake, for which I was mostly relieved and a tiny bit put out in a way I couldn't reconcile. The evening's topic was 'If I could turn back time', which meant that William and Sunil hummed or whistled the Cher song unconsciously at intervals for the entire hour and a half.

I listened to Fred wishing he had spent less time at work, then Sunil wishing he'd got to know his brother better ('You just think they're always going to be there, you know? And then one day they're not'), and wondered if it really had been worth coming.

There had been a couple of times when I'd thought the group might actually be helping. But for an awful lot of the time I was sitting among people I felt I had nothing in common with, droning on for the few hours they had company. I felt grumpy and tired, my hip ached on the hard plastic chair, and I thought I might have got just as much enlightenment about my mental state if I had been watching *EastEnders*. Plus the biscuits *were* rubbish.

Leanne, a single mother, was talking about how she and her older sister had argued about a pair of tracksuit bottoms two days before her sister had died. 'I accused her of taking them, because she was always nicking my stuff. She said she hadn't, but then she always said she hadn't.'

Marc waited. I wondered if I had any painkillers in my handbag.

'And then, you know, she got hit by the bus and the next time I got to see her was at the morgue. And when I was looking for dark clothes to wear to her funeral, you know what was in my wardrobe?'

'The tracksuit bottoms,' said Fred.

'It's difficult when things are unresolved,' said Marc. 'Sometimes for our own sanity we just have to look at the bigger picture.'

'You can love someone and also call them a prat for nicking your tracksuit bottoms,' said William.

That day I didn't want to speak. I was only there because I couldn't face the silence of my little flat. I had a sudden sneaking suspicion I could easily become one of those people who so crave human contact that they talk inappropriately to other passengers on trains or spend ten minutes picking things in a shop so they can chat to the assistant. I was so busy wondering whether it was symptomatic that I had just discussed my new physio support bandage with Samir at the mini-mart that I tuned out Daphne wishing she'd come back from work an hour earlier that particular day, then found she had dissolved, quietly, into tears.

'Daphne?'

'I'm sorry, everyone. But I've spent so long thinking in "if onlys". If only I hadn't stopped off for a chat with the lady at the flower stall. If only I'd left that stupid bought ledger and come home from work earlier. If only I'd just got back in time . . . maybe I could have persuaded him not to do what he did. Maybe I could have done one thing that persuaded him life was worth living.'

Marc leaned forward with the box of tissues and I placed it gently on Daphne's lap. 'Had Alan tried to end his life before, Daphne?'

She nodded and blew her nose. 'Oh, yes. Several times. He used to get what we called "the blues" from quite a young age. And I didn't like to leave him when they came because it was like . . . it was like he couldn't hear you. Didn't matter what you said. So quite often I would call in sick just to stay with him and jolly him along, you know? Make his favourite sandwiches. Sit with him on the sofa. Anything, really, just to let him know I was there. I always think that's why I never got a promotion at work when all the other girls did. I had to keep taking time off, you see.'

'Depression can be very hard. And not just on the sufferer.'

'Was he on medication?'

'Oh, no. But, then, it wasn't . . . you know . . . chemical.'

'Are you sure? I mean depression was under-diagnosed back in –'

Daphne lifted her head. 'He was a homosexual.' She said the word with its five full, clearly defined syllables, and looked directly at us, a little flushed, as if daring us to say anything in return. 'I've never told anyone that. But he was a homosexual, and I think he was sad because he was a homosexual. And he was ever such a good man and he wouldn't have wanted to hurt me, so he wouldn't have . . . you know . . . gone off and done things. He would have felt I'd be shamed.'

'What makes you think he was gay, Daphne?'

'I found things when I was looking for one of his ties. Those magazines. Men doing things to other men. In his drawer. I don't suppose you would have those magazines if you weren't.'

Fred stiffened slightly. 'Certainly not,' he said.

'I never mentioned them,' said Daphne. 'I just tucked them back where I found them. But it all started to click into place. He was never very keen on that side of things. But I thought I was lucky, you see, because I wasn't either. It's the nuns. They made you feel dirty for just about everything. So when I married a nice man who wasn't jumping on top of me every five minutes, I thought I was the luckiest woman on earth. I mean, I would have liked children. That would have been nice. But . . .' she sighed '. . . we never really talked about such things. You didn't in those days. Now I wish we had. Looking back, I keep thinking, What a waste.'

'You think if you'd talked honestly, it might have made a difference?'

'Well, times are different now, aren't they? It's fine to be homosexual. My dry cleaner is and he talks about his boyfriend to every Tom, Dick and Harry that walks in. I would have been sad to lose my husband, but if he was unhappy because of being trapped, then I would have let him go. I would have done. I never wanted to trap anyone. I only wanted him to be a bit happier.'

Her face crumpled, and I put my arm around her. Her hair smelt of lacquer and lamb stew.

'There, there, old girl,' said Fred, and stood up to pat her on the shoulder a little awkwardly. 'I'm sure he knew you only ever wanted the best for him.'

'Do you think so, Fred?' Her voice was tremulous.

Fred nodded firmly. 'Oh, yes. And you're quite right. Things were different back then. You're not to blame.'

'You've been very brave sharing that story, Daphne. Thank you.' Marc smiled sympathetically. 'And I have huge admiration for you picking yourself up and moving on. Sometimes just getting through each day requires almost superhuman strength.'

When I looked down, Daphne was holding my hand. I felt her plump fingers intertwine with mine. I squeezed hers back. And before I could think I began to talk. 'I've done something I wish I could change.'

Half a dozen faces turned to me. 'I met Will's daughter. She sort of landed in my life out of the blue and I thought that was going to be my way of feeling better about his death but instead I just feel like –'

They were staring. Fred was pulling a face.

'What?'

'Who's Will?' said Fred.

'You said his name was Bill.'

I slumped a little in my chair. 'Will is Bill. I felt weird about using his real name before.' There was a general release of breath around the room.

Daphne patted my hand. 'Don't worry, dear. It's just a name. Our last group we had a woman who invented the whole thing. Said she had a child died from leukaemia. Turned out she didn't even have a goldfish.'

'It's okay, Louisa. You can talk to us.' Marc gave me his Special Empathetic Gaze. I gave him a small smile back, just to show him I had received and understood. And that Will was not a goldfish. *What the hell?* I thought. My life is no more mixed up than any of theirs.

So I told them about Lily turning up and how I had thought I could fix her and bring about a reunion that would make everyone happy, and how I now felt stupid for my naivety. 'I feel like I've let Will – everyone – down again,' I said. 'And now she's gone and I keep asking myself what I could have done differently, but the real truth is I couldn't cope. I wasn't strong enough to take charge of it all and make it better.'

'But your things! Your precious things got stolen!'

Daphne's other plump, damp hand clamped onto mine. 'You had every right to be angry!'

'Just because she doesn't have a father doesn't give her the excuse to behave like a brat,' said Sunil.

'I think you were very nice to let her stay in the first place. I'm not sure I would,' said Daphne.

'What do you think her father might have done differently, Louisa?' Marc poured himself another cup of coffee.

I wished, suddenly, that we had something stronger. 'I don't know,' I said. 'But he had this way of taking charge. Even when he couldn't move his arms and legs you got the feeling he was capable. He would have stopped her doing stupid stuff. He would have got her straightened out somehow.'

'Are you sure you're not idealizing him? We do idealization in week eight,' said Fred. 'I keep turning Jilly into a saint, don't I, Marc? I forget that she used to leave her hold-ups hanging over the shower rail and it drove me absolutely potty.'

'Her father might not have been able to do anything to help her at all. You have no idea. They might have loathed each other.'

'She sounds like a complicated young woman,' said Marc. 'And it's possible that you gave her as many chances as you could. But . . . sometimes, Louisa, moving on means we do have to protect ourselves. And perhaps you understood that, deep down. If Lily simply brought chaos and negativity into your life, then for now, it's possible you did the only thing you could.'

'Oh, yes.' There were nods around the circle. 'Be kind to yourself. You're only human.' They were so sweet, smiling at me reassuringly, wanting me to feel better.

I almost believed them.

On Tuesday I asked Vera if she could give me ten minutes (I muttered vague things about Women's Troubles and she nodded, as if to say Women's Lives Were Nothing but Trouble, and murmured that she would tell me later about her fibroids). I ran to the quietest Ladies loo – the only place I could be sure Richard wouldn't see me – with my laptop in my bag. I threw a shirt over the top of my uniform, balanced the laptop near the basins and hooked into the thirty minutes' free airport Wi-Fi, positioning myself carefully in front of the screen. Mr Gopnik's Skype call came in dead on five o'clock, just as I whipped off my ringlets Irish-dancing-girl wig.

Even if I had seen nothing else of Leonard Gopnik than his pixellated face, I could have told you he was rich. He had beautifully cut salt-and-pepper hair, and gazed out of the small screen with natural authority, and spoke without wasting a word. Well, there was that and the gilt-framed old master on the wall behind him.

He asked nothing about my school record, my qualifications, my CV or why I was conducting an interview beside a hand-dryer. He looked down at some papers, then asked about my relationship with the Traynors.

'Good! I mean, I'm sure they would provide a reference. I've seen both of them recently, for one reason or another. We get on well, despite the – the circumstances of . . .'

'The circumstances of the end of your employment.' His voice was low, decisive. 'Yes, Nathan has explained a lot about that situation. Quite a thing to be involved in.'

'Yes. It was,' I said, after a short, awkward silence. 'But I felt privileged. To be part of Will's life.'

He registered this. 'What have you been doing since?'

'Um, well, I travelled a bit, Europe mostly, which was . . . interesting. It's good to travel. And get a perspective. Obviously.' I tried to smile. 'And I'm now working at an airport but it's not really –' As I spoke, the door opened behind me and a woman walked in, pulling a wheelie case. I shifted my computer, hoping he couldn't hear the sound of her entering the cubicle. 'It's not really what I want to be doing long term.' *Please don't wee noisily*, I begged her silently.

He asked me a few questions about my current responsibilities, and salary level. I tried to ignore the sound of flushing, and kept my gaze straight ahead, ignoring the woman who emerged.

'And what do you want –' As Mr Gopnik began to speak, she reached past me and started up the hand-dryer, which let out a deafening roar beside me. He frowned.

'Hold on one moment, please, Mr Gopnik.' I put my thumb over what I hoped was the microphone. 'I'm sorry,' I shouted at the woman. 'You can't use that. It's . . . broken.'

She turned towards me, rubbing perfectly manicured fingers, then back to the machine. 'No, it's not. Where's the out-of-order sign, then?'

'Burned off. Suddenly. Awful, dangerous thing.'

She fixed me, then the hand-dryer, with a suspicious look, removed her hands from under it, took her case and walked out. I wedged the chair against the door to stop anyone else coming in, shifting my laptop again so that Mr Gopnik could see me. 'I'm so sorry. I'm having to do this at work and it's a little . . .'

He was studying his paperwork. 'Nathan tells me you had an accident recently.'

I swallowed. 'I did. But I'm much better. I'm completely fine. Well, fine except I walk with a slight limp.'

'Happens to the best of us,' he said, with a small smile. I smiled back. Someone tried the door. I moved so that my weight was against it.

'So what was the hardest part?' Mr Gopnik said.

'I'm sorry?'

'Of working for William Traynor. It sounds like quite a challenge.'

I hesitated. The room was suddenly very quiet. 'Letting him go.' I said. And found myself unexpectedly biting back tears.

Leonard Gopnik gazed at me from several thousand miles away. I fought the urge to wipe my eyes. 'My secretary will be in touch, Miss Clark. Thank you for your time.' And then, with a nod, his face stilled and the screen went blank and I was left staring at it, contemplating the fact that I had blown it, yet again.

That night, on the way home, I decided not to think about the interview. Instead I repeated Marc's words in my head, like a mantra. I ran through the things that Lily had done, the uninvited guests, the theft, the drugs, the endless late nights, the borrowing of my things, and ran them through the prism of my group's counsel. Lily was chaos, disorder, a girl who took and gave nothing in return. She was young, and biologically related to Will, but that didn't mean I had to assume total responsibility for her or put up with the turmoil she left in her wake.

I felt a little better. I did. I reminded myself of something else Marc had said: that no journey out of grief was straightforward. There would be good days and bad days. Today was just a bad day, a kink in the road, to be traversed and survived.

I let myself into the flat, and dropped my bag, suddenly grateful for the small pleasure of a home that was just as I'd left it. I would allow some time to pass, I told myself, and then I would text her, and I would make sure our future visits were structured. I would focus my energies on getting a new job. I would think about myself for a change. I would let myself heal. I had to stop at that point because I was a little worried that I was starting to sound like Tanya Houghton-Miller.

I glanced at the fire escape. Step one would be getting back up on that stupid roof. I would climb up there by myself without having a panic attack and I would sit there for a full half-hour, breathe the air and stop letting a part of my own home have such a ridiculous hold on my imagination.

I took off my uniform and put on shorts and, just for confidence, Will's lightweight cashmere jumper, the one I had taken from his house after he died, comforted by the soft feel of it against my skin. I walked down the corridor and opened the window wide. It was just two short flights of iron steps. And then I would be up there.

'Nothing will happen,' I said aloud, and took a deep breath. My legs felt curiously hollow as I climbed out onto the fire escape, but I told myself firmly that it was just a feeling, the echo of an old anxiety. I could overcome it, just as I would overcome everything else. I heard Will's voice in my ear.

*C'mon, Clark. One step at a time.*

I grasped the rails tightly with both hands, and began to make my way up. I didn't look down. I didn't let myself think about what height I was at, or how the faint breeze recalled an earlier time gone wrong, or the recurring pain in my hip that never seemed to go away. I thought about Sam, and the fury that invoked made me push on. I didn't have to be the victim, the person to whom things just *happened*.

I told myself these things and made it up the second flight of steps as my legs began to shake. I climbed inelegantly over the low wall, afraid that they would give way under me, and dropped onto the roof on my hands and knees. I felt weak and clammy. I stayed on all fours, my eyes shut, while I let myself absorb the fact that I was on the roof. I had made it. I was in control of my destiny. I would stay there for as long as it took to feel normal.

I sat back on my heels, reaching for the solidity of the wall around me, and leaned back, taking a long, deep breath. It felt okay. Nothing was moving. I had done it. And then I opened my eyes and my breath stopped in my chest.

The rooftop was a riot of bloom. The dead pots I had neglected for months were filled with scarlet and purple flowers, spilling over the edges, like little fountains of colour. Two new planters mushroomed with clouds of tiny blue petals, and a Japanese maple sat in an ornamental pot beside one of the benches, its leaves shivering delicately in the breeze.

In the sunny corner by the south wall two grow-bags sat by the water tank, with little red cherry tomatoes dangling from their stalks, and another lay on the asphalt with small frilly green leaves emerging from the centre. I began to walk slowly towards them, breathing in the scent of jasmine, then stopped and sat down, my hand grasping the iron bench. I sank onto a cushion that I recognized from my living room.

I stared in disbelief at the little oasis of calm and beauty that had been created from my barren rooftop. I remembered Lily snapping the dead twig from a pot and informing me in all seriousness that it was a crime to let your plants die, and her casual observation in Mrs Traynor's garden, 'David Austin roses.' And then I remembered little unexplained bits of soil in my hallway.

And I sank my head into my hands.

# Chapter Seventeen

I texted Lily twice. The first time was to thank her for what she had done to my rooftop. *It's so gorgeous. I wish you had told me.* A day later, I texted to say I was sorry that things had become so tricky between us, and that if she ever wanted to talk more about Will, I would do my best to answer any questions. I added that I hoped she would go and see Mr Traynor and the new baby, as I knew as well as most that it was important to stay in touch with your family.

She didn't reply. I wasn't entirely surprised.

For the next two days I found myself returning to the rooftop, like someone worrying a loose tooth. I watered the plants, feeling a creeping, residual guilt. I walked around the glowing blooms, imagining her stolen hours up there, how she must have carried bags of compost and terracotta pots up the fire escape in the hours I was at work. But every time I thought back to how we had been together, I still went around in circles. What could I have done? I couldn't make the Traynors accept her in the way she needed to be accepted. I couldn't make her happier. And the one person who might have been able to was gone.

There was a motorbike parked outside my block. I locked the car and limped across the road to get a carton of milk after my shift, exhausted. It was spitting, and I put my head down against the rain. When I looked up, I saw a familiar uniform standing in the entrance to my block, and my heart lurched.

I walked back across the road straight past him, fumbling in my bag for my keys. Why did fingers always turn into cocktail sausages at moments of stress?

'Louisa.'

The keys refused to appear. I riffled through my bag a second time, dropping a comb, bits of tissue, loose change, and cursing. I patted my pockets, trying to work out where they might be.

'Louisa.'

Then, with a sickening drop of my stomach, I remembered where they were: in the pocket of the jeans I had changed out of just before leaving for work. Oh, *great*.

'Really? You're just going to ignore me? This is how we're doing this?'

I took a deep breath, and turned to him, straightening my shoulders a little. 'Sam.'

He looked tired too, his chin greyed with stubble. Probably just off a shift. It was unwise to notice these things. I focused on a point a little left of his shoulder.

'Can we talk?'

'I'm not sure there's any point.'

'No point?'

'I got the message, okay? I'm not even sure why you're here.'

'I'm here because I've just finished a crappy sixteen hour shift and I dropped Donna off up the road and I thought I might as well try to see you and work out what happened with us. Because I sure as hell don't have a clue.'

'Really?'

'Really.'

We glared at each other. Why had I not seen before how abrasive he was? How unpleasant. I couldn't understand how I had been so blinded by lust for this man when every part of me now wanted to walk away from him. I made one last futile search for my keys and fought the urge to kick the door.

'So, are you at least going to give me a clue? I'm tired, Louisa, and I don't like playing games.'

'*You* don't like playing games.' The words emerged in a bitter little laugh.

He took a breath. 'Okay. One thing. One thing and I'll go. I just want to know why you won't return my calls.'

I looked at him in disbelief. 'Because I'm many things, but I'm not a complete idiot. I mean I must have been – I saw the warning signs, and I ignored them – but, basically, I haven't returned your calls because you're an utter, utter knob. Okay?'

I stooped to pick up my things that had fallen on the ground, feeling my whole body heat rapidly, as if my internal thermostat had suddenly gone haywire. 'Oh, you're so good, you know? So bloody good. If it weren't all so sick and pathetic I'd actually be quite impressed by you.' I straightened up, zipping my bag. '*Look at Sam, the good father.* So *caring*, so *intuitive*. And yet what's really going on? You're so busy shagging your way through half of London you don't even notice that your own son is unhappy.'

'My son.'

'Yes! Because we actually listen to him, you see. I mean, we're not meant to tell outsiders what goes on in the group. And he won't tell you because he's a teenager. But he's miserable, not just for the loss of his mum but because you're busy swallowing your own grief by having an entire army of women traipse in and out of your bed.'

I was shouting now, my words tumbling over each other, my hands waving. I could see Samir and his cousin staring at me through the window of the shop. I didn't care. This might be the last time I ever got to say my piece.

'And, yes, yes, I know, I was stupid enough to be one of those women. So for him, and from me, you're a knob. And that's why I don't want to talk to you right now. Or ever, actually.'

He rubbed at his hair. 'Are we still talking about Jake?'

'Of course I'm talking about Jake. How many other sons have you got?'

'Jake isn't my son.'

I stared at him.

'Jake is my sister's son. Was,' he corrected himself. 'He's my nephew.'

These words took several seconds to filter into a form I could understand. Sam was gazing at me intently, his brow furrowed as if he, too, were trying to keep up.

'But – but you pick him up. He lives with you.'

'I pick him up on Mondays because his dad works shifts. And he stays with me sometimes, yes. He doesn't live with me.'

'Jake's . . . not your son?'

'I don't have any children. That I'm aware of. Though the whole Lily thing does make you wonder.'

I pictured him hugging Jake, mentally rewound half a dozen conversations. 'But I saw him when we first met. And when you and I were talking he rolled his eyes, like . . .'

Sam lowered his head.

'Oh, God,' I said. My hand went to my mouth. 'Those women . . .'

'Not mine.'

We stood there in the middle of the street. Samir was now in the doorway, watching. He had been joined by another of his cousins. To our left everyone at the bus stop turned away when they realized we knew they'd been watching us. Sam nodded at the door behind me. 'Do you think we could talk about this inside?'

'Yes. Yes. Oh. No, I can't,' I said. 'I seem to have locked myself out.'

'Spare key?'

'In the flat.'

He ran a hand over his face, then checked his watch. He was clearly drained, weary to the bone. I took a step backwards into the doorway. 'Look – go home and get some rest. We'll talk tomorrow. I'm sorry.'

The rain suddenly grew heavy, a summer dump, creating torrents in gutters and flooding the street. Across the road Samir and his cousins ducked back inside.

Sam sighed. He looked up at the skies and then straight at me. 'Hang on.'

Sam took a large screwdriver he had borrowed from Samir and followed me up the fire escape. Twice I slipped on the wet metal and his hand reached out to steady me. When it did, something hot and unexpected shot through me. When we reached my floor, he pushed the screwdriver deep into the hall window frame and started to lever upwards. It gave gratifyingly swiftly.

'There.' He wrenched it upwards, supporting it with one hand, and turned to me, motioning me through, his expression faintly disapproving. 'That was way too easy for a single girl living in this area.'

'You look nothing like a single girl living in this area.'

'I'm serious.'

'I'm fine, Sam.'

'You don't see what I see. I want you to be safe.'

I tried to smile, but my knees were trembling, my palms slippery on the iron rail. I made to step past him and staggered slightly.

'You okay?'

I nodded. He took my arm and half lifted, half helped me climb clumsily into my flat. I slumped down on the carpet by the window, waiting to feel normal again. I hadn't slept properly for days and felt half dead, as if the fury and adrenalin that had sustained me had all leached away.

Sam climbed in and closed the window behind him, eyeing the broken lock on the top of the sash. The hall was dark, the thrumming of the rain muffled on the roof. As I watched, he rummaged around in his pocket until, among other detritus, he picked out a small nail. He took the screwdriver and used the handle to knock the nail in at an angle to stop anyone opening it from outside. Then he walked heavily over to where I was sitting, and held out a hand.

'Benefits of being a part-time housebuilder. There's always a nail somewhere. 'C'mon,' he said. 'If you sit there you'll never get up.'

His hair was flattened from the rain, his skin glistening in the hall light, as I let him pull me to my feet. I winced, and he saw.

'Hip?'

I nodded.

He sighed. 'I wish you'd talk to me.' The skin beneath his eyes was mauve with exhaustion. There were two long scratches on the back of his left hand. I wondered what had happened the previous night. He disappeared into the kitchen and I heard running water. When he came back he was holding two pills and a cup. 'I shouldn't really be giving you these. But they'll give you a pain-free night.'

I took them gratefully. He watched me as I swallowed them.

'Do you ever follow rules?'

'When I think they're sensible.' He took the cup from me. 'So are we good, Louisa Clark?'

I nodded.

He let out a long breath. 'I'll call you tomorrow.'

Afterwards, I wasn't sure what made me do it. My hand reached out and took his. I felt his fingers close slowly around mine. 'Don't go. It's late. And motorbikes are dangerous.'

I took the screwdriver from his other hand, and let it fall onto the carpet. He looked at me for the longest time, then slid a hand over his face. 'I don't think I'm good for much just now.'

'Then I promise not to use you for sexual gratification.' I kept my eyes on his. 'This time.'

His smile was slow to come, but when it did, everything fell away from me, as if I had been carrying a weight I hadn't known.

*You never know what will happen when you fall from a great height.*

He stepped over the screwdriver, and I led him silently towards my bedroom.

I lay in the dark in my little flat, my leg slung over the bulk of a sleeping man, his arm pinning me pleasurably beneath it, and gazed at his face.

*— Fatal cardiac arrest, motorbike accident, suicidal teenager and a gang-related stabbing on the Peabody Estate. Some shifts are just a bit . . .*

*— Sssh. It's okay. Sleep.*

He had barely managed to get his uniform off. He had stripped to his T-shirt and shorts, kissed me, then closed his eyes and collapsed into a dead slumber. I had wondered whether I should cook him something, or tidy the flat so that when he woke I might look like someone who actually had a handle on life. But instead I undressed to my underwear and slid in next to him. For these few moments I just wanted to be beside him, my bare skin against his T-shirt, my breath mingling with his. I lay listening to his breathing, marvelling at how someone could be so still. I studied the slight bump on the bridge of his nose, the variation in the shade of the bristles that shadowed his chin, the slight curl at the end of his dark, dark eyelashes. I ran through conversations we had had, putting them through a new filter, one that pitched him as a single man, an affectionate uncle, and I wanted to laugh with the idiocy of it all, and cringe at my mistake.

I touched his face twice, lightly, breathing in the scent of his skin, the faint tang of antibacterial soap, the primal sexual hint of male sweat, and the second time I did so I felt his hand tighten reflexively on my waist. I shifted onto my back and gazed out at the streetlights, feeling, for once, that I was not an alien in this city. And finally, I found myself drifting . . .

His eyes open on mine. A moment later he realizes where he is.

'Hey.'

A lurch into waking. The peculiar dreamlike state that suffuses the small hours. *He is in my bed. His leg against mine.* A smile, creeping across my face. 'Hey yourself.'

'What time is it?'

I swivel to catch the digital readout of my alarm. 'A quarter to five.' Time settles into order, the world, reluctantly, into something that makes sense. Outside, the sodium-lit dark of the street. The minicabs and night buses rumble past. Up here it is just him and me in the night and the warm bed and the sound of his breathing.

'I can't even remember getting here.' He looks off to the side, his face faintly lit by the streetlights, frowning. I watch as memories of the previous day land softly, a silent, mental *Oh. Right.*

His head turns. His mouth, inches from mine. His breath, warm and sweet. 'I missed you, Louisa Clark.'

I want to tell him then. I want to tell him that I don't know what I feel. I want him but I'm frightened to want him. I don't want my happiness to be entirely dependent on somebody else's, to be a hostage to fortunes I cannot control.

His eyes are on my face, reading me. 'Stop thinking,' he says.

He pulls me to him, and I relax. This man spends each day out here, on the bridge between life and death. He understands. 'You think too much.'

His hand slides down the side of my face. I turn towards him, an involuntary reflex, and put my lips against his palm. 'Just live?' I whisper.

He nods, and then he kisses me, long and slow and sweet, until my body arches and I am just need and want and longing.

His voice is low in my ear. My name, pulling me in. He makes it sound like something precious.


The next three days were a blurred mass of stolen nights and brief meetings. I missed Idealization Week in the Moving On Circle because he turned up at the flat just as I was leaving and we somehow ended up an urgent mess of arms and legs, waiting for my egg-timer to go off so that he could dress and race to pick Jake up on time. Twice he was waiting for me when I returned from my shift, and with his lips on my neck, his big hands on my hips, the indignities of the Shamrock and Clover were, if not forgotten, swept aside along with last night's empties.

I wanted to resist him, but I couldn't. I was giddy, diverted, sleepless. I got cystitis and didn't care. I hummed my way through work, flirted with the businessmen, and smiled cheerfully at Richard's complaints. My happiness offended my manager: I could see it in his chewed cheek, the way he sought ever more feeble misdemeanours for which to tell me off.

I cared about none of it. I sang in the shower, lay awake

dreaming. I wore my old dresses, my brightly coloured cardigans and satin pumps, and let myself be enclosed in a bubble of happiness, aware that bubbles only ever existed for so long before they popped anyway.

'I told Jake,' he said. He had half an hour's break, and he and Donna had stopped outside my flat with lunch before I went off for a late shift. I sat beside him in the front seat of the ambulance.

'You told him what?' He had made mozzarella, cherry tomato and basil sandwiches. The tomatoes, grown in his garden, burst in little explosions of flavour in my mouth. He was appalled at how I ate when I was alone.

'That you'd thought I was his dad. He laughed more than I've seen him laugh for months.'

'You didn't tell him I told you his dad cried after sex, right?'

'I knew a man who did that once,' said Donna. 'But he really sobbed. It got sort of embarrassing. The first time I thought I'd broken his penis.'

I turned to her, open-mouthed.

'It's a thing. Really. We've had a couple in the rig, haven't we?'

'We have. You'd be amazed at the coital injuries we see.' He nodded at my sandwich, which was still on my lap. 'I'll tell you when your mouth's not full.'

'Coital injuries. Great. Because there aren't enough things in life to worry about.'

His gaze slid sideways as he bit into his sandwich, so that I blushed. 'Trust me. I'd let you know.'

'Just so we're straight, my old mucker,' said Donna, offering up one of her ever-present energy drinks, 'I am so totally not going to be your first responder for that one.'

I liked being in the cab. Sam and Donna had the no-nonsense wry manner of those who had seen pretty much every human condition, and treated it, too. They were funny and dark, and I felt oddly at home wedged between them, as if my life, with all its strangeness, was actually pretty normal.

These were the things I learned in the space of several snatched lunch hours:

- Almost no men or women over the age of seventy would complain about their pain or their treatment, even if a limb were actually hanging off.
- Those same elderly men or women would almost always apologize for 'making a fuss'.
- That the term 'Patient PFO' was not scientific terminology but 'Patient Pissed and Fell Over'.
- Pregnant women rarely gave birth in the back of ambulances. (I was quite disappointed by that one.)
- That nobody used the term 'ambulance driver' any more. Especially not ambulance drivers.
- There would always be a handful of men who would answer, when asked to describe how much pain they were in out of ten, with 'eleven'.

But what came through most, when Sam arrived back after a long shift, was the bleakness: solitary pensioners; obese men glued to a television screen, too large even to try to get themselves up and down their own stairs; young mothers who spoke no English, confined to their flats with a million small children, unsure how to call for help when it was needed; and the depressed, the chronically ill, the unloved.

Some days, he said, it felt like a virus: you had to scrub the melancholy from your skin along with the scent of antiseptic. And then there were the suicides, the lives ended under trains or in silent bathrooms, their bodies often unnoticed for weeks or months until somebody remarked on the smell, or wondered why so-and-so's post was now spilling out of their pigeonhole.

'Do you ever get frightened?'

He lay, oversized, in my little bath. The water had turned faintly pink with the blood from a patient's gunshot wound that had leaked all over him. I was a little surprised at how swiftly I had got used to having a naked man in the vicinity. Especially one who could move by himself.

'You can't do this job if you're frightened,' he said simply.

He had been in the army before he'd joined the paramedics; it was not an unusual career arc. 'They like us because we don't scare easy, and we've seen it all. Mind you, some of those drunk kids scare me far more than the Taliban ever did.'

I sat on the loo seat beside him and stared at his body in the discoloured water. Even with his size and strength, I shivered.

'Hey,' he said, seeing something pass across my face, and reached out a hand to me. 'It's fine, really. I have a very good nose for trouble.' He closed his fingers around mine. 'It's not a great job for relationships, though. My last girlfriend couldn't cope with it. The hours. Nights. The mess.'

'The pink bathwater.'

'Yeah. Sorry about that. The showers weren't working at the station. I should really have gone home first.' He looked at me in a way that showed me there had been no chance of him going home first. He pulled the plug to let some of the water drain away, then turned on the taps for more.

'So who was she, your last girlfriend?' I kept my voice level. I was not going to be one of *those* women, even if he had turned out not to be one of those men.

'Iona. Travel agent. Sweet girl.'

'But you weren't in love with her.'

'Why do you say that?'

'Nobody ever says "sweet girl" about someone they were

in love with. It's like the whole "we'll still be friends" thing. It means you didn't feel enough.'

He was briefly amused. 'So what would I have said if I had been in love with her?'

'You would have looked very serious, and said, "Karen. Complete nightmare," or shut down and gone all "I don't want to talk about it."'

'You're probably right.' He thought for a bit. 'If I'm honest I didn't really want to feel much after my sister died. Being with Ellen for the last few months, helping look after her, kind of knocked me sideways.' He glanced at me. 'Cancer can be a pretty brutal way to go. Jake's dad fell apart. Some people do. So I figured they needed me there. If I'm honest, I probably only held it together myself because we couldn't all go to pieces.' We sat in silence for a moment. I couldn't tell if his eyes had gone a bit red from grief or soap.

'Anyway. So, yes. Probably not much of a boyfriend back then. So who was yours?' he said, when he finally turned back to me.

'Will.'

'Of course. Nobody since?'

'Nobody I want to talk about.' I shuddered.

'Everyone's allowed their own way back, Louisa. Don't beat yourself up about it.'

His skin was hot and wet, making it hard for me to hold on to his fingers. I released them, and he began to wash his hair. I sat and watched him, letting the mood lift, enjoying the bunched muscles in his shoulders, the gleam of his wet skin. I liked the way he washed his hair: vigorously, with a kind of matter-of-factness, shaking off the excess water like a dog.

'Oh. I had a job interview,' I said, when he finished. 'For a thing in New York.'

'New York.' He raised an eyebrow.

242

'I won't get it.'

'Shame. I've always wanted an excuse to go to New York.' He slid slowly under the water so that only his mouth remained. It broke into a slow smile. 'But you'd get to keep the pixie outfit, yes?'

I felt the mood shift. And, for no reason at all other than that he didn't expect it, I climbed fully clothed into the bath and kissed him as he laughed and spluttered, suddenly glad of his solidity in a world where it was so easy to fall.

I finally made an effort to sort out the flat. On my day off I bought an armchair, and a coffee-table, and a small framed print, which I hung near the television, and those things somehow conspired to suggest someone might actually live there. I bought new bedding and two cushions and hung up all my vintage clothes in the wardrobe so that opening it now revealed a riot of pattern and colour, instead of several pairs of cheap jeans and a too-short Lurex dress. I managed to turn my anonymous little flat into something that felt, if not quite like a home, vaguely welcoming.

By some beneficence of the shift-scheduling gods, Sam and I both had a day off. Eighteen uninterrupted hours in which he did not have to listen to a siren, and I did not have to listen to the sound of pan pipes or complaints about dry-roasted peanuts. Time spent with Sam, I noted, seemed to go twice as fast as the hours I spent alone. I had pondered the million things we could do together, then dismissed half of them as too 'couple-y'. I wondered whether our spending so much time together was wise.

I texted Lily one more time. *Lily, please get in touch. I know you're mad at me, but just call. Your garden is looking beautiful! I need you to show me how to look after it, and what to do with the tomato plants, which have got really tall (is this right?). Maybe after we could go out dancing? x* I pressed send and stared at the little screen just as the doorbell rang.

'Hey.' He filled my doorway, holding a toolbox in one hand and a bag of groceries in the other.

'Oh, my God,' I said. 'You're like the ultimate female fantasy.'

'Shelves,' he said, deadpan. 'You need shelves.'

'Oh, baby. Keep talking.'

'And home-cooked food.'

'That's it. I just came.'

He laughed and dropped the tools in the hallway and kissed me, and when we finally untangled ourselves, he walked through to the kitchen. 'I thought we could go to the pictures. You know one of the greatest benefits to shift-working is empty matinées, right?'

I checked my phone.

'But nothing with blood in it. I get a bit tired of blood.'

When I looked up he was watching me.

'What? Don't fancy it? Or is that going to stamp all over your plans for *Zombie Flesh Eaters Fifteen*? . . . What?'

I frowned, and dropped my hand to my side. 'I can't get hold of Lily.'

'I thought you said she'd gone home?'

'She did. But she won't take my calls. I think she's really upset with me.'

'Her friends stole your stuff. You're allowed to be the one who's upset.'

He started to pull things out of the bag, lettuces, tomatoes, avocados, eggs, herbs, stacking them neatly in my near-empty fridge. He looked up at me as I texted her again. 'Come on. She could have dropped her phone, left it in some club, or run out of credit. You know what teenagers are like. Or she's just throwing a massive strop. Sometimes you need to let them work it out of their system.'

I took his hand and shut the fridge door. 'I need to show you something.' His eyes lit up briefly. 'Not that, no, you bad man. That will have to wait till later.'

Sam stood on the rooftop and gazed around him at the flowers. 'And you had no idea?'

'None at all.'

He sat down heavily on the bench. I sat next to him and we both stared at the little garden.

'I feel awful,' I said. 'I basically accused her of destroying everything she went near. And all the time she was creating this.'

He stooped to feel the leaves on a tomato plant, then straightened, shaking his head. 'Okay. So we'll go talk to her.'

'Really?'

'Yeah. Lunch first. Then cinema. Then we'll turn up on her doorstep. That way she won't be able to avoid you.' He took my hand and raised it to his lips. 'Hey. Don't look so worried. The garden is good news. It shows that her head's not in a totally bad place.'

He released my hand and I squinted at him. 'How come you always make everything better?'

'I just don't like seeing you sad.'

I couldn't tell him that I wasn't sad when I was with him. I couldn't tell him that he made me so happy I was afraid of it. I thought of how I liked having his food in my fridge, how I glanced at my phone twenty times a day waiting for his messages, how I conjured his naked body in my imagination in the quiet minutes at work and then had to think very hard about floor polish or till receipts just to stop myself glowing.

*Slow down*, said a warning voice. *Don't get too close.*

His eyes softened. 'You have a sweet smile, Louisa Clark. It's one of the several hundred things I like about you.'

I let myself gaze back at him for a minute. *This man*, I thought. And then I slapped my hands heavily on my knees. 'C'mon,' I said briskly. 'Let's go watch a movie.'

The cinema was almost empty. We sat side by side at the back in a seat where someone had knocked out the armrest, and Sam fed me popcorn from a cardboard bucket the size of a dustbin, and I tried not to think about the weight of his hand resting on my bare leg, because when I did I frequently lost track of what was happening with the plot.

The film was an American comedy about two mismatched cops who find themselves mistaken for criminals. It wasn't very funny, but I laughed anyway. Sam's fingers appeared in front of me, bearing a bulbous knobble of salted popcorn and I took it, and another, then, as an afterthought, kept hold of his fingers between my teeth. He looked at me and shook his head, slowly.

I finished the popcorn and swallowed. 'Nobody will see,' I whispered.

He raised an eyebrow. 'I'm too old for this,' he murmured. But when I turned his face to mine in the hot, dark air, and started to kiss him, he dropped the popcorn and his hand slid slowly up my back.

And then my phone rang. There was a hiss of disapproval from the two people at the front. 'Sorry. Sorry, you two!' (Given there were only four of us in the cinema.) I scrambled off Sam's lap and answered. A number I didn't recognize.

'Louisa?'

It took me a second to register her voice.

'Just give me a minute.' I pulled a face at Sam, and made my way out.

'Sorry, Mrs Traynor. I just had to – Are you still there? Hello?'

The foyer was empty, the cordoned-off queue areas deserted, the frozen-drinks machine churning its coloured ice listlessly behind the counter.

'Oh, thank goodness. Louisa? I wondered if I could speak to Lily.'

I stood, with the phone pressed to my ear.

'I've been thinking about what happened the other week and I'm so sorry. I must have seemed . . .' She hesitated. 'Look, I was wondering if you thought she would agree to see me.'

'Mrs Traynor –'

'I'd like to explain to her. For the last year or so I've . . . well, I've not been myself. I've been on these tablets and they make me rather dim-witted. And I was so taken aback to find you on my doorstep, and then I simply couldn't believe what you both were telling me. It all seemed so unlikely. But I . . . Well, I've spoken to Steven and he confirmed the whole thing and I've been sitting here for days and digesting it all and I just think . . . Will had a *daughter. I have a granddaughter.* I keep saying the words. Sometimes I think I dreamed it.'

I listened to the uncharacteristic flurry of her words. 'I know,' I said. 'I felt like that, too.'

'I can't stop thinking about her. I do so want to meet her properly. Do you think she'd agree to see me again?'

'Mrs Traynor, she's not staying with me any more. But yes.' I ran my fingers through my hair. 'Yes, of course I'll ask her.'

I couldn't focus on the rest of the film. In the end, perhaps realizing that I was simply staring at a moving screen, Sam suggested we leave. We stood in the car park by his bike and I told him what she'd said.

'There, see?' he said, as if I had done something to be proud of. 'Let's go.'

*

He waited on the bike across the road as I knocked on the door. I lifted my chin, determined that this time I would not let Tanya Houghton-Miller intimidate me. I glanced back, and Sam nodded encouragingly.

The door opened. Tanya was dressed in a chocolate linen dress and Grecian sandals. She looked me up and down as she had when we'd first met, as if my own wardrobe had failed some invisible test. (This was a little annoying as I was wearing my favourite checked cotton pinafore dress.) Her smile stayed on her lips for just a nanosecond, then fell away. 'Louisa.'

'Sorry to turn up unannounced, Mrs Houghton-Miller.'

'Has something happened?'

I blinked. 'Well, yes, actually.' I pushed my hair from the side of my face. 'I've had a call from Mrs Traynor, Will's mother. I'm sorry to bother you with this, but she'd really like to get in contact with Lily, and as she's not picking up her phone, I wondered if you'd mind asking her to call me?'

Tanya gazed at me from under perfectly plucked brows.

I kept my face neutral. 'Or maybe we could have a quick chat with her.'

There was a short silence. 'Why would you think *I* would ask her?'

I took a breath, picking my words carefully. 'I know you have strong feelings about the Traynor family, but I do think it would be in Lily's interests. I don't know if she told you but they had a rather difficult first meeting the other week and Mrs Traynor would really like the chance to start again.'

'She can do what she wants, Louisa. But I don't know why you're expecting me to get involved.'

I tried to keep my voice polite. 'Um . . . because you're her mother?'

'Whom she hasn't bothered to contact in more than a week.'

I stood very still. Something cold and hard settled in my stomach. 'What did you just say?'

'Lily. Hasn't bothered to contact me. I thought at least she might come and say hello after we got back from holiday but, no, that's plainly beyond her. Suiting herself, as usual.' She extended a hand to examine her fingernails.

'Mrs Houghton-Miller, she was meant to be with you.'

'What?'

'Lily. Was moving back in with you. When you got home from your holiday. She left my flat . . . ten days ago.'

# Chapter Eighteen

We stood in Tanya Houghton-Miller's immaculate kitchen and I stared at her shiny coffee machine with 108 knobs, which had probably cost more than my car, and ran through the previous week's events for the umpteenth time.

'It was around half twelve. I gave her twenty pounds for a taxi and asked her to leave her key. I just assumed she'd come home.' I felt sick. I walked the length of the breakfast bar and back again, my brain racing. 'I should have checked. But she tended to come and go as she pleased. And we . . . well, we'd had a bit of a row.'

Sam stood by the door, rubbing his brow. 'And neither of you has heard anything from her since.'

'I've texted her four or five times,' I said. 'I just assumed she was still angry with me.'

Tanya hadn't offered us coffee. She strolled to the stairwell, peered upstairs, then glanced at her watch, as if she were waiting for us to go. She did not look like a parent who had just discovered her child was missing. Periodically I heard the dull roar of a vacuum-cleaner.

'Mrs Houghton-Miller, has anyone here heard from her at all? Can you tell from your phone whether she's even read her texts?'

'I told you,' she said. Her voice was strangely calm. 'I told you this was what she was like. But you wouldn't listen.'

'I think we –'

She lifted a hand, stopping Sam. 'This is not the first time. Oh, no. She disappeared for days before, when she was meant to be at boarding-school. I blame them, of course. They were meant to know exactly where she was at all times. They only rang us when she'd been gone forty-eight hours and then we had to get the police involved. Apparently one of the girls in her dorm had lied for her. Why they couldn't tell who was and who wasn't there is completely beyond me, especially given the ridiculous fees we pay. Francis was all for suing them. He was called out of his annual board meeting to deal with it. It was a huge embarrassment.'

Upstairs there was a crash and somebody started to cry. Tanya walked to the kitchen door. 'Lena! Take them out to the park, for goodness' sake!' She came back into the kitchen. 'You know she gets drunk. She takes drugs. She stole my Mappin & Webb diamond earrings. She won't admit it, but she did. They were worth thousands. I have no idea what she did with them. She's taken a digital camera, too.'

I thought back to my missing jewellery and something in me tightened uncomfortably.

'So, yes. This is all rather predictable. I did tell you. And now, if you'll excuse me, I really have to go and sort the boys out. They're having a difficult day.'

'But you'll call the police, yes? She's sixteen years old and it's been almost ten days.'

'They won't be interested. Not once they know who it is.' Tanya held up a slender finger. 'Expelled from two schools for truanting. Cautioned for possession of a class-A drug. Drunk and disorderly. Shoplifting. What's the phrase? My daughter has "form". To be perfectly frank, even if the police do find her and bring her back here, she'll simply up and go again when it suits her.'

A wire had tightened across my chest, constricting my breath. Where would she have gone? Was that boy, the one who hung around outside my flat, involved? The nightclubbers who had been with Lily that drunken night? How had I been so distracted?

'Let's call them regardless. She's still very young.'

'No. I do not want the police involved. Francis is having a very tricky time at work right now. He's fighting to retain his place on the board. If they get wind that he's involved in some sort of police business that will be it.'

Sam's jaw tightened. He took a moment before he spoke. 'Mrs Houghton-Miller, your daughter is vulnerable. I really think it's time to get someone else involved.'

'If you call them I'll simply explain to them what I've just told you.'

'Mrs Houghton-Miller –'

'How many times have you met her, Mr Fielding?' She leaned back against the cooker. 'You know her better than I do, do you? You've been kept up nights waiting for her to come home? You've lost sleep? Had to explain her behaviour to teachers and police officers? Apologize to shop assistants for things she's stolen? Bail out her credit card?'

'Some of the most chaotic kids are those most at risk.'

'My daughter is a talented manipulator. She will be with one of her friends. Just as she has been before. I will guarantee that within the next day or two Lily will turn up here, drunk and screeching in the middle of the night, or knocking at Louisa's door, or begging for money, and you will probably have reason to wish she never had. Someone will let her in and she'll be sorry and contrite and terribly sad, and then a few days later, she'll bring a bunch of friends home or steal something. And the whole sorry cycle will revolve again.'

She pushed her golden hair back from her face. She and Sam stared at each other. 'I've had to undergo counselling to cope with the chaos my daughter has brought into my

252

life, Mr Fielding. It's hard enough coping with her brothers and their . . . behavioural difficulties. But one of the things you learn in therapy is that there comes a point when you have to take care of yourself. Lily is old enough to make her own decisions –'

'She's a child,' I said.

'Oh, yes – that's right. A child *you* turned out of your apartment some time after midnight.' Tanya Houghton-Miller held my gaze with the complacency of someone who had just been proven right. 'Not everything is black and white. Much as we would like it to be.'

'You're not even worried, are you?' I said.

She held my gaze. 'No, frankly. I've been here too many times before.' I made to speak again but she was ahead of me. 'Quite the saviour complex, haven't you, Louisa? Well, my daughter doesn't need saving. And if she did, I wouldn't be hugely convinced by your record so far.'

Sam's arm was around me even before I was able to take a breath. My retort formed, toxic, in my mouth, but she had already turned away. 'C'mon,' he said, propelling me out into the hallway. 'Let's go.'

We drove around the West End for several hours, slowing to peer at the groups of catcalling, staggering girls, and, more soberly, at the rough sleepers, then parked up and walked side by side along the dark archways under bridges. We put our heads around the doors of nightclubs, asking if anyone had seen the girl in the photographs on my mobile phone. We went to the club where she had taken me dancing, and to a couple more that Sam said were notorious haunts for under-age drinkers. We passed bus stops and fast-food joints, and the further we went the more I thought how ridiculous it was to try to find her among the thousands milling around the humming streets of central London. She could have been anywhere. She seemed to be everywhere. I texted her again, twice, to tell her we were urgently looking for her, and when we got back to my flat Sam rang various hospitals just to be sure she hadn't been admitted.

Finally we sat on my little sofa and ate some toast, he made me a cup of tea and we sat in silence for a bit.

'I feel like the worst parent in the world. And I'm not even a parent.'

He leaned forward, his elbows on his knees. 'You can't blame yourself.'

'Yes, I can. What kind of person turfs a sixteen-year-old out of their flat in the small hours without checking where she's actually going?' I closed my eyes. 'I mean, just because she's disappeared before doesn't mean she'll be okay now, does it? She'll be like one of those teenage runaways who disappear and nobody ever hears of them again until some dog out walking digs up their bones in the woods.'

'Louisa.'

'I should have been stronger. I should have understood her better. I should have thought harder about how young she is. Was. Oh, God, if something's happened I'll never forgive myself. And out there right now some innocent dog-walker has no idea that he's about to have his life ruined –'

'Louisa.' Sam put his hand on my leg. 'Stop. You're going round in circles. Irritating as she is, it's entirely possible Tanya Houghton-Miller's right and Lily will coast in or ring your bell in about three hours' time and we'll all feel like fools and forget what's happened until it all starts again.'

'But why won't she answer her phone? She must know I'm worried.'

'Perhaps that's why she's ignoring you.' He gave me a wry look. 'She may be enjoying making you sweat a little. Look, there's not much more we can do tonight. And I've got to go. I have an early shift.' He cleared away the plates and put them in the sink, leaning back against the kitchen cabinets.

'Sorry,' I said. 'Not exactly the most fun start to a relationship.'

He lowered his chin. 'This is a relationship now?'

I felt myself colour. 'Well, I didn't mean –'

'I'm kidding.' He reached out a hand and pulled me to him. 'I quite enjoy your determined attempts to convince me you're basically just using me for sex.'

He smelt good. Even when he smelt faintly of anaesthetic, he smelt good. He kissed the top of my head. 'We'll find her,' he said, as he left.

After he'd gone, I climbed up onto the roof. I sat in the dark, inhaling the scent of the jasmine she'd trained up the edge of the water tank, and ran my hand softly over the tiny purple heads of the aubretia that tumbled over the terracotta planters. I looked over the parapet, scanned the winking streets of the city and my legs didn't even tremble. I texted her again, then got ready for bed, feeling the silence of the flat close in around me.

I checked my phone for the millionth time, and then my email, just in case. Nothing. But there was one from Nathan:

Congratulations! Old man Gopnik told me this morning he's going to offer you the job! See you in NY, mate!

# Chapter Nineteen

*Lily*

Peter is waiting again. Out of the window, she sees him standing against his car. He spots her, gestures up and mouths, 'You owe me.'

Lily opens the window, glances across the road to where Samir is putting out a fresh box of oranges. 'Leave me alone, Peter.'

'You know what'll happen . . .'

'I've given you enough. Just leave me alone, okay?'

'Bad move, Lily.' He raises an eyebrow. He waits just long enough for her to feel uncomfortable. Lou will be home in half an hour. He hangs around so often she's pretty sure he knows this. Eventually he climbs back into his car, and pulls out onto the main road without looking. As he drives off he holds his phone out of the driver's window. A message: *Bad move, Lily.*

Spin the bottle. Such an innocent-sounding game. It had been her and four girls from her school and they had come up to London on an exeat. They had stolen lipsticks from Boots and bought too-short skirts in Top Shop and got into nightclubs for free because they were young and cute and doormen didn't ask too many questions if there were five of you and you were young and cute, and inside, over rum and Cokes, they had met Peter and his friends.

They had ended up in someone's flat in Marylebone at

two a.m. She couldn't entirely remember how they had got there. Everyone was sitting in a circle, smoking and drinking. She had said yes to everything that was offered her. Rihanna on the music system. A blue beanbag that smelt of Febreze. Nicole had been ill in the bathroom, the idiot. Time had slipped; two thirty, three seventeen, four . . . She lost track. Then someone had suggested Truth or Dare.

The bottle spun, careered into an ashtray, tipping butts and ash onto the carpet. Someone's truth, the girl she didn't know: on holiday the previous year she had engaged in phone sex with her ex-boyfriend while her grandmother slept in the twin bed beside her. The others reeled in fake horror. Lily had laughed.

'Niche,' said someone.

Peter had watched her the whole time. She had been flattered at first: he was the best-looking boy there by miles. A man, even. When he looked at her she refused to drop her eyes. She wasn't going to be like the other girls.

'Spin!'

She had shrugged when it pointed to her. 'Dare,' she had said. 'Always dare.'

'Lily never says no to anything,' said Jemima. Now she wonders whether there was something in the way she had looked at Peter when she said it.

'Okay. You know what that means.'

'Seriously?'

'You can't do that!' Pippa was holding her hands to her face in the way she did when she was being dramatic.

'Truth, then.'

'Nah. I hate truth.' So what? She knew these boys would be chicken. She stood, nonchalantly. 'Where. Here?'

'Oh, my God, Lily.'

'Spin the bottle,' said one of the boys.

It hadn't occurred to her to be nervous. She was a bit woozy and, anyway, she quite liked standing there, unbothered, while the other girls clapped and squealed and acted like idiots. They were such fakes. The same girls who would whack anyone on the hockey pitch and talk about politics and what careers in law and marine biology they were aiming for became stupid and giggly and girly in the presence of boys, flicking their hair and doing their lipstick, like they had spontaneously filleted out the interesting parts of themselves.

'Peter . . .'

'Oh, my God. Pete, mate. It's you.'

The boys, all catcalling and crowing to hide their disappointment, or perhaps relief, that it wasn't them. Peter, climbing to his feet, his narrow cat's eyes meeting hers. Different from the others: his accent spoke of somewhere tougher.

'Here?'

She shrugged. 'I don't mind.'

'Next door.' He gestured towards the bedroom.

She stepped neatly over the girls' legs as they walked through to the next room. One of the girls grabbed at her ankle, telling her not to, and she shook her off. She walked with a faint swagger, feeling their eyes on her as she left. *Dare. Always dare.*

Peter closed the door behind him and she glanced around her. The bed was rumpled, a horrid patterned duvet that you could tell from five yards hadn't been washed in ages, and left a faint musty trace in the atmosphere. There was a pile of dirty laundry in the corner, a full ashtray by the bed. The room fell silent, the voices outside temporarily stilled.

She lifted her chin. Pushed her hair back from her face. 'You really want to do this?' she said.

He smiled then, a slow, mocking smile. 'I knew you'd back out.'

'Who says I'm backing out?'

But she didn't want to do it. She didn't see his handsome features any more, just the cold glitter in his eyes, the unpleasant twist to his mouth. He put his hands on his zipper.

They stood there for a minute.

'It's fine if you don't want to do it. We'll go outside and say you're chicken.'

'I never said I wouldn't do it.'

'So what *are* you saying?'

She can't think. A low buzzing has started up in the back of her head. She wishes she hadn't come in here.

He stifles a theatrical yawn. 'Getting bored, Lily.'

A frantic knocking on the door. Jemima's voice. 'Lily – you don't have to do it. C'mon. We can go home now.'

'You don't *have* to do it, Lily.' His voice is an imitation, mocking.

A calculation. What's the worst that will happen – two minutes, at worst? Two minutes out of her life. She will not be a chicken. She will show him. She will show them all.

He is holding a bottle of Jack Daniel's loosely in one hand. She takes it from him, opens it and swigs from it twice, her eyes locked on his. Then she hands it back and reaches for his belt.

*Pictures or it didn't happen.*

She hears the boy's catcalling voice through the thumping in her ears, through the pain in her scalp as he grips her hair too tight. It is too late, by then. Way too late.

She hears the camera-phone click just as she looks up.

One pair of earrings. Fifty pounds in cash. One hundred. Weeks later and the demands keep coming. He sends her texts: *I wonder what would happen if I put this on Facebook?*

She wants to cry when she sees the picture. He sends it to

her again and again: her face, her eyes bloodshot, smudged with mascara. That thing in her mouth. When Louisa comes home she has to stuff the phone under the sofa cushions. It has become radioactive, a toxic thing she has to keep close.

*I wonder what your friends would think.*

The other girls don't talk to her afterwards. They know what she did because Peter flashed the picture to everyone as soon as they walked back into the party, ostentatiously adjusting his zipper, long after he had to. She had to pretend she didn't care. The girls stared at her and then looked away and she had known as soon as their eyes met hers that their tales of BJs and sex with unseen boyfriends had been fiction. They were fakes. They had lied about everything.

Nobody thought she was brave. Nobody admired her for not being chicken. She was just Lily, the slag, a girl with a cock in her mouth. It made her stomach go into knots even to think about it. She had swigged more Jack Daniel's and told them all to go to hell.

*Meet me at McDonald's Tottenham Court Road.*

By then her mother had changed the locks to her house. She couldn't take money from her purse any more. They had blocked her access to her savings account.

*I haven't got anything else.*

*Do you think I'm a mug, Little Rich Girl?*

Her mother had never liked the Mappin & Webb earrings. Lily had hoped she wouldn't even notice they were gone. She had made fake cooing faces at Fuckface Francis when he gave them to her, but she had muttered afterwards that she really didn't understand why he'd bought her heart-shaped diamonds when everybody knew they were common, and a pendant shape was far better against her bone structure.

Peter had looked at the glittering earrings as if she had handed him small change, then tucked them into his pocket.

He had been eating a Big Mac and there was mayonnaise in the corner of his mouth. She felt nauseous every time she saw him.

'Want to come and meet my mates?'

'No.'

'Want a drink?'

She shook her head. 'That's it. That's the last thing. Those earrings are worth thousands.'

He had pulled a face. 'I want cash next time. Proper cash. I know where you live, Lily. I know you got it.'

She felt as if she would never be free of him. He texted her at odd hours, waking her up, keeping her from sleep. That picture, again and again. She saw it in negative, burned onto her retinas. She stopped going to school. She got drunk with strangers, went out clubbing long after she really wanted to. Anything not to be alone with her thoughts and the relentless *ping* of her phone. She had moved to where he couldn't find her and he had found her, parking his car for hours outside Louisa's flat, a silent message. She even thought, a few times, about telling Louisa. But what could Louisa do? Half the time she was like a one-woman disaster area herself. So Lily's mouth would open and nothing would come out, then Louisa would start rattling on about meeting her grandmother or whether she had eaten something and she had realized she was on her own.

Sometimes Lily lay awake and thought about what it would have been like if her dad had been there. She could picture him in her head. He would have walked outside, grabbed Peter by his neck and told him never to come near his little girl again. He would have put his arms around her and told her it was all okay, that she was safe.

Except he wouldn't. Because he was just an angry quadriplegic who hadn't even wanted to be alive. And he would have looked at the pictures and been disgusted.

She couldn't blame him.

The last time, when she'd had nothing to bring him, he had shouted at her on a pavement behind Carnaby Street, calling her *worthless, a whore, a stupid little skank*. He had pulled up in his car and she had drunk two double whiskies because she was afraid to see him. When he'd started shouting at her and saying she was lying, she had started to cry.

'Louisa's chucked me out. My mum's chucked me out. I don't have anything.'

People hurried past, their eyes averted. Nobody stopped. Nobody said anything, because a man shouting at a drunk girl in Soho on a Friday night was nothing out of the ordinary. Peter swore, and turned on his heel, as if he was leaving, except she knew he wouldn't. And then the big black car had stopped in the middle of the street and reversed, its white lights glowing. The electric window hummed its way down. 'Lily?'

It took her a few seconds to recognize him. Mr Garside from her stepfather's business. His boss? A partner? He looked at her, and then at Peter. 'Are you all right?'

She glanced at Peter, then nodded.

He didn't believe her. She could tell. He had pulled over to the side of the road, in front of Peter's car, and walked across slowly in his dark suit. He had an air of authority, like nothing was going to faze him. She remembered, randomly, her mother talking about him having a helicopter. 'Do you need a ride home, Lily?'

Peter lifted his hand with the phone in it, just an inch. Just so she knew. And she opened her mouth and it came out. 'He has a bad picture of me on his phone and he's threatening to show it to everyone and he wants money and I don't have any left. I've given him what I can and I just don't have anything left. Please help me.'

Peter's eyes widened. He hadn't expected that. But she didn't care what happened. She just felt desperate, and tired, and she didn't want to carry all this by herself any more.

Mr Garside regarded Peter for a moment. Peter stiffened his shoulders and straightened, as if he were considering whether to run for his car.

'Is this true?' Mr Garside said.

'It's not a crime to have pictures of girls on your phone.' Peter smirked, an act of bravado.

'I'm well aware of that. It is, however, a crime to use them to extort money.' Mr Garside's voice was low and calm, as if it were perfectly reasonable to be discussing someone's naked pictures in the middle of the street. He moved his hand to his inside pocket. 'So what will it take to make you go away?'

'What?'

'Your phone. How much do you want for it?'

Lily's breath stopped in her throat. She looked from one man to the other. Peter was staring at him in disbelief.

'I'm offering you cash for the phone. On the basis that this is the only copy of that photograph.'

'I'm not selling my phone.'

'Then I have to advise you, young man, that I'll be contacting the police and identifying you through your car registration. And I have a lot of friends in the police force. Quite high-up friends.' He smiled a smile that wasn't really a smile at all.

Across the road a bunch of people spilled out of a restaurant, laughing. Peter looked at her and back at Mr Garside. He lifted his chin. 'Five grand.'

Mr Garside reached into his inside pocket. He shook his head. 'I don't think so.' He pulled out his wallet and counted out a bundle of notes. 'I think this will do. It sounds as though you've already been amply rewarded. The phone, please?'

It was as if Peter had been hypnotised. He hesitated for

just a moment, then handed Mr Garside his phone. Just like that. Mr Garside checked that the SIM card was in it, tucked it into his inside pocket, and opened the car door for Lily. 'I think it's time for you to leave, Lily.'

She climbed in, like an obedient child, hearing the solid *thunk* of the car door as it closed behind her. And then they were off, gliding smoothly down the narrow street, leaving Peter shell-shocked – she could see him in the wing mirror – as if he, too, couldn't believe what had just happened.

'Are you all right?' Mr Garside didn't look at her as he spoke.

'Is . . . is that it?'

He glanced sideways, then back at the road. 'I think so, yes.'

She couldn't believe it. She couldn't believe the thing that had hung over her for weeks could be fixed just like that. She turned to him, suddenly anxious. 'Please don't tell my mum and Francis.'

He frowned slightly. 'If that's what you want.'

She let out a long, silent breath. 'Thank you,' she said quietly.

He patted her knee. 'Nasty lad. You need to be careful with your friends, Lily.' He moved his hand back onto the automatic gearstick before she had even registered its presence.

He hadn't batted an eyelid when she had told him she had nowhere to stay. He had driven her to a hotel in Bayswater and spoken quietly to the receptionist, who had handed her a room key. She was relieved he hadn't suggested taking her to his house: she didn't want to explain herself to anyone else.

'I'll pick you up tomorrow when you're sober,' he said, tucking his wallet into his jacket pocket.

She had walked heavily up to Room 311, lain down on the bed fully clothed and slept for fourteen hours.

*

He called to say he would meet her for breakfast. She showered, took some clothes out of her rucksack and ran an iron over them in the hope that she looked a little more presentable. She was not good at ironing – Lena had done that sort of thing.

When she came downstairs to the restaurant he was already sitting there, reading a paper, a half-drunk cup of coffee in front of him. He was older than she remembered, his hair thinning on top, a faint crêpiness to the skin of his neck; the last time she had seen him had been at a company event at the races where Francis had drunk too much and her mother had hissed at him furiously whenever nobody else was about, and Mr Garside, catching it, had raised his eyebrows at Lily, as if to say, 'Parents, eh?'

She slid into the chair opposite him and he lowered his newspaper. 'Aha. How are you today?'

She felt embarrassed, as if last night she had been overly histrionic. As if it had all been a fuss over nothing. 'Much better, thank you.'

'Did you sleep well?'

'Very well, thank you.'

He had studied her for a minute over his glasses. 'Very formal.'

She smiled. She didn't know what else to do. It was too weird, being there with her stepdad's work colleague. The waitress offered her coffee and she drank it. She eyed the breakfast buffet, wondering if she was expected to pay. He seemed to sense her discomfort. 'Eat something. Don't worry. It's paid for.' He turned back to his paper.

She wondered whether he would tell her parents. She wondered what he had done with Peter's phone. She hoped he had slowed his big black car on the Thames embankment, lowered his window and hurled it into the swirling currents below. She wanted never to see that picture again. She rose and fetched a croissant with some fruit from the buffet. She was starving.

He sat reading as she ate. She wondered how they looked from outside – like any father and daughter probably. She wondered whether he had children.

'Don't you have to be at work?'

He smiled, accepted more coffee from the waitress. 'I told them I had an important meeting.' He folded his newspaper neatly and put it down.

She shifted uncomfortably in her seat. 'I need to get a job.'

'A job.' He sat back. 'Well. What kind of job?'

'I don't know. I kind of messed up my exams.'

'And what do your parents think?'

'They don't . . . I can't . . . They're not very happy with me right now. I've been staying with friends.'

'You can't go back there?'

'Not right now. My friend isn't very happy with me either.'

'Oh, Lily,' he said, and sighed. He looked out of the window, considering something for a minute, then glanced at his expensive watch. He thought for another moment, then called his office and told someone he was going to be late back from his meeting.

She waited to hear what he had to say next.

'You finished?' He put his newspaper into his briefcase, and stood up. 'Let's go and make a plan.'

She had not been expecting him to come to the room and was embarrassed by the state of it: the damp towels left on the floor, the television blaring trashy daytime programmes. She dumped the worst of it in the bathroom and shoved what was left of her belongings hastily into her rucksack. He pretended not to notice, just gazed out of the window, then turned back when she sat on the chair, as if he had only just seen the room.

'It's not a bad hotel, this,' he said. 'I used to stay here when I couldn't face the drive to Winchester.'

'Is that where you live?'

'It's where my wife lives, yes. My children are long grown-up.' He put his briefcase on the floor and sat on the edge of the bed. She got up and fetched the complimentary notepad from the bedside table, in case she needed to take notes. Her phone let out a chime and she glanced down. *Lily just call me. Louisa x*

She shoved it into her back pocket and sat down, the note-pad on her lap.

'So what do you think?'

'That you're in a tricky position, Lily. You're a bit young to be getting a job, to be frank. I'm not sure who would hire you.'

'I'm good at stuff, though. I'm a hard worker. I can garden.'

'Garden! Well, perhaps you could get work gardening. Whether that's going to bring in enough for you to support yourself is another matter. Have you got any references? Any holiday jobs?'

'No. My parents always gave me an allowance.'

'Mm.' He tapped his hands on his knees. 'You've had a difficult relationship with your father, haven't you?'

'Francis isn't my real father.'

'Yes. I'm aware of that. I know you left home some weeks ago. It all seems like a very sad situation. Very sad. You must feel rather isolated.'

She felt the lump swell in her throat and thought for a moment that he was reaching for a handkerchief, but it was then that he reached into his jacket pocket and pulled out a phone. Peter's phone. He tapped it, once, twice, and she saw a flash of her own image. Her breathing stalled in her chest.

He clicked on it, making it bigger. Her cheeks flooded with colour. He stared at the photograph for what felt like several years. 'You really have been quite a bad girl, haven't you?'

Lily's fingers closed in a fist around the hotel bedspread. She looked up at Mr Garside, her cheeks burning. His eyes didn't leave the picture.

'A very bad girl.' Eventually he looked up at her, his gaze even, his voice soft. 'I suppose the first thing we need to do is work out how you can repay me for the phone and the hotel room.'

'But,' she began, 'you didn't say –'

'Oh, come on, Lily. A live-wire like you? You must know that nothing comes for free.' He looked down at the image. 'You must have worked that out a while ago . . . You're obviously good at it.'

Lily's breakfast rose into her throat.

'You see, I could be very helpful to you. Give you somewhere to stay until you're back on your feet, a little leg up the career ladder. You wouldn't need to do very much in return. *Quid pro quo* – you know that phrase? You did Latin at your school, didn't you?'

She stood abruptly and reached for her rucksack. His hand shot out and took hold of her arm. With his free hand he tucked the phone slowly back into his pocket. 'Let's not be hasty about this, Lily. We wouldn't want me to have to show this little picture to your parents, would we? Goodness knows what they would think about what you've been up to.'

Her words stuck in her throat.

He patted the bedspread beside him. 'I would think very carefully about your next move. Now. Why don't we –'

Lily's arm flew back, shaking him off. And then she was wrenching the hotel-room door open and she was gone, feet pumping, racing down the hotel corridor, her bag flying out behind her.

London teemed with life into the small hours. She walked while cars nudged night buses impatiently along main roads, minicabs wove in and out of traffic, men in suits made their way home or sat in glowing office cubicles halfway to the sky, ignoring the cleaners who worked silently around them. She walked with her head low and her rucksack on her shoulder, and when she ate in late-night burger restaurants, she made sure her hood was up and that she had a free newspaper to pretend to read: there was always someone who would sit down at your table and try to get you to talk. *Come on, darling, I'm only being friendly.*

All the while she replayed that morning's events in her head. What had she done? What signal had she sent? Was there something about her that meant everyone assumed she was a whore? The words he had used made her want to cry. She felt herself shrink into her hood, hating him. Hating herself.

She used her student card and rode on underground trains until the atmosphere became drunk and febrile. Then it felt safer to stay above ground. The rest of the time she walked – through the glittering neon lights of Piccadilly, down the lead-dusted length of Marylebone Road, around the pulsing late-night bars of Camden, her stride long, pretending she had somewhere to be, only slowing when her feet began to ache from the unforgiving pavement.

When she got too tired she begged favours. She spent one night at her friend Nina's, but Nina asked too many questions and the sound of her chatting downstairs to her parents while Lily lay, soaking the grime out of her hair in the bath, made her feel like the loneliest person on earth. She left after break-fast, even though Nina's mum said she was welcome to stay another night, gazing at her with concerned maternal eyes. She spent two nights on the sofa of a girl she had met while clubbing, but there were three men sharing the flat, and she didn't feel relaxed enough to sleep and sat fully clothed, hugging her knees, watching television with the sound turned off until dawn. She spent one night at a Salvation Army hostel, listening to two girls argue in the next-door cubicle, her bag clutched to her chest under the blanket. They said she could have a shower, but she didn't like to leave her bag in the lockers while she got wet. She drank the free soup and left. But mostly she walked, spending the last of her cash on cheap coffee and Egg McMuffins and growing more and more tired and hungry until it was hard to think straight, hard to react quickly when the men in doorways said disgusting things or the staff in the café told her she'd made that one cup of tea last long enough, young lady, and it was time to move on.

And all the while she wondered what her parents were saying at that moment, and what Mr Garside would say about her when he showed them the pictures. She could see her mother's shocked face, Francis's slow shake of the head, as if this new Lily was of no surprise to him whatsoever.

She had been so stupid.

She should have stolen the phone.

She should have stamped on it.

She should have stamped on him.

She shouldn't have gone to that boy's stupid flat and behaved like a stupid idiot and broken her own stupid life, and that was usually the point at which she would start crying again and pull her hood further up around her face and –

# Chapter Twenty

'She's what?'

In Mrs Traynor's silence I heard disbelief, and perhaps (maybe I was being oversensitive) a faint echo of the last thing of hers I had failed to keep safe.

'And you've tried to call?'

'She's not picking up.'

'And she hasn't been in touch with her parents?'

I closed my eyes. I had been dreading this conversation. 'She's done this before, apparently. Mrs Houghton-Miller is convinced Lily will turn up any minute.'

Mrs Traynor digested this. 'But you aren't.'

'Something's not right, Mrs Traynor. I know I'm not a parent, but I just . . .' My words tailed away. 'Anyway. I'd rather be doing something than nothing, so I'm going to get back out walking the streets to find her. I just wanted you to know the truth about what was going on.'

Mrs Traynor was silent for a moment. And then she said, her voice measured but oddly determined, 'Louisa, before you go, would you mind giving me Mrs Houghton-Miller's telephone number?'

I called in sick, noting fleetingly that Richard Percival's cold 'I see,' was actually more ominous than his previous blustering protests. I printed off photographs – one of Lily's Facebook profile photographs, and one of the selfies she'd taken of the two of us. I spent the morning driving around central London. I parked on kerbs, leaving the hazard lights flashing, as I nipped into pubs, fast-food joints, nightclubs where the cleaners, working in the stale, dim air, peered up at me with suspicious eyes.

– *Have you seen this girl?*
– *Who wants to know?*
– *Have you seen this girl?*
– *Are you police? I don't want no trouble.*

Some people evidently thought it amusing to string me along for a bit – *Oh, that girl! Brown hair? Yeah, what was her name? . . . Nah. Never seen her before.* Nobody seemed to have seen her. And the further I travelled, the more hopeless it felt. What better place to disappear than London? A teeming metropolis where you could slide into a million doorways, mingle with crowds that never ended. I would gaze up at the tower blocks and wonder whether even now she was lying on someone's sofa in her pyjamas. Lily picked up people with ease, and had no fear of asking for anything – she could be with anyone.

And yet.

I wasn't entirely sure what drove me to keep going. Perhaps it was my cold fury at Tanya Houghton-Miller's semi-detached parenting; perhaps it was my guilt at having failed to do the thing I was criticizing Tanya for not doing. Perhaps it was just that I knew only too well how vulnerable a young girl could be.

Mostly, though, it was Will. I walked and drove and questioned and walked and held endless internal conversations with him as my hip began to ache, and I paused in my car, chewing stale sandwiches and garage chocolate and choking down painkillers to keep me going.

*Where would she go, Will?*
*What would you do?*
And – yet again – *I'm sorry. I let you down.*

*

*Any news?* I texted Sam. It felt odd speaking to him while having concurrent conversations with Will in my head, a strange infidelity. I just wasn't quite sure who I was being unfaithful to.

*Nope. I've called every ER department in London. How about you?*
*Bit tired.*
*Hip?*
*Nothing chewing a few Nurofen won't fix.*
*Want me to stop by after my shift?*
*I think I just need to keep looking.*
*Don't go anywhere I wouldn't go x*
*Very funny xxx*

'Did you try the hospitals?' My sister called from college, in her fifteen-minute break between HMRC: the Changing Face of Revenue Collection, and VAT: A European Perspective.

'Sam says there's nobody with her name has been admitted to any of the teaching hospitals. He's got people everywhere looking out for her.' I glanced behind me as I spoke, as if even then I half expected to see Lily walking out of the crowds towards me.

'How long have you been looking?'

'A few days.' I didn't tell her I'd barely slept. 'I – er – took time off work.'

'I knew it! I knew she was going to be trouble. Did your boss mind you taking time off? What happened about that other job, by the way? The one in New York? Did you do the interview? Please don't say you forgot.'

It took me a minute to work out what she was referring to. 'Oh. That. Yeah – I got it.'

'You *what?*'

'Nathan said they're going to offer it to me.'

Westminster was filling with tourists, lingering at gaudy stalls of Union Jack tat, their mobile phones and expensive cameras held aloft to capture the looming Houses of Parliament. I watched a traffic warden walking towards me and wondered if some anti-terrorism legislation prevented me parking where I'd stopped. I held up a hand, indicating that I was about to leave.

There was a short silence at the other end of the phone.

'Hang on – you're not saying you –'

'I can't even think about it right now, Treen. Lily's missing. I need to find her.'

'Louisa? *You* listen a minute. You have to take this job.'

'What?'

'This is the opportunity of a lifetime. If you had the faintest clue what I would give for a chance to move to New York . . . with guaranteed employment? A place to live? And you "can't think about it right now"?'

'It's not as simple as that.'

The traffic warden was definitely walking towards me.

'Oh, my God. This is it. This is the thing I was trying to talk to you about. Every time you get a chance to move forward, you just hijack your own future. It's like – it's like you don't actually want to.'

'Lily is *missing*, Treen.'

'A sixteen-year-old girl you barely know, with two parents and at least two grandparents, has buggered off for a few days like she's done before. Like teenagers sometimes do. And you're going to use this to throw away the greatest opportunity you're ever likely to be given? Jeez. You don't even really want to go, do you?'

'What the hell is that supposed to mean?'

'Far easier for you to just stick with that depressing little job and complain about it. Far easier for you to sit tight and not take a risk and make out that everything that happens to you is something you couldn't help.'

'I can't just up and leave while this is going on.'

'You're in charge of your own life, Lou. And yet you act like you're permanently buffeted by events outside your control. What is this – guilt? Is it that you feel you owe Will something? Is it some kind of penance? Giving up your life because you couldn't save his?'

'You don't understand.'

'No. I understand perfectly. I understand you better than you understand yourself. His daughter is *not your responsibility*. Do you hear me? None of this is your responsibility. And if you don't go to New York – an opportunity I can't even talk about because it makes me want to actually kill you – I'll never talk to you again. Ever.'

The traffic warden was at my window. I wound it down, pulling the universal face you make when your sister is going off on one at the other end of your phone and you're really sorry but you can't cut her short. He tapped his watch and I nodded, reassuringly.

'That's it, Lou. Think about it. Lily is not your daughter.'

I was left staring at my phone. I thanked the traffic warden, then wound up my window. And a phrase popped into my head: *he wasn't even my real dad.*

I drove around the corner, pulled up beside a petrol station and rifled through the battered old *A–Z* that lived in the footwell of my car, trying to remember the name of the road Lily had mentioned. Pyemore, Pyecrust, *Pyecroft*. I traced the distance to St John's Wood with my finger – would that take fifteen minutes to walk? It had to be the same place.

I used my phone and looked up his surname along with the street name, and there it was. Number fifty-six. My gut tightened with excitement. I started the ignition, wrenched the car into gear and headed out onto the road again.

*

Although separated by less than a mile, the difference between Lily's mother's house and her former stepfather's could not have been more pronounced. Where the Houghton-Millers' street was uniformly grand white stucco or red-brick houses, punctuated by yew topiary and large cars that seemingly never got dirty, Martin Steele's road appeared resolutely un-gentrified, a two-storey corner of London where house prices were spiralling but the exteriors resolutely refused to reflect it.

I drove slowly, past cars under canvas and an overturned wheelie-bin, and finally found a parking space near a small Victorian terraced house of the kind that existed in identikit lines all over London. I gazed at it, noting the peeling paint-work on the front door, the child's watering-can on the front step. Please let her be here, I prayed. Safe within those walls.

I climbed out of the car, locked it, and walked up to the front step.

Inside I could hear a piano, a fractured chord being repeated again and again, muffled voices. I hesitated, just a moment, and then I pressed the doorbell, hearing the sudden answering stop to the music.

Footsteps in the corridor, and then the door opened. A forty-something man, lumberjack shirt, jeans and day-old stubble, stood there.

'Yes?'

'I wondered . . . is Lily here please?'

'Lily?'

I smiled, held out a hand. 'You are Martin Steele, yes?'

He studied me briefly before he answered. 'I might be. And who are you?'

'I'm a friend of Lily's. I – I've been trying to get in contact with her and I understand that she might be staying here. Or that perhaps you might know where she is.'

He frowned. 'Lily? Lily Miller?'

'Well. Yes.'

He rubbed his hand against his jaw, and glanced behind him towards the hall. 'Could you wait there a moment, please?' He walked back down the corridor, and I heard him issuing instructions to whoever was at the piano. As he came back to me, a scale began playing, hesitantly and then with more emphasis.

Martin Steele half closed the door behind him. He dipped his head for a moment, as if he were trying to make sense of what I had asked him. 'I'm sorry. I'm slightly at a loss here. You're a friend of Lily Miller's? And you've come here why?'

'Because Lily said she came here to see you. You are – were – her stepfather?'

'Not technically, but yes. A long time ago.'

'And you're a musician? You used to take her to nursery? But you're still in contact. She told me how close you still were. How much it irritated her mother.'

Martin squinted at me. 'Miss –'

'Clark. Louisa Clark.'

'Miss Clark. Louisa. I haven't seen Lily Miller since she was five years old. Tanya thought it would be better for all of us when we split up if we broke off all contact.'

I stared at him. 'So you're saying she hasn't been here?'

He thought for a moment. 'She came once, a few years ago, but it wasn't great timing. We'd just had a baby and I was trying to teach and, well, to be honest, I couldn't work out what she really wanted from me.'

'So you haven't seen or spoken to her since then?'

'Apart from that one very brief occasion, no. Is she okay? Is she in some kind of trouble?'

Inside, the piano kept playing – *doh re mi fah soh lah ti doh. Doh ti lah soh fah mi re doh.* Up and down.

I waved a hand, already backing away down the steps. 'No. It's fine. My mistake. I'm sorry to have bothered you.'

I spent another evening driving around London, ignoring my sister's calls and the email from Richard Percival that was marked URGENT and PERSONAL. I drove until my eyes were reddened from the glare of lights and I realized I was now going to places I had already been, and I ran out of cash for petrol.

I drove home just after midnight, promising myself I would pick up my bank card, drink a cup of tea, rest my eyes for half an hour, then hit the road again. I took off my shoes and made some toast that I couldn't eat. Instead I swallowed another two painkillers and lay back on the sofa, my mind racing. What was I missing? There must be some clue. My brain buzzed with exhaustion, my stomach now permanently knotted with anxiety. What streets had I missed? Was there a chance she had gone somewhere other than London?

There was no choice, I decided. We had to let the police know. It was better to be thought stupid and overly dramatic than to risk something actually happening to her. I lay back and closed my eyes for five minutes.

I was woken three hours later by the phone ringing. I lurched upright, temporarily unsure where I was. Then I stared at the flashing screen beside me, and fumbled it up to my ear. 'Hello?'

'We've got her.'

'What?'

'It's Sam. We've got Lily. Can you come?'

In the evening crush that followed England losing a football match, the ill-temper and associated drink-related injuries, nobody had noticed the slight figure sleeping across two chairs in the corner, her hoodie pulled up high over her face. It was only when the triage nurse had gone person-to-person to ensure they were meeting waiting targets that someone shook the girl awake and she confessed reluctantly that she was just there because it was warm and dry and safe.

The nurse was questioning her when Sam, bringing in an old woman with breathing problems, caught sight of her at the desk. He had quietly instructed the nurses at the desk not to let her leave, and hurried out to call me before she could see him. He told me all this as we rushed into A and E. The waiting area had finally started to thin out, the fever-ridden children safely in cubicles with their parents, the drunks sent home to sleep it off. Only RTAs and stabbing victims, at this time of night.

'They've given her some tea. She looks exhausted. I think she's happy just to sit tight.'

I must have looked anxious at this point because he added, 'It's okay. They won't let her leave.'

I half walked, half ran along the strip-lit corridor, Sam striding beside me. And there she was, looking somehow smaller than she had done, her hair pulled into a messy plait, a plastic cup held between her thin hands. A nurse sat beside her, working through a pile of folders, and when she saw me and registered Sam, she smiled warmly, and stood up to leave. Lily's nails, I noticed, were black with grime.

'Lily?' I said. Her dark, shadowed eyes met mine. 'What – what happened?'

She looked at me, and then at Sam, her eyes huge and a little fearful.

'We've been looking everywhere. We were . . . My God, Lily. Where were you?'

'Sorry,' she whispered.

I shook my head, trying to tell her that it didn't matter. That nothing could possibly matter, that the only important thing was that she was safe and she was here.

I held out my arms. She looked into my eyes, took a step forward, and gently came to rest against me. And I closed my arms tight around her, feeling her silent, shaking sobs become my own. All I could do was thank some unknown God and offer up these silent words: *Will. Will – we found her.*

# Chapter Twenty-one

That first night home I put Lily in my bed and she slept for eighteen hours, waking in the evening for some soup and a bath, then crashing out for a further eight. I slept on the sofa, the front door locked, afraid to go out or even to move in case she vanished again. Sam dropped in twice, before and after his shift, to bring milk and to check on how she'd been, and we talked in whispers in the hall, as if we were discussing an invalid.

I rang Tanya Houghton-Miller to tell her that her daughter had turned up safely. 'I told you. You wouldn't listen to me,' she crowed triumphantly, and I put the phone down before she could say anything else. Or I did.

I called Mrs Traynor, who let out a long, shaking sigh of relief and didn't speak for some time. 'Thank you,' she said, finally, and it sounded like it came from somewhere deep in her gut. 'When can I come and see her?'

I finally opened the email from Richard Percival, which informed me that *As you have been given the requisite three warnings, it is considered that, given your poor attendance record and failure to carry out your contractual requirements, your employment at the Shamrock and Clover (Airport) is terminated with immediate effect.* He asked that I return the uniform ('including wig') at my earliest convenience *or you will be charged its full retail value.*

I opened an email from Nathan asking, *Where the hell are you? Have you seen my last email?*

I thought about Mr Gopnik's offer and, with a sigh, closed my computer.

*

On the third day I woke on the sofa to find Lily missing. My heart lurched reflexively until I saw the open hallway window. I climbed up the fire escape and found her seated on the roof, looking out across the city. She was wearing her pyjama bottoms, which I'd washed, and Will's oversized sweater.

'Hey,' I said, walking across the roof towards her.

'You have food in your fridge,' she observed.

'Ambulance Sam.'

'And you watered everything.'

'That was mostly him too.'

She nodded, as if that were probably to be expected. I took my place on the bench and we sat in companionable silence for a while, breathing in the scent of the lavender, whose purple heads had burst out of their tight green buds. Everything in the little roof garden had now exploded into gaudy life; the petals and whispering leaves bringing colour and movement and fragrance to the grey expanse of asphalt.

'Sorry for hogging your bed.'

'Your need was greater.'

'You hung up all your clothes.' She curled her legs neatly under her, tucking her hair behind an ear. She was still pale. 'The nice ones.'

'Well, I guess you made me think I shouldn't hide them in boxes any more.'

She shot me a sideways look and a small, sad smile that somehow made me feel sadder than if she hadn't smiled at all. The air held the promise of a scorching day, the street sounds muffled as if by the warmth of the sun. You could feel it already seeping through the windows, bleaching the air. Below us a bin lorry clattered and roared its way slowly along the kerbside to a timpanic accompaniment of beeps and men's voices.

'Lily,' I said, quietly, when it had finally receded into the distance, 'what's going on?' I tried not to sound too interrogative.

'I know I'm not meant to ask you questions and I'm not your actual family or anything, but all I can see is that something's gone wrong here and I feel . . . I feel like I . . . well, I feel we're sort of related and I just want you to trust me. I want you to feel you can talk to me.'

She kept her gaze fixed on her hands.

'I'm not going to judge you. I'm not going to report anything you say to anyone. I just . . . Well, you have to know that if you tell someone the truth, it will help. I promise. It will make things better.'

'Says who?'

'Me. There's nothing you can't tell me, Lily. Really.'

She glanced at me, then looked away. 'You won't understand,' she said softly.

And then I knew. I knew.

Below us it had become oddly quiet, or perhaps I could no longer hear anything beyond the few inches that separated us. 'I'm going to tell you a story,' I said. 'Only one person in the whole world knows this story because it was something I didn't feel I could share for years and years. And telling him changed the whole way I felt about it, and how I felt about myself. So here's the thing – you don't have to tell me anything at all, but I'm going to trust you enough to tell you my story anyway, just in case it will help.'

I waited a moment but Lily didn't protest, or roll her eyes, or say it was going to be *boring*. She wrapped her arms around her knees, and she listened. She listened as I told her about the teenage girl who, on a glorious summer evening, had celebrated a little too hard in a place she considered safe, how she had been surrounded by her girlfriends and some nice boys who seemed as if they came from good families and knew the rules, and how much fun it had been, how funny and crazy and wild, until some drinks later she realized nearly all the other girls had drifted away and the laughter had grown hard and the joke, it turned out, had been on her. And I told her, without going into too much detail, how that evening had ended: with a sister silently helping her home, her shoes lost, bruising in secret places and a big black hole where her recall of those hours should have been, and the memories, fleeting and dark, now hanging over her head to remind her every day that she had been stupid, irresponsible and had brought it all on herself. And how, for years, she had let that thought colour what she did, where she went and what she thought she was capable of. And how sometimes it just needed someone to say something as simple as *No. It wasn't your fault. It really wasn't your fault.*

I finished and Lily was still watching me. Her expression gave no clue to her reaction.

'I don't know what was – or is – going on with you, Lily,' I said carefully. 'It might be totally unrelated to what I've just told you. I just want you to know there is nothing so bad that you can't tell me. And there is nothing you could do that would make me close a door on you again.'

Still she didn't speak. I gazed out over the roof terrace, deliberately not looking at her.

'You know, your dad said something to me that I've never forgotten: "You don't have to let that one thing be the thing that defines you."'

'My dad.' She lifted her chin.

I nodded. 'Whatever it is that's happened, even if you don't want to tell me, you need to understand that he was right. These last weeks, months, don't have to be the thing that defines you. Even from the little I know of you, I recognise that you are bright and funny and kind and smart, and that if you can get yourself past whatever this is, you have an amazing future ahead.'

'How can you possibly know that?'

'Because you're like him. You're even wearing his jumper,' I added softly.

She brought her arm slowly to her face, placing the soft wool against her cheek, thinking.

I sat back on the bench. I wondered if I had pushed it too far, talking about Will.

But then Lily took a breath and, in a quiet, uncharacteristically flat voice, she told me the truth about where she'd been. She told me about the boy, and about the man, and an image on a mobile phone that haunted her, and the days she had spent as a shadow on the city's neon-lit streets. As she spoke she started to cry, shrinking into herself, her face crumpling like that of a five-year-old, so I moved across the seat and brought her in close to me, stroking her hair while she kept talking, her words now jumbled, too fast, too full, broken with sobs and hiccups. By the time she got to the last day, she was huddled into me, swallowed by the jumper, swallowed by her own fear and guilt and sadness.

'I'm sorry,' she sobbed. 'I'm so sorry.'

'You have nothing,' I said fiercely, as I held her, '*nothing* to be sorry for.'

That evening Sam came. He was cheerful, sweet and casual in his dealings with Lily, cooked us pasta with cream, bacon and mushrooms, when she said she didn't want to go out, and we watched a comedy film about a family who got lost in a jungle, a strange facsimile of a family ourselves. I smiled and laughed and made tea, but inside I simmered with anger I didn't dare show.

As soon as Lily went to bed I beckoned Sam onto the fire escape. We climbed up to the roof where I could be sure I wouldn't be heard, and as he sat down on the little wrought-iron bench I told him what she had told me in that spot, just a few hours earlier. 'She thinks it's going to hang over her for ever. He still has the phone, Sam.'

I wasn't sure I had ever been so furious. All evening, as the television burbled in front of me, I had recast the last weeks in a new light: I thought about the times the boy had hung around downstairs, the way Lily had hidden her phone under the sofa cushions when she thought I might see it, the way she had sometimes flinched when a new message came through. I thought of her stuttering words – of the way she described her relief when she thought she had been rescued – and then the horror of what was to come next. I thought about the arrogance of a man who had seen a young girl in distress and viewed it as an opportunity.

Sam motioned to me to sit down, but I couldn't keep still. I paced backwards and forwards across the roof terrace, my fists tight, my neck rigid. I wanted to throw things over the edge. I wanted to find Mr Garside. He came and stood behind me and rubbed at the knots in my shoulders. I suspected it was his way of making me stand still.

'I actually want to kill him.'

'It can be arranged.'

I looked round at Sam to see if he was joking, and was the tiniest bit disappointed when I saw he was.

It had grown chilly up there in the stiff night breeze and I wished I had brought up a jacket. 'Maybe we should just go to the police. It's blackmail, isn't it?'

'He'll deny it. There are a million places he could hide a phone. And if her mother was telling the truth nobody is going to believe Lily over a so-called pillar of the community. That's how these people get away with it.'

'But how do we get that phone off him? She won't be able to move forward while she knows he's out there, while that image is still out there.' I was shivering. Sam took his jacket off and hung it around my shoulders. It carried the residual warmth of him and I tried not to look as grateful as I felt.

'We can't turn up at his office or her parents will find out. We could email him? Tell him he has to send it back, or else?'

'He's hardly just going to cough it up. He might not even answer an email – that could be used as evidence.'

'Oh, it's hopeless.' I let out a long moan. 'Maybe she's just going to have to learn to live with it. Maybe we can convince her that it's as much in his interests to forget what happened as it is hers. Because it is, right? Maybe he'll just get rid of the phone himself.'

'You think she'll go with that?'

'No.' I rubbed my eyes. 'I can't bear it. I can't bear that he'll get away with it. That creepy, nasty, manipulative, limo-driving scumbag . . .' I stood up and gazed out at the city below me, feeling briefly despairing. I could see the future: Lily, defensive and wild, as she tried to escape the shadow of her past. That phone was the key to her behaviour, to her future.

*Think*, I told myself. *Think what Will would do*. He would not have let this man win. I had to strategize like he would. I watched the traffic creeping slowly past the front door of my block. I thought of Mr Garside's big black car, cruising the streets of Soho. I thought about a man who moved silently and easily through life, confident that it would always work his way.

'Sam?' I said. 'Is there a drug you could give that could stop someone's heart?'

He let that hang in the air for a moment. 'Please tell me you're kidding.'

'No. Listen. I've got an idea.'


She said nothing at first. 'You'll be safe,' I said. 'And this way nobody has to know a thing.' What moved me most was that she didn't ask me the question I had been asking myself ever since I outlined my plan to Sam. *How do you know this will actually work?*

'I've got it all lined up, sweetheart,' Sam said.

'But nobody else knows –'

'Anything. Just that he's hassling you.'

'Won't you get in trouble?'

'Don't worry about me.'

She pulled at her sleeve, then murmured, 'And you won't leave me with him. At all.'

'Not for one minute.'

She chewed her lip. Then she looked at Sam, and over at me. And something seemed to settle inside her. 'Okay. Let's do it.'

I bought a cheap, pay-as-you-go handset, called Lily's stepfather's workplace and got Mr Garside's mobile number from his secretary by pretending we had arranged to meet for a drink. That evening as I waited for Sam to arrive, I sent a text to Garside's number.

*Mr Garside. I'm sorry about hitting you. I just freaked. I want to sort it out. L*

He left it half an hour before responding, probably to make her sweat.

*Why should I talk to you, Lily? You were very rude after all the help I gave you.*

'Prick,' muttered Sam.

*I know. I'm sorry. But I do need your help.*

*This is not a one-way street, Lily.*

*I know. You just gave me a shock. I needed time to think. Let's meet up. I'll give you what you want, but you have to give me the phone first.*

*I don't think you get to dictate terms, Lily.*

Sam looked at me. I looked back at him, then began to type.

288

*Not even . . . if I'm a really bad girl?*

A pause.

*Now you've got my interest.*

Sam and I exchanged a look. 'I just did a little sick in my mouth,' I said.

*Tomorrow night then*, I typed. *I'll send you the address when I've checked my friend will be out.*

When we were sure he wouldn't respond, Sam put the phone into his pocket, where Lily couldn't see it, and held me for a long time.


I was almost ill with nerves the next day, and Lily was worse. We picked at our breakfast, and I let Lily smoke in the flat, and was almost tempted to ask for a cigarette myself. We watched a film and did some chores badly, and by seven thirty that evening, when Sam arrived, my head was buzzing so much I could barely speak.

'Did you send the address?' I asked him.

'Yup.'

'Show me.'

The phone message was simply the address of my flat and signed *L*.

He had responded: *I have a meeting in town and I'll be there shortly after eight.*

'You okay?' he said.

My stomach tightened. I felt as if I could hardly breathe. 'I don't want to get you into trouble. I mean – what if you get found out? You'll lose your job.'

Sam shook his head. 'Won't happen.'

'I shouldn't have pulled you into this mess. You've been so brilliant and I feel like I'm repaying you by putting you at risk.'

'We'll all be fine. Keep breathing.' He smiled reassuringly at me, but I thought I could detect a faint strain around his eyes.

He glanced over my shoulder and I turned. Lily was wearing a black T-shirt, denim shorts and black tights, and she had done her make-up so that she looked simultaneously very beautiful and very young. 'You all right, sweetheart?'

She nodded. Her skin, normally the slightly olive colour Will's had been, was unusually pale. Her eyes were huge in her face.

'It's all going to be fine, I'd be surprised if it takes longer than five minutes. Lou's been through it all with you, yes?' Sam's voice was calm, reassuring.

We had rehearsed it a dozen times. I wanted her to reach a point where she wouldn't freeze, where she could repeat her lines without thinking.

'I know what I'm doing.'

'Right,' he said, and clapped his hands together. 'Quarter to eight. Let's get ready.'

He was punctual, I had to give him that. At one minute past eight my buzzer rang. Lily took an audible breath, I squeezed her hand, and then she answered the entry-phone. *Yes. Yes, she's gone. Come up.* It didn't seem to occur to him that she might not be what he thought.

Lily let him in. Only I, watching through the crack in my bedroom door, could see the way her hand trembled as she reached for the lock. Garside ran his hand over his hair, glanced briefly around the hallway. He was wearing a good grey suit, and tucked his car keys into his inside breast pocket. I couldn't stop staring at him, at his expensive shirt, his beady, acquisitive eyes as they scanned the flat. My jaw tightened. What kind of man felt entitled to press himself on a girl forty years younger than he was? To blackmail the child of his own colleague?

He looked uncomfortable, far from relaxed. 'I've parked my car out the back. Will it be safe?'

'I think so.' Lily swallowed.

'You *think* so?' He took a step back towards the door. The kind of man who sees his car as an extension of some minuscule part of himself. 'And what about your friend? Whoever owns this place. They're not coming back?'

I held my breath. Behind me I felt Sam's steadying hand on the small of my back.

'Oh. No. It will be fine.' She smiled, suddenly reassuring. 'She won't be back for ages. Do come in. Would you like a drink, Mr Garside?'

He looked at her as if he were seeing her for the first time. 'So formal.' He took a step forward and finally closed the door behind him. 'Do you have Scotch?'

'I'll check. Come through.'

She began to walk to the kitchen, him following, removing his suit jacket. As they entered the living room, Sam walked past me out of the bedroom, strode across the hallway in his heavy boots and locked the inside door to the flat, placing the keys, jangling, in his pocket.

Garside, startled, turned and saw him, joined now by Donna. They stood there in uniform, against the door. He looked at them, then back at Lily, and faltered, trying to work out what was going on.

'Hello, Mr Garside,' I said, stepping out from behind the door. 'I believe you have something to return to my friend here.'

He actually broke out in a spontaneous sweat. Until then, I hadn't known it was physically possible. His eyes darted about for Lily, but as I had stepped out into the hall she had moved so that she was half behind me.

Sam stepped forward. Mr Garside's head reached just above his shoulder. 'The phone, please.'

'You can't threaten me.'

'We're not threatening you,' I said, my heart thumping. 'We would just like the phone.'

'You're threatening me just by blocking my exit.'

'Oh, no, sir,' said Sam. 'Actually *threatening* you would involve mentioning the fact that, if my colleague and I chose, we could pin you down right here and now and inject you with dihypranol, which would slow and ultimately stop your heart. Now *that* would be a threat, especially as nobody would question the word of the paramedic crew who had apparently tried to save you. And as dihypranol is one of the few drugs that leaves no trace in the bloodstream.'

Donna, her arms crossed across her chest, shook her head sadly. 'It's a shame, the way these middle-aged businessmen just drop like flies.'

'All sorts of health issues. They drink too much, eat too well, don't take enough exercise.'

'I'm sure this gentleman here isn't like that.'

'You'd hope not. But who knows?'

Mr Garside seemed to have shrunk by several inches.

'And don't even think of threatening Lily. We know where you live, Mr Garside. All paramedics have that information to hand if and when they need it. It's amazing what can happen if you piss off a paramedic.'

'This is outrageous.' He was blustering now, his face drained of colour.

'Yup. It really is.' I held out my hand. 'The phone, please.'

Garside glanced around him again, then finally reached into his pocket and handed it, to me.

I tossed it to Lily. 'Check it, Lily.'

I looked away, in deference to her feelings, while she did so. 'Delete it,' I said. 'Just delete it.' When I looked back, she had the phone, screen blank, in her hand. She gave a faint nod. Sam motioned to her to throw it to him. He dropped it to the floor and stamped down on it with his right foot, so that the plastic splintered. He crushed it with such violence that the floor shook. I found myself flinching, along with Mr Garside, every time Sam's heavy boot came down.

Finally, Sam stooped and gingerly picked up the tiny SIM card, which had skidded under the radiator. He examined it, and held it up in front of the older man. 'Was that the only copy?'

Garside nodded. Moisture was darkening his collar.

'Of course it's the only copy,' said Donna. 'A responsible member of the community wouldn't want to take the risk of something like that turning up anywhere, would he? Imagine what Mr Garside's family would say if his nasty little secret got out?'

Garside's mouth had compressed into a thin line. 'You've got what you wanted. Now let me leave.'

'No. I would like to say something.' My voice, I noted distantly, shook slightly with the effort of containing my fury. 'You are a sleazy, pathetic little man, and if I –'

Mr Garside's mouth hooked upwards in a sneer. The kind of man who had never once felt threatened by a woman. 'Oh, do be quiet, you ridiculous little –'

Something hard glittered in Sam's eyes and he sprang forward. My arm shot out to restrain him. I don't remember my other fist pulling back. I do remember the pain that shot through my knuckles as it made contact with the side of Garside's face. He reeled backwards, his upper body hitting the door, and I stumbled, not expecting the force of the impact. When he righted himself, I was shocked to see blood trickling from his nose.

'Let me out,' he hissed, through his fingers. '*This minute.*'

Sam blinked at me, then unlocked the door. Donna stepped away, just about allowing him through. She leaned towards him. 'Are you sure you don't want a dressing for that before you go?'

Garside kept his pace measured as he left, but as the door clicked shut behind him, we heard the sound of his expensive shoes picking up into a run down the corridor. We stood in silence until we couldn't hear them any more. And then, the sound of several people exhaling at once.

'Nice punch, Cassius,' said Sam, after a minute. 'Want me to take a look at that hand?'

I couldn't speak. I was bent double, swearing silently into my chest.

'Always hurts more than you think it will, doesn't it?' said Donna, patting my back. 'Don't stress, sweetheart,' she told Lily. 'Whatever he said to you, that old man is nothing. Gone.'

'He won't be back,' said Sam.

Donna laughed. 'He pretty much crapped himself. I think he'll be running a mile from you from now on. Forget it, darling.' She hugged Lily briskly, as you might someone who had toppled off a bike, then handed me the pieces of the broken phone to throw away. 'Right. I promised to pop round my dad's before our shift. See you later.' And then, with a wave, she was gone, her boots clumping cheerfully down the corridor.

Sam began to rummage through his medical pack to find a dressing for my hand. Lily and I walked into the living room where she sank down on the sofa. 'You did brilliantly,' I told her.

'You were pretty badass yourself.'

I examined my bloodied knuckles. When I looked up, the smallest grin was playing around her lips. 'He totally wasn't expecting that.'

'Neither was I. I'd never hit anyone before.' I straightened my face. 'Not that, you know, you should consider me any kind of moral example.'

'I've never considered you any kind of example, Lou.' She

grinned, almost reluctantly, as Sam came in, bearing some sterile bandage and a pair of scissors.

'You okay, Lily?' He raised his eyebrows.

She nodded.

'Good. Let's move on to something more interesting. Who fancies spaghetti carbonara?'

When she left the room, he let out a long breath, then stared at the ceiling for a moment, as if composing himself.

'What?' I said.

'Thank God you hit him first. I was afraid I was going to kill him.'

Some time later, after Lily had gone to bed, I joined Sam in the kitchen. For the first time in weeks some sort of peace had descended over my home. 'She's happier already. I mean, she bitched about the new toothpaste and left her towels on the floor, but in Lily terms she's definitely better.'

He nodded at this, and emptied the sink. It felt good having him in my kitchen. I watched him for a minute, wondering how it would feel to walk up and place my arms around his waist. 'Thank you,' I said instead. 'For everything.'

He turned, wiping his hands on the tea towel. 'You were pretty smart yourself, Punchy.' He reached out a hand and pulled me to him. We kissed. There was something so delicious about his kisses; the softness of them compared to the brute strength of the rest of him. I lost myself in him for a moment. But –

'What?' he said, pulling back. 'What's wrong?'

'You're going to think it's weird.'

'Uh, more weird than this evening?'

'I keep thinking about that dihypranol stuff. How much would it take to actually kill a person? Is this something you all carry routinely? It just . . . sounds . . . really dodgy.'

'You don't need to worry,' he said.

'You say that. But what if someone really hated you? Could they put it in your food? Could terrorists get hold of it? I mean, how much would they actually need?'

'Lou. There's no such drug.'

'What?'

'I made it up. There's no such thing as dihypranol. Totally invented.' He grinned at my shocked face. 'Funnily enough, I don't think I've ever had a drug that worked better.'

# Chapter Twenty-two

I was the last one to arrive at the Moving On meeting. My car wouldn't start again and I'd had to wait for the bus. When I got there the biscuit tin was just closing, a signal that the real business of the evening was about to begin.

'Today we're going to talk about faith in the future,' Marc said. I muttered my apology and sat down. 'Oh, and we only have an hour today because of an emergency Scouts meeting. Sorry about that, guys.'

Marc fixed each of us with his Special Empathetic Gaze. He was very keen on his Special Empathetic Gaze. Sometimes he would stare at me for so long I wondered if something was poking out of my nostril. He looked down, as if gathering his thoughts – or perhaps he liked to read his opening lines from a pre-prepared script.

'When someone we love is snatched from us, it often feels very hard to make plans. Sometimes people feel like they have lost faith in the future, or they become superstitious.'

'I thought I was going to die,' said Natasha.

'You are,' said William.

'Not helpful, William,' said Marc.

'No – honestly, for the first eighteen months after Olaf died, I thought I had cancer. I think I went to the doctor about a dozen times convinced I was getting cancer. Brain tumours, pancreatic cancer, womb cancer, even little-finger cancer.'

'There's no such thing as little-finger cancer,' said William.

'Oh, how would you know?' snapped Natasha. 'You have a smart answer for everything, William, but sometimes you should just keep your mouth shut, okay? It gets very tedious having you make a snarky comment about everything that someone says in this group. I thought I had little-finger cancer. My GP sent me for tests and it turned out I didn't. It might have been an irrational fear, yes, but you don't have to put down everything I say because, whatever you think, you don't know everything, okay?'

There was a brief silence.

'Actually,' said William, 'I work on an oncology ward.'

'It still stands,' she said, after a microsecond. 'You are insufferable. A deliberate agitator. A pain in the backside.'

'That's true,' said William.

Natasha stared at the floor. Or perhaps we all did. It was hard to tell, given I was studying the floor. She put her face into her hands for a moment, then looked up at him. 'You're not really, William. I'm sorry. I think I'm just having one of those days. I didn't mean to snap at you like that.'

'Still can't get little-finger cancer, though,' said William.

'So . . .' said Marc, as we tried to ignore Natasha cursing repeatedly under her breath '. . . I'm wondering whether any of you have reached a point where you can consider the prospect of life five years on. Where do you see yourself? What do you see yourself doing? Do you feel okay to imagine the future now?'

'I'll be happy if my old ticker's still ticking,' said Fred.

'All that internet sex putting it under strain?' said Sunil.

'That!' Fred exclaimed. 'That was a total waste of money. The first site, I spent two weeks emailing this woman from Lisbon – total cracker – and when I finally suggested we meet up for a bit of the old how's-your-father, she tried to sell me a condo in Florida. And then a man called Buffed Adonis private-messaged me to warn me off and tell me she was actually a one-legged Puerto Rican fella called Ramirez.'

'What about the other sites, Fred?'

'The only woman who said she'd meet me looked like my great-aunt Elsie, who kept her keys in her knickers. I mean, she was very sweet and all, but the old girl was so ancient I was almost tempted to check.'

'Don't give up, Fred,' said Marc. 'It might be that you're looking in the wrong places.'

'For my keys? Oh, no. I hang those by the door.'

Daphne decided she'd like to retire abroad in the next few years – 'It's the cold here. Gets into my joints.'

Leanne said she hoped to finish her philosophy master's. We gave each other the kind of deliberately blank looks you do when nobody wants to admit they had actually assumed she worked in a supermarket. Or maybe a slaughterhouse. William said, 'Well, you Kant.'

Nobody laughed, and when he realized nobody was going to, he sat back in his chair, and it might have been only me who heard Natasha muttering, 'Hah hah,' like Nelson in *The Simpsons*.

At first, Sunil didn't want to speak. Then he said he'd thought about it and he'd decided that in five years' time he'd like to be married. 'I feel like I've turned myself off for the past two years. Like I wouldn't let anyone get close to me because of what happened. I mean, what's the point of getting close to someone if you're only going to lose them? But the other day I started thinking about what I actually want out of life and I realized it was someone to love. Because you got to move on, right? You got to see some kind of future.'

It was the most I had heard Sunil speak in any meeting since I had started coming.

'That's very positive, Sunil,' said Marc. 'Thank you for sharing.'

I listened to Jake talk about going to college, and how he

wanted to train as an animator, and wondered absently where his father would be. Still weeping over his dead wife? Or happily ensconced with some newer version? I suspected the latter. Then I thought about Sam and wondered whether my offhand reference to a relationship had been wise. Then I wondered what we were in if it wasn't a relationship. Because there were relationships and relationships. And even as I mulled this over I realized that, if he asked, I wasn't sure which category we even fitted into. I couldn't help wondering whether the intensity of our search for Lily had acted as a kind of cheap glue, binding us together too quickly. What did we even have in common, other than a fall from a building?

Two days previously I had gone to the Ambulance Station to wait for Sam, and Donna had stood by her car chatting to me for a few minutes while he gathered his belongings. 'Don't mess him around.'

I turned, not sure if I had heard her correctly.

She had watched as an ambulance was unloaded by the shutters, and then rubbed her nose. 'He's all right. For a great lunk. And he really likes you.'

I hadn't known what to say.

'He does. He's been talking about you. And he doesn't talk about anyone. Don't tell him I said anything. I just . . . he's all right. I just want you to know.' She had raised her eyebrows at me then, and nodded, as if confirming something to herself.

'I've just realized. You're not in your dancing-girl outfit,' said Daphne.

There was a murmur of recognition.

'Did you get promoted?'

I was dragged from my thoughts. 'Oh. No. I got fired.'

'Where are you working now?'

'Nowhere. Yet.'

'But your outfit . . .'

I was wearing my little black dress with the white collar. 'Oh. This. It's just a dress.'

'I thought you were working at a themed bar for secretaries. Or maybe French maids.'

'Don't you ever stop, Fred?'

'You don't understand. At my age, the phrase "Use it or lose it" takes on a certain urgency. I might only have twenty or so stiffies left in me.'

'Some of us have never had twenty stiffies in us in the first place.'

We paused to give Fred and Daphne time to stop giggling.

'And your future? It sounds like it's all change for you,' said Marc.

'Well . . . I actually got offered another job.'

'You did?' There was a little ripple of applause, which made me blush.

'Oh, I'm not going to take it, but it's fine. I feel I've sort of moved on, just for being offered a job.'

William said: 'So what was the job?'

'Just something in New York.'

They all stared at me.

'You got a job offer in New York?'

'Yes.'

'A paid job?'

'With accommodation,' I said quietly.

'And you wouldn't have to wear that godawful shiny green dress?'

'I hardly think my outfit was a good enough reason to emigrate.' I laughed. Nobody else did. 'Oh, come on,' I said.

They were all still staring at me. Leanne's mouth might actually have been hanging open a little.

'*New York* New York?'

'You don't know the whole story. I can't go now. I have Lily to sort out.'

'The daughter of your ex-employer.' Jake was frowning at me.

'Well, he was more than my employer. But yes.'

'Does she have no family of her own, Louisa?' Daphne leaned forward.

'It's complicated.'

They all looked at each other.

Marc put his pad on his lap. 'How much do you feel you've really learned from these sessions, Louisa?'

I had received the package from New York: a bundle of documents, with immigration and health-insurance forms, clipped together with a thick piece of cream notepaper on which Mr Leonard M. Gopnik forwarded me a formal offer to work for his family. I had locked myself into the bathroom to read it, then read it a second time, converted the salary to pounds, sighed for a bit, and promised myself I would not Google the address.

After I'd Googled the address I resisted the brief urge to lie on the floor in a foetal position. Then I got a grip, stood up and flushed the loo (in case Lily wondered what I was doing there), washed my hands (out of habit), and took it all into my bedroom where I stuffed it into the drawer under my bed and told myself I would never look at it again.

That night she had knocked on my bedroom door shortly before midnight.

*Can I stay here? I don't really want to go back to my mum's.*

*You can stay as long as you want.*

She had lain down on the other side of my bed and curled up in a little ball. I watched her sleep, then pulled the duvet over her.

Will's daughter needed me. It was as simple as that. And,

whatever my sister said, I owed him. Here was a way to feel I hadn't been completely useless. I could still do something for him.

And that envelope proved I was someone who could get a decent job offer. That was progress. I had friends, a sort of boyfriend, even. This, too, was progress.

I ignored Nathan's missed calls and deleted his voicemail messages. I would explain it all to him in a day or two. It felt, if not like a plan, then as close to one as I was going to get right now.

Sam was due shortly after I got back on Tuesday. He texted at seven to say he was going to be late. He sent another at a quarter past eight, saying he wasn't sure what time he would make it. I'd felt flat all day, struggling with the stasis that comes from not having a job to go to, worries about how I was going to pay my bills, and being trapped in an apartment with someone else who similarly had nowhere to go and I was unwilling to leave by herself. At half nine the buzzer went. Sam was at the front door, still in uniform. I let him in and stepped out into the corridor, closing the front door behind me. He emerged from the stairwell and walked towards me, his head down. He was grey with exhaustion and gave off a strange, disturbed energy.

'I thought you weren't coming. What happened? Are you okay?'

'I'm being hauled up in front of Disciplinary.'

'What?'

'Another crew saw my rig outside the night we met Garside. They told Control. I couldn't give them a good answer as to why we were attending something that wasn't on the system.'

'So what happened?'

'I fudged it, said someone had come running out and asked

303

us for help. And that it had turned out to be a prank. Donna backed me up, thank God. But they're not happy.'

'It's not that bad, surely?'

'And one of the A and E nurses asked Lily how she knew me. And she said I'd given her a lift home from a nightclub.'

My hand went to my mouth. 'What does that mean?'

'The union's arguing my case. But if they find against me I'll be suspended. Or worse.' A new, deep furrow had etched it's way between his brows.

'Because of us. Sam, I'm so sorry.'

He shook his head. 'She wasn't to know.'

I was going to step forward and hold him then, to put my arms around him, rest my face against his. But something held me back: a sudden, unbidden image of Will, turning his face away from me, unreachable in his unhappiness. I faltered, then a second too late, reached out a hand instead and touched Sam's arm. He glanced down at it, frowning slightly, and I had the slightly discomfiting sensation that he knew something of what had just passed through my head.

'You could always give it up and raise your chickens. Build your house.' I heard my voice, trying too hard. 'You've got options! A man like you. You could do anything!'

He gave a half-smile that didn't reach his eyes. He kept staring at my hand.

We stood there for an awkward moment. 'I'd better go. Oh,' he said, holding out a parcel. 'Someone left this by the door. Didn't think it would last long in your lobby.'

'Come in, please.' I took it from him, feeling I had let him down. 'Let me cook you something badly. Come on.'

'I'd better get home.'

He walked back down the corridor before I could say anything else.

*

From the window, I watched him leave, walking stiffly back to his motorbike, and I felt a momentary cloud pass over me again. *Don't get too close.* And then I remembered Marc's advice at the end of the last session: *Understand that your grieving, anxious brain is simply responding to cortisol spikes. It is perfectly natural to be fearful of getting close to anyone.* Some days I felt as if I had two cartoon advisers constantly arguing on each side of my head.

In the living room Lily turned away from the television. 'Was that Ambulance Sam?'

'Yup.'

She went back to the television. Then the parcel grabbed her attention. 'What's that?'

'Oh. It was in the lobby. It's addressed to you.'

She stared suspiciously at it, as if she were still too conscious of the possibility of unpleasant surprises. Then she peeled back the layers of wrapping to reveal a leather-bound photograph album, its cover embossed with 'For Lily (Traynor)'.

She opened it slowly, and there, on the first page, covered with tissue, was the black and white photograph of a baby. Underneath it was a handwritten note.

*Your father weighed 9lb 2oz. I was absolutely furious with him for being so big, as I'd been told I'd have a nice small one! He was a very cross baby and kept me running ragged for months. But when he smiled . . . Oh! Old ladies would cross the road to tickle his cheeks (he hated this, of course).*

I sat down beside her. Lily flicked forward two pages and there was Will, in a royal blue prep-school uniform and cap, scowling at the camera. The note underneath read:

*Will hated that school cap so much that he hid it in the dog's basket. The second one he 'lost' in a pond. The third time his father*

*threatened to stop his pocket money, but he simply traded football
cards until he'd made it back. Even the school couldn't make him
wear it – I think he had a weekly detention until he was thirteen.*

Lily touched his face. 'I looked like him when I was small.'
'Well,' I said, 'he's your dad.'
She allowed herself a small smile, then turned to the next
page. 'Look. Look at this one.'
In the next photograph he smiled directly out at the
camera – the same skiing-holiday picture that had been in
his bedroom when we had first met. I gazed at his beautiful
face and the familiar wave of sadness passed over me. And
then, unexpectedly, Lily started to laugh. 'Look! Look at this
one!' Will, his face covered with mud after a rugby game,
another where he was dressed as a devil, taking a running
jump off a haystack. A page of silliness – Will as prankster,
laughing, human. I thought of the typed sheet Marc had given
me after I had missed Idealization Week: *It is important not to
turn the dead into saints. Nobody can walk in the shadow of a saint.*

*I wanted you to see your father before his accident. He was fiercely
ambitious and professional, yes, but I also remember times where he
slid off his chair laughing, or danced with the dog, or came home
covered with bruises because of some ridiculous dare. He once shoved
his sister's face into a bowl of sherry trifle (picture on right) because
she had said he wouldn't, and I wanted to be cross with him as it had
taken me simply ages to make, but you really could never be cross
with Will for very long.*

No, you never could. Lily flicked through the other pictures,
all with little notes beside them. This Will, rising from the pages,
was not a two-line piece in a newspaper, a careful obituary, a
solemn photograph illustrating a sad tale in a long-running

legal debate; this was a man – alive, three-dimensional. I gazed at each picture, distantly aware of each lump in my throat as it rose and was overcome.

A card had slid out onto the floor. I picked it up and scanned the two-line message. 'She wants to come and see you.'

Lily could barely tear her eyes from the album.

'What do you think, Lily? Are you up for it?'

It took her a moment to hear me. 'I don't think so. I mean, it's nice, but . . .'

The mood changed. She closed the leather cover, put it neatly to the side of the sofa and turned back to the television. A few minutes later, without saying a word, she moved up the sofa beside me and let her head fall onto my shoulder.

That night, after Lily had gone to bed, I emailed Nathan.

> I'm sorry. I can't take it. It's a long story, but I have Will's daughter living with me and a lot has been going on and I can't up and leave her. I have to do what's right. I'll try to explain in brief . . .

I ended,

> Thank you for thinking of me.

I emailed Mr Gopnik, thanking him for his offer and stating that due to a change in circumstances I was very sorry but I wouldn't be able to take the job. I wanted to write more, but the huge knot in my stomach seemed to have drained all the energy from my fingertips.

I waited an hour but neither of them responded. When I walked back into the empty living room to turn off the lights the photograph album was gone.

# Chapter Twenty-three

'Well, well . . . If it isn't the employee of the year.'

I put the bag containing my uniform and wig down on the counter. The tables of the Shamrock and Clover were already full by breakfast time; a plump forty-something businessman, whose drooping head suggested an early start on the hard stuff, gazed blearily up at me, cradling his glass between fat hands. Vera was at the far end, angrily shifting tables and people's feet to sweep under them as if she were chasing mice.

I was wearing a man's style blue shirt – it was easier to feel confident if you were wearing men's clothes, I had decided – and observed, distantly, that it was almost the same shade as Richard's. 'Richard – I wanted to talk to you about what happened last week.'

Around us the airport was half full of bank-holiday passengers; there were fewer suits than usual, and an undertow of small, crying children. Behind the till, a new banner offered the chance to 'Get Your Trip Off to a Good Start! Coffee, Croissant and a Chaser!' Richard moved briskly around the bar, placing newly filled cups of coffee and plastic-wrapped cereal bars on a tray, his brow furrowed in concentration. 'Don't bother. Is the uniform clean?'

He reached past me for the plastic bag and pulled out my green dress. He scanned it carefully under the strip-lights, his face set in a half-grimace, as if he were primed to spot unsavoury marks. I half expected him to sniff it.

'Of course it's clean.'

'It needs to be in a suitable condition for a new employee to wear.'

'It was washed yesterday,' I snapped.

I noticed suddenly that a new version of *Celtic Pan Pipes* was playing. Fewer harp strings. Heavy on the flute.

'Right. We have some paperwork in the back that you need to sign. I'll go and get it and you can do that here. And then that's it.'

'Maybe we could just do this somewhere a bit more ... private?'

Richard Percival didn't look at me. 'Too busy, I'm afraid. I have a hundred things to do and I'm one staff member down today.' He bustled past me officiously, counting aloud the remaining bags of Scampi Fries hanging by the optics. 'Six ... seven ... Vera, can you serve that gentleman over there, please?'

'Yes, well, that's what I wanted to talk to you about. I was wondering if there was any way you –'

'Eight ... nine ... The wig.'

'What?'

'Where's the wig?'

'Oh. Here.' I reached into my bag and pulled it out. I had brushed it before putting it in its own bag. It sat, like a piece of blonde roadkill, waiting to make some other person's head itch.

'Did you wash it?'

'Wash the wig?'

'Yes. It's unhygienic for somebody else to put it on without you washing it first.'

'It's made of cheaper synthetic fibres than a cut-price Barbie's. I assumed it would basically melt in a washing-machine.'

'If it's not in suitable condition for a future staff member to wear, I'm going to have to charge you for a replacement.'

I stared at him. 'You're charging me for the wig?'

He held it up, then stuffed it back into the bag. 'Twenty-eight pounds forty. I will, of course, provide you with a receipt.'

'Oh, my God. You really are going to charge me for the wig.'

I laughed. I stood in the middle of the crowded airport, as the planes took off, and I thought about what my life had become working for this man. I pulled my purse from my pocket. 'Fine,' I said. 'Twenty-eight pounds forty, you say? Tell you what, I'll round it up to thirty, you know, to include administrative expenses.'

'You don't need to –'

I counted out the notes, and slammed them onto the bar in front of him. 'You know something, Richard? I like working. If you'd looked beyond your bloody targets for five minutes you would have seen that I was somebody who actually wanted to do well. I worked hard. I wore your horrific uniform, even though it turned my hair static and made small children jig in the street behind me. I did everything you asked, including cleaning men's loos, which I'm pretty sure was not in my contract, and which, in actual employment law, I'm sure should have meant the provision of a Hazchem suit at least. I stood in for extra shifts while you searched for new bartenders because you've alienated every single member of staff who ever came through this door, and I have upsold your wretched dry-roasted peanuts even though they smell like someone breaking wind.

'But I'm not an automaton. I'm human and I have a life, and just for a short while I had responsibilities that meant I couldn't be the employee you – or I – would have liked. I came here today to ask for my job back – actually, to beg for my job back, as I still have responsibilities and I want a job. I *need* a job.

But I just realized I don't want this one. I'd rather work for free than spend another day in this miserable, soul-destroying pan-pipe-chuffing bar. I would rather clean toilets *for free* than work one more day for you.

'So thank you, Richard. You've actually prompted my first positive decision in as long as I can remember.' I rammed my purse into my bag, pushed the wig towards him, and made to leave. 'You can stick your job in the same place you can stick those peanuts.' I turned back. 'Oh, and that thing you do with your hair? All that gel stuff and the perfectly even top thing? Awful. It makes you look like Action Man.'

The businessman sat up on his bar stool and gave a little round of applause. Richard's hand went involuntarily to his head.

I glanced at the businessman, then back at Richard. 'Actually, forget the last bit. That was mean.'

And I left.

I was striding across the concourse, my heart still thumping, when I heard him. '*Louisa! Louisa!*'

Richard was half walking, half running behind me. I considered ignoring him, but finally came to a halt by the perfume concession. 'What?' I said. 'Did I miss a peanut crumb?'

He stopped, puffing slightly. He studied the shop window for a few seconds, as if he was thinking. Then he faced me. 'You're right. Okay? You're right.'

I stared at him.

'The Shamrock and Clover. It's a horrible place. And I know I've not been the greatest to work for. But all I can tell you is that, for every miserable directive I give you, my nuts are being squeezed ten times harder by Head Office. My wife hates me because I'm never home. The suppliers hate me because I have to cut their margins every single week because of pressure from shareholders. My regional manager says I'm underperforming on units shifted and if I don't pull it out of the bag I'm going to get sent to the North Wales Passenger Ferry branch. At which point my wife will actually leave me. And I won't blame her.

'I hate managing people. I have the social skills of a lamp-post, which is why I can't hang on to anyone. Vera only stays because she has the skin of a rhino and I suspect she's secretly after my job. So there – I'm sorry. I'd actually quite like to give you your job back because, whatever I said earlier, you were pretty good. Customers liked you.'

He sighed, and looked out over the milling crowds around us. 'But you know what, Louisa? You should get out while you can. You're pretty, you're smart, hardworking – you could get something way better than this. If I wasn't locked into a mortgage that I can barely afford, a baby on the way and payments to make on a fricking Honda Civic that makes me feel about 120 years old, believe me, I'd be taking off out of here faster than one of those planes.' He held out a hand with a payslip. 'Your holiday pay. Now go. Seriously, Louisa. Get out.'

I looked down at the little brown envelope in my hand. Around us the passengers moved at a crawl, pausing at outlet windows, checking for vanished passports, oblivious to what was going on in their midst. And I knew, with a weary inevitability, what was going to happen.

'Richard? Thanks for that, but . . . could I still have the job? Even if it's just for a bit? I do actually really need it.'

Richard looked as if he couldn't believe what I was saying. Then he let out a sigh. 'Actually, if you could do a couple of months it would be a massive relief. I'm right up the proverbial creek here. In fact, if you could start now I could make it over to the wholesalers to pick up the new beer mats.'

We swapped places; a little waltz of mutual disappointment.

'I'll call home,' I said.

'Oh. Here,' he said. We gazed at each other a moment longer, and then he handed me the plastic bag containing my uniform. 'I guess you'll be needing this.'

Richard and I settled into a routine of sorts. He treated me with a little more consideration, only asking me to do the Gents on the days when Noah, the new cleaner, failed to turn up, not commenting if he thought I was spending too long talking to customers (even if he did look a bit pained). In turn I was cheerful and punctual and careful to upsell when I could. I felt an odd responsibility towards his nuts.

One day he took me to one side and said that, while it was possibly a little premature, Head Office had told him they were looking to elevate one of the permanent staff to an assistant managerial position and if things carried on as they were he felt very much inclined to put my name forward. ('I can't risk promoting Vera. She'd put floor cleaner in my tea to get my job.') I thanked him and tried to look more delighted than I felt.

Lily, meanwhile, asked Samir for a job, and he said he would take her for a half-day's trial if she would do it for free. I handed her a coffee at seven thirty, and made sure she left the flat dressed and ready in time for her eight o'clock start. When I returned home that evening, she had apparently got the job, albeit on £2.73 an hour, which I discovered was the lowest rate he could legally pay her. She had spent most of the day moving crates in the back storeroom and putting prices on tins with an ancient sticker gun, while Samir and his cousin watched football on his iPad. She was filthy and exhausted, but curiously happy. 'If I last a month he says he'll consider putting me on the till.'

*

I had a shift change, so on Thursday afternoon we drove to Lily's parents' house in St John's Wood, and I waited in the car while Lily went in and collected some more clothes and the Kandinsky print that she had promised would look good in my flat. She emerged twenty minutes later, her face furious and closed. Tanya walked out into the porch, her arms folded, watching silently as Lily opened the boot and threw in an overstuffed holdall and, more carefully, the print. Then she climbed into the front seat and gazed straight ahead at the empty road. As Tanya closed the door behind her, there was a small possibility that she was wiping her eyes.

I put my key into the ignition.

'When I grow up,' Lily said, and perhaps only I could have detected the faint tremor in her voice, 'I am not going to be *anything* like my mother.'

I waited a moment, then started the car and we drove in silence back to my flat.

*Fancy the pictures tonight? I could do with some escapism.*
  *I don't think I should leave Lily.*
  *Bring her?*
  *I'd better not. Sorry, Sam x*

That evening I found Lily out on the fire escape. She looked up at the sound of the window opening and waved a cigarette. 'Thought it was a bit mean to keep smoking in your flat, given that you don't.'

I wedged the window open, climbed out carefully, and sat down on the iron steps beside her. Below us the car park simmered in the August heat, the scent of hot tarmac rising into the still air. A car with the bonnet up thumped bass from its sound system. The metal of the steps retained the warmth of a month of sunny afternoons and I leaned back, closing my eyes.

'I thought it would all work out,' Lily said.

I opened them.

'I thought if I could just get Peter to go away all my problems would be solved. I thought if I could find my dad I would feel like I belonged somewhere. And now Peter's gone, and Garside's gone, and I know about my dad and I have you. But nothing feels like I expected.'

I was about to tell her not to be silly. I was about to point out that she had come such a long way in a short time, that she had her first job, prospects, a bright future – the standard adult responses. But they sounded trite and patronizing.

At the end of the road a bunch of office workers huddled round a metal table by the pub's rear door. Later tonight it would be packed with hipsters and strays from the City, spilling out with drinks across the pavement, their raucous calls filtering in through my open window. 'I know what you mean,' I said. 'I've been waiting to feel normal again since your dad died. I feel like I'm basically going through the motions. I'm still in a crappy job. I still live in this flat, which I don't think is ever going to feel like home. I had a near-death experience, but I can't say it gave me wisdom or gratitude for life or anything. I go to a grief-counselling group full of people who are as stuck as I am. But I haven't really done anything.'

Lily thought about this. 'You helped me.'

'That's pretty much the one thing I hang onto most days.'

'And you have a boyfriend.'

'He's not my boyfriend.'

'Sure, Louisa.'

We watched the traffic crawl down towards the City. Lily took a final drag of her cigarette, and stubbed it out on the metal step.

'That's my next thing,' I said.

She had the grace to look slightly guilty. 'I know. I will stop. I promise.'

Across the rooftops the sun had started to slide, its orange glow diffused by the lead-grey air of the City evening.

'You know, Lily, perhaps some things just take longer than others. I think we'll get there, though.'

She linked her arm through mine and let her head rest on my shoulder. We watched the sun's gentle fall, and the lengthening shadows creeping towards us, and I thought about the New York skyline and that nobody was truly free. Perhaps all freedom – physical, personal – only came at the cost of somebody or something else.

The sun vanished, and the orange sky began to turn petrol-blue. When we stood up, Lily smoothed her skirt, then gazed at the packet in her hand. She pulled the remaining cigarettes abruptly from the wrapper and snapped them in half, then flung them into the air, a confetti of tobacco and white paper. She looked at me triumphantly and held up her hand. 'There. I am officially a smoke-free zone.'

'Just like that.'

'Why not? You said it might take longer than we thought. Well, that's my first step. What's yours?'

'Oh, God. Maybe I'll persuade Richard to let me stop wearing that godawful nylon wig.'

'That would be an excellent first step. It would be nice not to get an electric shock off every door handle in your flat.'

Her smile was infectious. I took the empty cigarette packet from her before she could litter the car park with that too, and stood back so she could climb through the window. She stopped and turned to me, as if she had suddenly thought of something. 'You know, you don't need to be sad just to stay connected to him.'

I stared at her.

'My dad. It's just a thought.' She shrugged and climbed back in through the window.

I woke the next day to find that Lily had already gone to work. She'd left a note saying she would bring some bread home at lunchtime as we were a bit short. I had drunk some coffee, had breakfast and put on my trainers to go for a walk (Marc: 'exercise is as good for your spirit as it is for your body!') when my mobile rang – a number I didn't recognize.

'Hello!'

It took me a minute. 'Mum?'

'Look out your window!'

I walked across the living room and gazed out. My mother was on the pavement waving vigorously.

'What – what are you doing here? Where's Dad?'

'He's at home.'

'Is Granddad okay?'

'Granddad's fine.'

'But you never come to London by yourself. You don't even go past the petrol station without Dad in tow.'

'Well, it was about time I changed, wasn't it? Shall I come up? I don't want to use up all the minutes on my new phone.'

I buzzed her in, and went around the living room, clearing the worst of last night's dishes, and by the time she reached the door I was standing there, arms open, ready to greet her.

She was wearing her good anorak, her handbag slung satchel-style over her shoulder ('Harder for muggers to snatch it') and her hair styled into soft waves around her neck. She was beaming, her lips carefully outlined in coral-pink lipstick, and clutching the family *A–Z*, which dated back to some time around 1983.

'I can't believe you came by yourself.'

'Isn't it wonderful? I actually feel quite giddy. I told a young man on the tube that it was the first time I'd been on the Underground in thirty years without someone holding my hand, and he moved a full four seats down the carriage. I got quite hysterical with laughter. Will you put the kettle on?' She sat, pulling off her coat, and gazed at the walls around her. 'Well now. The grey is . . . interesting.'

'Lily's choice.' I wondered fleetingly if her arrival was some great joke and Dad was about to barrel in through my front door, laughing at what a great eejit I was, believing Josie would come anywhere by herself. I put a mug in front of her. 'I don't understand. Why did you come without Dad?'

She took a sip of the tea. 'Oh, that's lovely. You always did make the best cup of tea.' She put it on the table, carefully sliding a paperback book under it first. 'Well, I woke up this morning and I thought about all the things I had to do – put a wash on, clean the back windows, change Granddad's bedding, buy toothpaste – and I just suddenly thought, Nope. I can't do it. I'm not going to waste a glorious Saturday doing the same thing I've done for thirty years. I'm going to have an adventure.'

'An adventure.'

'So I thought we could go to a show.'

'A show.'

'Yes – a show. Louisa, have you turned into a parrot? Mrs Cousins from the insurance brokers says there's a stall in Leicester Square where you can buy cheap tickets on the day for shows that aren't full. I was wondering if you'd like to come with me.'

'What about Treena?'

Mum waved a hand. 'Oh, she was busy. So what do you say? Shall we go and see if we can get some tickets?'

'I'll have to tell Lily.'

'Then go and tell her. I'll finish my tea, you can do something with that hair of yours, and we'll head off. I've got a one-day travelcard, you know! I might just hop on and off the Underground all day!'

We got half-price tickets to *Billy Elliot*. It was that or a Russian tragedy, and Mum said she'd been funny about Russians since someone had given her cold beetroot soup and tried to pretend that was how the Russians ate it.

She sat rapt beside me for the entire performance, nudging me and muttering at intervals, 'I remember the actual miners' strike, Louisa. It was very hard on those poor families. Margaret Thatcher! Do you remember her? Oh, she was a terrible woman. Always had a nice handbag, though.' When the young Billy flew into the air, apparently fuelled by his ambitions, she wept quietly beside me, a fresh white handkerchief pressed to her nose.

I watched the boy's dance teacher, Mrs Wilkinson, a woman whose ambitions had never lifted her beyond the confines of the town, and tried not to see anything of my own life. I was a woman with a job and a sort-of-boyfriend, sitting in a West End theatre on a Saturday afternoon. I totted these things up as if they were little victories against some foe I couldn't quite identify.

We emerged into the afternoon light dazed and emotionally spent. 'Right,' said Mum, tucking her handbag firmly under her arm (some habits die hard). 'Tea at a hotel. C'mon. We'll make a day of it.'

We couldn't get into any of the grand ones, but we found a nice hotel near Haymarket with a tea selection that Mum approved of. She asked for a table in the middle of the room and sat there remarking on every person who walked in, noting their dress, whether they looked like they came from 'abroad', their lack of wisdom in bringing small children, or little dogs that looked like rats.

'Well, look at us!' she would exclaim every now and then, when it grew quiet. 'Isn't this nice?'

We ordered English Breakfast tea (Mum: 'That's just posh for normal tea, yes? None of those weird flavours?') and the 'Afternoon Tea Fancy Plate' and we ate tiny crustless sandwiches, little scones that weren't as good as Mum made and cakes in gold foil. Mum talked for half an hour about *Billy Elliot* and how she thought we should all do this once a month or so and she bet that my father would love it if we could get him down here.

'How is Dad?'

'Oh, he's fine. You know your father.'

I wanted to ask, but was too afraid. When I looked up, she was gazing at me a little beadily. 'And no, Louisa, I am not doing my legs. And, no, he's not happy. But there are more important things in life.'

'What did he say about you coming here today?'

She snorted, and covered it up with a little coughing fit. 'He didn't believe I was going to. I told him about it when I brought him up his tea this morning, and he started to laugh, and if I'm honest with you it annoyed me so much I got dressed and I just went.'

My eyes widened. 'You didn't tell him?'

'I already had told him. He's been leaving messages on this phone thing all day, the eejit.' She peered at the screen, then tucked it neatly back into her pocket.

I sat and watched her fork another little scone delicately onto her plate. She closed her eyes in pleasure as she took a bite. 'This is just marvellous.'

I swallowed. 'Mum, you're not going to get divorced, are you?'

Her eyes shot open. 'Divorced? I'm a good Catholic girl,

Louisa. We don't divorce. We just make our men suffer for all eternity!'

I paid the bill, and we disappeared to the Ladies, a cavernous room of walnut-coloured marble and expensive flowers, overseen by a silent attendant who stood by the basins. Mum washed her hands twice, thoroughly, then sniffed the various hand lotions lined up against the sink, pulling faces in the mirror depending on what she liked. 'I shouldn't say so, given my opposition to the patriarchy and all, but I do wish one of you girls had a nice man.'

'I've met someone,' I said, before I realized I'd said it.

She turned to me, a lotion bottle in her hand. 'You haven't!'

'He's a paramedic.'

'Well, that's smashing. A paramedic! That's almost as useful as a plumber. So when are we going to meet him?'

I faltered. 'Meet him? I'm not sure it's . . .'

'It's what?'

'Well. I mean, it's early days. I'm not sure it's that kind of –'

My mother unscrewed the lid of her lipstick and stared into the mirror. 'It's just for sex, is that what you're saying?'

'Mum!' I glanced at the attendant.

'Well, what are you saying?'

'I'm not sure I'm ready for a real relationship just yet.'

'Why? What else have you got going on? Those ovaries won't go in the freezer, you know.'

'So why didn't Treena come?' I said, hurriedly changing the subject.

'She couldn't find a sitter for Thom.'

'You said she was busy.'

Mum's eyes darted across to my reflection. She pressed her lips together and snapped her lipstick back into her handbag. 'She seems to be a little cross with you right now, Louisa.' She activated Maternal X-ray Vision. 'Have you two had a falling out?'

'I don't know why she always has to have opinions about everything I do.' I heard my own voice, the sulky tones of a twelve-year-old.

She fixed me with a look.

So I told her. I sat up on the marble basin, and Mum took the easy chair, and I told her about the job offer and why I couldn't possibly take it, how we had lost Lily and found her again, and how she was finally beginning to come out of the other side. 'I've arranged for her to meet Mrs Traynor again. So we're moving forward. But Treena just won't listen, although if Thom were going through half the same thing she'd be the first person saying I couldn't walk away from him.'

I felt relieved telling my mother. She, of all people, would understand the ties of responsibility. 'So that's why she's not talking to me.'

My mother was staring at me.

'Jesus, Mary, and Joseph, have you lost your mind?'

'What?'

'A job in New York with all the trimmings and you're sticking around here to work in that godawful place at the airport? Did you hear this?' She turned to the attendant. 'I can't believe she's my own daughter. Honest to God, I wonder what happened to the brains she was born with.'

The attendant shook her head slowly. 'No good,' she said.

'Mum! I'm doing the right thing!'

'For whom?'

'For Lily!'

'You think nobody other than you could have helped get that girl back on her feet? Well, did you speak to this chap in New York and ask him whether you could defer the job offer a few weeks?'

'It's not that kind of a job.'

'How would you know? You don't ask, you don't get. Isn't that right?'

The attendant nodded slowly.

'Oh, Jesus. When I think about it . . .'

The attendant gave my mother a hand towel and she fanned her neck vigorously with it. 'Listen to me, Louisa. I've got one brilliant daughter stuck at home weighed down with responsibility because she made a bad choice early on – not that I don't love Thom to bits, but I'll tell you, I want to cry my heart out when I think of what Treena could have become if she'd just had that boy a bit later. I'm stuck looking after your father and Granddad, and that's fine. I'm finding my way. But this should not be the most you have to look forward to in your life, you hear me? Not a bunch of half-price tickets and a fancy tea every now and then. You should be out there! You're the one person in our family with an actual ruddy chance! And to hear you've just chucked it away for the sake of some girl you barely even know!'

'I did the *right thing*, Mum.'

'Maybe you did. Or maybe it wasn't actually an either/or situation.'

'You don't ask, you don't get,' said the attendant.

'There! This lady knows. You need to get back there and ask this American gentleman is there any way you can come along a bit later . . . Don't you look at me like that, Louisa. I've been too soft on you. I haven't pushed you when I should have done. You need to get yourself out of that dead-end job of yours and start living.'

'The job is gone, Mum.'

'Gone my pearly-handled backside it is. Have you actually asked them?'

I shook my head.

Mum huffed and adjusted the scarf around her neck. She pulled two pound coins from her purse and pressed them into the hand of the attendant. 'Well, I have to say, haven't you done a grand job! You could eat your supper off this floor. And it all smells simply gorgeous.'

The attendant smiled at her warmly, and then, almost as an afterthought, held up a finger. She peered out of the door, then walked to her cupboard, unlocking it swiftly with a bunch of keys. She emerged and pressed a bar of floral soap into Mum's hands.

Mum sniffed it and sighed. 'Well, that is just *heaven*. Just a little piece of heaven.'

'For you.'

'For me?'

The woman closed Mum's hands around it.

'Well, aren't you the kindest? May I ask your name?'

'Maria.'

'Maria, I'm Josie. I'm going to make sure I come back to London and use your toilet the very next time I'm here. Do you see that, Louisa? Who knows what happens when you break out a little? How's that for an adventure? And I got the most gorgeous bar of soap from my lovely new friend Maria here!' They clasped hands with the fervency of old acquaintances about to be parted, and we left the hotel.

I couldn't tell her. I couldn't tell her that that job haunted me from the moment I woke until I went to sleep. Whatever I said to anyone else, I knew I would always regret to my bones missing the chance to live and work in New York. That no matter how much I told myself there would be other chances, other places, this would be the lost opportunity I carried, like a cheap handbag I regretted buying, wherever I went.

And sure enough, after I had waved her off on the train to

my, no doubt, bemused and blustering father, and long after I had made a salad for Lily from bits that Sam had left in the fridge, when I checked my email that night there was a message from Nathan.

> I can't say I agree, but I do get what you're doing. I guess Will would have been proud of you. You're a good person, Clark x

# Chapter Twenty-four

These are the things I learned about being a parent, while not actually being a parent. That whatever you did you would probably be wrong. If you were cruel or dismissive or neglectful, you would leave scars upon your charge. If you were supportive and loving, encouraging and praising them for even their smallest achievements – getting out of bed on time, say, or managing not to smoke for a whole day – it would ruin them in different ways. I learned that if you were a *de facto* parent all these things applied but you had none of the natural authority you might reasonably expect when feeding and looking after another person.

With all this in mind, I loaded Lily into the car on my day off and announced that we were going to lunch. It would probably go horribly wrong, I told myself, but at least there would be two of us there to shoulder it.

Because Lily was so busy staring at her phone, with her earphones plugged in, it was a good forty minutes before she looked out the car window. She frowned as we approached a signpost. 'This isn't the way to your mum and dad's.'

'I know.'

'Then where are we going?'

'I told you. To lunch.'

When she had stared at me long enough to accept that I wasn't going to elaborate, she squinted out the window for a while. 'God, you're annoying sometimes.'

Half an hour later we pulled up at the Crown and Garter, a red-brick hotel set in two acres of parkland, about twenty minutes south of Oxford. Neutral territory, I had decided, was the way forward. Lily climbed out and shut the door emphatically enough to send me the message that this was *actually still quite annoying*.

I ignored her, put on a slick of lipstick and walked into the restaurant, letting Lily follow.

Mrs Traynor was already at a table. When Lily saw her, she let out a little groan.

'Why are we doing this again?'

'Because things change,' I said, and propelled her forwards.

'Lily.' Mrs Traynor rose to her feet. She had evidently been to a hairdresser, and her hair was once again beautifully cut and blow-dried. She was wearing a little make-up, too, and those two things conspired to make her look like the Mrs Traynor of old: self-possessed, someone who understood that appearances were, if not everything, at least the foundation of something.

'Hello, Mrs Traynor.'

'Hi,' Lily mumbled. She didn't reach out a hand, but positioned herself at the seat beside mine.

Mrs Traynor registered this, but gave a brief smile, sat down and summoned the waiter. 'This restaurant was one of your father's favourites,' she said, placing her napkin on her lap. 'On the rare occasions I could persuade him to leave London, this is where we would meet. It's rather good food. Michelin-starred.'

I looked at the menu – *turbot quenelles with a frangipane of mussels and langoustine, smoked duck breast with cavalo nero and Israeli couscous* – and hoped very much that as Mrs Traynor had suggested this restaurant she would pay.

'It looks a bit fussy,' said Lily, not lifting her head from the menu.

I glanced at Mrs Traynor.

'That's exactly what Will said too. But it is very good. I think I'll have the quail.'

'I'll have the sea bass,' Lily said, and closed the leather-bound menu.

I stared at the list in front of me. There was nothing here I even recognized. What was *rutabaga*? What was *ravioli of bone marrow and samphire*? I wondered if I could ask for a sandwich.

'Are you ready to order?' The waiter appeared beside me. I waited as the others reeled off their choices. Then I spotted a word I recognized from my time in Paris. 'Can I have the *joues de boeuf confites*?'

'With the potato gnocchi and asparagus? Certainly, Madame.'

Beef, I thought. I can do beef.

We talked of small things while waiting for our starters. I told Mrs Traynor that I was still working at the airport but was being considered for a promotion and tried to make it sound like a positive career choice rather than a cry for help. I told her Lily had found a job, and when she heard what Lily was doing, Mrs Traynor didn't shudder, as I had secretly been afraid she might, but nodded. 'That sounds eminently sensible. It never hurts to get your hands dirty when you're starting out.'

'It's not got any prospects,' Lily said firmly. 'Unless you count being allowed to move onto the till.'

'Well, neither does having a paper round. But your father did that for two years before he left school. It instils a work ethic.'

'And people always need tins of frankfurters,' I observed.

'Do they really?' said Mrs Traynor, and looked briefly appalled.

We watched as another table was seated beside us, an elderly woman lowered with much fuss and exclamation into a chair by two male relatives.

'We got your photograph album,' I said.

328

'Oh, you did! I had wondered. Did . . . did you like it?'

Lily's eyes flickered towards her. 'It was nice, thank you,' she said.

Mrs Traynor took a sip of her water. 'I wanted to show you another side of Will. I feel sometimes as if his life has been rather taken over by what happened when he died. I just wanted to show that he was more than a wheelchair. More than the manner of his death.'

There was a brief silence.

'It was nice, thank you,' Lily repeated.

Our food arrived, and Lily grew silent again. The waiters hovered officiously, filling water glasses when their levels fell by a centimetre. A breadboard was offered, removed and re-offered five minutes later. The restaurant filled with people like Mrs Traynor: well-dressed, well-spoken, people for whom *turbot quenelles* was a standard lunch and not a conversational minefield. Mrs Traynor asked after my family, and spoke warmly of my father. 'He did such a very good job at the castle.'

'It must be strange, not going back,' I said, then winced internally, wondering if I'd breached some invisible line.

But Mrs Traynor just gazed at the tablecloth in front of her. 'It is,' she agreed, and nodded, her smile a little tighter, then drank some more water.

The conversation carried on like this through our starters (smoked salmon for Lily, salad for Mrs Traynor and me), stalling and moving forward in fits and starts, like someone learning to drive a car. It was with some relief that I saw the waiter approach with our main courses. My smile disappeared as he placed my plate in front of me. It did not look like beef. It looked like soggy brown discs in a thick brown sauce.

'I'm sorry,' I said to the waiter. 'I ordered the beef?'

He let his gaze hang on me for a moment. 'This is the beef, Madame.'

We both stared at my plate.

'*Joues de boeuf?*' he said. 'Beef cheeks?'

'Beef *cheeks?*'

We both stared at my plate and my stomach did a little flip. 'Oh, of course,' I said. 'I – yes. Beef cheeks. Thank you.'

Beef cheeks. I was too afraid to ask from which end they came. I wasn't sure which would be worse. I smiled at Mrs Traynor, and set about nibbling my gnocchi.

We ate in near silence. Mrs Traynor and I were both running out of conversational options. Lily spoke little, and when she did say something it was spiky, as if she were testing her grandmother. She toyed with her food, a reluctant teen dragged along to a too-fancy lunch with the grown-ups. I ate mine in small forkfuls, trying not to listen to the little voice that kept squeaking in my ear: *You're eating cheeks! Actual cheeks!*

Eventually we ordered coffee. When the waiter had gone, Mrs Traynor removed her napkin and put it on the table. 'I can't do this any longer.'

Lily's head lifted. She looked at me and back at Mrs Traynor.

'The food is very nice and it's lovely hearing about your jobs and all, but this really isn't going to move us forward, is it?'

I wondered if she was going to leave, whether Lily had pushed her too far. I saw the surprise in Lily's face and realized she was thinking it too. But instead Mrs Traynor pushed away her cup and saucer, and leaned forward over the table. 'Lily, I didn't come to impress you with a fancy lunch. I came to say I'm sorry. It's hard to explain how I was when you turned up that day, but that unfortunate meeting was not your fault, and I want to apologize that your introduction to this side of your family has been so . . . inadequate.'

The waiter approached with the coffee, and Mrs Traynor lifted her hand without turning. 'Can you leave us for two minutes, please?'

He backed away swiftly with his tray. I sat very still. Mrs Traynor, her face taut and her voice urgent, took a breath. 'Lily, I lost my son – your father – and in truth I probably lost him some time before he died. His death took away everything my life was built on: my role as a mother, my family, my career, even my faith. I have felt, frankly, as if I descended into a dark hole. But to discover that he had a daughter – that I have a granddaughter – has made me think all might not be lost.'

She swallowed.

'I'm not going to say that you've returned part of him to me, because that wouldn't be fair on you. You are, as I've already grasped, very much your own person. You've brought me a whole new person to care about. I hope you'll give me a second chance, Lily. Because I would very much like – no, *dammit* – I would *love* for us to spend time together. Louisa tells me you're a strong character. Well, you should know that it runs in your family. So we'll probably butt heads a few times, just as I did with your father. But essentially, if nothing else comes of today, you must know this.'

She took Lily's hand and gripped it. 'I'm so very glad to know you. You've changed everything so much simply by existing. My daughter, your aunt Georgina, is flying over next month to meet you, and has already been asking if the two of us might go over to Sydney and stay with her at some point. I have a letter from her for you in my handbag.'

Her voice dropped. 'I know we can never make up for your father not being here, and I know I'm not – well, I'm still climbing out of things rather – but . . . do you think . . . perhaps . . . . you could find some room for a rather difficult grandmother?'

Lily stared at her.

'Might you at least . . . give it a go?'

Mrs Traynor's voice cracked slightly on the last sentence.

There was a long silence. I could hear the beating of my heart in my ears. Lily looked at me, and after what seemed like an eternity, she looked back at Mrs Traynor. 'Would you . . . would you want me to come and stay with you?'

'If you wanted to. Yes, I would like that very much.'

'When?'

'When can you come?'

I'd never seen Camilla Traynor anything less than composed, but at that moment her face crumpled. Her other hand crept across the table. After a second's hesitation, Lily took it, and they gripped each other's fingers tightly across the white linen, like survivors of a shipwreck, while the waiter stood holding his tray, unsure when he could safely move forward again.

'I'll bring her back tomorrow afternoon.'

I stood in the car park as Lily hung back by Mrs Traynor's car. She had eaten two puddings – her chocolate molten pot and my own (I had completely lost my appetite by then) and was casually examining the waistband of her jeans. 'You're sure?' I wasn't sure which of them I was directing this to. I was conscious how fragile this new *entente cordiale* was, how easy it would be for it to flare up and go wrong.

'We'll be fine.'

'I don't have work tomorrow, Louisa,' Lily called out. 'Samir's cousin does Sundays.'

It felt odd leaving them there, even if Lily was beaming. I wanted to say 'no smoking', and 'no swearing' and maybe even 'How about we do this some other time?' but Lily waved and climbed into the passenger seat of Mrs Traynor's Golf with barely a backward glance.

It was done. Out of my hands.

Mrs Traynor turned to join her.

'Mrs Traynor? Can I ask you something?'

She stopped. 'Camilla. I think you and I are beyond formalities, don't you?'

'Camilla. Did you ever speak to Lily's mother?'

'Ah. Yes, I did.' She stooped to pick some tiny weed out of a border. 'I told her I was hoping to spend a lot of time with Lily in the future. And that I was quite conscious that in her eyes I was no kind of maternal role model, but that, frankly, none of us appeared to be ideal in that role, and it would behove her to think carefully, for once, about putting her child's happiness before her own.'

My jaw might have dropped a little. '"Behove" is an excellent word,' I said, when I could speak.

'It is rather, isn't it?' She straightened. The faintest hint of mischief glinted in her eyes. 'Yes. Well. The Tanya Houghton-Millers of this world hold no fears for me. I think we'll rub along just fine, Lily and I.'

I made to move back to my car, but this time Mrs Traynor stopped me. 'Thank you, Louisa.'

Her hand lay on my arm. 'I didn't d—'

'You did. I'm very much aware that I have an awful lot to thank you for. At some point I hope I can do something for you.'

'Oh, you don't need to. I'm fine.'

Her eyes searched mine, and she gave me a small smile. Her lipstick, I noticed, was perfect. 'Well, I'll ring you tomorrow about dropping Lily home.'

Mrs Traynor tucked her handbag under her arm and walked back to her car, where Lily was waiting.

I watched the Golf disappear, and then I called Sam.

A buzzard wheeled lazily in the azure sky above the field, its enormous wings suspended in the shimmering blue. I had offered to help him finish some bricklaying but we had done one row (I had handed him the bricks). The sultry heat was such that he had suggested we had a cold beer during our break, and somehow after we had lain back in the grass for a while, it had proven impossible to get up again. I had told him the story of the beef cheeks and he had laughed for a full minute, trying to straighten his face when I protested that *If they had only called them something else* and *I mean, it's like being told you're eating chicken buttock or something*. Now I was stretched out beside him, listening to the birds and the gentle whisper of the grass, watching the peach-coloured sun slide gently towards the horizon, and thought, when I was managing not to worry whether Lily had used the word *pussy-whipped* yet, that life was not all bad.

'Sometimes when it's like this I think I might not bother building the house at all,' said Sam. 'I might just lie in a field till I get old.'

'Good plan.' I was chewing a grass stalk. 'Except the rain-water shower is going to seem a lot less appealing in January.'

I felt his laugh, a low rumble.

I had come straight to him from the restaurant, inexplicably unbalanced by the unexpected absence of Lily. I didn't want to be in the flat alone. When I had pulled up in the gateway of Sam's field, I had sat as my car engine ticked its way to sleep and watched him, content in his own company, scraping mortar onto each brick and pressing it to the next, wiping the sweat from his brow on his faded T-shirt, and I had felt something in me unwind. He had said nothing about the slight awkwardness of our last few conversations and I was grateful.

A solitary cloud drifted across the blue. Sam shifted his leg closer to mine. His feet were twice the size of my own.

'I wonder whether Mrs T has got her photographs out again. You know, for Lily.'

'Photographs?'

'Framed pictures. I told you. She didn't have a single one of Will anywhere that time Lily and I went to her house. I was quite surprised when she sent the album because a little bit of me had wondered if she'd destroyed them all.'

He was silent, thinking.

'It's odd. But when I thought about it, I don't have any pictures of Will on display either. Maybe it just takes a while to . . . to be able to have them looking at you again. How long did it take you to have your sister by your bed again?'

'I never took her down. I like having her there, especially looking like . . . like she used to look.' He lifted his arm above his head. 'She used to give it to me straight. Typical big sister. When I think I've got something wrong, I look at that picture and I hear her voice. *Sam, you great lunk, just get on with it.*' He turned his face towards me. 'And, you know, it's good for Jake to see her around. He needs to feel that it's okay to talk about her.'

'Maybe I'll put one up. It will be nice for Lily to have pictures of her dad in the flat.'

The hens were loose and a few feet away two of them shivered into a patch of dirt, ruffling their feathers and wiggling, sending up little clouds of dust. Poultry, it turned out, had personalities. There was the bossy chestnut, the affectionate one with the piebald comb, the little bantam that had to be plucked out of the tree every evening and put to bed in the coop.

'Do you think I should text her? To see how it's going?'

'Who?'

'Lily.'

'Leave them. They'll be fine.'

'I know you're right. It's weird. I was watching her in that restaurant and she's so much more like him than I first realized. I think Mrs Traynor – Camilla – could see it, too. She kept blinking at Lily's mannerisms, like she was suddenly remembering stuff Will did. There was this one time when Lily raised an eyebrow, and neither of us could take our eyes off her. She did it just like he used to.

'So what do you want to do tonight?'

'Oh . . . I don't mind. You choose.' I stretched out, feeling the grass tickle my neck. 'I might just lie here. If you happened to fall gently on top of me at some point that would be okay.'

I waited for him to laugh, but he didn't.

'So . . . shall we . . . talk about us?'

'Us?'

He pulled a blade of grass through his teeth. 'Yup. I just thought . . . well, I wondered what you thought was going on here.'

'You make us sound like a maths problem.'

'Just trying to make sure we don't have any more misunderstandings, Lou.'

I watched him discard the grass, and pick a new blade. 'I think we're good,' I said. 'Well, I'm not going to accuse you of having a neglected child this time. Or a trail of imaginary girlfriends.'

'But you're still holding back.'

It was gently said, but it felt like a kick.

I pushed myself up on my elbow, so that I was looking down on him. 'I'm here, aren't I? You're the first person I call at the end of the day. We see each other when we can. I wouldn't call that holding back.'

'Yup. We see each other, we have sex, eat some nice meals.'

'I thought that was basically every man's dream relationship.'

'I'm not every man, Lou.'

We gazed at each other in silence for a minute. I no longer felt relaxed. I felt wrong-footed, defensive.

He sighed. 'Don't look like that. I don't want to get married or anything. I'm just saying . . . I've never met any woman who wanted less to talk about what might be going on.' He shaded his eyes with his hand, squinting slightly into the sun. 'It's fine if you don't want this to be a long-term thing. Well, okay, it's not, but I just want an idea of what you're thinking. I guess, since Ellen died, I've realized life is short. I don't want . . .'

'You don't want what?'

'To waste time on something that isn't going anywhere.'

'*Waste time?*'

'Bad choice of words. I'm not good at this stuff.' He pushed himself upright.

'Why does it have to *be* anything? We have fun together. Why can't we just let it run and, I don't know, see what happens?'

'Because I'm human. Okay? And it's hard enough to be around someone who is still in love with a ghost, without them also acting like they're just using you for sex.' He raised his hand, covering his eyes. 'Jesus Christ, I can't believe I just said that out loud.'

My voice, when it emerged, cracked a little. 'I'm not in love with a ghost.'

This time he didn't look at me. He pushed himself to a seated position and rubbed at his face. 'Then let him go, Lou.'

He climbed heavily to his feet and walked off to the railway carriage, leaving me staring behind him.


Lily arrived back the following evening, slightly sunburned. She let herself into the flat and walked past the kitchenette, where I was unloading the washing-machine, wondering for the fifteenth time whether to call Sam, and flopped onto the sofa. As I stood at the counter and watched, she put her feet on the coffee-table, picked up the remote control and flicked on the television.

'So how was it?' I said, after a moment had passed.

'Okay.'

I waited for something more, braced for the remote control to be hurled down, for her to stalk off muttering, *That family is impossible*. But she simply changed channels.

'What did you do?'

'Not much. Talked a bit. Actually, we gardened.' She turned round, resting her chin on her hands on the back of the sofa. 'Hey, Lou. Have we got any of that cereal with the nuts left? I'm starving.'

# Chapter Twenty-five

*Are we talking?*
  *Sure. What do you want to say?*

Sometimes I look at the lives of the people around me and I wonder if we aren't all destined to leave a trail of damage. It's not just your mum and dad who fuck you up, Mr Larkin. I gazed around me, like someone suddenly handed clear glasses, and saw that pretty much everyone bore the brutal imprint of love, whether lost, whipped away from them or simply vanished into a grave.

Will had done it to all of us, I saw now. He hadn't meant to, but even in simply refusing to live, he had.

I loved a man who had opened up a world to me but hadn't loved me enough to stay in it. And now I was too afraid to love a man who might love me in case ... In case what? I turned it over in my head in the silent hours after Lily had retreated to the glowing digital distractions of her room.

Sam didn't call. I couldn't blame him. What would I have said, anyway? The truth was that I didn't want to talk about what we were because I didn't know.

It wasn't that I didn't love being with him. I suspected I became slightly ridiculous around him – my laugh goofy, my jokes silly and puerile, my passion fierce and surprising even to myself. I felt better when he was there, more the person I wanted to be. More of everything. And yet.

*And yet.*

To commit to Sam was to commit to the likelihood of

more loss. Statistically most relationships ended badly and, given my mental state over the past two years, my chances of beating the odds were pretty low. We could talk around it, we could lose ourselves in brief moments, but love ultimately meant more pain. More damage – to me or, worse, to him.

Who was strong enough for that?

I wasn't sleeping properly again. So I slept through my alarm and, despite tearing my way up the motorway, arrived late for Granddad's birthday. In celebration of his eighty years, Dad had brought out the foldaway gazebo we had used for Thomas's christening, which flapped, mossy and listless, at the end of the garden where, through the open door that led to the back alley, a succession of neighbours popped in and out, bringing cake or good wishes. Granddad sat in the middle of it all on a plastic garden chair, nodding at people he no longer recognized, only occasionally gazing longingly towards his folded copy of the *Racing Post*.

'So this promotion,' Treena was on tea-duty, pouring from an oversized pot and handing out cups, 'what exactly does it mean?'

'Well, I get a title. I balance the till at the end of every shift and I get to hold a set of keys.' *This is a serious responsibility, Louisa*, Richard Percival had said, bestowing them with as much gravitas and pomposity as if he were handing me the Holy Grail. *Use them wisely.* He actually said those words. *Use them wisely.* I wanted to say, What else am I going to do with a set of bar keys? Plough a field?

'Money?' She handed me a cup and I sipped at it.

'A pound an hour extra.'

'Mm.' She was unimpressed.

'And I don't have to wear the uniform any more.'

She scrutinized the *Charlie's Angels* jumpsuit I had put on that morning in honour of the occasion. 'Well, I guess that's something.' She pointed Mrs Laslow towards the sandwiches.

What else could I say? It was a job. Progress of sorts. I didn't tell her about the days when it felt like a peculiar form of torture to work somewhere where I was forced to watch each plane taxi on the runway, gather its energy like a great bird, then launch itself into the sky. I didn't tell her how putting on that green polo shirt each day made me feel somehow as if I had lost something.

'Mum says you've got a boyfriend.'

'He's not really my boyfriend.'

'She said that as well. What is it, then? You just bump uglies once in a while?'

'No. We're good friends –'

'So he's a pig.'

'He's not a pig. He's gorgeous.'

'But crap in the sack.'

'He's wonderful. Not that it's any of your business. And smart, before you –'

'Then he's married.'

'He is not married. Jesus, Treen. Will you just let me explain? I like him, but I'm not sure I want to get involved just yet.'

'Because of the long queue of other handsome, employed single sexy men waiting to snap you up?'

I glared at her.

'I'm just saying. Gift horses and all that.'

'When do you get your exam results?'

'Don't change the subject.' She sighed and opened a new carton of milk. 'Couple of weeks.'

'What's wrong? You're going to get top marks. You know you will.'

'But what's the difference? I'm stuck.'

I frowned.

'There are no jobs in Stortfold. But I can't afford the rent in London, not with childcare for Thom on top. And nobody gets top dollar when they're first starting out, even with top marks.'

She poured another cup of tea. I wanted to protest, to say it wasn't so, but I knew only too well how tough the job market was. 'So what will you do?'

'Stay here for now, I suppose. Commute, maybe. Hope that Mum's feminist metamorphosis won't stop her picking Thom up from school.' She raised a small smile that wasn't a smile at all.

I had never seen my sister down. Even if she felt it, she ploughed on, like an automaton, a firm advocate of the 'short walk and snap out of it' school of depression. I was trying to work out what to say when there was a sudden commotion on the food table. We looked up to see Mum and Dad facing off over a chocolate cake. They were talking in the lowered, sibilant voices of people who did not want others to know they were arguing, but not enough to stop arguing.

'Mum? Dad? Everything okay?' I walked over.

Dad pointed at the table. 'It's not a homemade cake.'

'What?'

'The cake. It's not homemade. Look at it.'

I looked at it – a large, lavishly iced chocolate cake, decorated with chocolate buttons between the candles.

Mum shook her head in exasperation. 'I had an essay to write.'

'An essay. You're not at school! You always do a homemade cake for Granddad.'

'It's a nice cake. It's from Waitrose. Daddy doesn't mind that it's not homemade.'

'Yes, he does. He's your father. You do mind, don't you, Granddad?'

Granddad looked from one to the other, and gave a tiny shake of his head. Around us, the conversation stuttered to a halt. Our neighbours eyed each other nervously. Bernard and Josie Clark never argued.

'He's just saying that because he doesn't want to hurt your feelings.' Dad harrumphed.

'If his feelings aren't hurt, Bernard, why on earth should yours be? It's a chocolate cake. It's not like I ignored his whole birthday.'

'I just want you to give priority to your family! Is that too much to ask, Josie? One homemade cake?'

'I'm here! There's a cake, with candles! Here's the ruddy sandwiches! I'm not off sunning myself in the Bahamas!' Mum put her pile of plates heavily on the trestle table and folded her arms.

Dad went to speak again but she shut him up with a raised hand. 'So, Bernard, you devoted family man, you, exactly how much of this little lot did you put together, eh?'

'Uh-oh . . .' Treena moved a step closer to me.

'Did you buy Daddy's new pyjamas? Did you? Did you wrap them? No. You wouldn't even know what bloody size he is. You don't even know what bloody size your own pants are because I BUY THEM FOR YOU. Did you get up at seven o'clock this morning to fetch the bread for the sandwiches because some eejit came back from the pub last night and decided he needed to eat two rounds of toast and left the rest of the loaf out to get stale? No. You sat on your arse reading the sports pages. You gripe away at me for weeks on end because I've dared to claim back twenty per cent of my life for myself, to try to work out whether there is anything else I can do before I shuffle off this mortal coil, and while I'm still doing your washing, looking after Granddad and doing the dishes, you're there harping on at me about a shop-bought fecking cake. Well, Bernard, you can take the fecking shop-bought cake that is apparently such a sign of neglect and disrespect and you can shove it up your –' she let out a roar '– up your . . . well . . . There's the kitchen, there's my ruddy mixing bowl, you can make one your ruddy self!'

With that, Mum flipped the cake plate upwards, so that it landed nose down in front of Dad, wiped her hands on her apron, and stomped up the garden to the house.

She stopped when she got to the patio, wrenched her apron over her head, and threw it to the ground. 'Oh, yes! Treena? You'd better show your daddy where the recipe books are. He's only lived here twenty-eight years. He can't possibly be expected to know himself.'

After that, Granddad's party didn't last long. The neighbours drifted away, conferring in hushed tones, and thanking us effusively for the *lovely* party, their eyes flickering towards the kitchen. I could see they felt as thrown as I did.

'It's been brewing for weeks,' Treena muttered, as we cleared the table. 'He feels neglected. She can't understand why he won't just let her grow a little.'

I glanced to where Dad was grumpily picking up napkins and empty beer cans from the grass. He looked utterly miserable. I thought of my mother at the London hotel, glowing with new life. 'But they're old! They're meant to have all this relationship stuff sewn up!'

My sister raised her eyebrows.

'You don't think . . . ?'

'Of course not,' said Treena. But she didn't sound quite as convinced as she might have done.

I helped Treena tidy the kitchen, and played ten minutes of Super Mario with Thom. Mum stayed in her room, apparently working on her essay, and Granddad retreated with some relief to the more reliable consolations of *Channel 4*

*Racing.* I wondered if Dad had gone down the pub again, but as I stepped out of the front door to leave, there he was, sitting in the driver's seat of his work van.

I knocked on the window and he jumped. I opened the door and slid in beside him. I'd thought maybe he was listening to sports results but the radio was silent.

He let out a long breath. 'I bet you think I'm an old fool.'

'You're not an old fool, Dad.' I nudged him. 'Well, you're not old.'

We sat in silence, watching the Ellis boys wheel up and down the road on their bikes, wincing in unison when the littler one took a skid too fast and slid halfway across the road.

'I want things to stay the same. Is that so much to ask?'

'Nothing stays the same, Dad.'

'I just . . . I just miss my wife.' He sounded so bleak.

'You know, you could just enjoy the fact that you're married to someone who still has a bit of life in her. Mum's excited. She feels like she's seeing the world through new eyes. You've just got to allow her some room.'

His mouth was set in a grim line.

'She's still your wife, Dad. She loves you.'

He finally turned to face me. 'What if she decides that I'm the one with no life? What if all this new stuff turns her head and . . .' He gulped. 'What if she leaves me behind?'

I squeezed his hand. Then I thought better and leaned over and gave him a hug. 'You won't let that happen.'

The wan smile he gave me stayed with me the whole way home.

Lily came in just as I was leaving for the Moving On Circle. She had been with Camilla again, and arrived home, as she often did now, with black fingernails from gardening. They had created a whole new border for a neighbour, she said

345

cheerfully, and the woman had been so pleased she had given Lily thirty pounds. 'Actually, she gave us a bottle of wine too but I said Granny should keep that.' I noted the unselfconscious 'Granny'.

'Oh, and I spoke to Georgina on Skype last night. I mean it was morning there, because it's Australia, but it was really nice. She's going to email me a whole load of pictures of when she and my dad were little. She said that I really look like him. She's quite pretty. She has a dog called Jakob and it howls when she plays the piano.'

I put a bowl of salad and some bread and cheese on the table for Lily as she chatted on. I wondered whether to tell her that Steven Traynor had called again, the fourth time in as many weeks, hoping to persuade her to go and see the new baby. 'We're all family. And Della is feeling much more *relaxed* about things now that the baby is safely here.' Maybe that was a conversation for another time. I reached for my keys.

'Oh,' she said. 'Before you go. I'm going back to school.'

'What?'

'I'm going back to the school near Granny's house. Do you remember? The one I told you about? The one I actually liked? Weekly boarding. Just for sixth form. And I'm going to live with Granny at weekends.'

I had missed a leaf with the salad dressing. 'Oh.'

'Sorry. I did want to tell you. But it's all happened really fast. I was talking about it, and just on the off-chance Granny rang up the school and they said I'd be welcome, and you'll never guess what — my friend Holly's still there! I spoke to her on Facebook and she said she can't wait for me to come back. I mean, I didn't tell her everything that's happened, and I probably won't tell her any of it, but it was just really nice. She knew me before it all went wrong. She's just . . . okay, you know?'

I listened to her talking animatedly and fought the sensation that I had been shed, like a skin. 'When is all this going to happen?'

'Well, I need to be there for the start of term in September. Granny thought it would probably be best if I moved quite soon. Maybe next week?'

'Next *week*?' I felt winded. 'What – what does your mum say?'

'She's just glad I'm going back to school, especially since Granny's paying. She had to tell the school a bit about my last school and the fact that I didn't take my exams, and you can tell she doesn't like Granny much, but she said it would be fine. "If that's actually going to make you happy, Lily. And I do hope you're not going to treat your grandmother the way you've treated everyone else."'

She cackled at her own impression of Tanya. 'I caught Granny's eye when she said that, and Granny's eyebrow went up the tiniest bit but you could totally see what she thought. Did I tell you she's dyed her hair? A sort of chestnut brown. She looks quite good now. Less like a cancer patient.'

'Lily!'

'It's all right. She laughed when I told her that.' She smiled to herself. 'It was the kind of thing Dad would have said.'

'Well,' I muttered, when I'd caught my breath, 'sounds like you've got it all worked out.'

She shot me a look. 'Don't say it like that.'

'Sorry. It's just . . . I'll miss you.'

She beamed, an abrupt, brilliant smile. 'You won't miss me, silly, because I'll still be back down in the holidays and stuff. I can't spend all my time in Oxfordshire with old people or I'll go mad. But it's good. She just . . . she feels like my family. It doesn't feel weird. I thought it would, but it doesn't. Hey, Lou . . .' She hugged me, exuberantly. 'You'll still be my friend. You're basically the sister I never had.'

I hugged her back and tried to keep the smile on my face.

'Anyway. You need your privacy.' She disentangled herself and pulled a piece of gum from her mouth, folding it carefully into a torn piece of paper. 'Having to listen to you and Hot Ambulance Man shagging across the corridor was actually pretty gross.'

*Lily is going.*

 *Going where?*

 *To live with her grandmother. I feel strange. She's so happy about it. Sorry. I don't mean to talk about Will-related things all the time, but I can't really talk to anyone else.*

Lily packed her bag, cheerfully stripping my second bedroom of nearly every sign she had ever been there, apart from the Kandinsky print and the camp bed, a pile of glossy magazines and an empty deodorant canister. I dropped her at the station, listening to her non-stop chatter and trying not to look as unbalanced as I felt. Camilla Traynor would be waiting at the other end.

'You should come up. We've got my room really nice. There's a horse next door that the farmer across the way says I can ride. Oh, and there's quite a nice pub.'

She glanced up at the departures board, and bounced on her toes, suddenly seeing the time. 'Bugger. My train. Right. Where's platform eleven?' She began to run briskly through the crowd, her holdall slung over her shoulder, her legs long in black tights. I stood, frozen, watching her go. Her stride had grown longer.

Suddenly she turned and, spotting me by the entrance, waved, her smile wide, her hair flying up around her face. 'Hey, Lou!' she yelled. 'I meant to say to you. Moving on doesn't mean you loved my dad any less, you know. I'm pretty sure even he would tell you that.'

And then she was gone, swallowed by the crowd.

Her smile was like his.

*She was never yours, Lou.*

*I know. It's I suppose she was the thing I felt was giving me a purpose.*

*Only one person can give you a purpose.*

I let myself absorb these words for a minute.

*Can we meet? Please?*

*I'm on shift tonight.*

*Come to mine after?*

*Maybe later in the week. I'll call you.*

It was the 'maybe' that did it. There was something final in it, the slow closing of a door. I stared at my phone as the commuters swarmed around me and something in me shifted too. Either I could go home and mourn yet another thing I had lost, or I could embrace an unexpected freedom. It was as if a light had gone on: the only way to avoid being left behind was to start moving.

I went home, made myself a coffee and stared at the grey wall. Then I pulled out my laptop.

Dear Mr Gopnik,

My name is Louisa Clark and last month you were kind enough to offer me a job, which I had to turn down. I appreciate that you will have filled your position by now, but if I don't say this I will regret it for ever.

I really wanted your job. If the child of my former employer hadn't turned up in trouble, I would have taken it like a shot. I do not want to blame her for my decision, as it was a privilege to help sort things out for her. But I just wanted to say that if you ever need someone again I really hope you might consider getting in touch.

I know you are a busy man so I won't go on, but I just needed you to know.

With best wishes
Louisa Clark


I wasn't sure what I was doing but at least I was doing something. I pressed send, and with that tiny action, I was suddenly filled with purpose. I raced into the bathroom and ran the shower, stripping off my clothes and tripping on my trouser legs in my hurry to get out of them and under the hot water. I began to lather my hair, already planning ahead. I was going to go to the ambulance station, and I was going to find Sam and I was –

The doorbell rang. I swore and grabbed a towel.


'I've had it,' my mother said.

It took me a moment to register that it was actually her standing there, holding an overnight bag. I pulled my towel around me, my hair dripping onto the carpet. 'Had what?'

She stepped in, closing the front door behind her. 'Your father. Grumbling incessantly at me about everything I do. Acting as if I'm some kind of harlot just for wanting a little time to myself. So I told him I was coming here for a little break.'

'A break?'

'Louisa, you have no idea. All the mumping and grumping. I can't stay set in stone, you know? Everyone else gets to change. Why can't I?'

It was as if I'd come halfway into a conversation that had been going on for an hour. Possibly in a bar. After hours.

'When I started that feminist consciousness course, I

thought a fair bit of it was exaggerated. Man's patriarchal control of woman? Even the unconscious kind? Well, they only had the half of it. Your father simply can't see me as a person beyond what I put on the table or put out in bed.'

'Uh –'

'Oh. Too much?'

'Possibly.'

'Let's discuss it over some tea.' My mother walked past me and into the kitchen. 'Well, this looks a bit better. I'm still not sure about that grey, though. It washes you right out. Now, where are your teabags?'

My mother sat on the sofa and, as her tea grew cold, I listened to her litany of frustration and tried not to think about the time. Sam would be arriving for his shift in half an hour. It would take twenty minutes to get over to the ambulance station. And then my mother's voice would lift and her hands would end up somewhere around her ears and I knew I was going nowhere.

'Do you know how stifling it is to be told you're never going to be able to change? For the rest of your life? Because nobody else wants you to? Do you know how awful it is to feel stuck?'

I nodded vigorously. I did. I really did. 'I'm sure Dad doesn't mean for you to feel like that – but listen, I –'

'I even suggested he take a course at the night school. Something he might like – you know, repairing antiques or life drawing or something. I don't mind him looking at the nudies! I thought we could grow together! That's the kind of wife I'm trying to be, the kind that doesn't even mind her husband looking at nudies, if it's in the name of culture . . . But he's all "What would I want to go down there for?" It's like he's got the ruddy menopause. And as for the rabbiting on about me not shaving my legs! Oh, my days. He's so hypocritical. Do you know how long the hairs in his nostrils are, Louisa?'

'N-no.'

'I'll tell you! He could wipe his plate with them. For the last fifteen years, I've been the one telling the barber to give him a trim up there, you know? Like he's some kind of child. Do I mind? No! Because that's the way he is. He's a human being! Nose hair and all! But if I dare not to be as smooth as a ruddy baby's bottom he acts like I've turned into flipping Chewbacca!'

It was ten minutes to six. Sam would be heading out at half past. I sighed, and pulled my towel around me.

'So . . . um . . . how long do you think you'll be here?'

'Well, now, I don't know.' Mum took a sip of her tea. 'We've got the social services bringing Granddad his lunch now so it's not like I've got to be there all the time. I might just stay for a few days. We had a lovely time last time I was here, didn't we? We could go and see Maria in the toilets tomorrow. Wouldn't that be nice!'

'Lovely.'

'Right. Well, I'll make up the spare bed. Where is the spare bed?'

We had just stood up when the buzzer went again. I opened the door, expecting a random pizza delivery, but there stood Treena and Thom and, behind them, his hands jammed into his trouser pockets like a recalcitrant teenager, my father.

She didn't even look at me. She just walked in past me. 'Mum. This is ridiculous. You can't just run away from Dad. How old are you? Fourteen?'

'I am not running away, Treena. I am giving myself breathing space.'

'Well, we're going to sit here until you two have sorted this ridiculous thing out. You know he's been sleeping in his van, Lou?'

'What? You didn't tell me that.' I turned to Mum.

She lifted her chin. 'You didn't give me a chance, with all your talking.'

Mum and Dad stood there not looking at each other.

'I have nothing to say to your father right now,' Mum said.

'Sit down,' said Treena. 'The both of you.' They shuffled towards the sofa, casting mute glances of resentment at each other. She turned to me. 'Right. Let's make tea. And then we're going to sort this out as a family.'

'Great idea!' I said, sensing my chance. 'There's milk in the fridge. Tea's on the side. Help yourselves. I've got to pop out for half an hour.' And before anyone could stop me I had whipped on a pair of jeans and a top and was running out of the flat with my car keys.

I saw him even as I turned the car into the ambulance-station car park. He was striding towards the ambulance, his pack slung over his shoulder, and something inside me lurched. I knew the delicious solidity of that body, the soft angles of that face. He turned and his step faltered, as if I had been the last thing he had expected to see. Then he turned back to the ambulance, hauling open the rear doors.

I walked towards him across the tarmac. 'Can we talk?'

He lifted an oxygen tank like it was a tin of hairspray, securing it in its holder. 'Sure. But it'll have to be some other time. I'm on my way out.'

'It won't wait.'

His expression didn't flicker. He stooped to pick up a pack of gauze.

'Look. I just wanted to explain . . . what we were talking about. I do like you. I really like you. I just – I'm just scared.'

'We're all scared, Lou.'

'You're not scared of anything.'

'Yeah. I am. Just not stuff you'd notice.'

He stared at his boots. And then he saw Donna running towards him. 'Ah, hell. I've got to go.'

I jumped into the rear of the ambulance. 'I'll come with you. I'll get a taxi home from wherever you're headed.'

'No.'

'Ah, come on. Please.'

'So I can get in even more trouble with Disciplinary?'

'Red Two, reports of a stabbing, young male.' Donna threw her pack into the back of the ambulance.

'We have to go, Louisa.'

I was losing him. I could feel it, in the tone of his voice, the way he wouldn't look at me directly. I climbed out of the back, cursing my lateness. But Donna took me by the elbow and steered me towards the front. 'For God's sake,' she said, as Sam made to protest. 'You've been like a bear with a sore head all week. Just sort this thing out. We'll drop her before we get there.'

Sam walked briskly around to the passenger door and opened it, casting a glance at the controller's office. 'She'd make a great relationship counsellor.' His voice hardened. 'If we were, you know, in a relationship.'

I didn't need telling twice. Sam climbed into the driving seat and looked at me as if he were going to say something, then changed his mind. Donna began sorting out equipment. He started the ignition and put the blue light on.

'Where are we headed?'

'*We* are headed to the estate. About seven minutes away with blues and twos. *You* are headed to the high street, two minutes from Kingsbury.'

'So I've got five minutes?'

'And a long walk back.'

'Okay,' I said. And realized, as we sped forward, that I really had no idea what to say next.

# Chapter Twenty-six

'So, here's the thing,' I said. Sam indicated and swung out onto the road. I had to shout as the siren was so loud.

His attention was on the road ahead. He glanced at the computer readout on the dashboard. 'What have we got, Don?'

'Possible stabbing. Two reports. Young male collapsed in stairwell.'

'Is this really a good time to talk?' I said.

'Depends what you want to say.'

'It's not that I don't want a relationship,' I said. 'I just still feel a bit mixed up.'

'Everyone's mixed up,' said Donna. 'Every bloke I go out with starts our date with how he's got trust issues.' She looked at Sam. 'Oh. Sorry. Don't mind me.'

Sam kept his eyes straight ahead. 'One minute you're calling me a dick because you've decided I'm sleeping with other women. Next you're keeping me at arm's length because you're still attached to someone else. It's too –'

'Will is gone. I know that. But I just can't leap in like you can, Sam. I feel like I'm only just getting back on my feet after a long time of . . . I don't know . . . I was a mess.'

'I know you were a mess. I picked up that mess.'

'If anything, I like you too much. I like you so much that if it went wrong it would feel like that again. And I'm not sure I'm strong enough.'

'How is *that* going to happen?'

'You might go off me. You might change your mind. You're

a good-looking bloke. Some other woman might fall off a building and land on you and you might like it. You could get ill. You could get knocked off that motorbike.'

'ETA two minutes,' said Donna, gazing at the satnav. 'I'm not listening, honest.'

'You could say that about anyone. So what? So we sit there and do nothing every day in case we have an accident? Is that really how to live?' He swerved to the left so that I had to hang on to my seat.

'I'm still a doughnut, okay?' I said. 'I want to be a bun. I really do. But I'm still a doughnut.'

'Jesus, Lou! We're all doughnuts! You think I didn't watch my sister being eaten by cancer and know that my heart was going to break, not just for her but for her son, every day of my life? You think I don't know how that feels? There's only one response, and I can tell you this because I see it every day. You *live*. And you throw yourself into everything and try not to think about the bruises.'

'Oh, that's lovely,' said Donna, nodding.

'I'm *trying*, Sam. You have no idea how far I've come.'

And then we were there. The sign for Kingsbury estate loomed in front of us. We drove in through a huge archway, past a car park and into a darkened courtyard, where Sam pulled up and swore softly. 'Dammit. We were meant to drop you off.'

'I didn't like to interrupt,' said Donna.

'I'll wait here till you get back.' I crossed my arms.

'There's no point.' Sam jumped out of the driver's door and grabbed his pack. 'I'm not going to jump through hoops to convince you to be with me. Oh, crap. The bloody signs are missing. He could be anywhere.'

I gazed out at the forbidding maroon-brick buildings. There were probably twenty stairwells in those blocks and none you would have wanted to walk around without the company of a large bodyguard.

Donna shrugged her way into her jacket. 'The last time I came here – heart attack – it took four tries to find the right block, and that gate was locked. We had to find a caretaker to unlock it before we could bring in the mobile unit. By the time I made it to the right flat the patient was dead.'

'Two gang shootings here last month.'

'You want me to call in a police escort?' said Donna.

'No. No time.'

It was eerily quiet, even though it was barely eight p.m. These were estates in a part of the city where only a few years ago children might have been playing out on bikes, sneaking cigarettes and catcalling long into the evening. Now residents double-locked their doors long before dark, and windows were braced with decorative metal bars. Half the sodium lights had been shot out, and the odd remaining one flickered intermittently, as if uncertain whether it was safe to shine.

Sam and Donna, now outside the cab, were talking, their voices lowered. Donna opened the passenger door, reached in and handed me a high-visibility jacket. 'Right. Put that on and come with us. He doesn't feel safe leaving you here.'

'Why couldn't he –'

'Oh, you two! For God's sake! Look, I'm going to head this way, you follow him that way. Okay?'

I stared at her.

'Sort it out afterwards.' She strode off, her walkie-talkie buzzing in her hand.

I followed close behind Sam as we went along one length of concrete walkway, then another.

'Savernake House,' he muttered. 'How the hell are we sup-posed to know which one is Savernake?' The radio hissed.

'Control, can we have some guidance? No signs on these buildings, and no idea where this patient is.'

'Sorry,' the voice said apologetically. 'Our map doesn't show individual block names.'

'Want me to head off that way?' I said, pointing in front of us. 'Then we'll have three walkways covered. I've got my phone with me.' We halted in a stairwell that reeked of urine and the stale fat of old takeaway cartons. The walkways sat in shadow, only the occasional muffled burble of a television behind the windows suggesting life deep within each small flat. I had expected a distant commotion, some vibration in the air that would lead us to the injured. But this was eerily still.

'No. Stay close, okay?'

I saw that having me there was making him nervous. I wondered whether I should just leave, but I didn't want to find my way out by myself.

Sam stopped at the end of the walkway. He turned, shaking his head, his mouth compressed. Donna's voice crackled across the radio: 'Nothing this end.' And then we heard a shout.

'There,' I said, following the sound. On the other side of the square, in the half-light, we saw a crouching figure, a body on the ground under the sodium lights.

'Here we go,' said Sam, and we started to run.

Speed was everything in his job, he had once told me. It was one of the first things paramedics were taught – the difference a few seconds could make to someone's chances of survival. If the patient was bleeding out, had had a stroke or a heart attack, it could be those critical few seconds that kept them alive. We bolted along the concrete walkways, down the reeking, dingy stairs, and then we were across the worn grass towards the prostrate figure.

Donna was already down beside her.

'A girl.' Sam dropped his pack. 'I'm sure they said it was a man.'

As Donna checked her for injuries, he called into Control.

'Yup. Young male, late teens, Afro-Caribbean appearance,' the dispatcher responded.

Sam clicked off his radio. 'They must have misheard. It's like bloody Chinese whispers some days.'

She was about sixteen, her hair neatly braided, her limbs sprawled as if she had recently fallen. She was strangely peaceful. I wondered, fleetingly, if that was how I had looked when he'd found me.

'Can you hear me, sweetheart?'

She didn't move. He checked her pupils, her pulse, her airways. She was breathing, and there was no obvious sign of injury. Yet she seemed completely non-responsive. He checked all around her a second time, staring at his equipment.

'Is she alive?'

Sam's eyes met Donna's. He straightened up and glanced around him, thinking. He gazed up at the windows of the estate. They stared down at us like blank, unfriendly eyes. Then he motioned us over and spoke quietly. 'Something's not right. Look, I'm going to do the drop-hand test. And when I do, I want you to head for the rig and start the engine. If it's what I think it is we need to get out of here.'

'Drugs ambush?' muttered Donna, her gaze sliding behind me.

'Might be. Or turf-related. We should have had a Location Match. I'm sure this is where Andy Gibson had that shooting.'

I tried to keep my voice calm. 'What's the drop-hand test?'

'I'm going to lift her hand and drop it from above her face. If she's acting, she'll move her hand rather than hit her own face. They always do. It's like a reflex. But if there's someone watching, I don't want them to get wind that we've worked it out. Louisa, you act like you're going to get some more equipment, okay? I'll do it once you've texted me to say you're at the rig. If anyone's near it, don't go in. Just turn round and come straight back to me. Donna, get your pack together, and ready. You go after her. If they see two of us leaving together they'll know.'

He handed me the keys. I picked up a bag, as if it were mine, and started to walk briskly towards the ambulance. I was suddenly conscious of unseen people watching from the shadows; my heartbeat was thumping in my ears. I tried to make my face expressionless, my movements purposeful.

The walk along the echoing concourse felt achingly long. When I reached the ambulance, I let out a sigh of relief. I reached for the keys, opened the door, and as I stepped up, a voice called from the shadows, 'Miss.' I glanced behind me. Nothing. 'Miss.'

A young boy appeared from behind a concrete pillar, another behind him, a hoodie pulled forward to obscure his face. I took a step back towards the rig, my heart racing. 'I've got back-up on the way,' I said, trying to keep my voice steady. 'There's no drugs in here. You both need to back off. Okay?'

'Miss. He's by the bins. They don't want you to get to him. He's bleeding real bad, miss. That's why Emeka's cousin is faking it out there. To distract youse. So youse'll go away.'

'What? What do you mean?'

'He's by the bins. You got to help him, miss.'

'What? Where are the bins?'

But the boy glanced warily behind him, and when I turned to ask again, they had disappeared into the shadows.

I glanced around, trying to work out where he meant. And then I spied it, over by the garages – the protruding edge of a bright green plastic rubbish container. I edged along the shadows of the ground-floor walkway, out of view of the main square, until I saw an open doorway out to the refuse area. I ran over, and there, tucked behind the recycling bin, a pair of legs sprawled, tracksuit bottoms soaked with blood. His upper half was slumped under the containers and I crouched down. The boy turned his head and groaned quietly.

'Hello? Can you hear me?'

'They got me.'

Blood seeped stickily from what looked like two wounds to his legs. 'They got me . . .'

I grabbed my phone and called Sam, my voice low and urgent. 'I'm over by the bins, to your right. Please. Come quick.'

I could see him, looking around slowly until he spotted me. Two elderly people, Samaritans from a previous age, had appeared beside him. I could see them asking questions about the fallen girl, their faces blanketed with concern. He gently placed a blanket over the faking cousin, asking them to watch over her, then walked briskly towards the rig with his bag, as if to get more equipment. Donna had vanished.

I opened the bag he'd given me, ripping open a pack of gauze and placing it over the boy's leg, but there was so much blood. 'Okay. Someone's coming to help. We'll have you in the ambulance in a moment.' I sounded like someone out of a bad film. I had no idea what else to say. *Come on, Sam.*

'You gotta get me out of here.' The boy groaned. I put my hand on his arm, trying to keep calm. *Come on, Sam. Where the hell are you?* And suddenly I heard the rig's engine starting, and there it was, reversing through the garages towards me at some speed, its engine whining in protest. It bumped to a halt, and Donna jumped out. She ran towards me, threw open the back doors. 'Help me put him in,' she said. 'We're getting out of here.'

There was no time for gurneys. Somewhere above I heard shouting, multiple footsteps. We shouldered the boy towards the ambulance, shoving him into the back. Donna slammed the doors behind him and I ran for the cab, my heart racing, and threw myself in, locking the doors. I could see them now, a gang of men, racing towards us around the upper floor, hands raised with – what? Guns? Knives? I felt something grow liquid inside me. I looked out of the window. Sam was walking along the open space, his face turned to the sky: he had seen them too.

Donna saw before he did: the gun, raised in the man's hand. She swore loudly and slammed the rig into reverse, steering it round the garage, headed straight for the grassed area where Sam was still walking towards us. I could just make him out, the green of his uniform growing larger in the passenger mirror.

'Sam!' I yelled out of my window.

He glanced at me, then up at them. 'Leave the ambulance alone,' he yelled at the men, over the whine of the ambulance's reverse gear. 'Back off, all right? We're just doing our jobs.'

'*Not now, Sam. Not now,*' Donna said, under her breath.

The men kept running, peering over as if calculating the quickest way down, relentless, moving forward like a tide. One vaulted nimbly over a wall, swinging his way easily down a flight of stairs. I wanted to skid out of there so badly I was limp with it.

But Sam was still walking towards them, his hands raised, palms up. 'Leave the ambulance, boys, okay? We're just here to help.' His voice was calm and authoritative, betraying none of the fear that I felt. And then I saw through the back window that the men had slowed. They were walking now, not running. A distant part of me thought, *Oh, thank God.* The boy lay behind us, still moaning.

'That's it,' said Donna, leaning around. 'Come *on*, Sam. In you come. Come on over here now. And we can get the –'

*Bang.*

The sound cut through the air, amplified in the empty space so that I felt, briefly, as if my whole head had expanded and contracted with the sound. And then, too quickly –

*Bang.*

I yelped.

'*What the f—*' Donna yelled.

'We need to get out of here, man!' the boy shouted.

I looked back, willing Sam to get in. *Get in now. Please.* But Sam had gone. No, not gone. There was something on the ground: a high-visibility jacket. A green stain on the grey concrete.

Everything stopped.

No, I thought. No.

The ambulance screeched to a halt. Then Donna was out, and I was running after her. Sam was motionless and there was blood, so much blood, seeping outwards in a steadily expanding pool around him. In the distance the two old people scrambled stiffly towards the safety of their door, the girl who was supposedly immobile sprinting across the grass at the speed of an athlete. And the men were still coming, running down the upper walkway towards us. I tasted metal in my mouth.

'*Lou! Grab him.*' We hauled Sam towards the back of the rig. He was leaden, as if he were deliberately resisting. I pulled at his collar, his armpits, my breath coming in short bursts. His face was chalk-white, huge black shadows under his half-closed eyes, as if he had not slept for a hundred years. His blood against my skin. Why had I not known how warm blood is? Donna was already in the rig, hauling at him, and we were pushing, heaving, a sob in my throat as I pulled at his arms, his legs. '*Help me!*' I was shouting, as if there was anyone who could. '*Help me!*'

And then he was in, his leg at the wrong angle, and the doors slammed behind me.

*Crack!* Something hit the top of the rig. I screamed and ducked. Some part of me thought absently, *Is this it? Is this how I die, in my bad jeans, while a few miles away my parents argue about birthday cakes with my sister?* The boy on the gurney was screaming, his voice shrill with fear. And then the ambulance skidded forwards, steering right as the men approached us from the left. I saw a hand rise, and thought I heard a gunshot. I ducked again instinctively.

'*Bloody hell!*' Donna swore and swerved again.

I raised my head. I could make out the exit. Donna steered hard left, then right, the ambulance almost on two wheels as she hurled it around the corner. The wing mirror clipped a car. Someone dived towards us but Donna swerved once more and kept going. I heard the *thump* of an angry fist on the side. And then we were out on the road, and the young men were behind us, slowing to a furious, defeated jog as they watched us go.

'*Jesus.*'

The blue light on, Donna radioing ahead to the hospital, words I couldn't make out through the thumping in my ears. I was cradling Sam's face, grey and covered with a fine sheen, his eyes glassy. He was completely silent.

'What do I do?' I yelled at Donna. '*What do I do?*' She screeched around a roundabout and her head swivelled briefly towards me. 'Find the injury. What can you see?'

'It's his stomach. There's a hole. Two holes. There is so much blood. Oh, God, there's so much blood.' My hands came away red and glossy. My breath came in short bursts. I felt, briefly, as if I might faint.

'I need you to be calm now, Louisa, okay? Is he breathing? Can you feel a pulse?'

I checked, felt something inside me sag with relief. 'Yes.'

'I can't stop. We're too close. Elevate his feet, okay? Push up his knees. Keep the blood near his chest. Now make sure his shirt is open. Rip it. Just get to it. Can you describe the wound?'

That stomach, which had lain warm and smooth and solid against mine, now a red, gaping mess. A sob escaped my throat. 'Oh, God . . .'

'Don't you panic now, Louisa. You hear me? We're nearly there. You have to apply pressure. Come on, you can do this. Use the gauze from the pack. The big one. Whatever, just stop him bleeding out. Okay?'

She turned back to the road, sending the ambulance the wrong way up a one-way street. The boy on the gurney swore softly, now lost in his own private world of pain. Ahead, cars swerved obediently out of the way on the sodium-lit road, waves parting on the tarmac. A siren, always a siren. '*Paramedic down. I repeat paramedic down. Gunshot wound to the abdomen!*' Donna yelled into the radio. '*ETA three minutes. We're going to need a crash cart.*'

I unwrapped the bandages, my hands shaking, and ripped open Sam's shirt, bracing myself as the ambulance tore round corners. How could this be the man who had been arguing with me just fifteen minutes earlier? How could someone so solid just be ebbing away in front of me?

'Sam? Can you hear me?' I was crouched over him now on my knees, my jeans darkening red. His eyes closed. When they opened, they seemed to fix on something far away. I put my face down so that I was directly in his field of vision and for a second his eyes locked onto mine and I saw a flicker of something that could have been recognition.

I took hold of his hand, as he had once held mine in another ambulance, a million years ago. 'You're going to be okay, you hear me? You're going to be okay.'

Nothing. He didn't even seem to register my voice.

'Sam? Look at me, Sam.'

Nothing.

I was there, back in that Swiss room, Will's face turning away from mine. Losing him.

'No. Don't you dare.' I placed my face against his, my words falling his ear. 'Sam. You stay with me, you hear?' My hand was on the gauze dressing, my body over his, juddering with the rocking of the ambulance. There was the sound of sobbing in my ears and I realized it was my own. I turned his face with my hands, forcing him to look at me. 'Stay with me! You hear me? Sam? *Sam! Sam!*' I had never known fear like it. It was in the stilling of his gaze, the wet warmth of his blood, a rising tide.

The closing of a door.

'*Sam!*'

The ambulance had stopped.

Donna leaped into the back. She ripped open a clear plastic pouch, pulling out drugs, white padding, a syringe, injected something into Sam's arm. With shaking hands she hooked him up to a drip, and placed an oxygen mask over his face. I could hear beeping outside. I was trembling violently. 'Stay there!' she commanded, as I made to scramble out of her way. 'Keep that pressure. That's it – that's good. You're doing great.' Her face lowered to his. 'Come on, mate. Come on, Sam. Nearly there.' I could hear sirens as she worked, still talking, her hands swift and competent on the equipment, always busy, always moving. 'You're going to be fine, my old mucker. Just hang on in there, okay?' The monitor was flickering green and black. The sound of beeping.

Then the doors opened again, flooding the ambulance with swinging neon light, and there were paramedics, green uniforms, white coats, hauling out the boy, still complaining

366

and swearing, then Sam, lifting him gently away from me. Blood swilled on the floor of the ambulance and as I made to stand up I slipped and put a hand out to right myself. It came back red.

Their voices receded. I caught a flash of Donna's face, white with anxiety. A barked instruction: '*Straight to theatre.*' I was left standing between the ambulance doors, watching as they ran with him, their boots clumping across the tarmac. The doors of the hospital opened and swallowed him, and as they closed again, I was alone in the silence of the car park.

# Chapter Twenty-seven

Hours spent on hospital seating have a strange, elastic quality. I had hardly noticed them when I waited for Will during his check-ups; I had read magazines, pecked out messages on my phone, strolled downstairs for too-strong hospital coffee on an overpriced concourse, worried about car-parking charges. Moaned without really meaning it about how long these things always took.

Now I sat on a moulded plastic chair, my mind numb, my gaze fixed on a wall, unable to tell how long I had been there. I couldn't think. I couldn't feel. I just existed: me; the plastic chair, the squeaky linoleum under my bloodied tennis shoes.

The strip-lighting overhead was a harsh constant, illuminating the nurses who walked briskly past, barely giving me a second look. Some time after I had come in, one of them had been kind enough to show me a bathroom so that I could clean my hands, but I could still see Sam's blood in the dips around my nails, rust-coloured cuticles that hinted at a not-so-distant atrocity. Pieces of him in pieces of me. Pieces of him where they shouldn't be.

When I closed my eyes I heard the voices, the sharp *thwack* of the bullet hitting the roof of the ambulance, the echo of the shot, the siren, the siren, the siren. I saw his face, the brief moment when he had looked at me and there had been nothing – no alarm, nothing except perhaps a vague bemusement at finding himself there on the floor, unable to move.

And I kept seeing those wounds, not neat little holes like gunshot injuries in movies, but living, pulsing things, pushing out blood as if they were trying maliciously to rid him of it.

I sat motionless on that plastic chair because I didn't know how to do anything else. Somewhere at the end of that corridor were the operating theatres. He was in there right now. He was alive or he was dead. He was being wheeled to some distant ward, surrounded by relieved, high-fiving colleagues, or someone was pulling that green cloth up over his –

My head sank into my hands and I listened to my breath, in and out. In and out. My body smelt unfamiliar: of blood and antiseptic and something sour left over from visceral fear. Periodically I would observe distantly that my hands were trembling, but I wasn't sure if it was low blood sugar or exhaustion, and somehow the thought of trying to find food was way beyond me. Movement was beyond me.

My sister had texted me some time ago.

*Where are you? We're going for pizza. They are talking, but I need you here as United Nations.*

I hadn't answered. I couldn't work out what to say.

*He is talking about her hairy legs again. Please come. This could get ugly. She has a fearsome aim with a doughball.*

I closed my eyes and I tried to remember what it felt like, a week ago, to lie on the grass beside Sam, the way his stretched-out legs were so much longer than mine, the reassuring scent of his warm shirt, the low rumble of his voice, the sun on my face. His face, turning towards mine to steal kisses, the way he looked secretly pleased after every one. The manner in which he walked, set slightly forward yet his weight so centred, the most solid man I had ever met – as if nothing could knock him down.

I felt the buzz and pulled my phone from my pocket, read my sister's message. *Where are you? Mum getting worried.* I checked the time: 10:48 p.m. I couldn't believe I was the same person who had woken that morning and dropped Lily at the station. I leaned back in the chair, thought for a moment and began to type. *I'm at the City hospital. There's been an accident. I'm fine. I'll be back when I know*

when I know

My finger hovered over the keys. I blinked and, after a moment, pressed send.

And I closed my eyes and prayed.

I came to with a start at the sound of the swing doors. My mother was walking briskly down the corridor, her good coat on, her arms already outstretched.

'What the hell happened?' Treena was close behind, dragging Thom, in his pyjamas with an anorak over the top. 'Mum didn't want to come without Dad and I wasn't going to be left behind.' Thom looked at me sleepily and waved a damp hand.

'We had no clue what had happened to you!' Mum sat down beside me, studying my face. 'Why didn't you say?'

'What's going on?'

'Sam has been shot.'

'Shot? Your paramedic man?'

'With a gun?' said Treena.

It was then that my mother registered my jeans. She gazed at the red stains, disbelieving, and turned mutely to my father.

'I was with him.'

She pressed her hands to her mouth. 'Are you okay?' And then, when she saw the answer was yes, at least physically, 'Is . . . is he okay?'

The four of them stood before me, their faces immobilized by shock and concern. I was suddenly utterly relieved to have them there. 'I don't know,' I said, and as my father stepped forward to take me in his arms, I finally began to cry.

*

We sat for several years, my family and I, on those plastic chairs. Or something close to that. Thom fell asleep on Treena's lap, his face pale under the strip-lights, his battered cuddly cat pressed into the silky soft space between his neck and chin. Dad and Mum sat on each side of me and at any time one of them would hold my hand or stroke the side of my face and tell me it was going to be okay. I leaned against Dad and let the tears fall silently, and Mum wiped my face with her ever-present clean handkerchief. Periodically she would head off on a recce trip around the hospital for hot drinks.

'She'd never have done that by herself a year ago,' Dad said, the first time she disappeared. I couldn't tell whether it was said admiringly or with regret.

We spoke little. There was nothing to say. The words repeated in my head like a mantra – *Just let him be okay. Just let him be okay. Just let him be okay.*

This is what catastrophe does: it strips away the fluff and the white noise, the *should I really* and the *but what if*. I wanted Sam. I knew it with a stinging clarity. I wanted to feel his arms around me, hear him talking, and sit in the cab of his ambulance. I wanted him to make me a salad with things he had grown in his garden and I wanted to feel his warm, bare chest rise and fall steadily under my arm while he slept. Why had I not been able to tell him that? Why had I wasted so much time worrying about what was not important?

Then, as Mum came through the doors at the far end, bearing a cardboard holder with four teas in it, the doors to the theatres opened and Donna emerged, her uniform still smeared with blood, trailing her hands through her hair. I stood. She slowed in front of us, her expression grave, her eyes red-rimmed and exhausted. For a moment I thought I might pass out. Her eyes met mine. 'Tough as old boots, that one.'

As I let out an involuntary sob, she touched my arm. 'You

did good, Lou,' she said, and let out a long, shaky breath. 'You did good tonight.'

He spent the night in intensive care, and was transferred to a high-dependency unit in the morning. Donna called his parents, and said she would stop by his place after she'd had some sleep to feed his animals. We went in to see him together shortly after midnight, but he was asleep, still ashen, a mask obscuring most of his face. I wanted to move closer to him but I was afraid to touch him, hooked up as he was to all those wires and tubes and monitors.

'He really is going to be okay?'

She nodded. A nurse moved silently around the bed, checking levels, taking his pulse.

'We were lucky it was an older handgun. A lot of kids are getting hold of semi-automatics now. That would have been it.' She rubbed at her eyes. 'It'll probably be on the news, if nothing else happens. Mind you, another crew dealt with the murder of a mother and baby on Athena Road last night, so it's possible it won't be news at all.'

I tore my gaze from him, and turned to her. 'Will you carry on?'

'Carry on?'

'As a paramedic.'

She pulled a face, as if she didn't really understand the question. 'Of course. It's my job.' She patted me on the shoulder and turned towards the door. 'Get some sleep, Lou. He probably won't wake up until tomorrow anyway. He's about eighty-seven per cent fentanyl right now.'

My parents were waiting when I stepped back into the corridor. They didn't say anything. I gave a small nod. Dad took my arm and Mum patted my back. 'Let's get you home, love,' she said. 'And into some clean things.'

It turns out there is a particular tone of voice that emanates from an employer who, several months previously, had to listen to how you couldn't come to work as you had fallen off the fifth floor of a building, and now would like to swap shifts because a man who may or may not be your boyfriend has been shot twice in the stomach.

'You – he has – what?'

'He was shot twice. He's out of intensive care but I'd like to be there this morning when he comes to. So I was wondering if I could swap shifts with you.'

There was a short silence.

'Right . . . Uh. Okay.' He hesitated. 'He was actually shot? With an actual gun?'

'You can come and inspect the holes, if you like.' My voice was so calm I almost laughed.

We discussed a couple more logistical details – calls that needed to be made, a visit from Head Office, and before I rang off, Richard grew silent for a moment. Then he said, 'Louisa, is your life always like this?'

I thought of who I had been just two and a half years ago, my days measured in the short walk between my parents' house and the café; the Tuesday-night routines of watching Patrick running or supper with my parents. I looked down at the rubbish bag in the corner, which now contained my bloodstained tennis shoes. 'Possibly. Although I'd like to think it's just a phase.'

After breakfast, my parents left for home. My mother didn't want to go, but I assured her that I was fine, and that I didn't know where I would be for the next few days so there would be little point in her staying. I also reminded her that the last time Granddad was left alone for more than twenty-four hours he had eaten his way through two pots of raspberry jam and a tin of condensed milk in lieu of actual meals.

'You really are all right, though.' She held her hand to the side of my face. She said it as though it wasn't a question, although it clearly was.

'Mum, I'm fine.'

She shook her head and made to pick up her bag. 'I don't know, Louisa. You do pick them.'

She was taken aback when I laughed. It might have been leftover shock. But I like to think it was then that I realized I wasn't afraid of anything any more.

I showered, trying not to look at the pink water that ran from my legs, and washed my hair, bought the least limp bunch of flowers I could find at Samir's, and headed back to the hospital for ten a.m. Sam's parents had arrived several hours previously, the nurse told me, as she led me to the door. They had headed over to the railway carriage with Jake and Jake's father to fetch Sam's belongings.

'He wasn't very with it when they came but he's making more sense now,' she said. 'It's not unusual when they're recently out of theatre. Some people just bounce back quicker than others.'

I slowed as we reached the door. I could see him now through the glass, his eyes closed, as they had been last night, his hand, strapped up to various monitors, lying motionless alongside his body. There was stubble on his chin and while he was still ghostly pale, he looked a little more like himself.

'You sure I'm okay to go in?'

'You're Louise, right? He's been asking for you.' She smiled and wrinkled her nose. 'Give us a shout if you get tired of that one. He's lovely.'

I pushed the door slowly and his eyes opened, his face turning slightly. He looked at me then, as if he were taking

374

me in, and something inside me weakened with relief.

'Some people will do anything to beat me on the scar front.' I closed the door behind me.

'Yeah. Well.' His voice emerged as a croak. 'I've gone right off that game.' He gave a small, tired smile.

I stood, shifting my weight from one foot to the other. I hated hospitals. I would do almost anything never to enter one again.

'Come here.'

I put the flowers on the table and walked over to him. He moved his arm, motioning for me to sit on the bed beside him. I sat, and then, because it felt wrong to be looking down at him, I lay back, positioning myself carefully, wary of dislodging something, of hurting him. I placed my head on his shoulder and felt the welcome weight of his head come to rest against mine. His lower arm lifted, gently hooking me in. We lay there in silence for a while, listening to the soft-shoe shuffle of the nurses outside, the distant conversation.

'I thought you were dead,' I whispered.

'Apparently some amazing woman who shouldn't have been in the back of the ambulance managed to slow my blood loss.'

'That's some woman.'

'I thought so.'

I closed my eyes, feeling the warmth of his skin against my cheek, the unwelcome scent of chemical disinfectant emanating from his body. I didn't think about anything. I just let myself exist in the moment, the deep, deep pleasure of being there next to him, of feeling the weight of him beside me, the space he took up in the atmosphere. I shifted my head and kissed the soft skin on the inside of his arm, and felt his fingers trace their way gently through my hair.

'You scared me, Ambulance Sam.'

There was a long silence. I could hear him thinking the million things he chose not to say.

'I'm glad you're here,' he said eventually.

We lay there for a bit longer, in silence. And when the nurse finally came in and raised an eyebrow at my proximity to various important tubes and wires, I climbed reluctantly off the bed and obeyed her instructions to get some breakfast while she did her medical thing. I kissed him, a little self-consciously, and when I stroked his hair his eyes lifted slightly at the corners and I saw, with gratitude, something of what I was to him. 'I'll be back after my shift,' I said.

'You might bump into my parents.' He said it as a warning.

'That's fine,' I said. 'I'll make sure I'm not wearing my Fuck Da Police T-shirt.'

He laughed, then grimaced, as if laughing were painful.

I fussed around a little while the nurses were seeing to him, doing the things that people do at patients' bedsides when they're simply looking for an excuse to hang around; I put out some fruit, disposed of a tissue, organized some magazines that I knew he wouldn't read. And then it was time to go. I had made it as far as the door when he spoke. 'I heard you.'

My hand was outstretched, ready to open it. I turned.

'Last night. When I was bleeding out. I heard you.'

Our eyes locked. And in that moment everything shifted. I saw what I had really done. I saw that I could be somebody's centre, their reason for staying. I saw that I could be enough. I walked back, took Sam's face in my hands and kissed him fiercely, feeling hot tears fall unchecked onto his face, his arm pulling me in tightly as he kissed me back. I pressed my cheek against his, half laughing, half weeping, oblivious to the nurses, to anything except the man before me. Then, finally, I turned and walked downstairs, wiping my face, laughing at my tears, ignoring the curious faces of the people who passed.

The day was beautiful, even under strip-lights. Outside birds sang, a new morning dawned, people lived and grew and got better and looked forward to getting older. I bought a coffee and ate an over-sweet muffin and they tasted like the most delicious things I had ever had. I sent messages to my parents, to Treena, to Richard, telling him I would be in shortly. I texted Lily: *Thought you might want to know Sam is in hospital. He got shot but he's okay. I know he'd love it if you dropped him a card. Or even just a text if you're busy.*

The answer pinged back within seconds. I smiled. How did girls of that age type so quickly when they did everything else so slowly?

*OMG. I just told the other girls and I'm basically now the coolest person they know. Seriously though give him my love. If you text me his details I'll get him a card after school. Oh and I'm sorry for showing off to him in my pants that time. I didn't mean it. Like not in a pervy way. Hope you guys are really happy. Xxx*

I didn't wait to respond. I looked at the hospital cafeteria and the shuffling patients and the bright blue day through the skylight and my fingers hit the keys before I knew what I was saying.

*I am.*

# Chapter Twenty-eight

Jake was waiting under the porch when I arrived at the Moving On Circle. It was raining heavily, dense clouds the colour of heather abruptly unleashing a thunderstorm that overwhelmed gutters and soaked me in the ten seconds it took to run across the car park.

'Aren't you going in? It's filthy out –'

He stepped forward, and his lanky arms enfolded me in a swift, awkward hug as I reached the door.

'Oh!' I lifted my hands, not wanting to drip all over him.

He released me and took a step back. 'Donna told us what you did. I just – you know – wanted to say thanks.'

His eyes were strained, and shadowed, and I realized what these last days must have been like for him, so close to having lost his mother. 'He's tough,' I said.

'He's bloody Teflon,' he said, and we laughed awkwardly, in the way British people do when they're experiencing great emotion.

In the meeting, Jake spoke unusually volubly, about the fact that his girlfriend didn't understand what grief was like for him. 'She doesn't get why some mornings I just want to stay in bed with the covers over my head. Or why I get a bit panicky about things happening to people I love. Literally nothing bad has happened to her. Ever. Even her pet rabbit is still alive and it's, like, nine years old.'

'I think people get bored of grief,' said Natasha. 'It's like you're allowed some unspoken allotted time – six months, maybe – and then they get faintly irritated that you're not "better". It's like you're being self-indulgent hanging on to your unhappiness.'

'Yes!' There was a murmur of agreement from around the circle.

'I sometimes think it would be easier if we still had to wear widows' weeds,' said Daphne. 'Then everyone could know you were still grieving.'

'Maybe like learner plates, so, you know, you got a different set of colours after a year. Maybe move from black to a deep purple,' said Leanne.

'Coming up all the way to yellow when you were really happy again,' Natasha grinned.

'Oh, no. Yellow is awful with my complexion.' Daphne smiled cautiously. 'I'll have to stay a bit miserable.'

I listened to their stories in the dank church hall – the tentative steps forward over tiny, emotional obstacles. Fred had joined a bowling league, and was enjoying having another reason to go out on Tuesdays, one that didn't involve talking about his late wife. Sunil had agreed to let his mother introduce him to a distant cousin from Eltham. 'I'm not really into the whole arranged-marriage thing but, to be honest, I'm having no luck with other methods. I keep telling myself she's my mother. She's hardly going to set me up with someone horrible.'

'I think it's a lovely idea,' said Daphne. 'My mother would probably have spotted which tree my Alan barked up long before I did. She was ever such a good judge.'

I viewed them as if I were on the outside of something looking in. I laughed at their jokes, winced internally at their tales of inappropriate tears or misjudged comments. But what became clear as I sat on my plastic chair and drank my instant coffee was that I had somehow found myself on the other side. I had crossed a bridge. Their struggle was no longer my struggle. It wasn't that I would ever stop grieving for Will, or loving him, or missing him, but that my life seemed to have somehow landed back in the present. And it was with a growing satisfaction that I found, even as I sat there with people I now knew and trusted, I wanted to be somewhere else: beside a large man in a hospital bed who I knew, to my utter gratitude, would even now be glancing up at the clock in the corner, wondering how long it was going to take me to get to him.

'Nothing from you tonight, Louisa?'

Marc was looking at me, one eyebrow raised.

I shook my head. 'I'm good.'

He smiled, perhaps recognizing something in my tone. 'Good.'

'Yes. Actually, I think I don't need to be here any more. I'm . . . okay.'

'I knew there was something different about you,' said Natasha, leaning forwards and eyeing me almost suspiciously.

'It's the shagging,' said Fred. 'I'm sure that's the cure. I bet I'd have got over Jilly much faster with all the shagging.'

Natasha and William exchanged a strange look.

'I'd like to come until the end of the term, if it's okay,' I said to Marc. 'It's just . . . I've come to think of you all as my friends. I might not need it, but I would still like to come for a bit longer. Just to make sure. And, you know, to see everyone.'

Jake gave a small smile.

'We should probably go dancing,' said Natasha.

'You can come for as long as you want,' said Marc. 'That's what we're here for.'

My friends. A motley group, but then most friends are.

Orecchiette cooked *al dente*, pine-nuts, basil, home-grown tomatoes, olives, tuna and Parmesan cheese. I had made the pasta salad to the recipe Lily gave me over the phone as she was fed instructions by her grandmother.

'Good invalid food,' Camilla shouted, from some distant kitchen. 'Easy to digest if he's spending a lot of time lying down.'

'I'd just buy him a takeaway,' muttered Lily. 'Poor man's suffered enough.' She cackled quietly. 'Anyway, I thought you preferred him lying down.'

I walked along the hospital corridor later that evening feeling quietly proud of my little Tupperware box of domesticity. I had made this supper the night before and now carried it in front of me like a badge of honour, half hoping someone would stop me and ask what it was. *Yes, my boyfriend is recuperating. I bring him food every day. Just little things he might fancy. You know I grew these tomatoes myself?*

Sam's wounds were beginning to heal, the internal damage clearing. He tried to get up too often, and was grumpy about being stuck in bed and worried about his animals, even though Donna, Jake and I had set up a reasonably good animal husbandry schedule.

Two to three weeks, the consultants reckoned. If he did what he was told. Given the extent of his injuries he had been lucky. More than one conversation had taken place in my presence where medical professionals had murmured, 'A centimetre the other way and . . .' I sang la-la-la-la-la-la in my head during those conversations.

I reached his corridor and buzzed myself in, cleaning my hands with the antibacterial foam, as I pushed at the door with my hip.

'Evening,' said the nurse with glasses. 'You're late!'

'Had to go to a meeting.'

'You just missed his mum. She brought him the most delicious homemade steak and ale pie. You could smell it all the way down the ward. We're still salivating.'

'Oh.' I lowered my box. 'That's nice.'

'Good to see him tuck in. The consultant will be round in about half an hour.'

I was just about to put the Tupperware into my bag when my phone rang. I pressed answer, still wrestling with the zip.

'Louisa?'

'Yes?'

'It's Leonard Gopnik.'

It took me two seconds to register his name. I made to speak, then stood very still, glancing around me stupidly as if he could be somewhere nearby.

'Mr Gopnik.'

'I got your email.'

'Right.' I put the food container on the chair.

'It was an interesting read. I was pretty surprised when you turned down my job offer. As was Nathan. You seemed suited to it.'

'It's like I said in my email. I did want it, Mr Gopnik, but I . . . well . . . things came up.'

'So is this girl doing okay now?'

'Lily. Yes. She's in school. She's happy. She's with her family. Her new family. It was just a period of . . . adjustment.'

'You took that very seriously.'

'I'm not the kind of person who can just leave someone behind.'

There was a long silence. I turned away from Sam's room and gazed out of the window at the car park, watching as an oversized 4x4 tried and failed to negotiate its way into a too-small parking space. Forwards and backwards. I could see it wasn't going to fit.

'So here's the thing, Louisa. It's not working out with our new employee. She's not happy. For whatever reason she and my wife are not really comfortable with each other. By mutual agreement she's leaving at the end of the month. Which leaves me with a problem.'

I listened.

'I would like to offer you the job. But I don't like upheaval, especially when it involves people close to me. So I guess I'm calling because I'm trying to get a clear picture of what it is you actually want.'

'Oh, I did really want it. But I –'

I felt a hand on my shoulder. I spun around, and there was Sam, leaning against the wall. 'I – er –'

'You got another position?'

'I got a promotion.'

'Is it a position you want to stay in?'

Sam was watching my face.

'N-not necessarily. But –'

'But obviously you have to weigh it all up. Okay. Well, I imagine that I've probably caught you by surprise with this call. But on the back of what you wrote me, if you're genuinely still interested I'd like to offer you the job. Same terms, to start as soon as possible. That's as long as you're sure that it's something you really want. Do you think you can let me know within forty-eight hours?'

'Yes. Yes, Mr Gopnik. Thank you. Thank you for calling.'

I heard him click off. I looked up at Sam. He was wearing a hospital dressing gown over his too-short hospital night-shirt. Neither of us spoke for a moment.

'You're up. You should be in bed.'

'I saw you through the window.'

'One ill-timed breeze and those nurses are going to be talking about you till Christmas.'

'Was that the New York guy?'

I felt, oddly, busted. I put my phone in my pocket and reached for the Tupperware container. 'The position came up again.' I watched his gaze slide briefly away from me. 'But it's . . . I've only just got you back. So I'm going to say no. Look, do you think you can manage some pasta after your epic pie? I know you're probably full, but it's so rare that I manage to cook something that's actually edible.'

'No.'

'It's not that bad. You could at least try –'

'Not the pasta. The job.'

We stared at each other. He ran his hand through his hair, glancing down the corridor. 'You need to do this, Lou. You know it and I know it. You have to take it.'

'I tried to leave home before, and I just got even more messed up.'

'Because it was too soon. You were running away. This is different.'

I gazed up at him. I hated myself for realizing what I wanted to do. And I hated him for knowing it. We stood in the hospital corridor in silence. And then I saw he was rapidly losing colour from his face. 'You need to lie down.'

He didn't fight me. I took his arm and we made our way back to his bed. He winced as he lay back carefully on the pillows. I waited until I saw colour return to his face, then lay down beside him and took his hand.

'I feel like we just sorted it all out. You and me.' I laid my head against his shoulder, feeling my throat constrict.

'We did.'

'I don't want to be with anyone else, Sam.'

'Pfft. Like that was ever in doubt.'

'But long-distance relationships rarely survive.'

'So we are in a relationship?'

I started to protest and he smiled. 'I'm kidding. Some. *Some* don't survive. I'm guessing some do, though. I guess it depends how much both sides want to try.'

His big arm looped around my neck and pulled me to him. I realised I was crying. He wiped at my tears gently with his thumb. 'Lou, I don't know what will happen. Nobody ever does. You can set out one morning and step in front of a motorbike and your whole life can change. You can go to work on a routine job and get shot by a teenager who thinks that's what it takes to be a man.'

'You can fall off a tall building.'

'You can. Or you can go to visit a bloke wearing a nightie in a hospital bed and get the best job offer you can imagine. That's life. We don't know what will happen. Which is why we have to take our chances while we can. And . . . I think this might be yours.'

I screwed my eyes shut, not wanting to hear him, not wanting to acknowledge the truth in what he was saying. I wiped at my eyes with the heels of my hands. He handed me a tissue and waited while I wiped the black smears from my face.

'Panda-eyes suit you.'

'I think I might be a bit in love with you.'

'I bet you say that to all the men in intensive care.'

I turned over and kissed him. When I opened my eyes again he was watching me.

'I'll give it a go, if you will,' he said.

It took a moment for the lump in my throat to subside enough for me to be able to speak. 'I don't know, Sam.'

'You don't know what?'

'Life is short, right? We both know that. Well, what if you're my chance? What if you are the thing that's actually going to make me happiest?'

# Chapter Twenty-nine

When people say autumn is their favourite time of year, I think it's days like this that they mean: a dawn mist, burning off to a crisp clear light; piles of leaves blown into corners; the agreeably musty smell of gently mouldering greenery. Some say you don't really notice the seasons in the city, that the endless grey buildings and the microclimate caused by traffic fumes mean there is never a huge difference; there is only inside and out, wet or dry. But on the roof it was clear. It wasn't just in the huge expanse of sky but in Lily's tomato plants, which had pushed out swollen red fruit for weeks, the hanging strawberry pots providing an intermittent array of occasional sweet treats. The flowers budded, bloomed and browned, the fresh green growth of early summer giving way to twiggy stalks and space where foliage had been. Up on the roof you could already detect the faintest hint in the breeze of the oncoming winter. An aeroplane was leaving a vapour trail across the sky and I noted that the streetlights were still on from the night before.

My mother emerged onto the roof in her slacks, gazing around her at the guests, and brushing moisture droplets from the fire escape off her trousers. 'It really is quite something, this space of yours, Louisa. You could fit a hundred people up here.' She was carrying a bag containing several bottles of champagne, and put it down carefully. 'Did I tell you, I think you're very brave getting up the confidence to come up here again?'

'I still can't believe you managed to fall off,' observed my sister, who had been refilling glasses. 'Only you could fall off a space this big.'

'Well, she was drunk as a lord, love, remember?' Mum headed back to the fire escape. 'Where did you get all the champagne from, Louisa? This looks awful grand.'

'My boss gave it to me.'

We had been cashing up a few nights previously, chatting (we chatted quite a lot now, especially since he'd had his baby. I knew more about Mrs Percival's water retention than I think she would have been entirely comfortable with). I had mentioned my plans and Richard had disappeared, as if he hadn't been listening. I had been ready to chalk it up as just another example of how Richard was still basically a bit of a wazzock, but when he re-emerged from the cellars a few minutes later he was holding a crate containing half a dozen bottles of champagne. 'Here. Sixty per cent off. Last of the order.' He handed me the box and shrugged. 'Actually, sod it. Just take them. Go on. You've earned them.'

I had stuttered my thanks and he had muttered something about them being not a great vintage and the last of the line, but his ears had gone a tell-tale pink.

'You could try to sound a bit pleased that I didn't actually die.' I passed Treena a tray of glasses.

'Oh, I got over my "I wish I was an only child" thing ages ago. Well, maybe two years or so.'

Mum approached with a packet of napkins. She spoke in an exaggerated whisper: 'Now, do you think these will be okay?'

'Why wouldn't they be?'

'It's the Traynors, isn't it? They don't use paper napkins. They'll have linen ones. Probably with a coat of arms embroidered on them or something.'

'Mum, they've travelled to the roof of a former office block in east London. I don't think they're expecting silver service.'

'Oh,' said Treena. 'And I brought Thom's spare duvet and pillow. I thought we might as well start bringing bits and bobs down every time we come. I've got an appointment to look at that after-school club tomorrow.'

'It's wonderful that you've got it all sorted out, girls. Treena, if you like, I'll mind Thom for you. Just let me know.'

We worked around each other, setting out glasses and paper plates, until Mum disappeared to fetch more inadequate napkins. I lowered my voice so that she couldn't hear. 'Treen? Is Dad really not coming?'

My sister grimaced, and I tried not to look as dismayed as I felt.

'Is it really no better?'

'I'm hoping that when I'm gone they'll have to talk to each other. They just skirt around each other and talk to me or Thom most of the time. It's maddening. Mum's pretending she doesn't care that he didn't come down with us, but I know she does.'

'I really thought he'd be here.'

I had seen my mother twice since the shooting. She had signed up for a new course – modern English poetry – at the adult education centre and now grew wistful at symbols everywhere. Every blown leaf was a sign of impending decrepitude, every airborne bird a sign of hopes and dreams. We had gone once to a live reading of poetry on the South Bank, where she had sat rapt and applauded twice into the silence, and once to the cinema, then on to the loos at the smart hotel, where she had shared sandwiches with Maria in the two easy chairs of the cloakroom. Both times, when we had found ourselves alone, she had been oddly brittle. 'Well, aren't we having a lovely time?' she would say repeatedly, as if challenging me to disagree. And then she would grow quiet or exclaim about the insane price of sandwiches in London.

Treena pulled the bench across, plumping up the cushions she had brought up from downstairs. 'It's Granddad I worry about. He doesn't like all the tension. He changes his socks four times a day and he's broken two of the buttons on the remote control by over-pressing.'

'God – there's a thought. Who would get custody?'

My sister stared at me in horror.

'Don't look at me,' we said in unison.

We were interrupted by the first of the Moving On Circle, Sunil and Leanne, emerging from the cast-iron steps, remarking on the size of the roof terrace, the unexpectedly magnificent view over the east of the City.

Lily arrived at twelve on the dot, throwing her arms around me and letting out a little growl of happiness. 'I *love* that dress! You look completely gorgeous.' She was sun-kissed, her face open and freckled, the tiny hairs on her arms bleached white, clad in a pale blue dress and gladiator sandals. I watched her as she gazed around the roof terrace, clearly delighted to be there again. Camilla, making her way slowly up the fire escape behind her, straightened her jacket and walked over to me, an expression of mild admonishment on her face. 'You could have waited, Lily.'

'Why? You're not some old person.'

Camilla and I exchanged wry glances, and then, almost impulsively, I leaned forward and kissed her cheek. She smelt of expensive department stores and her hair was perfect. 'It's lovely that you came.'

'You've even looked after my plants.' Lily was examining everything. 'I just assumed you'd kill them all. Oh, and this! I like these. Are they new?' She pointed to two pots I had bought at the flower market the previous week, to decorate the roof for today. I hadn't wanted cut flowers, or anything that might die.

'They're pelargoniums,' said Camilla. 'You won't want to leave them up here over the winter.'

'She could put fleece over them. Those terracotta pots are heavy to take down.'

'They still won't survive,' said Camilla. 'Too exposed.'

'Actually,' I said, 'Thom's coming to live here and we're not sure he would be safe on the roof, given what happened to me, so we're shutting it off. If you'd like to take those with you afterwards . . .'

'No,' Lily said, after a moment's thought. 'Let's leave it. It will be nice to just think of it like this. As it was.'

She helped me with a trestle table, and talked a little of school – she was happy there but struggling slightly with the work – and of her mother, who was apparently making eyes at a Spanish architect called Felipe, who had bought the house next door in St John's Wood. 'I feel almost sorry for Fuckface. He doesn't know what's about to hit him.'

'But you're okay?' I said.

'I'm fine. Life is pretty good.' She popped a crisp into her mouth. 'Granny made me go and see the new baby – did I tell you?'

I must have looked startled. 'I know. But she said someone had to behave like a grown-up. She actually came with me. She was epically cool. I'm not meant to know but she bought a Jaeger jacket specially. I think she needed more confidence than she let on.' She glanced over at Camilla, who was chatting to Sam over by the food table. 'Actually, I felt a bit sad for my grandfather. When he thought nobody was looking he kept gazing at her, like he felt a bit sad at how it had all turned out.'

'And how was it?'

'It's a baby. I mean, they all look the same, don't they? I think they were on their best behaviour, though. It was all a bit "And how is school, Lily? Would you like to fix a date to

390

come and stay? And would you like to hold your aunt?" Like *that* doesn't sound completely weird.'

'You'll go and see them again?'

'Probably. They're all right, I suppose.'

I glanced over at Georgina, who was talking politely to her father. He laughed, slightly too loudly. He had barely left her side since she had arrived. 'He calls me twice a week to chat about stuff, and Della keeps going on about how she wants me and the baby to "build a relationship", like a baby can do anything except eat and scream and poo.' She pulled a face.

I laughed.

'What?' she said.

'Nothing,' I said. 'It's just good to see you.'

'Oh. And I brought you something.'

I waited as she pulled a little box out of her bag, and handed it to me. 'I saw it at this totally tedious antiques fair that Granny made me go to and I thought of you.'

I opened the box carefully. Inside, on dark blue velvet, was an art-deco bracelet, its cylindrical beads alternate jet and amber. I picked it up and held it in my palm.

'It's a bit out there, right? But it reminded me of –'

'The tights.'

'The tights. It's a thank-you. Just – you know – for everything. You're about the only person I know who would like it. Or me, for that matter. Back then. Actually, it totally goes with your dress.'

I held out an arm and she put it on my wrist. I rotated it slowly. 'I love it.'

She kicked at something on the ground, her face briefly serious. 'Well, I think I kind of owe you some jewellery.'

'You owe me nothing.'

I looked at Lily, with her new confidence and her father's eyes, and thought of everything she had given me without even knowing it. And then she punched me quite hard on the arm. 'Right. Stop being all weird and emotional. Or you're totally going to ruin my mascara. Let's go downstairs and fetch the last of the food. Ugh, did you know there's a Transformers poster gone up in my bedroom? And one of Katy Perry? Who the *hell* have you got as a new flatmate?'

The rest of the Moving On Circle arrived, making their way with varying degrees of trepidation or laughter up the iron steps – Daphne stepping onto the roof with loud exclamations of relief, Fred holding her arm, William vaulting nonchalantly over the last step, Natasha rolling her eyes behind him. Others paused to exclaim at the bundle of white helium balloons, bobbing in the thin light. Marc kissed my hand and told me it was the first time something like this had taken place the whole time he had been running the group. Natasha and William, I noticed with amusement, spent a lot of time talking alone.

We put the food on the trestle table and Jake was on bar duty, pouring the champagne and looking curiously pleased at the responsibility. He and Lily had skirted around each other at first, pretending the other was invisible, as teenagers do when they're in a small gathering and conscious that everyone will be waiting for them to speak to each other. When she finally made her way over to him she shoved out her hand with exaggerated courtesy and he looked at it for a moment before giving a slow smile.

'Half of me would like them to be friends. The other can think of nothing more terrifying,' Sam murmured into my ear.

I slid my hand into his back pocket. 'She's happy.'

'She's gorgeous. And he's just split up with his girlfriend.'

'What happened to living life to the full, mister?'

He let out a low growl.

'He's safe. She's now tucked away in Oxfordshire for most of the year.'

'Nobody's safe with you two.' He lowered his head and kissed me and I let everything else disappear for a luxurious second or two. 'I like that dress.'

'Not too frivolous?' I held out the pleats of the striped skirt. This part of London was full of vintage-clothes stores. I had spent the previous Saturday lost in rails of ancient silks and feathers.

'I like frivolous. Although I'm a bit sad that you're not wearing your sexy pixie thing.' He stepped back from me as my mother approached, bearing another pack of paper napkins.

'How are you, Sam? Still healing up nicely?' She had visited Sam twice in hospital. She had become deeply concerned at the plight of those left to rely on hospital catering and brought him homemade sausage rolls and egg-mayonnaise sandwiches.

'Getting there, thanks.'

'Don't you do too much today. No carrying. The girls and I can manage just fine.'

'We should probably start,' I said.

Mum glanced again at her watch, then scanned the roof terrace. 'Shall we give it another five minutes? Make sure everyone gets a drink?'

Her smile – fixed and too bright – was heartbreaking. Sam saw it. He stepped forward and took her arm. 'Josie, do you think you could show me where you've put the salads? I just remembered I didn't bring the dressing from downstairs.'

'Where is she?'

A ripple passed through the small crowd by the table. We turned towards the bellowing voice. 'Jesus Christ, is it really up here, or is Thommo sending me on another wild-goose chase?'

'Bernard!' My mother put down the napkins.

My father's face appeared above the parapet, scanning the rooftop. He climbed the last of the iron steps and blew out his cheeks as he surveyed the view. A light film of sweat shone on his forehead. 'Why you had to do the damn thing all the way up here, Louisa, I have no idea. Jaysus.'

'Bernard!'

'It's not a church, Josie. And I have an important message.'

Mum gazed around her. 'Bernard. Now is not the –'

'And my message is – *these*.'

My father bent over and with exaggerated care pulled up his trouser legs. First the left, and then the right. From my position on the other side of the water tank I could see that his shins were pale and faintly blotchy. The rooftop fell silent. Everyone stared. He extended one leg. 'Smooth as a baby's backside. Go on, Josie, feel them.'

My mother took a nervous step forward and stooped, sliding her fingers up my father's shin. She patted her hand around it.

'You said you'd take me seriously if I had my legs waxed. Well, there you are. I've done it.'

My mother stared at him in disbelief. 'You got your *legs* waxed?'

'I did. And if I'd had any idea you were going through pain like that, love, I would have kept my stupid mouth shut. What fecking torture is that? Who the hell thinks *that* is a good idea?'

'Bernard –'

'I don't care. I've been through hell, Josie. But I'd do it again if it means we can get things back on track. I miss you. *So much*. I don't care if you want to do a hundred college courses – feminist politics, Middle Eastern studies, macramé for dogs, whatever – as long as we're together. And to prove to you exactly how far I'd go for you, I've booked myself in again next week, for a back, sack and – What is it?'

'Crack,' said my sister, unhappily.

'Oh, God.' My mother's hand flew to her neck.

Beside me Sam had started to shake silently. 'Stop them,' he murmured. 'I'm going to bust my stitches.'

'I'll do the lot. I'll go the full-plucked ruddy chicken if it shows you what you mean to me.'

'Oh, my days, Bernard.'

'I mean it, Josie. That's how desperate I am.'

'And this is why our family doesn't do romance,' muttered Treena.

'What's a crack, back and wax?' asked Thomas.

'Oh, love, I've missed the bones of you.' My mother put her arms around my father's neck and kissed him. The relief on his face was almost palpable. He buried his head in her shoulder and then he kissed her again, her ear, her hair, holding her hands, like a small boy.

'Gross,' said Thomas.

'So I don't have to do the –'

My mother stroked my father's cheek. 'We'll cancel your appointment first thing.'

My father visibly relaxed.

'Well,' I said, when the commotion had died down, and it was clear from Camilla Traynor's blanched complexion that Lily had just explained to her exactly what my father had planned to endure in the name of love, 'I think we should do one last check of everyone's glasses, and then maybe . . . we should start?'

What with the merriment over Dad's grand gesture, Baby Traynor's explosive nappy change, and the revelation that Thomas had been dropping egg sandwiches onto Mr Antony Gardiner's balcony (and his brand-new replacement Conran wicker-effect sun chair) below, it was another twenty minutes before the rooftop grew silent. Amid some surreptitious scanning of notes and clearing of throats, Marc stepped into the middle. He was taller than I'd thought – I had only ever seen him sitting down.

'Welcome, everyone. First, I'd like to thank Louisa for offering us this lovely space for our end-of-term ceremony. There's something rather appropriate about being this much closer to the heavens . . .' He paused for laughter. 'This is an unusual final ceremony for us – for the first time we have some faces here who aren't part of the group – but I think it's a rather lovely idea to open up and celebrate among friends. Everyone here knows what it's like to have loved and lost. So we're all honorary members of the group today.'

Jake stood beside his father, a freckle-faced, sandy-haired man, who, unfortunately, I couldn't look at without picturing him weeping after coitus. Now he reached out and gently pulled his son to him. Jake caught my eye and rolled his. But he smiled.

'I like to say that although we're called the Moving On Circle, none of us moves on without a backward look. We move on always carrying with us those we have lost. What we aim to do in our little group is ensure that carrying them is not a burden that feels impossible to bear, a weight keeping us stuck in the same place. We want their presence to feel like a gift.

'And what we learn through sharing our memories and our sadnesses and our little victories with each other is that it's okay to feel sad. Or lost. Or angry. It's okay to feel a whole host of things that other people might not understand, and often for a long time. Everyone has his or her own journey. We don't judge.'

'Except the biscuits,' muttered Fred. 'I judge those Rich Teas. They were shocking.'

'And that, impossible as it may feel at first, we will each get to a point where we can rejoice in the fact that every person we have discussed and mourned and grieved over was here, walking among us – and whether they were taken after six months or sixty years, we were lucky to have them.' He nodded. 'We were lucky to have them.'

I looked around the faces I had grown fond of, rapt with attention, and I thought of Will. I closed my eyes and recalled his face, his smile and his laugh, and thought of what loving him had cost me, but mostly of what he had given me.

Marc looked at our little group. Daphne dabbed surreptitiously at the corner of her eye. 'So . . . what we usually do now is just say a few words acknowledging where we are. It doesn't have to be much. It's just a closing of a door on this little bit of your journey. And nobody has to do it, but if you do, it can be a nice thing.'

The group exchanged embarrassed smiles and, briefly, it seemed that nobody would say anything at all. Then Fred stepped up. He adjusted his handkerchief in his blazer pocket and straightened a little. 'I'd just like to say thank you, Jilly. You were a smashing wife and I was a lucky man for thirty-eight years. I will miss you every day, sweetheart.'

He stepped back, a little awkwardly, and Daphne mouthed, 'Very nice, Fred,' to him. She adjusted her silk scarf, and then she stepped forwards too. 'I just wanted to say . . . I'm sorry. To Alan. You were such a kind man, and I wish we'd been able to be honest about everything. I wish I'd been able to help you. I wish – well, I hope you're okay, and that – that you've got a nice friend, wherever you are.'

Fred patted Daphne's arm.

Jake rubbed the back of his neck, then stepped forward, blushing, and faced his father. 'We both miss you, Mum. But we're getting there. I don't want you to worry or anything.' When he finished his father hugged him, kissing the top of his head, and blinked hard. He and Sam exchanged small smiles of understanding.

Leanne and Sunil followed, each saying a few words, fixing their eyes on the sky to hide awkward tears or nodding silent encouragement at each other.

William stepped forward and silently placed a white rose at his feet. Unusually short of words, he gazed down at it briefly, his face impassive, then stepped back. Natasha gave him a little hug and he swallowed suddenly, audibly, then folded his arms across his chest.

Marc looked at me, and I felt Sam's hand close around mine. I smiled at him and shook my head. 'Not me. But Lily would like to say a few words, if that's okay.'

Lily was chewing her lip as she stepped into the middle. She glanced down at a bit of paper she had written on, then appeared to change her mind and screwed it into a ball. 'Um, I asked Louisa if I could do this even though, you know, I'm not a member of your group. I didn't know my dad in person and I never got to say goodbye to him at his funeral and I thought it would be nice to say a few words now that I sort of feel I know him a bit better.' She gave a nervous smile, and pushed a strand of hair from her face. 'So. Will . . . Dad. When I first found out you were my real father, I'll be honest, I was a bit freaked out. I'd hoped my real dad was going to be this wise, handsome man, who would want to teach me stuff and protect me and take me on trips to show me amazing places that he loved. And what I actually got was an angry man in a wheelchair who just, you know, killed himself. But because of Lou, and your family, over the last few months I've come to understand you a bit better.

'I'll always be sad and maybe even a bit angry that I never got to meet you, but now I want to say thank you too. You gave me a lot, without knowing it. I think I'm like you in good ways – and probably a few not-so-good ways. You gave me blue eyes and my hair colour and the fact that I think Marmite is revolting and the ability to do black ski runs and . . . Well, apparently you also gave me a certain amount of mood iness – that's other people's opinion, by the way. Not mine.'

There was a little ripple of laughter.

'But mostly you gave me a family I didn't know I had. And that's cool. Because, to be honest, it wasn't going *that* well before they all turned up.' Her smile wavered.

'We're very happy *you* turned up,' Georgina called out.

I felt Sam's fingers squeeze mine. He wasn't meant to be standing so long but, typically, he refused to sit down. *I'm not a bloody invalid.* I let my head rest against him, fighting the lump that had risen to my throat.

'Thanks, G. So, um, Will . . . *Dad*, I'm not going to go on and on because speeches are boring and also that baby is going to start wailing any minute, which will totally harsh the mood. But I just wanted to say thank you, from your daughter, and that I . . . love you and I'll always miss you, and I hope if you're looking down, and you can see me, you're glad. That I exist. Because me being here sort of means *you're* still here, doesn't it?' Lily's voice cracked and her eyes filled with tears. Her gaze slid towards Camilla, who gave a small nod. Lily sniffed, and lifted her chin.

'I thought maybe now would be a good time for everyone to release their balloons?'

There was a barely perceptible release of breath, a few shuffled steps. Behind me the handful of members of the Moving On Circle murmured among themselves, reaching into the gently bobbing bundle for a string.

Lily was the first to step forward, holding her white helium balloon. She lifted her arm, then, as an afterthought, picked a tiny blue cornflower from one of her pots, and tied it carefully

399

to the string. Then she raised her hand and, after the briefest hesitation, released the balloon.

I watched as Steven Traynor followed, saw Della's gentle squeeze of his arm. Camilla released hers, then Fred, Sunil, then Georgina, her arm linked with her mother's. My mother, Treena, Dad, blowing his nose noisily into his handkerchief, and Sam. We stood in silence on the roof and watched them sail upwards, one by one into the clear blue sky, growing smaller and smaller until they were somewhere infinite, unseen.

I let mine go.

# Chapter Thirty

The man in the salmon-coloured shirt was on his fourth Danish pastry, wedging great iced wads of it into his open mouth with chubby fingers, and periodically sluicing it down with a pint of cold lager. 'Breakfast of champions,' muttered Vera, as she walked past me with a tray of glasses and made a fake gagging noise. I felt a fleeting, reflexive gratitude that I was no longer in charge of the Gents.

'So, Lou! What does a man have to do to get some service around here?' A short distance away, Dad had perched himself on a stool and was leaning over the bar, examining the various beers. 'Do I need to show a boarding card to buy a drink?'

'Dad –'

'Quick trip to Alicante? What do you think, Josie? Fancy it?'

My mother nudged him. 'We should look into it this year. We really should.'

'You know, it's not a bad aul' place this. Once you get past the daft idea of actual kids being allowed in an actual pub.' Dad shuddered and glanced behind him to where a young family, their flight evidently delayed, had spread a mixture of Lego and raisins all over the table while they eked out two coffees. 'So what do you recommend, sweetheart, eh? What's good on the old pumps?'

I eyed Richard, who was approaching with his clipboard. 'It's all good, Dad.'

'Apart from those outfits,' said Mum, eyeing Vera's too-short green Lurex skirt.

'Head Office,' said Richard, who had already endured two conversations with my mother about the objectification of women in the workplace. 'Nothing to do with me.'

'You got any stout there, Richard?'

'We have Murphy's, Mr Clark. It's a lot like Guinness, although I wouldn't say as much to a purist.'

'I'm no purist, son. If it's wet and it says "beer" on the label it'll do for me.'

Dad smacked his lips in approval and the glass was set down in front of him. My mother accepted a coffee with her 'social' voice. She used it almost everywhere in London now, like a visiting dignitary being shown around a production line: *So that's a lah-tay, is it? Well, that looks simply lovely. And what a clever machine.*

My father patted the bar stool beside her. 'Come and sit down, Lou. Come on. Let me buy my daughter a drink.'

I glanced over at Richard. 'I'll have a coffee, Dad,' I said. 'Thank you.'

We sat at the bar in silence, as Richard served us, and my father made himself at home, as he did in every bar he ever sat in, nodding a greeting to fellow bar dwellers, settling on his stool as if it were his favourite easy chair. It was as if the presence of a row of optics and a hard surface on which to rest his elbows created an instant spiritual home. And at all times he kept within inches of my mother, patting her leg appreciatively or holding her hand. They barely left each other alone, these days, heads pressed together, giggling like teenagers. It was utterly revolting, according to my sister. She told me before she set off for work that she had almost preferred it when they weren't talking. 'I had to sleep with earplugs last Saturday. Can you imagine the horror? Granddad looked quite white over breakfast.'

Outside, a small passenger plane slowed on the runway

and taxied towards the terminal, a man in a reflective jacket waving paddles to guide it in. Mum sat, handbag balanced on her lap, and gazed at it. 'Thom would love this,' she said. 'Wouldn't he love this, Bernard? I reckon he'd stand at that window all day.'

'Well, he can come now, can't he, now he's just up the road? Treena could bring him here at the weekend. I might come too if the beer's any good.'

'It's lovely what you've done, letting them come and stay in your flat.' Mum watched the plane disappear from view. 'You know this will make all the difference to Treena, with her starting salary and all.'

'Well. It made sense.'

'Much as we'll miss them, we know she can't live with us for ever. I know she appreciates it, love. Even if she doesn't always show it.'

I didn't really care that she didn't show it. I had realized something the moment she and Thom walked through my front door with their cases of belongings and posters, Dad behind them bearing the plastic crate of Thom's favourite Predacons and Autobots. It was at that exact point that I finally felt okay about the flat Will's money had paid for.

'Did Louisa mention that her sister is moving down here, Richard?' My mother now operated on the basis that pretty much everyone she met in London was her friend, and therefore keen to hear all developments in the Clark household. She had spent ten minutes this morning advising Richard on his wife's mastitis, and couldn't see any reason why she shouldn't pop along and see his baby. Then again, Maria from the hotel toilets was actually coming for tea in Stortfold in two weeks' time, with her daughter, so she wasn't entirely wrong. 'Our Katrina's a great girl. Smart as a whip. If you ever need any help with your accounts, she's your woman.'

'I'll bear it in mind.' Richard's gaze met mine and slid away.

I glanced up at the clock. A quarter to twelve. Something inside me fluttered.

'You all right, love?'

You had to hand it to her. My mother never missed a thing.

'I'm fine, Mum.'

She squeezed my hand. 'I'm so proud of you. You know that, don't you? Everything you've achieved these past few months. I know it hasn't been easy.' And then she pointed. 'Oh, look! I knew he'd come. There you go, sweetheart. This is it!'

And there he was. A head taller than everyone else, and walking a little tentatively through the crowd, his arm braced slightly in front of him, as if he were wary even now that someone would bump into him. I saw him before he saw me, and my face broke into a spontaneous smile. I waved vigorously, and he saw me, and gave a nod.

When I turned back to my mother she was watching me, a small smile playing around her lips. 'He's a good one, that one.'

'I know.'

She gazed at me for the longest time, her face a mixture of pride and something a little more complicated. She patted my hand. 'Right,' she said, climbing off her bar stool. 'Time to have your adventures.'

I left my parents at the bar. It was better that way. It was hard to get emotional in front of a man who liked to quote sections of the managerial handbook for LOLs. Sam had a brief chat with my parents – my father kept breaking in with occasional *nee-naw* noises – and Richard asked after Sam's injuries and laughed nervously when Dad mentioned that at least he'd done better than my last boyfriend. It took three goes for Dad to convince Richard that, no, he wasn't joking about

Dignitas, and a terribly sad business it had all been. That might have been the point at which Richard decided he was actually quite glad I was leaving.

I extricated myself from Mum's embrace, and we walked across the concourse in silence, my arm linked in Sam's, trying to ignore the fact that my heart was thumping and that my parents were probably still watching me. I turned to Sam, faintly panicked. I'd thought we would have more time.

He looked at his watch and up at the departures board. 'They're playing your tune.' He handed over my little wheeled case. I took it and tried to raise a smile.

'Nice travelling threads.'

I looked down at my leopard-print shirt, and the Jackie O sunglasses I had tucked into my top pocket. 'I was going for a 1970s jet-set vibe.'

'It's a good look. For a jet-setter.'

'So,' I said. 'I'll see you in four weeks . . . It's meant to be nice in New York in the autumn.'

'It'll be nice whatever.' He shook his head. 'Jesus. "Nice". I hate the word "nice".'

I looked down at our hands, which were entwined. I found myself staring at them, as if I had to memorize how his felt against mine, as if I had failed to revise for some vital exam that had come too soon. A strange panic was welling inside me, and I think he felt it because he squeezed my fingers.

'Got everything?' He nodded towards my other hand. 'Passport? Boarding pass? Address of where you're going?'

'Nathan is meeting me at JFK.'

I didn't want to let him go. I felt like a magnet gone awry, being pulled between two poles. I stood aside as other couples stepped towards Departures together, towards their adventures, or extracted themselves tearfully from each other's arms.

He was watching them too. He stepped back from me gently,

and kissed my fingers before releasing my hand. 'Time to go,' he said.

I had a million things to say and none I knew how. I stepped forward and kissed him, like people kiss at airports, full of love and desperate longing, kisses that must imprint themselves on their recipient for the journey, the weeks, the months ahead. With that kiss, I tried to tell him the enormity of what he meant to me. I tried to show him that he was the answer to a question I hadn't even known I had been asking. I tried to thank him for wanting me to be me, more than he wanted to make me stay. In truth I probably just told him I'd drunk two large coffees without brushing my teeth.

'You take care,' I said. 'Don't rush back to work. And don't do any building stuff.'

'My brother's coming to take over the brickwork tomorrow.'

'And if you do go back, don't get hurt. You are totally crap on the not-getting-shot thing.'

'Lou. I'm going to be fine.'

'I mean it. I'm going to email Donna when I get to New York and tell her I'll hold her personally responsible if anything else happens to you. Or maybe I'll just tell your boss to put you on desk duty. Or send you to some really sleepy station in north Norfolk. Or maybe make you wear bulletproof vests. Have they thought of issuing bulletproof vests? I bet I could buy a good one in New York if –'

'Louisa.' He pushed a lock of hair back from my eyes. And I felt my face crumple. I placed it against his and clenched my jaw and breathed in the scent of him, trying to embed some of that solidity into myself. And then, before I could change my mind, I let out a strangled 'Bye' that might have been a sob or a cough or a stupid half-laugh, I'm not sure even I could tell. And I turned and walked briskly towards security, pulling my case behind me, before I could change my mind.

I flashed the new passport, the ESTA that was my key to my future at a uniformed official, whose face I could barely make out through my tears. And then as I was waved through, almost on impulse, I spun on my heel. There he was, standing against the barrier, still watching. We locked eyes, and he lifted a hand, his palm open, and I lifted mine slowly in return. I fixed that image of him in my imagination – the way he tilted forward, the light on his hair, the steady way he always looked at me – somewhere where I could draw it up on lonely days. Because there would be lonely days. And bad days. And days when I wondered what the hell I had just agreed to be part of. Because that was all part of the adventure too.

*I love you*, I mouthed, not sure if he could even see the words from here.

And then, holding my passport tight in my hand, I turned away.

He would be there, watching as my plane gathered speed and lifted into the great blue sky beyond. And, with luck, he would be there, waiting, when I came home again.

# Acknowledgements

Thank you, as ever, to my agent, Sheila Crowley, and my editor Louise Moore, for their continuing faith and endless support. Thanks to the many talented people at Penguin Michael Joseph who help turn a raw draft into something glossy on legions of bookshelves, particularly: Maxine Hitchcock, Francesca Russell, Hazel Orme, Hattie Adam-Smith, Sophie Elletson, Tom Weldon, and all the unsung heroes who help get us authors out there. I love being part of your team.

Huge gratitude to everyone who works alongside Sheila at Curtis Brown for your support, especially Rebecca Ritchie, Katie McGowan, Sophie Harris, Nick Marston, Kat Buckle, Raneet Ahuja, Jess Cooper, Alice Lutyens, Sara Gad and of course Jonny Geller. In the US, thank you to the inimitable Bob Bookman. It's in the box, Bob!

Thank you for friendship, advice and wisdom-filled lunches on related stuff to Cathy Runciman, Maddy Wickham, Sarah Millican, Ol Parker, Polly Samson, Damian Barr, Alex Heminsley, Jess Ruston and all at Writersblock. You all rock.

Closer to home, thank you to Jackie Tearne (I will be up to date with email one day, I promise!), Claire Roweth, Chris Luckley, Drew Hazell, and everyone who helps me do what I do.

Thank you also to the cast and crew of Me Before You. To be there as my characters were made flesh was an extraordinary privilege, and one I will never forget. You were all, uniformly, brilliant (but especially you, Emilia and Sam).

Thanks and love to my parents – Jim Moyes and Lizzie

Sanders – and most of all to Charles, Saskia, Harry and Lockie. My world.

And a final thank you to the legions of people who wrote, via Twitter or facebook or my website, caring enough about Lou to want to know what happened to her. I might not have considered writing this book if she hadn't continued to live so vividly in your imaginations. I'm so glad she did.